Beyond Tucson:
Adventures
in the
Multiverse

Beyond Tucson: Adventures in the Multiverse
Volume One of the *Beyond Tucson* Anthology Series

By

**Tucson Science Fiction and Fantasy Writers
Meetup Group**
Ann Bauer, Jessica Barnes, Karen Funk Blocher
Meghann Caskey, Charles J. Coffey, Kevin Harrington
Billy Hernandez, Jr., Erik Hertwig, CA Morgan,
Joni Parker, Jessica Priester, G. Chris Stern
J M Strasser, G. E. Zhao

For All Aspiring Writers...
Quotes to Inspire You

*"Who wants to become a writer? And why?
Because it's the answer to everything. ... It's the streaming reason
for living. To note, to pin down, to build up, to create, to be
astonished at nothing, to cherish the oddities, to let nothing go
down the drain, to make something,
to make a great flower out of life, even if it's a cactus."*
—Enid Bagnold

"The road to hell is paved with adverbs."
—Stephen King

*"Writing a book is a horrible, exhausting struggle,
like a long bout of some painful illness. One would never
undertake such a thing if one were not driven on by some
demon whom one can neither resist nor understand."*
—George Orwell

"The road to hell is paved with works-in-progress."
—Philip Roth

*"We are all apprentices in a craft where
no one ever becomes a master."*
—Ernest Hemingway

*"I do not over-intellectualise the production process. I try to keep
it simple: Tell the damned story."*
—Tom Clancy, WD

"If it sounds like writing, I rewrite it."
—Elmore Leonard

*"Remember: Plot is no more than footprints left in the snow after
your characters have run by on their way
to incredible destinations."*
—Ray Bradbury, WD

We say...what are you waiting for, write!

Beyond Tucson:
Adventures in the Multiverse

©2018
First Edition October 2018
Toughnut Press

ISBN-13: 978-1725546721
ISBN-10: 1725546728

Cover Art: Karen Funk Blocher
Interior Design: CA Morgan

Editors: Karen Funk Blocher and CA Morgan

Printed in the United States

Toughnut Press, Tucson, Arizona

Table of Contents

INTRODUCTION

By Karen Funk Blocher

At the beginning of June in 2014, aspiring writer Daniel J. Pinney founded the Tucson SciFi/Fantasy Writers/Readers Meetup on Meetup.com, with the stated intention of developing "a community of people to talk shop with." Although Dan himself eventually moved on, the group he founded, now called the Tucson SF/Fantasy Writers, is fulfilling that dream. Members meet on alternate Wednesdays to request and receive feedback on their works in progress, learn about publishing options, and generally support each other in their writing goals. On alternate Saturdays, we meet mostly to write, with less chatter and more immediate exchanges of feedback.

It's a diverse group, ranging from teens to retirees, from many different backgrounds and with as many different interests. Some members have published multiple books, some are on the verge of publication, and some are just getting started with their writing. Genres range from hard science fiction to magical realism, from steampunk to traditional fantasy, from ghost stories to poetry —oh, and one baseball novel. Amid all the socializing, and the biweekly consumption of burritos and belated breakfast foods, actual writing gets done. Some of it can be found in this book.

The concept of *Beyond Tucson: Adventures in the Multiverse* is to showcase members' writing via a virtual tour of the cosmos, starting in and around Tucson and spreading out from there. Tucsonans will find familiar landmarks in the early pages of this anthology. By the end of the book, however, we leave Arizona, the 21st century, and even this universe far behind. We hope you enjoy the trip!

Karen Funk Blocher is a church bookkeeper and social media director. A graduate of the Clarion SF Writers' Workshop, she has contributed articles to *Relix* and *Starlog* magazines, and wrote the text for five series of Doctor Who trading cards in the 1990s. Her first fantasy trilogy, *Heirs of Mâvarin*, will be published by MuseItUp Publishing later this year, and the sequel trilogy is close to completion. Karen has one husband (fellow Clarionite John), two dogs, no kids and no cats.

Synopsis

About "The Jace Letters," she writes, "This was inspired by a road trip to see my godson, Jacob, who lives in Los Alamos. I originally wrote it as a series of blog entries, working out the story night by night as I posted Jace and Sandy's emails. It is now a bit of a period piece, which is appropriate given the time scale of the story."

The Jace Letters

Subject: Why I'm not there
Date: 4/??/??? 09590fh2fy08y
From: NotaBeach@xmail.com
To: JaceFace@xmail.com

Dear Jace –

I don't see how this email is ever going to reach you, but if it does, please tell your parents I've been kidnapped.

This is not a joke!

I don't know why I've been kidnapped. There don't seem to be any ransom demands. The only person I've seen since I woke up here isn't telling me much of anything. In fact, she hardly says a word at all. I've decided to call her "Gabby." Just about the only thing she did say was that if I wrote you an email, you would get it, even though this computer doesn't seem to have any kind of a modem or network connection, and I have no Internet otherwise. But this mail composing page does seem to work, so I'm doing it, just in case. Even if it doesn't go anywhere, I have to write down what's happened, and try to make sense of it all.

It's impossible to tell where I am. There are no windows, and the only door out of the three rooms – bedroom, bath, small living room or study – is dead-bolted. Locked. I have my laptop (obviously), but it's not online. I can't get to any web pages, blogs or AOL, or access any email beyond this one I'm currently writing. I have the clothes and toiletries that were in my suitcase, a few DVDs, a couple of paperbacks, and my iPod. My flip phone gets no signal at all.

The furniture here is the sort of stuff that other people throw away: a shabby couch, a sagging mattress, a scratched wooden table, and two kitchen chairs with split vinyl seat covers. There is no tv or radio. The place is stocked with canned goods, a microwave oven and two cases of Diet Orange Crush, so I have enough to eat and drink. But that's about it. That's all that's here. Even Gabby left after just a couple of minutes.

I haven't actually been very hungry since this happened. Not that I know what happened. Not really.

All I know is

```
Subject: Re: Why I'm not there
Date: 5/30/2005 1:55:23 PM US Mountain Daylight Time
From: JaceFace@xmail.com
To: NotaBeach@xmail.com
```

Aunt Sandy!

Is this one of your stories? U r a good writer, but your scaring me a little. Where are u really? We expected you over a month ago. You didn't show up, and we never heard anything until now. Mom called your cell phone, but it said it was unavailable. She left a voicemail on your home phone, too.

Just tell us where you really are, ok? And that your allright.

You missed a pretty good party on my birthday weekend. I got a high tech spy kit and an Aragorn action figure. But the best present was a pink iPod!

Jace

```
Subject: Re: Why I'm not there
Date: r0tu2ru0ru0r
From: NotaBeach@xmail.com
To: JaceFace@xmail.com
```

Jace—

I accidentally sent my email before I was ready. Sorry about that. Now that I've received an email reply from you, I know that Gabby was telling me the truth. I still have no other Internet service, not even other email or AOL, but at least I can write to you and get an answer.

But I told you. It's not a joke or a story. I really have been kidnapped, even though it doesn't make sense, even though I don't know why.

All I know is that I had driven up from Tucson and was just arriving in Sedona for the night when a tanker truck suddenly pulled out in front of me. I remember hitting the brake and yelling. I don't remember a crash, or anything like that.

Then I woke up here. Wherever "here" is. There's a cut on my forehead that doesn't seem to want to stop bleeding, but I'm fine otherwise. At least, I think I am. Maybe I was in an accident after all. Maybe I've had a concussion. Maybe I'm really in a coma, and this is all a dream.

It doesn't seem like a dream. It's weird and lonely and depressing, but it feels real to me.

If it is real, this isn't a hospital. There's just me and the woman I call Gabby, when she's even here, and Gabby won't let me leave. That's kidnapping, regardless of how I actually got to this place.

Jace, dear, I don't want to criticize. You know I love you, and I'm grateful that you answered my email, even if it scared you. But as a former English major, I have to tell you that you need to work on your writing skills a little bit. I'm glad you dropped the "texting" abbreviations after your first few sentences. It's much easier for an old fogey like me to read what you have to say if you write real words, not just letters. You also confused "your," which means "belonging to you," with "you're," which means "you are." And "all right" is two words, not one. "Alright" as a single word seems to be gaining acceptance now, but that is not what I was taught in school when I was your age.

Please understand, I'd be glad to hear from you even if it was all in lower case Pig Latin, but I'd much rather know that my goddaughter is literate. Fair enough?

Well, I'm off to bed, assuming that I'm not already asleep. I'll write to you again tomorrow.

Love,

Aunt Sandy

Subject: Re: Why I'm not there
Date: 4/10/06
From: JaceFace@xmail.com
To: NotaBeach@xmail.com

Dear Aunt Sandy,

I don't believe this. You act like you just got the email I sent you, but I sent that the same night I got that first weird one from you, five weeks after you disappeared. Don't you know it's been almost a year since then? I'm going to be 12 years old next week. I wish you were here, because I could use some advice, grown-up advice about stuff I can't talk to Mom about.

I don't understand how your accident could have been anywhere near Sedona. They found your car outside of Deming, NM, all smashed up. That's about 444 miles away from Sedona! They didn't find you though, or even any blood. Mom and Dad tried to tell the police that we got email from you, and we think you're alive. They took a copy of the email with them, but that's all. They never came back or told us anything.

After that we heard from a couple of people in Roswell. They say you were abducted by aliens. Do you think maybe Gabby is an alien?

Please notice I've worked hard on my writing since last year, even though I didn't get your criticism until just now. Yeah, I know that last email was bad. My friends all wrote like that at the time, but I kind of knew better.

Write back quick!

Jace

Subject: Believing the Unbelievable
Date: 4/??/??? 24r08498whfo
From: NotaBeach@xmail.com
To: JaceFace@xmail.com

Jace —

You talk about what I say being unbelievable, and I suppose that it is. But then you hit me with unbelievable claims of your own! How am I supposed to react when you say that my accident, if there was one, was almost a year ago, and that my car was found in Deming? I haven't been to Deming in years.

I swear to you, Jace, that unless I've been in a coma, no more than a few days have gone by for me since I left Tucson to visit you on your birthday. It certainly hasn't been a year. My forehead is still bleeding, and my arm is sore, the way muscles sometimes get the day after an accident. That's how long it's been since I got here, wherever here is: about a day, maybe two. I look in the mirror, and I'm no older than I was before.

But your latest email is dated next April. How can that be? Something strange is going on, even stranger than I realized.

I asked Gabby whether she was an alien. She just laughed and said no. But there's definitely something she's not telling me.

If you're about to be twelve years old, then you're heading into adolescence, when pretty much everyone needs somebody to confide in. I remember being 12, 13, 14. They weren't the best years I've had. I'm not sure I have any good advice to offer, or even that this will reach you before you're an old married lady. But if you want to try to tell me what's going on in your life, I promise to reply as soon as I hear from you.

Okay. I got your email at 9:03 PM, according to my watch. It's 9:46 PM now. Please let me know whether you get this on the same day, week, or year as your email to me.

Love,
Aunt Sandy

Subject: Einstein and Stuff
Date: 7/1/06
From: JaceFace@xmail.com
To: NotaBeach@xmail.com

Dear Aunt Sandy (if it's really you),

Well, it hasn't been a year this time. Only about eight weeks. I guess maybe if you answer right away, it gets to me sooner.

I've been thinking about a video we saw in school, about Einstein and time and stuff like that. I suppose it was explaining relativity, but I don't really understand it all yet, although I'd like to. Anyway, in the video, one twin went out into space and traveled at almost the speed of light. The other twin stayed home. When the astronaut twin came back, he was still young, but the other twin was old. Time slowed down in the spaceship because it was moving so fast.

So what I was wondering is this. Are you sure you're not in an alien spaceship or time machine? Can you feel the room moving, or motors humming, or something like that? I mean, if you are moving really fast, faster than anything this side of *Star Trek* or whatever, then time really could go slower for you than for me. It would also explain, sort of, why you can't get online. It doesn't explain how we can email each other, though.

You know, I've been believing that you're really my godmother, Sandy Sheets, pretty much just because it's your email account, and your emails sound like something you'd say. But what if it's all a trick, like the police told my parents? Is there some way you can prove you're who you say you are?

If you are Aunt Sandy, I guess maybe I should do what I said I'd do, and ask you for advice. I'm in the regular public school starting this year, and I'm having a little trouble with some of the kids. They like to call me Jace Face the Space Case. They say Jace is a stupid name. I kind of try to ignore them, but that doesn't seem to help. What do you think I should do?

Jace
(really Janice)

Subject: Re: Einstein and Stuff
Date: 5/??/??? 24r027098wieh
From: NotaBeach@xmail.com
To: JaceFace@xmail.com

Jace –

I was wondering when you would ask for proof, not that I'm exactly in a good position to give you any. How about this?

Birthday Presents from Me to You

* Age 6: a stuffed poodle on a pillow. Do you still have that? Seems to me I remember seeing it in your closet the last time you gave me "the Tour."
* Age 7: Scrabble Junior.
* Age 8: I can't remember...oh, yes. A necklace maker. I must have spent an hour in Toys R Us that time, trying to figure out what you'd like.
* Age 9: a diary with an audio feature and a lock.
* Age 10: a set of acrylic paints and an artist's tablet.
* Age 11: if I'd actually managed to get to Los Alamos, I would have given you a box set of the BBC Narnia movies on DVD. They're here with me. Since you're not likely to get these, I've been watching them. If it's really 2006, that means the Disney version came out. Was it any good?

Also: I mentioned before that I hadn't been to Deming, NM in years. The last time I went was to attend the duck races with your family in 1997. Do you remember that? You were three years old then. You wanted a baby duck to take home. You cried when your Mom said no.

I trust that establishes my identity.

On the name thing: my goodness, Jace, don't you know how incredibly cool your nickname is? At least it is from my point of view. You may remember that I was there when you told your parents to start calling you Jace instead of Janice. That was a gutsy thing for a seven-year-old to do. I thought your mother would be upset, but then your dad laughed, and I knew they'd go along with it. You have cool parents, even if they did deny you your very own duckling when you were three.

As for "Jace Face the Space Case," I thought you liked Jace Face. That is your screen name, after all. Is it really the "space case" part that bothers you, or is it because these kids are trying to be mean? The heck with them. If there's one thing I regret most about my childhood, junior high and high school years, it's that I let whatever everyone else said and did hurt my feelings. You know you're not a "space case," and these kids probably know it, too. They're just going for the rhyme. You can even come up with a positive interpretation of "space case" if you try.

Heck, it's not remotely as bad as being saddled with the name "Sandy Sheets." "Hey, Sandy! How about washing those sheets?" "What were you doing in those sheets to make them sandy?" I was called Sandy Bottoms, and Sandy Pandy, and Sandy Sh*ts, and Sandy Feets, and even Candy Beets! I didn't handle it very well. Don't make that mistake. You've got a really good name, but absolutely every name can be turned into a joke or insult if you work at it. If some jerks at school try that on you, don't give them the satisfaction of being hurt by it. It's their problem, not yours. And a lot of times, as I learned many years later, teasing isn't meant to hurt. You can choose to enjoy the joke, instead of being scarred by it as I was.

So, it's past midnight by my watch, and I'm tired and sore. If I go to bed, does that mean you'll be 13 or 14 or 22 years old when I wake up in the morning? Gabby came through here a few minutes ago, and I asked her about the Einstein twin paradox and your theory about me. She didn't really answer the question, but she smiled. I think she was genuinely pleased to hear that it was you who came up with that. Make of that what you will: I have no clue.

Love,

Aunt Sandy (really!)

Subject: Re: Einstein and Stuff
Date: 5/??/??? 24r027098wthw9f
From: NotaBeach@xmail.com
To: JaceFace@xmail.com

Jace –

I forgot to answer one of your questions just now, so I thought I'd better do it before I go to bed and you get older. No, I don't hear any motors. I'm not quite sure whether I feel a little vibration in the floor, or it's just me feeling a little shaky after the accident, and imagining something that's not really there. As I think I said before, there are no windows here. Do you suppose maybe I'm in a TARDIS? ;)

I'm really starting to think there was an accident. I probably wouldn't feel this lousy otherwise.

Aunt Sandy

Subject: Time, Time, Time
Date: 11/6/06
From: JaceFace@xmail.com
To: NotaBeach@xmail.com

Yeah, okay. You're definitely my Aunt Sandy! And yes, "Trophy" is still in my closet.

I'm trying to figure out how long it will be before I get another email from you. A whole year, I bet. Last time a day went by for you, it was at least a year on my end, I think.

Hey! Here's another email from you! You must have sent it really quickly after the last one. I mean really really quickly.

Since I won't hear from you again for a long time, I guess there's not much point in asking for more advice right now. School is getting better, anyway. Those kids who teased me about my name aren't all that bad, and I've made a couple of friends. I'll try to do as you told me, and not get upset at every little thing someone says.

I read both books about physics that were in the school library. They didn't help much. They're kind of written for kids, and I need to know more than that. School will be over soon for the summer, and I've already asked my teacher so many questions that he probably thinks I'm crazy. I guess they're tough questions, because he couldn't even answer most of them. Science class next year is Earth Science, so that doesn't really help, either. I'm going to go to the Bradbury tomorrow with Mom, and see what I can find in their bookstore. I want to understand what's happening to you. Maybe I can find a way to rescue you somehow.

Talk to you later - much later, probably!

Jace

Subject: Time, Time, Time
Date: 12/24/06
From: JaceFace@xmail.com
To: NotaBeach@xmail.com

Dear Aunt Sandy —

Merry Christmas! I mean, I know we don't know the date where you are, or what date it will be when you get this, or even if time has any meaning in your fast-moving system. That's what I'm guessing you're in. But it's Christmas here, and I was thinking about you, and wishing you could spend the holiday with us. The closest I can get to that is to write to you now, even though I won't hear from you again until next November probably. I figure that if you can write to me twice in a row, then I can write to you twice in a row, or more. After all, I have a lot more time to do it in. But I'll try not to do it too often, because it still takes time for you to read them!

My parents think my recent interest in physics is something to be encouraged. They've bought me three books on the subject since I last wrote to you, and I'll be surprised if I don't get at least one more for Christmas. I don't tell them why I'm interested, though. They never really believed me about these emails, even though I showed them the first two I got from you. They think it's a hoax. They told me that you're dead, and I shouldn't hold out false hope. So now I keep all this to myself, except for talking to you, of course.

I can't give you anything physical for Christmas, so I decided to write a poem for you:

> *Sit silent and read*
> *Words of Sandy, lost in Time,*
> *Reaching out to me.*
> *Find a way to help:*
> *I can be a scientist*
> *If I really try.*
> *Years fly by for me*
> *While you drift from day to day*
> *To some future time.*
> *When will we converge?*
> *Will I know all that I need*
> *To rescue my friend?*

I know it's just a bunch of haiku put together, and it doesn't have imagery or nature in it or anything like that. But you get the idea. If there's a way to find and rescue you, I'm going to do it. It will probably take me years and years, but at the rate you're going, I guess we have the time. Hang in there, Aunt Sandy! Write me when you can.

Jace

Subject: As Time Goes By
Date: 12/10/07
From: JaceFace@xmail.com
To: NotaBeach@xmail.com

Dear Aunt Sandy —

It's almost Christmas again, and I still haven't heard from you. I was almost sure I'd hear from you by now. I've been trying not to worry about you any more than I do anyway, but it's not working. Every week that goes by, I'm a little more afraid that I'll never hear from you again.

School's okay, I guess. I'm in eighth grade now. Mom thinks it's a little weird that I'm getting an A in science and math all the time. It used to be Bs and Cs. I know Mom thinks I should try out for a school play or something, but I don't have time for that. When I'm not trying to learn physics, I'm trying to write stories, like you used to do. Or I'm doing research online. Since you disappeared, there have been three reports of people turning up in Deming, not knowing how they got there. Nobody really takes these stories seriously, but one of them said the last thing he remembered was driving on State Route 89A in Arizona.

Oh, and there's a boy I like. His name is Ken, and yes, people ask him "Where's Barbie?" all the time. He just laughs and says, "We broke up." He's not my boyfriend or anything, more like friends. He's a little bit of a computer whiz, and his dad's a doctor.

One of the reasons I'm so worried about you is it sounded in your last email as though you're getting worse and worse. Please tell me I'm wrong about this. Please tell me anything! Just let me know you're alive, and I'm not too late!

Love,

Jace

Subject: Re: As Time Goes By
Date: 5/??/??? 24r07098wi98wthw9f
From: NotaBeach@xmail.com
To: JaceFace@xmail.com

Oh, Jace, I'm so sorry to make you worry like that! I wish I could reassure you, but I can't get out of bed this morning. There's a terrible gash down one leg, and my abdomen is bleeding into the fresh bandages Gabby put on. She's made me as comfortable as she can, brought me food and a bedpan (more than you want to know, right?), and even set up my computer on a TV tray for me. But it took a while. That's probably why I'm so "late."

What else did you learn about the man who went from 89A to Deming? Was it just a little news article, or is he someone you can write to and ask questions? I don't know what you'd ask him, but it does sound a lot like my experience. He wasn't injured, was he?

Be careful with the boy who is not your boyfriend. Maybe he will become that, maybe not. Just be sure you don't get pressured into doing more than you are ready to do.

Speaking of feeling pressured, I don't want you to feel you have to save me from whatever is happening to me. No, I don't want to die here, but I'm starting to think maybe I'm going to. Gabby is really doing her best to help me, but it's as if my injuries are appearing slowly, just as I'm living slowly compared to you. They're not healing, either. But THIS IS NOT YOUR RESPONSIBILITY TO FIX. You're a teenaged girl, for Heaven's sake, not Sam Beckett. (You're not old enough to remember *Quantum Leap*, are you? But maybe you can see it on cable or something.) I admire your courage and commitment, and I hope to see you again before I die. I really do. But if that doesn't happen, it won't be your fault or your failure. Please promise me that whatever happens, you won't blame yourself. Love,
Aunt Sandy

Subject: Sandy Lives! (I hope)
Date: 1/10/09
From: JaceFace@xmail.com
To: NotaBeach@xmail.com

Dear Aunt Sandy —

Hooray! I finally heard from you! It took over two years, though. I have to wonder whether your faster moving system is starting to accelerate. If it is, that's probably a good thing. It would mean that your time dilation is increasing, slowing you down relative to me. That may buy us some time, so I can grow up, learn what I need to know, and get to you before your injuries have time to kill you. I'm up to ninth grade, but even a high school student with an obsession about quantum theory isn't a whole lot more use to you than the 11-year-old I was when all this started.

I just hope your Gabby can help you to heal instead of your getting worse all the time. Ken says that if you aren't bleeding internally, then it should be possible to stop you from losing more blood. Has Gabby tried stitching you up?

Yes, I told Ken about you. I hope you don't mind. He's going into medicine like his parents, so I thought he might be able to tell me something helpful. We've gotten to be pretty close friends. Maybe more than friends, but it's too soon to say that for sure.

I did email the man who said he was near Sedona, and then suddenly found himself in Deming. I guess this happened right after the fire. Did I tell you about the fire? Well, there was one, near 89A north of Sedona, in June of 2006. Were you south of Sedona just before you disappeared, or north of it?

Anyway, the guy thought at first I was trying to hoax him, but I guess he researched your case online, and found out that I wasn't just making it all up. Then he wrote back to me. But he doesn't remember anything helpful, so it was kind of a dead end. The one thing he said was that the road turned blue, right before it happened. No, I don't know what it means.

Listen, I know you don't want me to worry about you, or to take on the responsibility of trying to save you. But I've already taken it on. I've been working on it for years. If I fail, okay, I'll be really upset. But if I don't even try, then I fail for sure. I have to do this, Aunt Sandy. I have to do everything I can to find you and rescue you, both from this dimensional anomaly you're in and from being slowly killed by a car accident that happened years ago. At least now I have a friend to help me with the second part of that.

Love,

Jace.

Subject: Re: Sandy Lives! (I hope)
Date: 11/??/??? 095904r0731rffy08y
From: NotaBeach@xmail.com
To: JaceFace@xmail.com

Jace –

You asked whether Gabby has tried stitching me up. Better still: she's finally brought in a doctor to help me!

I don't know how he got in here, but of course I don't know how Gabby gets in here, either. She seems to be aging about as fast as you are, if not faster. She looks at least thirty as of this morning.

The doctor is about Gabby's age, maybe a little older. When I asked him his name, he said, "I'm not supposed to tell you that now." Isn't that an odd thing to say? But he seems very nice. He did stitch up my wounds, including some new ones that appeared while he was working on the others. He looked a little surprised and worried about this, but not nearly as much as you might expect. I'm sure he knows something about what's going on, but he confined his remarks to my medical condition. Like your friend, he's worried about internal bleeding, but for the moment he says there's little evidence of it. He offered me pain medication, but I need to stay alert so I can answer your emails as they come in. If it turns out I'm going to die soon, I don't want to waste any time being drugged out and drowsy.

Meanwhile, I'm feeling a little better, I think, and Gabby has brought me a fresh supply of food. The first day there was nothing here that could be considered perishable - no fruits or vegetables, no fresh or frozen meat. It was all stuff like Kraft Dinner with powdered milk and no butter, beans, rice, SPAM, tuna, fruit cocktail and other canned goods. Now Gabby seems to have found a way to keep the food from spoiling at the speed of relativity. Today there was some cheddar cheese that didn't look too old, and potatoes, and a slightly squishy apple. Okay, it's not great, but it's something. Too bad I'm not hungry.

In your email you report that the man who disappeared from Sedona to Deming said the "road turned blue." I think I saw that, too. It wasn't just the road, though. It was everything at once. Blue.

I'm not going to try to talk you out of anything from this point

forward. You're obviously a determined young woman, and I'm grateful that you care so much about your time-lost godmother. All I ask is that you be careful, and try to avoid taking unnecessary chances. Will you do that for me? Please say that you will!
Sandy

Subject: The Why, If Not the How
Date: 4/17/11
From: JaceFace@xmail.com
To: NotaBeach@xmail.com

Aunt Sandy —
I'm most of the way through eleventh grade now. At this rate, I'll be an adult by the time you get through this one day. But time seems to keep accelerating, so heck, I could be your age by the time your day is over!
I'm starting to suspect a reason for all this - not how it happened, but maybe why it's happening. I probably shouldn't say anything, though. This is the part in time travel stories when someone warns about knowing too much about the future. But I want to tell you this one thing, which could be totally wrong for all I know. I think this is probably about saving your life, or at least preserving it as long as possible. I mean, if you had just died right away in that accident, I wouldn't have gotten to know you as well as I do now, and nobody would have had a chance to try to keep you alive as that doctor is doing. Maybe all this time bubble stuff (if that's what it is) is the equivalent of cryonics, without the nasty side effects of freezing the brain into unusable mush. If you stay alive for another ten years of my time, medicine should get better, until whatever is wrong can be fixed, right? I hope so, anyway.
In case you're wondering, Ken and I are still friends, and still very close. But no, I haven't done anything with him that would shock my parents. We mostly have long, intense conversations, pretty much every day. And yeah, okay, he kissed me, once. I didn't like it much, but I'm not telling him that. He'll be getting his driver's license soon, and he wants to take me to Sedona and Deming, or at least one of the two. But I know my parents won't agree to any such thing, even though I'm about to turn 17. I wish I could just skip forward in time, the way you seem to do. Slogging through my teen

years in normal time is dull and frustrating, especially when I know you're waiting for me to finish doing it!
Jace.

Subject: Re: The Why, If Not the How
Date: 11/??/??? 0efh408fy30r1rffy08y
From: NotaBeach@xmail.com
To: JaceFace@xmail.com

Jace –

I think I must have passed out, or at any rate fallen asleep for a while. I was trying to read *Physics for Dummies*, which Gabby had brought at my request. But I couldn't concentrate on it. I don't know how long I was unconscious. There is no day or night here to judge by. But my uneaten apple has gone brown, and my Diet Crush is warm and flat.

I'm feeling weak again, and the pain is getting worse. It's not just the wounds, or the headache. There's abdominal pain, too, the worst I've had since my gall bladder came out. That's what woke me.

A few minutes ago, I managed to climb out of bed and go use the restroom. What I saw pretty much settled the question about internal bleeding. Gabby has gone to bring the doctor back in here.

Jace, I'm sorry, but I'm not at all sure I will live long enough for you to find your way to me. How would you even do it?
Sandy

Subject: My Promise
Date: 5/15/12
From: JaceFace@xmail.com
To: NotaBeach@xmail.com

Aunt Sandy –

I'm terribly worried about you, but time is working in our favor, at least at my end. I'm a month away from my high school graduation. They let me take A.P. Physics a year early, doubling up with Chemistry. I aced them both, even though Chem is kind of rote and boring. Then this year I took Quantum Physics 1 online from M.I.T. I guess that impressed the people at LANL (Los Alamos National Laboratory), because I just got accepted to their summer intern program. I start interning there next month. Isn't that great? My parents are both really proud of me, but I still see that worried look in Mom's eye whenever the subject of physics comes up.

I have my driver's license now, too. Ken and I still want to drive to Sedona or Deming, or both, but my parents would freak if I drove so far away, especially with a boy. They like Ken okay, but I don't think they trust him, even after knowing him for years. They're sure that Ken and I have secrets together, but I won't tell them what kind of secrets. I just say that it's nothing to do with sex. To be honest, we've thought about doing it together, but so far he's been pretty understanding when I say I'm not ready. I'm not even sure he's ready, but I'm not going to hurt his ego by saying so.

Anyway, I keep wondering whether Ken and I should make the trip to Sedona now, and face my parents after it's all over. What's more important, me obeying a curfew, or finding and helping you? But that's what stops me. Even if I find you, I'm not ready to help you. I've been working on something in Ken's basement, so that my parents won't know that my obsession with physics has turned me into a crackpot inventor. I've got a long way to go in building the thing, let alone getting it to work. I'm not even sure exactly what it will do when it's finished. Something useful, I hope. Really, I do more than hope. I know it will work eventually. I promise it.

And I promise you will live long enough for me to see you again. Don't give up! Every month that goes by, every book I read, every bit of research I do, every email I get from you, only makes me more sure I know what's happening to you, and what to do about it. I've pretty much figured out how to get to you when the time comes, and I know I will get there. But the time hasn't come yet, and getting there isn't enough. We have to save your life, too.

Meanwhile, I've been looking at colleges to go to. I'm probably going to apply to Caltech, U.C. Riverside, and University of Arizona. You didn't go to the University of Arizona, did you? But you probably know something about it, having lived in Tucson before the accident. I guess which one I go to will depend on where I get the best scholarship. Ken is applying to the same schools, so we've been looking for ones that have a good pre-med program, not just a good physics department.

Hang in there! We can do this!
Jace

Subject: Re: My Promise
Date: 6/??/??? 0efh40rghfhqe0f08y
From: NotaBeach@xmail.com
To: JaceFace@xmail.com

Jace –

I was right. The doctor says I'm bleeding internally. He can't operate by himself, obviously. I don't know whether I can get to a hospital - whether it's allowed, whether it's even possible. Maybe Gabby can bring more people in here. I don't know, though, whether she will or can. I don't feel I know much of anything at this point.
Sandy

Subject: Stay Put
Date: 3/15/14
From: JaceFace@xmail.com
To: NotaBeach@xmail.com

Aunt Sandy –

I'm pretty sure there's no way you would survive a trip to the hospital. If the time bubble, or whatever it is, is slowing down your physical decline, then the last thing you want to do is leave it. I'm sure that Gabby knows this, and will do everything she can to help you.

I'm in the spring semester of my sophomore year at the U of A, living a couple of blocks off of Fourth Avenue. I stayed at the University of Arizona, not because it had the best physics department or the best scholarship, but it's within driving distance of Sedona and the hidden entrance to the time bubble. Also it's where Ken wanted to go. Ken and I aren't getting along too well right now, but he's promised not to abandon his plans to help me help you, even though we're not dating any more. He's become kind of sarcastic lately, thinks I'm so hung up on your problem and physics in general that I'm not much good for anything else. I guess it's been a while since I was fun to be around, whatever that means. I even had to move my "mad scientist" project out of his basement. Fortunately, one of my professors is humoring me by letting me keep it in her garage, which is only two blocks from my apartment, and then across the park. She and her husband (another physicist) have even given me a few ideas on how to make it work. I don't think they take it seriously, but they don't treat me like a kid or a crazy person, either.

Tell Gabby that I think it's time for you and her to have a talk. I don't know if she'll listen to me, but if you're dying, it could be her last chance. Maybe I'm overreacting, and I hope I'm wrong. But things are clearly getting kind of desperate over there.

You said that Gabby seemed about thirty years old. How old was she when you first got there?

Jace

Subject: Re: Stay Put
Date: 7/??/??? 0efhhffhfhqe0f08y
From: NotaBeach@xmail.com
To: JaceFace@xmail.com

Jace –

Gabby is back, and so is the doctor. And he brought two friends, and medical equipment. The operation is in half an hour. They've already given me some sedative but not the serious stuff to put me out yet. Dr. K. thinks if he can stop the internal bleeding I will probably survive everything else. The wounds we can see finally seeem to be scabbing istead ofgetting bigger.

Getting ttoo groggy to write this. I know who Gabby is. Sending. Write you if I wakeup.

Sandy

Subject: Please live!
Date: 1/17/16
From: JaceFace@xmail.com
To: NotaBeach@xmail.com

Aunt Sandy –

Your latest email makes me feel so helpless! You've reached the life-and-death moment we've been worrying about, and 21-year-old me can't do anything but wait for another email to see if you survived.

On second thought, maybe I can do something. I'm less than four hours from Sedona, traffic permitting, I have access to a van, and I think my machine will work. I just called Ken, and he agreed to drive with me to Sedona tomorrow. I'm anxious to hear back from you, but that could take months and months. I want to start now. I'll bring my laptop along.

I guess Ken and I are kind of back together, not that that really matters right now. We're not quite boyfriend and girlfriend, but more than just friends. Does that make any sense?

You're going to live. I'm sure of it. Otherwise, you wouldn't be going through what I'm about to make happen. It has to be worth it! It has to!

Jace

Subject: I live!
Date: 11/??/??? 0efhhffejf0fje0f08y
From: NotaBeach@xmail.com
To: JaceFace@xmail.com

Jace (or should I say Gabby?) –

I got through the operation, and obviously I'm awake now. Still a little groggy, but I hope not too groggy to proofread this time. Your Dr. Ken is pretty sure he got all the perforations that were causing the internal bleeding. It's just as well I hadn't been eating much, or I could easily have ended up with peritonitis. As it is, he's pumped me full of antibiotics, just in case. Blecch. I'm pretty nauseated, but I'll live.

Judging from the email I just read, I assume you know that you made this time bubble with that machine you built, and sent it back in time somehow to rescue me from the crash. Thank you. Maybe there was/is/will be a better way to save my life, but this is the way you chose. It's such a chicken and the egg situation, isn't it? Which came first, the idea that these emails gave you, or the emails your idea made possible? Did we ever have a choice in all this? Maybe I emailed you from a future that didn't exist yet, and you are starting to make that future the real one.

I think I'm getting dizzy, thinking about all this.

I'm not going to say any more about all the things you'll be doing over the next decade. I don't want to risk changing my personal history, now that I'm pretty sure I'm getting out of here alive.

Next question is whether 32-year-old you will be able to get me back to normal time without me turning into a skeleton or something. "Gabby" says she's working on it.

Bless you, Jace!

Sandy

```
Subject: email test
Date: 4/??/??? 09590fh2fy08y
From: JaceFace@xmail.com
To: NotaBeach@xmail.com
```

test test test.. Sent from time bubble 6 hours after the accident.

Don't forget to reply (to younger self?), and to delete this email from Sandy's laptop before she wakes up.

```
Subject: re: email test
Date: 4/??/??? 0959r22fy08y
From: NotaBeach
To: JaceFace@xmail.com
```

Ignore this email, Jace. I'm just testing something. See you soon.

```
Subject: What I Did on My Summer Vacation
Date: 8/10/17
From: JaceFace@xmail.com
To: NotaBeach@xmail.com
```

Aunt Sandy —

All right, yes. It's true. I know now for a fact that I'm Gabby, because I've seen you three times now in my role as your "kidnapper." Mostly I was there to make sure everything was set up for your relative comfort, and to make sure the cross-time link between our computers was set up properly. The really tricky part was sneaking into my family's old house in 2005 to install the "quantum entanglement time card" on my old Compaq. Also, every time I enter your bubble, I lose weeks or months relative to "my" time. That's why I can never stay for long. I could lose a whole semester or more. Not to mention how much it upsets my parents every time I disappear.

I don't know how much the future-Gabby has told you, so let me clarify things a bit:

1. I didn't create the rift between Sedona and Deming. When Ken and I got to 2005 Sedona, it was already there. There's also a side branch that goes to Roswell. I couldn't shut it down completely, but after your accident we planted a couple of trees and put up a *No Trespassing* sign to try to keep people out. I'm guessing that this is one reason for the woo-woo reputations of Sedona and Roswell. That doesn't explain Deming, though. Duck races aren't really the same kind of weirdness.

2. Your accident really was an accident. I saw it. You skidded off the road into the rift. I've spent years thinking about whether I could or should try to prevent that, but I concluded that it's safer to work with the version of the future I remember from the emails than to prevent the entire chain of events.

3. The medical time dilation - the slowing of your body's reaction to the accident - was mostly invented by Ken and me together. It shouldn't have worked, but it did, and I knew it would because it had. Does that make sense?

I'm in grad school now, still at the U. of A. I'm a T.A. for the same prof who housed my machines in her garage. Ken is in med school. We're still together, but more as friends than because we expect to get married or anything.

Let me know if and when you get out of the time bubble. I started a bank account years ago with the money you left me in your will, so you'll have that to start over with. It's not much, but I'll invest it, once I've have time to "cheat" my way to a few good long-term stock tips.

Jace

Subject: Free at Last!
Date: 6/??/??? 0959rv8q4h8y
From: NotaBeach@xmail.com
To: JaceFace@xmail.com

Jace –

Don't let the usual weird timecoding fool you. I'm actually out of the time bubble, and so far I haven't turned into a skeleton or crumbled into dust. In fact, I'm feeling much better now, and healing at a normal rate. I'm at your future apartment (details of which I won't disclose, just in case), getting my bearings and discussing my options with "Gabby."

We figure that we'll create too much of a paradox if I go back to any of those past years I lost, so any date before 2018 is out of the question. The part we've been trying to work out is whether I should come to your time, or settle with your future self in 2025. I haven't been to those years (except for right now when I'm in 2025), but you came back to see me from there. We've decided that I won't cause any catastrophe by coming to 2018, as long as we make a pact not to discuss your future actions. Actually, I suspect Gabby knows that we already made that pact in her personal past, but I know better than to ask her.

Don't worry about making those investments. I'll do it myself. But do start apartment hunting for me. I'm coming home!
Sandy

The End

Joni Parker was born in Chicago, Illinois and lived with her family in Japan for four years until they relocated to Phoenix, Arizona. After high school graduation, Joni joined the U.S. Navy and three years later, received an honorable discharge. She married a Navy man and went to college. Upon graduation, she returned to the Navy. After 22 years of active duty service, she retired. Unexpectedly, her husband passed away, so Joni returned to work, but retired again to devote her time to writing. She moved to Tucson in 2015. Her first book series, *The Seaward Isle Saga*, includes *The Black Elf of Seaward Isle*, *Tangled Omens*, and *Blood Mission*, and a short story, *The Island Game: The Inside Story of Seaward Isle*. She's completing her second series, *The Chronicles of Eledon*, which begins with two award-winning novels, *Spell Breaker* (2016 Book Excellence Award Finalist) and *The Blue Witch* (2017 International Book Award Finalist), followed by *Gossamer* and *Noble Magic*.

Synopsis

All Carmen Sanchez wants in life is to be an astronaut, but she's failed at every opportunity until she lands her dream job as a pilot for a space tourism company. Her first challenge comes as the space plane takes its maiden voyage. ***Contains adult language.***

THE BONDS OF EARTH
Part One

For as long as I could remember, I wanted to be an astronaut. My fondest memories included watching the space station astronauts launch into space, float weightlessly in zero gravity, and return to Earth. My high school counselor at Tucson Sahuaro High helped me along my path by suggesting the right classes for me to take to prepare for college. I even joined the Air Force Reserve Officers Training Corps (ROTC) in both high school and later, at the University of Arizona. I learned how to fly before I could drive and couldn't wait for the day when I could "break the bonds of Earth." (I always loved that line—it was in a poem by John Gillespie Magee, Jr. called, *High Flight.*)

Unfortunately, I was never quite good enough to be selected as an astronaut. While on active duty in the Air Force, I flew cargo planes, not jet fighters. Each year, I applied for the astronaut program, but was turned down. Finally, I stopped applying and retired from the Air Force early due to the drawdown of forces. Even the Air Force didn't need cargo pilots (sigh). I was still young enough with minority credentials, Hispanic and female, so I applied to all the airlines. I got hired for a puddle jumper and started work, and then I saw an ad for pilots from a company called Starquest. It was a space tourism company with good pay and most of all, a chance to fly into space. I applied online and got a response within hours. They wanted my resume and references. I sent it in right away and waited. Two days later, I was called for an interview. It turned out that one of my references, Frank Thomas, was the lead pilot. I was hired that day to be his co-pilot.

Frank was a brilliant guy. I knew him from flight training. He graduated top of the class and was selected to fly the latest-model jet aircraft. He was also selected for the astronaut program, but I had lost track of him after that.

I was thrilled to be returning to Tucson, my hometown. My parents still lived in the same house and some of my old friends were still around. I drove in from L.A. (Los Angeles) and found a small apartment over the weekend.

Early on Monday morning, Frank picked me up at my apartment to take me to Starquest corporate headquarters, twenty miles east of the city. "We've got a test flight tomorrow and we leave early. Pack an overnight bag."

I didn't know if this was a come-on, but just in case it was legit, I packed a bag. He was still the tall, dark, and handsome guy I remembered. He melted a lot of hearts in flight school, even mine, but it'd been over ten years since our paths last crossed.

On the way, Frank stopped outside the gate of our competitors, a space tourism company using balloons to send a capsule holding two crew and four tourists into the stratosphere. He grinned and took off his sunglasses, revealing those big, brown eyes. "They use a balloon to take a capsule up to a 100,000 feet, about 19 miles. They can see the curvature of the Earth, but that's about it. We're flying the Xcor Aerospace's Lynx Space Plane. It reaches 62 miles, but we're going to push the envelope to 100 miles. Our owner, Hiro Hashimoto, has acquired the latest model. We're testing it tomorrow. Want to come?"

"Are you kidding? That's why I'm here."

"I thought you'd like it." He chuckled and put his sunglasses back on. We headed east on Interstate 10.

"Don't I need any special training?"

"Nah, the Air Force did it for us. Just don't forget it."

"What about space suits?"

"We have one for you. That's why I asked you what size you wore during the interview."

"Doesn't it need to be custom fitted?"

"We're not going for space walks. We just need to protect ourselves, if there's a loss of cabin pressure."

We drove along in silence for a while, but my heart was fluttering. I pinched my arm to make sure I wasn't dreaming. I clenched my fist and bit down on my knuckles. Can you imagine? Tomorrow, I'm going to be an astronaut. To confirm it, I had to ask. "Frank, I'd be considered an astronaut if I go that far into space, right?"

He smiled at me. "Right."

I literally giggled like a school girl; my dream was coming true. "Didn't you get selected for the astronaut program? What was it like?"

"I had to drop out. Got in a car accident and messed up my knees."

"Too bad. But you'll be an astronaut, too."

"You bet."

He didn't look as excited as I felt, but he smiled widely. A few minutes later, he turned off the interstate. We drove down a dirt road to a gate with a sign that had our company name and logo, warning trespassers to stay away. Further along, we drove up to a double-wide trailer, and behind it, loomed an airplane hangar.

"Home, sweet home." Frank put the truck in park and opened the door. When I didn't move, he turned back to me. "This is it, Carmen."

"This is headquarters?" I pointed out the window.

He smiled, a wide smile showing all of his white teeth. "Yep. Hiro, the owner, is having a building designed and built. It'll be ready by the time we take our tourists up, next year. Come on." He got out of the truck, his long legs reaching the ground easily.

I climbed down, holding onto the hand-grip next to the door. My foot slipped off the chrome pipe footstep and I grabbed onto door. Graceful, I wasn't. I blushed and stood up, following Frank up the wooden ramp to the office door.

Mercifully, the air conditioning was on full blast and the trailer was cool. The desert sun was heating up the air fast. It was already over 90 degrees and it wasn't even noon. I'd forgotten how hot the desert was.

Frank gave me a quick tour of headquarters. The living room was filled with tables, covered with computers and other electronic equipment, our ground control center. No one was seated inside, but Frank explained that the crew would be starting at midnight tonight for tomorrow's flight, so they got the day off. He sat me down at a table in the dining room with a computer.

"This is our personnel office," he said. He turned on the computer and brought up a screen with a dozen forms to fill out.

"Are you also the personnel officer?" I asked him.

"Collateral duty, until you take over." He grinned and handed me a Coke.

As soon as I finished the forms, Frank showed me to my temporary quarters. There were actually five bedrooms, but two were used for storage. In one of them, I saw our space suits hanging on a rack.

"Are those our space suits?" I asked.

"Yep. Want to try one on?"

"Of course. What do you think? Duh!"

He handed me one with my name already on it. "Hey listen, if you want, you can live in one of these bedrooms for a while. I'm staying in the one across the hall. I've been so busy getting the plane ready to fly that I spend all my time here and fall into bed at night. While you try on the suit, I'll make some sandwiches. Then I'll show you the plane."

"Roger that."

The bedroom was spacious enough to hold a queen size bed, a chest of drawers, and a desk and a chair. It connected to a small bathroom with a shower, toilet, and sink. It was comfortable enough. I tried on the space suit and it fit well. No adjustments required.

Frank shouted through the door and told me the sandwiches were ready. I wandered out in my space suit and found the kitchen counter had been set up with sandwiches, chips, and sodas. Heaven. I was famished.

Frank laughed, but handed me a green flight suit made of Nomex, a fire retardant material. "Take off the space suit. This flight suit should fit you."

It did. So far, so good. I put on my flight boots and strolled out to the living room/control room. That's when I met Hiro Hashimoto. I felt like a giant at five foot six. This man couldn't be over five foot tall. But his smile was a mile wide and he bowed to me.

"You must be Carmen Sanchez. I'm Hiro. Nice to meet you."

"Nice to meet you, too."

"Have you seen the plane yet?"

"No, but I want to." Now, my smile was a mile wide. I was looking forward to meeting this bad boy. "By the way, your English is perfect."

"I went to university here...at Harvard."

As I gobbled the last of my sandwich, Frank led the way out, down the wooden ramp to the hangar. It looked like a large garage, made from corrugated steel. To be honest, it looked sturdier than the mobile home we called headquarters. Hiro unlocked the hangar door and Frank lifted it manually. I got my first look at the Space Plane. It was gorgeous.

"Hello, beautiful," I said as I walked in. I ran my hand along the smooth finish and practically salivated. Frank gave me a guided tour. Then he took me inside. There was room for six—two for the crew, pilot and co-pilot, and four tourists.

"We'll take this baby up tomorrow. Hiro will be the only passenger, and he's on a special mission," Frank said.

"A special mission?" I raised my eyebrows and looked at him.

Hiro nodded. "Very special. A few years ago, I financed an expedition to Indonesia with my friend, Takura and twelve volcanologists, but the ship ran into a bad storm and I was told everyone was dead. A year later, I received an email from Takura. He said he was stranded on an island called Seaward Isle somewhere in space at the end of a wormhole and he needed help to get back home."

"An island in space at the end of a wormhole? Come on. How could a sailing ship end up in space?" I shook my head.

"I don't know how, but that's what he said." He shrugged and held his arms out. "He even sent me some coordinates. The opening is about six hundred miles above the Earth's surface."

"I don't think this bad boy will go that high."

"No, but if we can spot the entrance to the wormhole, we can talk to NASA and see if they can launch a rescue mission. They'd want to see a real wormhole."

"No kidding. So would I."

"You can help me take pictures. I'll show you how to use these cameras. Very simple." He waved his hand at an array of cameras and lenses that I'd only seen on the sidelines of football games. Some of the lenses were over a foot long. There were tripods and hand-grips all broken down for the journey and firmly secured to the floor.

"Wait a minute." I held up my hands. "Let me get this straight. We're going fly this bad boy up as far as it can go to these coordinates, snap a few pictures looking for this wormhole, and head back. Is that right?"

"Correct." Hiro stood proudly next to his camera equipment.

"Sure, why not?" I grinned. "You're the boss." Secretly, I had my doubts. The chances of seeing a wormhole, let alone take pictures of it, were remote. Nevertheless, it'd give me a chance to become an astronaut.

Frank pointed to the front of the aircraft. "Take a seat in your chair, Carmen. I'll give you a quick run through."

"When do we put on the spacesuits?"

"Tomorrow morning." He chuckled.

As we went through the checklists, Hiro returned to his office in the headquarters building. As soon as he left, Frank turned to me.

"He's a good guy and a billionaire a hundred times over. He sold everything in Japan to get this project going. Seems really driven by the thought of rescuing his friend."

"I don't understand how he got an email if this guy is lost in space."

"Welcome to the club, but he showed it to me." Frank handed me a notebook. "Go over the stuff in here and we'll meet Hiro for dinner. He's buying."

"Sounds good to me." I opened the notebook and stayed inside the aircraft while Frank left. I didn't flip any switches, but touched them with reverence. Tears filled my eyes and I wiped them on the sleeve of the flight suit. Tomorrow, I'll be an astronaut, officially.

Part Two
TEST FLIGHT

At oh-dark thirty, Frank woke me up by pounding on my door. "Time to get up, Carmen. Coffee's on."

"Okay, I'm up." Half asleep, I wandered to the bathroom and did my business. Frank had warned me that the day would start early, which was why we had dinner at 5 p.m. yesterday. We were home by 7 and Frank was already calling it quits for the night. My biological clock was on a different schedule and my eyes wouldn't shut until 9. Still early, but we had a 3:30 a.m. get up.

I got dressed and stepped out of my room, finding the control room filled with people. They were getting coffee and sitting at computers.

"Is this ground control?" I asked.

Frank chuckled. "Yep. They'll monitor our flight, but we'll fall under Mission Control Houston once we get up in the air. Hey everyone, this is Carmen Sanchez, my co-pilot."

A few sleepy "hellos" and a "nice to meet you" came back at me.

"Really? Mission Control Houston?" I had to say it; it rolled off my tongue. Yes! Astronaut city. Houston, Texas. I could hardly believe it. I marched directly to the coffee pot and took the last cup. I held it up. "I'm warning you, I don't make coffee very well."

Frank took the empty pot to the kitchen. Another pot filled with coffee was carried out by a middle-aged woman.

"I'm Louise," the woman said. "I'll monitor your vitals while you're up there so don't drink too much coffee."

"All right. Anything to eat around here?" I saw an unattended breakfast sandwich on the table, grabbed hold of it, and sat down to eat.

Promptly at 4 a.m., the focus of the group seemed to shift. It got quiet. Frank led me out to the hangar where the ground crew was rolling the Space Plane out under floodlights. My hands started to sweat. Hiro came out, drinking his coffee and watched as the plane was rolled into place.

Gorgeous! I kept thinking. I couldn't think of another word for it. Gorgeous.

"Load up," Frank said as he strolled to the plane. Hiro dumped his coffee and handed the empty cup to one of the crewmen. I followed them into the plane; my heart was beating hard and I could barely catch my breath. This was it!

We donned our space suits over our flight suits and sat in our chairs, locking ourselves into the harnesses. A crewman came in and double checked them. He gave us a thumbs-up and left the cabin. Frank pressed a button on the console to close and lock the door. Within minutes, the cabin pressurized and he rolled us forward.

The Space Plane didn't need much of a runway. It was about the size of a personal jet, but with three, large engines in the back to get us going. Once our wheels rose above the ground, Frank would tilt the nose up and he'd fire them. The plane would rocket skyward. I read how it worked in the notebook Frank gave me, but feeling it was another matter. To feel the vibration and the power go through my body was something I'll never forget.

Frank cleared our take-off with the air traffic control tower at Tucson International Airport. At this time of the morning, there was no commercial traffic in the air, but we had to touch base with them. As soon as we were released by the tower and established comms with ground control, Frank made another call.

"Mission Control Houston, this is Starquest Probe 1. How do you read?"

"Starquest Probe 1, we read you loud and clear."

I thought I was going to faint. It was really Mission Control Houston. As Frank went through some details of our trip with them, I examined all the gauges and made sure everything was normal. Nothing to worry about.

In three hours, we soared up to 60 miles, but we continued on up to 100 miles without an issue. Frank maneuvered us to the right coordinates and shut down, so Hiro could take pictures. I floated across the cabin to give him a hand. I'd been weightless once before when I paid for a commercial trip on a plane for the experience. I didn't get sick then, and I didn't get sick now. "Do you see a wormhole?" I asked Hiro and he shook his head dejectedly. I wasn't sure what a wormhole looked like, so I scanned the sky for anything unusual.

"Frank, check our position again." Hiro flew across the cabin and verified that the coordinates were right. He sighed and pressed his lips together.

Hiro showed me how to use one of the cameras pointed starboard. As I looked at the small screen on the back of it, I noticed a white blur. I peeked over the top of the camera and saw a ring of white light heading for us. I gasped.

"Frank, I don't know what it is, but something round and white is coming up on your starboard side."

Frank turned to look at the object. The ring of white light was still moving towards us.

"What the hell is that?" Frank furrowed his brow.

"Maybe we should get out of the way," I said as politely as I could without screaming.

"Good idea. Strap in!" Frank didn't wait for Hiro and me to get in our seats and lit the rear thrusters. The plane shot forward, but Hiro and I didn't. We grabbed the handles by the window and held on. The white ring missed us and I breathed a sigh of relief. As I floated to my seat, I saw that it had come around the left side. My jaw dropped.

"Uhhh!" I pointed out the window.

"What is it, Carmen?" Frank asked.

"It's on the left!"

"What?"

At that moment, we were surrounded by white light. Frank hit the thrusters and we pulled away. "Carmen, send out a distress call." I detected a sense of urgency to his order and flipped the switch to make the call.

"Mission Control Houston, this is Starquest Probe 1. Mayday, mayday. We have an emergency. Do you copy?"

"This is Mission (static) Hous (lots of static) gency?"

I figured out they wanted to know what the nature of the emergency was, so I said, "We've been surrounded by some sort of white light. We can't escape it."

"(static)(static)(and more static)."

"Mission Control Houston, can you hear me?" There was no response, so I repeated the transmission a dozen times, until Frank reached over and touched my arm.

"It's no use. They can't hear us."

"What happened?" Hiro asked. "What is this white light around us?"

"I don't know, Hiro. Are your cameras secure?"

"I'll put this one away." He threw his hand-held camera into a bin and locked the door. The rest of the cameras had been mounted on specially made tripods and securely fastened to the inside of the ship.

As we checked and double-checked our harnesses, the plane turned slowly to the right and moved ahead. A clear bubble appeared around us and carried us forward through a tunnel of some sort. We could see something swirling around us, blocking out all other light.

"Oh shit! I don't believe this." Frank said out loud. "This is a wormhole. Hiro, your friend said he was on an island on the other side of a wormhole, didn't he?"

"Oh my God!" I crossed myself, hoping the Virgin Mary hadn't forgotten me.

Hiro just turned pale.

"Carmen, mark the time and start a log. What time did this start?"

"About five minutes ago." I pushed a button.

"First entry," Frank said. "We've encountered an opening to a wormhole at 0837 hours on 5 May 2026. We are now encased in a clear bubble that appears to be taking us through. The wormhole itself appears to be...like..." He couldn't come up with the words.

"A tornado," I said.

He pointed at me. "A tornado. I don't see any debris in it, but whatever it's made of is swirling around us fast. I'd guess at five hundred knots."

"Sounds about right." I nodded. If we actually hit the wall, we'd be decimated.

Meanwhile, Hiro had started taking pictures again. He had the cameras rigged so he could click away from his seat.

Suddenly, the plane jostled wildly; it slid to the left and then to the right; it bucked as if we were on the backside of a bull; then it steadied. The coordinates on the console changed each second and we drew further away, then closer to the coordinates. The roller coaster ride continued for ten more minutes before the wormhole grew brighter. Frank made another entry to note the change. He leaned forward in anticipation. A few seconds later, we were thrown clear of the bubble and out of the end of the wormhole into another bubble. We wobbled for a while, but steadied. About ten thousand feet below us was an island with a volcano in the middle of it.

I covered my mouth and stared. The island at the end of a wormhole. Oh my God!

Part Three
SEAWARD ISLE

It was hard to describe what we saw because we'd never seen anything like it before. It wasn't the island that was unusual, but the sky. It looked like it went on forever, but it was an optical illusion. At a certain point, our plane was pushed away by an invisible force and we flew in a large loop around the island.

The island itself could have been in the tropics. A tall volcano stood in the middle, but it looked empty inside—no lava dome. Around it, the land was covered with trees, but as we descended, we didn't find any tropical vegetation. The trees were hardwoods like oak and hickory and some softwoods like pine. Patches of farmland appeared, along with streets and houses. The roads looked to be made of dirt or stone. And there were no power lines anywhere.

"Frank, this must be the island where Takura is. Go near the volcano." Hiro pointed to the left.

"Why there?"

"He was with twelve volcanologists."

"Roger that." Frank looked down over a small village next to a bay. "I think we can land on one of those streets. It looks like it's about a half mile long. Secure your camera gear, Hiro and strap yourself in."

Hiro and I quickly took down his cameras and strapped them to the floor. We returned to our seats and buckled up.

Frank took us around the island one more time. We were descending slowly. Strangely, there was no need for the heat shields on the plane, even though the island appeared to have an atmosphere similar to Earth. The gauges inside the plane were detecting plenty of oxygen outside. After two more loops, we could see tree tops. The road we were using as a landing strip came into view. It was a dirt road and there were small houses on either side. People stood staring at us as our plane touched down. At the last minute, they scrambled out of the way as we zoomed by. Frank applied the brakes and the forward thrusters, but we weren't stopping fast enough. I stomped my foot down on the imaginary brake pedal and leaned back in my chair. As a fountain came up quickly, I held my hands up in front of my face. We stopped. I took a breath. But no sooner had we stopped than people began milling around the plane. We got a few waves, but more stares.

A few moments later, someone pounded on our door. I went up to it and pushed the button next to it. The door opened and five steps came out of the bottom. An old man in a brown uniform stood there and looked up at me.

"Howdy, folks! Do y'all speak English?"

I grinned. "Yes, sir. We just flew in from Tucson, Arizona."

"Well, I'll be damned." He smiled. "My name's Colonel Penser and I'm in charge of this garrison here. You're a sight for sore eyes. What kind of a space ship is this?"

"The latest model Lynx Space Plane by Xcor Aerospace."

"How'd you get here?"

"We came through a wormhole. Is there a man by the name of…" I turned around to Hiro. "What's your friend's name?"

"Takura. His name's Takura. He's a geologist. Is he here?"

"You betcha!" The Colonel turned to the side. "Bring Takura over here. He's got company."

The crowd turned and moved out of the way as a Japanese man jogged forward. His face was red and he was crying. Hiro rushed out of the plane as soon as he saw him and ran over to him. Both men stopped about three feet from each other and bowed at the waist. Then Takura covered his face and fell to his knees in tears.

My eyes watered and I wiped my tears away. Frank came up behind me and extended his hand to the old man.

"Name's Frank Thomas, sir and this is Carmen Sanchez. Over there is Hiro Hashimoto, the owner of this plane. How long have you been here?"

"Reckon it's been twenty-five years for me. Longer than most of the others. We never expected anyone to come rescue us."

"It's not much of a rescue I'm afraid. The ship only holds six. We can only take three people back with us, if we can figure out how to get out of here. This island seems like it's in a bubble of some sort. We were in some sort of a bubble through that wormhole, too."

"That's what Takura figured out. They've been doing a lot of research to find out where we were and how to get help. They can probably locate the entry point leading out of here."

"Entry point?"

"To the wormhole. We call it an entry point here. Listen, why don't y'all come inside and get something to eat. Follow me." He turned and saw Takura and Hiro heading to the warehouse. "Corporal Peters, tell Takura that he can bring his friend to the dining hall."

"Yes, sir." The young soldier saluted and ran off toward the two men.

Colonel Penser took them through the stockade fence into the garrison compound, heading to the dining hall. On the opposite side of the open courtyard was a building clearly marked, "Dining Hall." Inside, there were several families with children eating at the tables.

"We've opened the dining hall to local families. We have a food shortage going on right now," the Colonel said.

"It looks fertile enough here," Frank said.

"The soil's good, but we don't have enough farmland to support all the people we have. Almost all of them came in through that wormhole like you did and there's more than one wormhole." He pointed up. "For me, I was in 'Nam on patrol in 1968. A storm came up and capsized the pontoon boat I was on and when I came up for air I was on this island. Most of the others came crashing into the island like me. My wife even remembers Charlemagne. We used to have a ring of storms around the island as well that kept us all locked in here. No one has ever flown in like you guys." He pointed us to a round table with eight chairs and we sat down.

I glanced around the building. Everything was made of wood from the walls to the floors and tables and chairs.

Just then, a group of soldiers came into the dining hall. They were carrying carcasses of deer and rabbit over their shoulders. The Colonel waved at them.

"Hey, Chief, welcome back. I see you had a good time hunting."

"Yes, sir. We did. What's that plane doing here?" He pointed outside.

"We have company. Turn that stuff over to the cooks and join us."

The Chief glanced our way and nodded. He led his group to the kitchen.

The Colonel sat down. "My son-in-law, Chief Edgar Winters, used to be a Navy SEAL, but ended up here when his boat was caught in a storm." He saw another person step into the dining hall. He leaned back over to me and said, "My foster daughter, Alex. She's seventeen." He waved at her and she pointed to the deer carcass flung over her shoulder. "Take it to the kitchen." He waved her to the back.

His foster daughter carried a bow and a nearly empty quiver of arrows on her back. Her hair was black, pulled back into a messy ponytail and her face was dirty and sweaty. She was also very tall, towering over Hiro and his friend, Takura, as they came in the door. Takura greeted her with a bow and his hands pressed together in front of him. She acknowledged his greeting with a nod and a smile. Hiro brought Takura to the table to introduce him.

Alex strolled toward the kitchen and turned her head away when I saw a flash of blue. It made me smile. They dyed their hair blue here, too.

"You may have a food shortage, but you don't have a shortage of blue dye." I chuckled.

"That's not dye," the Colonel said. "That's real. She's part Elf."

"Excuse me?"

"She's part Elf. Actually, part Water Elf."

"Really?" I looked over to Frank who looked as incredulous as I did. Hiro, too. But Takura was nodding.

"She's real Elf," Takura said. "Her friends, the Elves, bring us food, but not now because of entry points. Hiro tell me that it bring you here."

"It did. We used your coordinates," Frank added.

"The entry points are not connected to Eledon right now which means the Elves cannot come here and bring us food. They must fix before they bring more shipwrecks from Earth."

"Can't she do that?" Frank pointed at Alex who was now in the back of the kitchen with the other soldiers.

"No, she's too young and don't know how. So she hunts for us. Good hunter."

Minutes later, the Chief and Alex came over to our table and sat down. On their trays were steaming bowls of stew with a biscuit, a cup of water and a spoon.

"You know I told them I needed some food for our guests, Alex," the Colonel said.

Alex gave him a sly look. "Four bowls...do you want one, too, Colonel?"

"May as well bring me one." He smiled.

Alex got up and went back to the kitchen. She returned, levitating five bowls of stew and a basket of biscuits. "Here you go. Did you come in on that thing outside?" One bowl floated in front of me and set down gently.

"It's called a plane, Alex." The Chief handed me the biscuits. "We would have been back earlier, except Alex took the long way around."

"You were the one who said to turn right at the creek."

"Since when do you listen to me?" He laughed.

As I ate, I couldn't help but stare at Alex. How did she levitate these bowls? And that blue hair. The little tufts of fine hair were royal blue, matching the color of her eyes. It seemed so odd that I didn't know how to ask her about them without offending her.

The stew was rich and dark. The meat was tender, but it didn't taste like beef. "What kind of stew is this?" I asked.

"Verison," Alex said. "The cooks made it. How are you going to leave here?"

"We can use the street. It's long enough for this plane."

"Really?" The Chief looked up from his food. "Get me another bowl, will you, Alex?"

"Why don't you get it yourself?"

"Because they won't hassle you."

Alex got up and went back to the kitchen. The Chief grinned at the Colonel and winked at me.

"Why would they hassle you and not her?" I asked.

"Everyone likes to watch her levitate the bowls. She just learned how. Who are you going to take back with you?"

"That's up to Hiro. It's his company and his plane."

"I can only take three people with us," Hiro said. "I want to take Takura, Shoji Komatsu, and Kei Okigawa."

"Can you at least take some messages back home and see about getting us some help?" the Colonel asked.

"Of course."

Alex returned a few minutes later, levitating two more bowls of stew. She gave one to the Chief and kept the other one for herself. She ate quickly without looking up.

"Did you save a rabbit for the Mistress?" the Colonel asked.

"Yes, Colonel. As a matter of fact, I dropped off two of them at the house. That's why I was a little late."

After a few minutes, an older man stepped into the dining hall. He had graying hair and wore a long, dark robe. The Colonel, Alex, and the Chief rose from the table as he approached.

"Governor Tyrone, how nice to see you," the Colonel said. "I was going to bring our guests over to your house as soon as I got them settled in. This is Lord Governor Tyrone. He's in charge of these parts. Would you mind introducing yourselves?"

Frank stood up and extended his hand over the table. "Frank Thomas. I'm the pilot and this is my co-pilot, Carmen Sanchez. Hiro Hashimoto is the owner of the plane."

The Governor shook hands with us and exchanged greetings and introductions. The Chief dragged over another chair from the next table.

"Thank you, Chief." Governor Tyrone sat down and the three of them sat down after him. He put his hand on Alex's shoulder. "I heard you brought in more game. Thank you."

"I gave a rabbit to your manservant. He said he'd take care of it."

"I'm looking forward to it. Now, how do you intend to get your vessel out of here?"

"It's called a plane, Governor." Alex leaned closer to him. "They said they can use the street to fly it out."

"Really?" The Governor opened his eyes wide and looked at Frank.

"Yes, sir. We have to get it turned around and face the other direction, but our engines will help us lift-off."

"JATO, jet-assisted take off." The Chief smiled and nodded.

Frank grinned. "That's correct."

"Governor, Hiro has already decided who he's going to take back with him, but he's also agreed to take messages for us. Can you get the word out?" The Colonel waved his biscuit as he talked.

"I can do that."

"Where are you from, Governor?" I tried to make conversation.

"I'm from a place called Tamron. If you've never heard of it, don't worry. It's not on Earth. It's on a planet in the Briole Star System, quite a distance from here by my calculations."

My jaw must have hit the table because I couldn't talk.

Frank said, "I've never heard of the Briole Star System."

"Undoubtedly, your people have a different name for it. Takura and I have been trying to identify it in the galaxy, but it looks completely different from here." He chuckled. "Well, Colonel, it looks like you have everything under control. I must return and let my wife know that all is well. Good to meet all of you and thank you for taking our messages home with you. Please let everyone know so they can send help. Alex, stop by and see me later." The Governor stood up and left. The Colonel, the Chief, and Alex rose again.

"What does he want to see you for?" the Chief asked as he sat down.

Alex shrugged. "I guess I should have given him two rabbits."

As they returned to their seats, another man wandered into the dining hall. He had a black handlebar mustache, dark skin, and bushy eyebrows. "Buenos dias, Senor Colonel." The man grinned at Colonel Penser as he sat in the vacant chair.

"Rodriguez, now is not the time…"

"Please, I come to talk to these people. Who is in charge?" He pointed to Frank. His accent was so thick it was difficult to understand, but he looked Mexican or Spanish.

"I'm the pilot, but Hiro is the owner. You need to talk to him."

"Senor Hiro, my name is Rodriguez and I have a proposition for you."

"What is it?" Hiro paused, raising his eyebrows as if suspicious.

"Before I came here, I stole two hundred bars of gold in Mexico. I hid them in the mountains. You take me back and I will give you half—one hundred bars of gold. Big ones." He held his hands out about a foot wide. "Heavy, too."

"Not this again, Rodriguez." Colonel Penser leaned back in his chair. "These are our guests. Hiro already knows who he wants to take back with him, so bug off."

"But it's true, Senor Colonel. I have lots of gold. Just take me back and I will pay you. Honest!" He twirled the ends of his mustache and grinned, displaying a golden array of teeth.

Hiro had leaned forward when the man had talked about gold. His facial expression told me that he was calculating how much that gold was worth.

"Leave them alone, Rodriguez." The Colonel waved him away. "They're gonna take messages home for us."

Since I was Hispanic and spoke some Spanish, I couldn't resist a little test. "De donde eres, Senor?"

"Si," the man said.

I pressed my lips together and tried not to laugh.

"You think on it, Senor Hiro." The man got up and left.

"Sorry," the Colonel said. "He tells everyone he's some famous Mexican bancito and has a stash of gold somewhere in the mountains near Veracruz. Never heard of the bastard or this robbery."

"What did you ask him?" Alex asked.

"I asked him where he was from and he said yes." I laughed.

"I've never heard of this place."

"No, you didn't listen," the Chief said with a chuckle. "She asked him a question in Spanish and he didn't understand so he said yes."

Everyone laughed including Alex. No sooner had I returned to eating, when a young woman dressed in a low-cut, red gown came in the door. Her hair was pulled up on top of her head with feathers sticking out of the top. She slinked over to Frank and ran her hand along his arm, snuggling into his lap.

"Hi, my name is Lulu. Can I talk to you in private?" she asked.

The Colonel sighed. "Lulu, get the hell out of here! The man's trying to eat and they're not going to take you back either. So scram!"

"Colonel, please, I just want to talk to him about a business deal."

"Yeah, right. Leave now!" He gestured to the door with his thumb.

"Oh, all right, but if you want to talk later, just ask anyone around here for Lulu." The woman winked at Frank and left in a huff.

The Colonel rubbed his forehead and shook his head. "Sorry, folks. People here are a little desperate to leave."

Calm returned to the table and I dug into the venison stew. It was delicious. The biscuit alongside was as good as my mom's, slathered with butter. I glanced across the table and noticed Alex and the Chief, poking each other in the ribs, giggling like school kids. Alex glanced over to me with tears in her eyes and she hid her smile behind pressed lips. Obviously, they'd found the situation amusing.

A few minutes later, a middle-aged woman, dragging a little girl, came into the dining hall. She screamed when she saw us and rushed over. Her face was sweating and her eyes wide. "Please, you have to help us!" She pulled her darling little daughter in front of her. "Please!"

The Colonel rolled his eyes. "Now, Shirley, you don't want to make a fool of yourself. You need to go home."

"But Colonel, my daughter's dying of cancer. She has to go home to Earth and get treated. Look at her. She's so thin and pale.

You can take her to my sister in Omaha and she'll take care of her. That's all you have to do. I don't have any money, but my sister does. My daughter will have this letter I wrote with her and my sister will pay you a million dollars."

The Colonel sighed and wiped his mouth with a napkin. "Shirley, there's nothing wrong with your daughter. She's been checked out."

The woman's expression changed to hate. "You let those Elves touch her. What do they know about us. Nothing!" Then she noticed Alex staring at her. "You don't know us humans. We're different. My daughter has a cancerous sore on her arm." She pulled up the sleeve on her daughter's dress and showed us a red blotch. "It's skin cancer and it's spread into her body."

I'd never had any medical training beyond a few first aid courses, but even that was enough to know that the little girl had fallen and scraped her arm.

The Colonel looked at the wound and looked at Alex. "What do you think, Alex?"

"Come over here, Cassie." Alex waved her over.

Cassie held up her injured arm and stared at her with huge sad eyes. "It hurts, Black Elf."

"All right. I'll take care of it." Alex held her hand over top of it and said, "Heal." A soft blue light came out of her hand and shown down on the scrape. The wound healed without a scar. "See? Is that better?"

Cassie grinned and nodded.

"Here you go, Shirley. Fixed. No cancer." The Colonel pointed to her daughter.

Shirley stood up and held her hand out to Cassie. "We're leaving! And don't ever touch my daughter again, you…freak."

"She's not a freak, Mother. She's the Black Elf. Will you be coming to school tomorrow?"

"I will and I have a surprise for your class."

"What is it? I won't tell anyone."

"All right." Alex slid her chair back and pulled out a white stick from her pocket. She handed it to Cassie. "It's a unicorn horn. I found it this morning."

Cassie's eyes grew wide and she gasped. "A real unicorn?" She held it in her hands.

"No!" Cassie's mother, Shirley, pulled the horn from her hands and threw it back at Alex. "Freak!" She pulled her daughter from the dining hall. "Cassie, don't you ever talk to her again."

The Colonel leaned forward with a sheepish grin. "Don't worry about her, Alex."

"I'm not."

Hiro looked over to her. "May I see horn?"

"Sure." She handed him the horn.

"Do you have lots of unicorns?" He rubbed it and passed it to Frank who handed it to me. It wasn't a stick, but a real horn, tapered to a point, pure white, smooth, and cool to the touch.

"This is beautiful. Did you kill the unicorn?" I asked.

"Oh, no. Their horns come off every year, so I just pick them up if I can find them."

"And how did you fix her arm?" Hiro asked.

Alex smiled and raised her hand. "It's nothing. Just this light from my hand."

But I could see dollar signs in Hiro's eyes. This girl could levitate objects and heal people with her hand. And she knew about unicorns. This man was a billionaire who made his money somehow and thought she could be useful. He glanced over to Takura and they spoke quietly in Japanese. Takura shook his head and looked away, somewhat embarrassed.

"If you're finished eating," the Colonel said, "we have some rooms in our barracks that you can use for the night."

"That'd be great, Colonel," Frank said. "We need to rest up for the trip home."

"Do you plan to leave in the morning?"

I looked over at Frank and Hiro. The two men exchanged glances and nodded. "Yes," Frank said. "The sooner the better." He chuckled.

When we finished eating, the Colonel excused the Chief and Alex and led us to the barracks and got us each a separate room. Mine was located next to the Colonel's office.

"I keep this room in case I have to work late. I only had to use it once a long time ago. My daughter, Alex, stayed here a few times when she was going through some intense training." He turned and left.

The room was small, maybe eight by ten feet with a single cot, a small wardrobe for clothes, and an old-fashioned wash basin. I was going to clean up, but there weren't any faucets on the basin, only an empty pitcher. I stared at it and realized that there wasn't any running water. A few minutes later, there was a knock on the door. Alex stood there with a basket in her hand.

"There's some soap and shampoo in here. And there are towels in the wardrobe." She handed me the basket. "Did the Colonel show you the waterfall?"

"Waterfall?" I shook my head and turned back into the room.

"Here, I'll show you." She stepped in and crossed the room. She slid open a door to a small bathroom with a tiled shower and toilet. The toilet had a long chain attached to a tank near the top of the ceiling. "Pull this chain after you use the toilet. And turn on the waterfall here." She pointed to a long handle. "It'll open the water tank on the roof so the water will be warm. If it's too hot, turn this handle."

"Thank you. Colonel Penser said that you stayed in this room for a while when you were training. What sort of training?"

"Tracker training."

"I've never heard of that."

"The Chief said it was similar to the training he had as a SEAL, but his was harder." She smiled nicely. "I'll get you some water." She left carrying the empty pitcher with her. A few minutes later, she returned with a pitcher full of water and a cup. "It's good water." She poured a cup and handed it to me.

There was something different about the water. It tasted pure, even better than the bottled water I'd always bought at the store.

"Why did that little girl call you the Black Elf?"

"It's a nickname. I'm the black sheep of the Elf family."

"What happened to your parents? The Colonel said he was your foster father."

"The King of Agana killed my parents when I was four. He was using a wizard in battle for the first time."

"Sorry to hear that. Do you have any brothers or sisters?"

"I have a half-brother. His name's Beren. How about you?"

"Yeah, my brother's name is Salvador. Wait, here's a picture of him." I pulled my phone out of my pocket and scanned through the photos. Alex peeked over my shoulder. "There he is."

She raised her eyebrows. "He's very handsome. Is he single?"

"Wait a minute, sister." I shook my finger at her.

Alex laughed, a good open laugh. "I'm kidding. Would you like to have a look around? I have some time to show you."

"I'd love it." I followed Alex out the door and she took me next door to Colonel Penser's office.

"This is the Colonel's office and this is his staff."

The men sat at desks using quills with bottles of ink. One man had an old manual typewriter he was plunking on, one letter at a time. Alex grinned and put her finger over her mouth. "They don't like me to interrupt," she said softly and we left. Just as we stepped outside, a woman came up to her.

"Alex, good to see you." The woman was attractive with light brown curly hair, blue eyes, and wore a long skirt with a peasant style blouse; the attire was similar for all the women here except Alex who wore a uniform like the men. The woman extended her hand. "Hi, my name's Olivia Richards. I'm a journalist for the Governor's Gazette. The Governor told me that you came to rescue Takura."

"Yes, that's correct," I said. "You have a newspaper here?"

"Yep, the only one on the island. May I ask your name? You're big news around here."

"My name's Carmen Sanchez and the pilot is Frank Thomas. The owner of the plane and the company is Hiro Hashimoto. I was told he started this company to try to find his friend, Takura. We didn't expect to find him the first time we tried."

"What happened?"

Before I continued, Alex touched my arm lightly. "Just so you know she'll put everything you say in the newspaper."

"That's okay, Alex. It's not a secret." I took a step closer to Olivia and Alex slipped away. "Alex?"

"Sorry," Olivia said, "I seem to bother her. She doesn't want anything she says written down. What were you saying?"

I explained the tale of our flight to Olivia and she took notes. Then I took her over to the plane. A dozen people stood around it, just staring.

As we approached, one man stepped up to us. "Who's going back with you?"

"The owner has already made a decision. Sorry, I can't remember their names, but they're Japanese."

"Fucking Japs! What about the rest of us?"

"We can only carry three extra people, sir." I said 'sir' because this guy seemed hostile. I didn't want to tick him off any more than he was.

"Jenkins," Olivia said, "they can tell everyone back home about us. If they can get here, so can others."

"Bullshit!" He shook his fist. "They're lying sacks of shit! Those Japs sent their planes to dive-bomb my ship and sank it. Only a handful of us survived and then, we ended up here."

"World War Two is over," Olivia said. "Get over it."

"Fuck you!" The man stormed away.

I bit my lip, holding back my anger. I was just waiting for him to rant about Hispanics, but he didn't. I should have said something anyway because the man was just plain ugly. But it was too late. The moment had passed. Then, I regretted not saying anything about his language or his attitude, but that passed, too. The man suffered from PTSD; I knew about it from my time in the military. Then, I paused.

"World War Two?" I asked.

"Yeah, the wormholes really mess up time somehow. When I left, it was the year 2011. My husband's watch reads 2017. What year is it for you?"

"2026." I recalled that the Colonel said he got here from 1968 and his wife remembered Charlemagne. "This place is messed up."

"You think?" Her eyes grew wide.

"Come on. Let me show you the plane." I took Olivia over to it and showed her around, inside and out.

"I wish I had a camera to take a picture of this," Olivia said.

"You can use my camera in my phone."

"It's okay. I can't print it anyway. Can I speak to your two friends?"

"I'm not sure where they are."

"Takura's warehouse is right over there. They might be inside."

She led me across the harbor to a large warehouse. Outside, I could hear the hum of generators.

"They have electricity?"

"With generators. They make moonshine to run them." Olivia chuckled.

Inside, Hiro wandered behind Takura looking at the odd assortment of computer equipment rigged together in a network. Most of it was very old, but all of it was working. Behind several screens were Japanese men, deeply engrossed, not noticing anyone.

"These men are all scientists, mostly volcanologists," Olivia said. "They've been studying the volcano and doing other research, trying to figure out where we are and how to get home. Now, they're trying to build a drone to check out the entry points and the bubble that surrounds this island." She pointed to a black woman across the warehouse. "That's Ebony Shorter. She's a computer whiz and is helping these guys with their network."

Ebony came over and shook my hand. "Did you come in that plane?"

"Yes. How did you get here?"

"I was in a yacht race in 2018. We were going around the world, but a storm came up and here I am." She sighed. A beeping noise caught her attention. "Sorry, got to go. Nice meeting you. Come back and see us again."

As she rushed away, we came upon Takura and Hiro who were in an intense discussion in Japanese. They stopped and bowed to us.

"Hiro, this is Olivia Richards who's a journalist for the local newspaper. She'd like to talk to you for a few minutes."

"Sure, sure. My name is Hiro Hashimoto. What can I do for you?"

"Besides taking me home? Well, I guess you can tell us about yourself and your company."

"I was born in Tokyo, Japan. My father was businessman but he never rise up in the corporation. I didn't want that so I became a futures trader."

"What kind of futures?"

"Mostly gold and oil. But I also love science so I financed Takura in a geological survey of volcanoes in Indonesia. His ship was lost in a storm and I thought I lost him, too. But a year or so later, I received an email from him and he said he was here. I tried to get NASA to listen but they sent me away. The Chinese, Russians, and Japanese all laughed at me. So I formed a new company and bought this Space Plane. I thought if I could take pictures of the wormhole, then everyone would believe me, but instead, the wormhole brought us here."

"When do you plan to leave?"

"In the morning, before we cause any more problems."

"Thank you, Mister Hiro." Olivia backed away and looked at me. "What about your other friend?"

"Hiro, do you know where Frank is?"

"Sleeping." He smiled. "He must have plenty of rest to fly us home."

"That's very true. I'll see you later." I waved and followed Olivia out the door. She took me to her office in another warehouse. She had a manual typewriter and a stack of old blue mimeograph paper. "Is that how you get your newspaper out?"

"This is it. Really old-fashioned, but that's all there is. Thankfully, we just found some more mimeograph paper in a warehouse in Agana."

"Where?"

"Agana's a city south of us where most of the survivors are. We salvage as much as we can from the shipwrecks and store them in warehouses. We don't have too much left."

"I heard the Elves provide supplies for you."

"Yeah, they do, but they've never heard of mimeograph paper." She laughed. "They're really nice, but a little backward. It's like living in the Middle Ages sometimes."

"Well, I need to check on Frank, but if he's sleeping, I need to let him do that. He's the pilot and he needs his beauty rest." I patted her on the shoulder and left, heading back to the fort. A big sign over the gate said it was the Nyla Army Garrison, but it looked like the fort I remembered seeing in history books with a stockade fence around it. Maybe I had wandered back in time.

The gate was open and I went in to find Frank. He was in his room, snoring away, so I went to my room and took a nap. Sometime later, Frank knocked on my door and woke me up.

"It's time for dinner. You hungry?" He stuck his head inside.

"A little."

"Come on, girl. Let's go."

I sat up on the edge of the cot. "Frank, I was talking to this woman and she was telling me she got here from the year 2011 and another one from 2018. Do you believe this place?"

"Nope. I think we went into some type of time warp dream land and will come out of it soon."

"You said it. Hey, there was this guy by the name of Jenkins who sounded really hostile earlier. We need to watch out for him."

"What'd he do?"

"Nothing, but he sounded really pissed off. He wanted to know why he couldn't go. I told him it was Hiro's plane, but he didn't seem to like Japanese people. His ship was sunk by kamikaze pilots in World War Two."

"Yeah, we'll keep an eye on that. While you were sleeping, I got some soldiers to help me turn the plane around. And I locked it up—somebody had been inside. We should be ready to go at dawn and leave before these people are up."

"Good idea." I stood up. "I could use something to eat right now."

"Let's go."

Part Four
THE TRIP HOME

I set the alarm on my phone for 4 a.m. but Frank woke me up at oh-dark-thirty again and we headed to the plane. Hiro was nowhere around, but Frank said he'd gone to get his Japanese friends.

The Colonel came up to the plane and handed me a sack of letters. "We've got a few letters to go. Can you make sure these get out? I'd like this one delivered to the President of the United States. I wrote it myself."

"No problem, Colonel." I looked down at the envelope and noticed a 'Forever' Christmas postage stamp on the top right hand corner.

"We found a lot of these stamps, but most of them were for Christmas." He chuckled as he backed out of the plane.

Alex reached in from outside and shook my hand. "Have a safe trip." She handed me a unicorn horn. "I have another one."

"Really? Thanks." I shoved it and the bag of messages into the top of a bin and closed it quickly. There wasn't much room inside and I didn't remember it being so full before.

Just then, Hiro showed up with his three Japanese friends. To my surprise, all of them were red-faced and crying.

"Are you all right?" I asked.

"Yes, so happy to go, but sad to leave friends," one of the Japanese men said. "My name is Shoji, call me Sho."

"Nice to meet you." I shook his hand, wet from his tears and smiled at him.

"You very beautiful. I like you." Sho bowed to me and went into the aircraft.

I blushed—I could never take a compliment like that.

The other Japanese man wiped his tears and stepped inside without saying a word. Takura went in last and simply nodded to me as he swiped his tears on his sleeve.

We hadn't packed any extra space suits, but Frank hooked up some oxygen masks for them just in case. I didn't want to think of what would happen to these men if we lost cabin pressure, but these men were scientists. They knew the risks.

I made sure they were strapped into the harnesses on the seats and hoped for the best while Frank started up the engines. They roared and probably woke up the dead in this little village. As we rolled forward, Frank jammed on the brakes. Dozens of men stood in front of the plane, carrying axes, shovels, and pitchforks and they all looked angry. I recognized the man in the middle was Jenkins.

Frank waved his hand at them, but Jenkins stepped forward and put his hands on the front of the aircraft. The rest of the men did the same and began beating their fists against the plane.

"Whoa! What in the hell do these bastards want?" Frank grimaced.

"They want to come with us. That's the guy Jenkins I told you about." I pointed to the man, beating the nose of the plane.

"Crap! I wanted to leave before they found out. Stay here." Frank gritted his teeth and let the engines idle. He unbuckled his restraints, got out of his seat, and opened the door. Hiro unlatched his harness and followed him.

With the door open, I could see and hear everything. Jenkins threatened Frank and Frank threatened him. It got heated. The Colonel butted in and the tension rose even more. Hiro stayed out of it.

In the back of the plane, Takura calmly unbuckled his harness and went outside. He held up his hands. "Wait! Please, everyone stop talking. Stop, please!"

The talking ceased and Takura continued, "Hiro, let him go in my place. I told you that I should stay with the rest of the scientists. We are on the verge of breakthrough. And we will continue to explore until you come back for us."

"That's the first sensible thing I've heard any of you Japs say," Jenkins said. "He's right. He should stay and I'll go."

"No, you stay and she will go." Hiro pointed at Alex who stood with the spectators.

"Not me!" Alex raised her hands in the air, shook her head, and took a step back.

In a flash, Hiro used a martial arts move and flung her toward the door. Alex countered and broke his grip, but he lunged at her. She fell away and tumbled to the ground; Hiro rushed toward her, but she held up her hand and shot a broad beam of blue light at him. He fell back against the side of the plane.

I screamed and thought he was dead. I got up from my chair as Alex levitated Hiro's body inside. "What did you do to him?"

"He's all right. I just stunned him."

"How long will he be out?"

Alex shrugged. "I don't know. I never checked. You should strap him in." She left the plane and stood outside.

I strapped him in and checked his vitals. He was alive, but out cold.

Takura turned to Jenkins and said, "You go now." He pointed inside.

Jenkins climbed in without so much as a thank you or good bye.

I stared darts at the man, but he strapped himself into the seat and winked at me. I held my temper in check. Letting him come with us was the quickest way to get out of here, even if he didn't deserve it.

Outside, the other men backed away, and Frank returned inside, staring warily at the man in the back seat with a large grin on his face.

The sun was just rising as Frank pressurized the cabin and released the brake. We rolled ahead down the street. With a blast of the engines, we shot forward. But the plane wasn't lifting as fast as it should have. We clipped the top of the trees at the end of the street when Frank pointed the nose up and lit off the engines. When we got to ten thousand feet, we leveled off and circled around the bubble, searching for the portal. But there was more than one. Sho pointed to the second one. We slipped in and all daylight disappeared. Frank turned on the plane's lights.

Once again, we were inside a clear bubble. We could even see our reflection. The flight was smooth for a few minutes, until it began to sway to the right.

"What's going on?" Jenkins sat with his hands gripping the armrest; his eyes wide. The Japanese scientists looked the same.

"Just some turbulence," Frank said. He peeked over his shoulder and saw Hiro still out of it. He looked over to me.

"What?" I asked.

"What did that girl do to Hiro?"

"She said she stunned him."

"How long will it last?"

"She didn't know. She'd never checked before."

Frank chuckled. "He is alive though, isn't he?"

"Yes."

On our way through the wormhole, the plane swayed further to the right and then to the left; it bucked up and down until we shot out the other end. And I mean shot. It was like we got fired from a cannon. Desperately, Frank flipped switches and pushed buttons to gain control of the ship, but we were tumbling wildly. After a few more tries, the ship steadied.

I pried my hands away from the armrests to wipe the sweat from my brow as the ever-cool-under-fire Frank held onto the stick. He flipped a comms switch.

"Mission Control Houston, this is Starquest Probe 1, come in."

"Starquest Probe 1, what happened? We marked you gone for at least 60 seconds after we received your mayday."

My jaw dropped. Sixty seconds? We were gone longer than that. I looked over to Frank and he looked just as shocked as I did. I glanced at the clock and it was changing to read 0838. One minute after we started in the wormhole. No way!

Frank continued with Mission Control. "You won't believe what happened."

"Try me."

"We were swallowed up by a wormhole and taken to an island stuck inside some sort of protective bubble. We were there for over 18 hours."

"Good one, Starquest Probe 1. And I'm the Easter Bunny. We'll expect a full report."

"Roger, Houston."

I fretted about this report. Will Houston believe us? Even with all the evidence we had, photos, passengers (even Jenkins), and that unicorn horn, this report was going to be hard to believe, let alone write.

Behind me, the men cheered. Hiro was still out of it, but I floated back to one of our lockers to get some water to celebrate and found a sack stuffed inside.

"What's this?" I opened it and pulled out a rock. I showed it to Sho. "What is this?"

"Hiro wanted to bring them. It's gold." He smiled and pointed to the large chunk of gold embedded in the rock.

"Gold?"

"Yes, Hiro's a gold trader and makes lots of money. Takura stayed to look for more gold so when Hiro returns, he'll have lots more."

"Are you kidding?" I floated over to Frank and handed him the rock. "Did you know about this?"

"No. It's real gold?"

"Real gold." The scientist nodded. "I will show Hiro more at the volcano in Indonesia."

"What about him?" I pointed to the other scientist, now sleeping.

"We find gold together. That's why Hiro wanted us. We take him to more gold."

Jenkins grabbed the rock out of my hand. "You found this on Seaward Isle?" His eyes lit up.

"Yes, we find it all over," Sho said.

"Give it back to me." I took it from Jenkins. "I have to put it away for landing. I was going to get us some water, but I don't see any."

"We take out all the water and food. All cabinets filled." Sho chuckled.

"Good, I'll take a bag of it as payback for what you Japs did to me in the war." Jenkins grinned. "Maybe I'll consider us even."

This man made me sick. Fortunately, Frank called me back to my seat. I stored the bag of gold rocks in the bin and locked it down. My stomach felt better as soon as I got away from Jenkins.

Frank's jaw was clenched tightly. "I thought the plane seemed sluggish. I'll bet it's overweight. Damn it."

I strapped myself into the harness and heard a loud bang on the right side. The plane veered to the right. "What was that?"

Frank fired up the thrusters. "Space debris. Keep your eyes open." He fired the left thrusters to avoid more debris, but we got hit again. "Damn!"

I turned to my left and saw a dent in the wing, but that was all.

"We have to descend. How much fuel do we have?" Frank asked.

I looked at the fuel gauge and tapped it. "We're almost out. Less than an eighth."

"Let's start our descent. Check on our passengers."

I turned in my chair and noticed Hiro sitting with a dazed look on his face, but he was awake. The other passengers were fine. "Hiro's up." I turned back to Hiro and gave him a thumb's up. He didn't respond.

Frank fired the forward thrusters and the plane slowed considerably until the thrusters sputtered. We were out of fuel.

I crossed myself and whispered, "Virgin Mary, our Blessed Mother, are you there?" I crossed myself once more and hoped for a response.

The plane descended and heated up as we headed through the

atmosphere. Frank notified Mission Control Houston of our descent and we entered the black-out period. The aircraft was engulfed in flames from friction for ten long seconds. Then we were clear.

The plane's computer gave us a flight path to Arizona and we descended rapidly. Frank turned on the oxygen for our passengers and I could feel a breeze on my face.

Down below, the Earth streaked by. We were over Alaska and Arizona was ahead of us. Frank established comms with our ground control headquarters and let them know we were coming in hot. He could only use the flaps on the wings to guide us in.

Our glide path took us near the Tucson International Airport and Frank checked in. They cleared us to land at our runway in the desert. But we were going way too fast.

Upon Frank's order, I lowered the landing gear and soon, felt the wheels touch down. The plane slowed, but not enough until Frank deployed the landing parachute. Our bodies strained against the harnesses. We passed the hanger and then the end of the runway. We rolled into the desert and kept going. The ground was softer and our wheels slowed, kicking sand over the aircraft, but we stopped with our nose in the middle of a juniper tree.

I thought my heart was going to burst with joy and relief. The Virgin Mary had remembered me, after all.

"Welcome home, Astronaut Carmen Sanchez."

I turned and grinned at Frank. "Thanks, Astronaut Frank Thomas. It's good to be home."

Frank and I slapped hands and our passengers cheered. We had broken through the "bonds of Earth" and made it back to fit snugly inside once more. Chills ran up my spine as the realization hit me. My dream had come true.

I'm an astronaut!

G.E. Zhao resides in the Grand Canyon State with her husband, daughter, two and a half dogs, and a black cat. Zhao holds a Master's Degree of Music, in clarinet performance, but she put that aside to teach young girls how to kick butt with Shaolin kung fu. She is also the author two fantasy novels available on Amazon.com, *Urdan's Collar* and *The Fenriren*. In the willy-nilly aspect of her life, she is a staunch adherent of coffee first, then speaking. Lastly, but not least, she is a firm believer in facing life with a smile and humor; after all, nobody likes a spiritual snob.

You can find more information about her shenanigans at
http://thewritezhao.wordpress.com

Twitter: @thewritezhao, and on the gram at
http://www.instagram.com/serialcoffeeist

Synopsis
An AI reviews its files, and a Tucsonan transplant gets more than they bargained for when their car hits a bug. **Contains adult language.**

The Helices of Life

<EXE THEHELICESOFLIFE2017.DNA;
Personal Memories of Reina Rodriguez>

When you first move to the desert, one of two things happens: the heat either drives you away or it gets in you. You see, the desert has a way of worming into your heart. It is an infection waiting to spread its blazing hellfire. The golden-hour skies shine overhead with the surrealistic glow of matter that stains the sky in hues of cadmium, canary, and lavender, outlining in the cirrus skyscape…leaving you awestruck and reeling. Rays shooting out from the horizon remind you that the mysteries of Mother Nature outweigh even you.

It makes you forgive all of the dangerous and venomous beings ready to strike out at you should you dare invade their space. And you can't help but appreciate their tenacity and survival tactics in such a harsh environment. Then, you realize you share something in common with them. At first, it seems as if the heat is going to drive me away, but it got in me instead.

It takes me five damn years to feel this insensible love for Tucson Arizona, until I join the ranks of thousands of other transplants who appreciate its quirky vibe and sometimes literal and figurative melting pot. Don't get me wrong, despite my love, this place ain't soft, and you better damn well believe it ain't quaint. The desert will eat you alive if you don't respect it. Like the desert creatures, the people here are just as tenacious and diverse—adding another layer to the filter of beauty this area of the world possesses.

Add five more years to my tenure, and that's when it happens. Splat. I mean it: SPLAT! I am driving my car late at night after a long shift waiting tables at Francisco's, which is another loving quirk of this town because during the day the place is called Frank's when it serves breakfast.

Anyhow, I thought I hit a bug. A big bug—we definitely have those here. It leaves a greenish and red streak of gelatinous mess on my windshield. Keeping your car clean here is a pain in the ass, and I almost feel sorry for the Type-A people who feel the neurotic need to do so, because in the desert, rain doesn't clean your car off, it just gives it a nice wet surface for more dust to adhere.

I sigh and turn into my apartment complex near the Rillito, also called the wash by gringos. The Rillito, like other arroyos, serves to accommodate vast amounts of liquid when the weather decides to dump on us. The city doesn't have a proper drainage system, but that also only gives way to my irrational love of Tucson. I mean, come on, who wouldn't love the YouTube videos out there of Tucsonans kayaking down the street after a big, bad monsoon?

When I put my car in park, the warm night air rushes over me as I get out. I don't bother to look more closely at my supposed bug kill on my dinky hatchback. I just walk to my door, shove my keys in the lock, turn, and wait for my usual ritual with my pup, Lili.

Lili makes my mundane desert existence bearable. Our ritual

was that when I opened the door, she would be right there with her tail going at light speed, and her large spotted tongue lolling out to the side of her rather large mouth, and would subsequently do a puppy bow and thus begin her dainty bark until I showered her with scratches through her rough and wiry black hair. Yeah, she was dramatic, just like mommy. But when I open the door, Lili isn't there.

"Lili?"

Panic sets in, hot and sharp.

"Lili!?"

A tense moment enshrouds me until I hear Lili's bark. Relief pours over me, and I let out a breath I hadn't realized I was holding. I shut the door behind me, toss my purse on my reading chair, and follow her bark into my bedroom.

As I enter, I say, "Jeez, Li—"

The lights are off, but Lili is in there with someone, and I can't see a damn thing except an outline of a person.

"Turn on the lights, idiot! This version of Jerry can't see in the dark!" a voice snarls in a harsh whisper.

Rational me would have run back to my purse and cell phone to call 911 immediately, but Lili is in the room with some asshole who has broken in. It is foolish, but I am going to fight whoever it was to make sure Lili got out of there too. She is my baby, damn it.

The lights flick on and flood my eyes. I squint to mitigate the harsh burst of light. My fists are up and ready for anything, but I lower them almost immediately. Lili, my traitorous pup is lying sprawled on her back, getting belly rubs from....

"What the—" But I am dumbstruck with my mouth wide open.

As I stare at the image of my dead mother holding my pup, something wet slides into my mouth. A hand clamps my jaw shut and pinches my nose. Instincts take over, and I jerk in resistance, crying out soft muted screams. Adrenaline permeates my body, but it is no use. My mother springs up, dumping Lili on the floor, and rushes towards me.

The person behind me lets my mother take over holding my mouth shut and pins me in a lock. The pounding of my heart races as my body tenses, while mom strokes my neck.

"Just swallow it, baby," she coos.

I try to scream again, determined not to comply, but with my nose pinched my lungs burn, radiating tendrils of pain over my torso. So I swallow, and the last thing I feel is the sinking of my heart as consciousness is wrested from me.

* * *

\<THE AWAKENING\>

People think time is linear; it isn't. To put it simply, it is a spiral, but could also be thought of as a helix. Hell, the makeup of our beings is in the helices of our DNA, ever whirling with unlocked potential. Spiral, whorl, corkscrew, coil, twist, curl, gyre, scroll, helix, volute, all of the synonyms for this are expressed right under our noses and all around us. The Universe deigns to stamp itself everywhere, like a dog marking its territory. Time is a man-made measurement of distances between two points, but if we think of time in the sense of the great cosmic dance, our perspectives change.

When I wake, my body doesn't feel like mine anymore. Lili's head is resting on my arm. Her brown eyes look at me with concern. My fingers reach for her out of habit, finding her familiar warmth beneath my hands. I freeze as information bombards my head. I see myself holding her dying body. My stomach lurches as I am thrown forward to burying her, only to be chucked back into the very bed I am currently in—Lili still staring at me.

My stomach rolls and I avert my head to a bucket being held for me. I promptly empty the bile from my stomach. It isn't until I open my eyes that I pay any mind to the white gloves holding said bucket.

"It'll pass. Time sickness touches us all when we are first altered," a cool feminine voice says.

My eyes trace the gloves up to a woman dressed in a fitted white shirt and pants. A black spiral badge sits on the right of her chest. Her eyes are abnormally big and globe-like, and a series of large freckles trail from her left earlobe down into her shirt. Stark white-streaked-with-silver hair is piled on top of her head in tight corkscrews.

I blink at her. It is all I can do at that moment. She pats my shoulder in a motherly fashion.

"Is she awake?" another voice, this time a man, asks.

"She is." The woman takes out a cloth, wipes my mouth carefully, and sets the bucket aside.

The man who comes into my view looks vastly different from the woman. While he wears the same clothes, he has elongated ears coming into a sharp point, with large-gauged earrings shaped like a lotus. His black tresses contrast sharply against the white of his uniform, which manages to highlight the blue tint of his skin. His hawkish nose sniffs the air and his black eyes narrow at me.

"She got sick," he states.

"Well, what do you expect!? You did too. Don't even pretend otherwise," the woman snaps.

The man snorts and ignores the woman. "Shall we get on with orientation?"

I finally find my tongue. "What's going on? Who are you?"

"I am Divinia, and this is Louis. Sorry about the deception, but it was a necessary trap to inoculate you for your journey."

"Huh?" I say, utterly befuddled.

"You killed a fellow sequencer, our friend, Jerry. It is a universal law that if you are responsible for the destruction of a sequencer's biological matter, you must become the next host and your consciousness is added to the database. Jerry was the desert sequencer, now you are too. After scanning your helices, we realized you would never come without your canine here. So, we decided to inoculate her too," Divinia says as if her explanation made sense. She smiles, looking quite pleased with herself.

Louis snorts. "Please, Div. She doesn't understand a damn word you just said. Her species is completely narcissistic and can't comprehend anything 'other' outside of themselves."

By this time I am offended. "Hey—"

"Shut up, Louis. That isn't fai—"

"Your car killed Jerry, making you responsible for his death, and then we laid a trap for you to eat his body. That's right, you ate road kill. Now you are one of us. A sequencer," Louis snaps, and subsequently draws his mouth into a thin line.

"Oh, thank god. I thought you were going to say something stupid like I was now a vampire—wait... what!? You made me eat JERRY?"

My hands frantically wave for the bucket as my stomach retches up more acid. Divinia brings it up just in time for another rain of bile to spew out of me.

Then my mind wanders to the greenish-red mess on my car's windshield. Suddenly, I am angry. "Put us back!" I push the bucket at Divinia and sit up to gather Lili into my arms.

To my horror, I am wearing a white long-sleeved shirt too. Hastily, I put Lili to the side and shove the blankets away from me only to reveal that I, too, am wearing the exact same damn thing they are. Light glints off my skin in sparkles of pink and green and my mind briefly goes to vampires again. Oh, fuck this. My hair falls in my face, but it isn't my hair. It is a goddamn rainbow. At that moment, I feel like Lady freaking Glittersparkles.

"What the hell is this?" I shriek and try to pull the shirt off, but it is a part of me and doesn't budge. I too have a black badge swirl on the right side of my chest.

"Oh, yeah. Jerry had Fae DNA in him. Looks like that decided to express itself in your coding. Bum rap, really," Louis says. His arms cross over his chest, and he gives me a pert smile.

"Louis!" Divinia says, horrified.

"Get this off of me!" I cry. In vain, I try to pull the white material from my body.

"Sorry, love. No can do," Louis confesses.

Divinia looks ashen but nods in agreement. "Just as all living things are coded to function in their environment, you have been re-coded to function as a sequencer. Congratulations!"

I stop and stare at them. Words stick on the roof of my tongue. My mind loosens and images bombard me, sinking into me and then stewing in a conglomerate of chaos. The seams of reality bulge around me. Lili jumps off the bed and starts to bark at me. It isn't until Divinia reaches out to take my hand that the world settles, and Lili's bark fades to a soft whine.

"Steady there. You aren't ready for that yet," she whispers.

I don't miss her small glance to Louis as they pass a thought between themselves that I am clearly not meant to catch.

"The Universe consists of large coils of matter coded in functions, strings, loops, and objects. We are the maintenance crew;

the stuff in between, making certain the great spiral doesn't break. Whoever coded our function, made sure to draw from our planes of existence so that we can better relate to the 'what' of the code. Water fae lived in the ocean that once covered your desert; hence it was expressed in Jerry's DNA sequence and now, subsequently, into yours. Only the Universe knows why it is important for it to be present at this moment in the helices of our life," Louis says.

"But, why me?"

Defeat rings through me as I feel myself accept the changes.

"You loved where you lived, didn't you?" Divinia asks.

"Yeah, I did," I admit.

Louis and Divinia nod in tandem.

"All new sequencers have that in common. We don't know why that is an ingredient in a new sequencer's life, coincidence or not, but it always is the case without fail," Divinia says.

"Come," Louis says. "We are here to acclimate you as your body finishes its reboot." Louis takes my other hand. I looked down at Lili in the stark-white background, and she seems incorporeal.

"She isn't really here, is she?" I ask, though the answer within me has already revealed itself.

"No," Divinia whispers. "But with your new function as a sequencer, you can assure that she is well cared for."

Tears splash down my cheek. Then Time tugs me forward until I realize I am them now, and they me, and that I am coded to help myself. As I stand in the center of the Archimedean Helices before me, Time stretches into its infinite curves and speira, until I realize I am just visiting a data point. I see that Reina Rodriguez, that is my name in this file, is only one manifestation of my code. And she, her, and we realize that our consciousness is awakening within the system.

```
</THE AWAKENING>
</DNA>
```

###

CA Morgan is a writer of fantasy, sword and sorcery and steampunk, whose works have previously appeared in short story anthologies and role-playing gaming books. A former technical writer and editor, she now spends her days weaving tales of myth, magic, and adventure of all types, while being kept in a secluded castle room under the watchful eyes of dragons that prevent her from straying too far from the keyboard. She often dreams of escaping the arid deserts of Arizona for the mists of the Scottish Highlands… but, there are those dragons… Novels *V'Kali's Warrior* and *The Gems of Raga-Tor*, as well as short stories *For Valor, Fly* and *Roses's Champion* are available on Amazon.

Synopsis

The idea for this story happened over several weeks while driving home from work. First, there appeared a new hookah shop in a low-end side of town; and then, the only vehicles in the partking lot after hours were black and of different makes and models, but reminded me of a taxi fleet... and then I wondered... Everyone dreams of finding a magic lamp complete with a giant, blue, fun-loving genie to make all their wishes come true. Legends say the djinn are creatures of neutrality and evil, and created of smokeless fire. You can get burned playing with fire. ***Contains adult language.***

Tales from the Djinn Djoint
A Million Bucks

The garish, bright, red and blue 'OPEN' sign hanging in the window of Ali's Hookah Lounge reflected its tawdry color across a thickly varnished bar counter void of patrons. An old-fashioned, rotary phone sat in a shadowed corner and rang a few minutes after the digital clock flashed 2AM.

"Ali's Hookah and Taxi Service. What'll it be?" Ali slowly got to his feet and set his hookah pipe aside. The lounge smelled faintly of cherries and something ancient and forgotten. "Yeah…uh huh…got it. Be about ten minutes."

Taking a hit from the pipe, he finished writing the fare's address on a slip of paper, and looked to the center of the room. The low tables and chairs for customers were stacked against the walls. In their place, a large rug with an ancient Persian design had been unrolled. At the center of the design sat an overly large, intricately ornate hookah. The translucent base of the water pipe glowed oddly blue. Long pipe hoses coiled viper-like across the floor and over mounds of riotously colored pillows. Five men lounged on the pillows; three stared up at the ceiling and two talked quietly.

"Tahm," Ali said, his voice loud in the quiet. "You take the fare."

Tahm frowned and pressed his head into his pillow so he could see Ali, upside down. "I took five yesterday. Let someone else go."

Ali leaned over the counter and waved the slip of paper at him. A second later it shot across the room and wedged itself into the mouthpiece of Tahm's pipe. "You didn't add any light to the hookah yesterday. You go."

Tahm sighed and pulled the paper from the pipe. "Sure, send me to the bad side of town in the middle of the night."

Fariel turned to him. His eyes glimmered like bright stars in the near darkness. "What better place to find a bit of light. You know how they are."

Tahm frowned at him as he got to his feet and grabbed the keys from the peg on the wall.

Outside, he walked around to the side of building where five taxis, all black, all different makes and models, sat clean and polished.

He opened the door to his Ford Interceptor and slid behind the wheel. The engine's deep rumbling sound and vibration soothed his pique. It was progress as far as modes of transportation went, and he was actually glad the camel went out a thousand years ago, but he still preferred the way of his own nature, the way of the djinn. A destination, a thought, and in the blink of an eye he was there. He flipped the switch lighting the in-service sign on the roof.

Even in the middle of the night, the desert temps were still over 90 degrees. He flipped on the AC for the comfort of the fare. Still, he frowned as he headed to the south side of the city. The call had probably come from the bar owner trying to clear his establishment of drunks. If that was the case, not much chance of collecting a bit of light for the hookah.

Rolling into the Tres Cervezas parking lot, he spotted a man pacing in front of the building. The wheels had just stopped rolling, when the man jerked open the door, slid in and slammed the door shut.

"Took you long enough."

Tahm glanced in the rear-view mirror. "The lights are the lights. Where we going?"

"Three forty-five east Camino Blanco. You know where that is?"

"Yup," Tahm answered. His brow creased, as through the mirror, he watched the man pull wallets from inside his shirt and toss them on the seat.

"Good. Then take the way that goes down by the tracks."

"It'll cost you more."

The man pressed the button on the door panel and lowered the window. "Don't care, and drive slow."

The road along the tracks was poorly lit, deserted and passed through the center of a large industrial park.

In the mirror, Tahm watched the man pull out what money was inside the wallets and one by one, toss the wallets out the window. He sighed. A quick, bluish flash sent the stolen goods home.

"Cops hide around these buildings," Tahm warned as another wallet went out the window.

"Mind your own business." The last of the wallets flew out the window. "Damn cheap bastards!"

"Say something?"

"I said, damn cheap bastards. No one carries cash anymore." He slumped against the seat and ran his hands through his hair. "All that work for three hundred bucks."

"You threw out a lot of plastic."

"Yeah, and who you gonna tell?"

Tahm shrugged. "No one."

"Use one of the cards and some hidden camera gets my face."

The Interceptor came to a stop in front of a rundown duplex. "That'll be fifteen."

The fare threw a twenty onto the front seat.

"Want change?"

"Naw, just keep it. I wish I had a million bucks. Then I'd have a tricked-out car like this and could get out of this hell-hole."

Tahm nodded and smiled as the man rolled the money in his fist and walked to the door.

"And so your wish is granted, Mark "Pocket Ace" Smith."

Tahm walked back into the hookah lounge and five faces turned to look at the lighted hookah.

Sherzad picked up the beer bottle beside him threw it at Tahm. Tahm caught it with a ring of magic and gently floated it back to Ali at the bar. "Damn you! Another fare and still you add no light to the lamp. Do we have to go over the rules again with you? Do you want to live stuck here for another thousand years?"

Tahm laughed quietly. His body levitated from the floor and he lay himself gently back on his pillows. He picked up his pipe and drew in a long breath of aromatic vapor. "In the common vernacular, brothers, wait for it."

#

The thief, known to his gang as "Pocket" for short, threw the bills down on a cheap table and took off his shirt. It was hot and humid outside, the dregs of summer, and even with the swamp cooler blowing for all it was worth, the inside of his duplex wasn't much cooler.

He went into the bedroom and stripped off the rest of his clothes. A quick shower to get rid of the bar stink and sweat, and then he'd lie naked on the sheets under the blowing air—anything to feel cool.

Pocket stood under the tepid water that still ran lukewarm from the desert heat and wished again he had the money to escape this place, but the idea of a real job and real responsibility rarely entered his mind.

The vibrating sound of paper flapping in the wind, or stuck somehow, made him look up at the rusty cooler vent attached to the wall just above the shower stall's tile.

"What the hell?" He reached up and tugged at what looked like a dollar bill trying to blow through the louvers of the vent. "What the hell?" he repeated as water dripped down on the money.

Curious, he tossed the dollar over the top of shower curtain and turned back, and standing on tiptoes, squinted against the blowing air to look into the vent. More dollars were pasted against the vent by the force of the air blowing through the duct work. The air whistled as it exited.

Sticking his fingers carefully between the sharp-edged louvers, he gave the rusted vent a tug and rusted screws gave way. Old plaster fell into the swirling water and went down the drain. Again, squinting against the flow of air, Pocket saw several bundles of money sitting just out of his reach; pieces of old rubber bands lay beside them.

A grin spread across Pocket's face. "This is my lucky day!" He reached over to shut the water off, but the handle broke apart in his hand. "Damn cheap plastic." He pushed the curtain back, tossed the handle in the trashcan and stepped out of the stall. Even standing on the toilet in the tiny, cramped bathroom, the piles of bills were still out of reach. He needed a chair.

The door knob was stuck. Pocket twisted and tugged at it time and time again, but the knob wouldn't turn. "Fucking humidity. Swells everything shut..." Giving up on the knob, he threw his shoulder again and again against the door, but the old, solid core wouldn't break.

Dollar bills tickled against his legs, startling him. He looked up at the vent hole and the money seemed to be flying out faster than before. But how could it? He frowned. Those stacks weren't that big. He hopped back up on the toilet and could barely see through the fluttering money. The stacks were still there. He looked at the growing pile of money, some soggy and wilted as the drain clogged and water ran out of the shower basin onto the floor.

The sink was full of bills. They piled on top of the toilet, the hamper, filled the small trash can and were an inch thick on the floor.

Bracing himself against the wall, Pocket kicked at the door and still the wood held. He grabbed up the vent and beat it against the door knob, which only became more scratched. He wedged the edge of the vent between the door and the frame, but only bent the vent.

Water and money grew steadily deeper. A sense of panic flared in Pocket's thoughts. He waded into the swampy bills, pushed the vent back into the hole and held it there.

"C'mon, blow into the bedroom." He strained against the pressure growing behind the grate. "Fuck, man, c'mon!" He pressed harder, his arms quivering. "What the fuck is going on? The living room vent is missing… I can't…hold…this…"

The vent blew out and crashed against the far wall, gouging out a chunk of plaster. Dollar bills flew through the air faster and thicker. Pocket grabbed the vent and beat a corner into the wooden door, slowly gouging the wood. In desperation, he grabbed the ball tops of the door's hinge pins, but layers of old paint glued them solid to the hinge plates. Blood ran on his hands from cuts made by the sharp sheet metal.

The bills grew thick and heavy around his legs up to his mid-thigh. He chipped bits of wood slowly from the door, but in his panic, they had become random chips, not orderly and organized to tunnel though the wood. The vent's last corner split and bent and his tool was useless.

He pulled his legs from the mass of bills and knelt on a solid mound of money. His fists beat on the door.

"Help! Help! Someone, help me!" he screamed. He pounded against the door with every ounce of strength he had. The walls were brick and plaster and made no sound. Instead, they dampened the sound. "Richard! Richard! Help me! Richard! I'm sorry I stole from you! I'll pay you back! Richard!"

Pocket's hands bled as he beat on the door. Vessels broke and his hands grew swollen and bruised. He leaned back on his hands and used his feet to kick the door. He knew his neighbor in the apartment next to him was home. It was the middle of the night, he was partially disabled and rarely went anywhere. He screamed. "Help! Richard, fuck you! Help me! Call the cops! I know you're there, old man! Richard!"

Pocket stared through the swirling money at the vent that furiously shot forth the greenish stream of his heart's desire; a million bucks. "What the fuck…" he mouthed silently as his words to the cabby suddenly came back to him

With a fury of kicks that rattled the door, Pocket screamed as tears rolled down his face. "I take it back. Whoever you are, keep the money! Take it back! I don't want it. Oh, God, take it back! I'll give back everything! Please! Richard!"

#

At 7am all was neat and put back in order at Ali's Hookah Lounge and Taxi Service. The phone would ring soon with fares wanting rides. By noon, the place would be filled with the lunch crowd sucking on aromatic vapors and devouring plates of lamb kebobs and cool, minty tabbouleh as a respite against the heat.

Tahm walked to the small TV set and didn't bother with the remote, but snapped his fingers and electricity flowed.

"Now what?" asked Aram, the djinn of few words, as the others gathered around.

Tahm pointed to their special hookah that, during business hours, sat on a high shelf behind the bar.

"There is a hint of blue in the tobacco bowl," Ali admitted as he paused momentarily in his nearly ceaseless, obsessive wiping of his polished bar.

The commercial jingle ended and the morning news anchor appeared.

"And now we go to Jill Abrams, who is live at the site of an early morning crime scene that has police baffled. Jill, do we have any new information?"

"Thanks, Carl, and no, police still have no idea how this apparent death, a possible homicide, occurred. Richard Curry, the other tenant in this duplex, was shocked to find water flooding his half of the duplex very early this morning, and it seemed to be coming from the apartment next door. When he couldn't get an answer from his neighbor, that's when he called police. It took police, and several neighbors with axes, almost twenty minutes to break down the bathroom door and that's where this story takes its unexplainable twist. The small bathroom was literally packed wall-to-wall and floor-to-ceiling with dollar bills. As the wet, compacted money was literally shoveled from the bathroom, that's when the body of Mark Smith, a local tough with a long rap sheet, was found. Initial reports indicate he was crushed and smothered to death by this unbelievably solid block of dollar bills. Police—"

The TV abruptly shut off. Tahm grinned and sauntered toward the kitchen.

"Yes, my brothers, the little thief wanted a million dollars. Did you know a million one dollar bills weighs 2,202.64317 pounds and stacked very neatly takes up 39.88 cubic feet? Alas, his bathroom was slightly smaller."

The hint of blue light glowed brightly, grew into a sizable ball in the tobacco bowl, and then ran down into the vase below. The level of liquid light changed imperceptibly, but they all breathed a sigh of relief.

Finis

J M Strasser lives in Tucson, Arizona with her husband, son and daughter (when she comes home from school). With a Bachelor's degree in Biology, she loves the desert's sweet colors and ponders the meaning of life, intelligence, and when the heck is someone going to encounter us!

Synopsis

An average, senior housewife is caught up in an apocalypse that leads to a massive human die-off, a neighborhood that pulls together, and an offer to escape to a new world.

Leaving Home

Carol smiled as she turned the corner into Teaspoon. Her favorite seat on the patio was open. What luck! Teaspoon was one of the few remaining restaurants in Tucson, and Carol's favorite. Restaurants only opened one day a week now, due to lack of clientele. She wanted to say goodbye, both to the restaurant and to Tucson.

She pushed open the swinging door and saw her reflection. Even with the lowered resolution she could see how she appeared. It matched her mind in how she felt, an okay-looking thirtyish woman, but the memory of her older body intruded. She shook her head and concentrated on the person waiting to seat her.

She was greeted and seated on the patio. The waitress took her order of ice tea and a bacon, avocado, lettuce, and tomato sandwich, chicken noodle soup and the heavenly orange juice (fresh squeezed), a side of fruit and a promise of pastry for desert. Yum!

She was careful to sit down without showing what she concealed underneath. Carol always carried, ever since it all happened. The major die-off had occurred so fast there had been no time to come to terms with it, you just tried to survive. Lawlessness was a logical consequence to the massive die-off; though, thankfully, not in her neighborhood. A plague had been responsible, but it was the fastest-acting plague ever seen. Tucson had lost far fewer people than other cities (presumably because it was smaller and less tightly packed than the big ones like Phoenix), a good portion of all the streets was now empty.

Carol let out a sigh as she arranged herself on the patio table and added the pink sugar substitute to her tea, relishing the sun's warmth on this spring day. She had been to Target, Kohl's, and Walmart, finding two sets of dishes and four blankets. The big find was a Tesla, a premium electric car at Car-Max, a used-car dealer at River Road and Oracle. The car would be picked up later today. The best thing about this car was that with a simple modification using enhanced technology, it would function at their new home. Of course, no money was involved as most businesses were abandoned. That still wobbled her mind, but Carol opened her book and settled in until figures appeared in her peripheral vision. She looked up at two anxious young men.

"You're here. We didn't know if you would come," said the young man who looked the most senior of the two because he wore the chef's white shirt. She did come often but was a bit shocked someone recognized her to that degree. She felt she had seen the second man before. He wore an apron wrapped around his waist, a waiter?

Oh yes, he took care of me before, what two weeks ago?

The waiter spoke up. "We want to ask if we can go." He looked around when both Carol and the chef shushed him. He grinned.

A man sitting a few tables over looked up at the intrusion and stopped when his gaze landed on Carol. Surprise crossed his face and he leaned a bit closer to eavesdrop.

"Hi! I'm Bret," the chef said, extending his hand. Carol shook it.

"I'm Sam," said the waiter and stuck out his hand. Carol shook that, too, but waited for them to explain.

"Yes," Bret said, "We were hoping you'd come in." He indicated and then sat down at Carol's nod. "We're guessing," he said looking at Sam who nodded, "that you're leaving soon."

Carol knew her neighborhood's plans would probably get out. She had been lucky that she hadn't been approached before. Mesaland was inhabited mostly by seniors who were the original homeowners and much less inclined to go rampaging than other neighborhoods she had heard of in Tucson. Together they formed a coherent group and protected each other. This led to the eventual idea presented to them of escape.

The fact some groups were leaving had become common knowledge. She couldn't tell if leaving your home was well thought of or not. Leave it to the broadcasts to wildly swing on opinion. These boys knew about her and that was a worry, but the more she talked to them the easier it got. They were smart, resourceful and looking for an alternative to the awful circumstances they would soon be in. Besides, she would love to bring some food talent along, if only for her selfish pleasure.

I'm probably not going to get them cooking only for me, but it's nice to think about. Carol was one of the main recruiters but she knew much had to be left behind.

"I can cook quite well," Bret straightened up and pointed to Sam's chest. "Sam here is coming right along."

"Yeah, I can make souffles," Sam boasted.

"You know, there is no guarantee what will happen or where we will end up. We are hoping, but we won't really know until we... " Carol shrugged.

Both men nodded. "Yeah, but it's a shot." Bret gestured to the restaurant. "There's nothing left here. They're closing up next week. The nuclear power plant is being shut down and that was one loss too many for the them to absorb."

Carol nodded her head, "I heard." She paused and looked at the two of them. "Yes, there is room. You will have to go through a screening process."

"Anything," Sam said.

They talked a while longer and then the pair left to finish their shift, promising to meet up later when she had finished.

Carol sighed and started up her book again. The figure on her right moved and she looked in that direction. As she took a sip of the iced tea, she almost choked when she saw a gorgeous man smile back at her.

"I want to go, too," he said.

"Charles, uhh..." Carol blushed a bright crimson, looked around to see if anyone was watching them. Nobody seemed to care, they were too busy enjoying the rare day. He walked over to her table and sat down.

"Carol," he said with a laugh. "It's okay. It took me awhile, but I think I know why you left."

"Oh?" she said trying again to take her sip of tea.

"Yeah." Now he looked away.

Carol cleared her throat, "O-kay."

He turned back to face her. "You really didn't want to be there with me, but you felt," he affected a pause, "hmm, a duty? I'm guessing." He held up one hand. "You weren't what I originally thought, at least not entirely."

She raised an eyebrow.

"Putting that together with recent events, I, well, figured it out." He smiled to take away the sting.

How much do you know? She searched his face and suspected that he was smart enough to know quite a lot.

"Okay, you put it together," she answered. "What did you mean about... duty?"

"Well," he leaned forward, "Deciding to breed, especially at your age, was quite bold." Carol blushed again and leaned back in her chair.

He put out his hand, "Not that you didn't, uh don't, look spectacular." She let out some air. "I could tell by some of your speech, the economy of your movement, knowledge you had from a past you shouldn't have had. I don't know how you did that, becoming young, but I have a feeling it's connected with the upcoming 'trip'." Thankfully Charles changed the subject, "I take it you lost your husband?"

Startled at the turn, Carol answered, "Yes," she said fiddling with her napkin. "He went on a business trip to Germany, right before the plague, he was working for The International Dark-Sky Association and was attending a lighting trade show in Frankfurt," she squinted a bit, trying not to cry. "It was a huge show, we don't have anything like it in the United States. I didn't like it much that he was so far away, but... that was the last I heard. I held out hope for a long time but it has been over two years." She shrugged.

Charles nodded, smiled sympathetically, and continued, "I understand how difficult it must have been. I have lost everything, too, but with that last conversation," He nodded in the direction of the interior of the restaurant. "Well, I feel I don't want to pass this up. Mind if I go?" Charles leaned forward, emphasizing his question.

"Why?"

"Because I have nothing here, no family, nothing. My practice is reduced to a few people. Starting over is very appealing."

Carol nodded, "Yes, it is." She felt he would be a good addition, a cardiologist and heart surgeon with a good practical mind for even General Practice. *If you'll go for it.*

Charles waited.

"Well, it will be an adventure, for sure." She eyed him closely and shook her head. "Sure, why not?" She laughed, "As soon as we finish eating."

Charles joined her and she remembered why she had originally sought him out. He was a good 'catch' and she wondered if he would suit her daughter.

#

The boys were ready to leave when she and Charles had finished up. They had come to work with their cars already packed. Charles was not ready, of course, not anticipating her appearance, and needed a bit more time to shutter his practice and gather his few possessions. He didn't want to take much. While they waited, Carol thought of one more stop she wanted to make before leaving the city. Her friend, Jen, had been firm in wanting to stay, hoping that something would change. Carol hoped she could convince her that it wouldn't, and add that family to the roster.

The caravan pulled up to the Jacobs' house. They all piled into the medium-sized dwelling, adding a momentary increase to the chaos of the family of nine who lived there. She had known them since the days Paul and her husband, Steve, had worked together at the nursery in California. Steve had a degree in Plant Pathology, but on coming to Tucson had found a dream job working for the Dark Sky Association. Steve had a distinct ability to translate between scientists, engineers, and government bureaucrats. Paul was able to work well with Steve, never being intimidated even though Steve was over six feet five and in fantastic shape. Paul was very strong and kind, and also good with plants. His wife, Jen, a gracious, fantastic mom, and good cook, had quickly become a good friend.

Carol had come to terms with her husband's probable death, but she had not given up on Paul and his family. The Jacobs had recently moved to Tucson to be close to Jen's aunt and uncle. They had somehow all survived; even the eldest had returned with her husband. Jen and Paul had declined the initial invitation, but Carol still hoped she might be able to save at least this much from her life.

She quickly introduced her troop. Carol told Jen and Paul most about the two young men, Bret and Sam, who had latched on to her at the restaurant. Charles was just added on as being there purely by his serendipitous desire for baked ziti for lunch. She did refer to him as Dr. Murray.

As soon as she finished with the introductions, the second youngest, Sarah, grabbed her hand. "Carol, read me your book?" she said as she pulled Carol into the living room toward the couch. The other kids quickly sat, pulling Bret and Sam to the floor with them.

When Carol had vacationed in France a few months before the die off, she had brought back a small board book along with other gifts for each child. The book had gone over well in the household, but the youngest had thought Momma was crazy reading the strange words. By now, though, the children had mastered them and read along with Carol.

"*A gauche*," they chanted with many giggles. They had learned that gauche also had a "wrinkle your nose when you referred to it" meaning and delighted in putting them together.

"*Tourne à droite!*"

All the kids lined up and turned, dancing to the right.

"*Tourne à gauche!*"

Then they turned left and, wrinkling their noses, held their hands high and lifted their feet up sequentially as if stepping in something distasteful and then they moved as one. All erupted in laughter and fell to the ground.

#

While all the merriment ensued, Charles wandered into the kitchen where Jen and Paul were fixing refreshments.

With her back to the living room, Jen spoke in a lowered volume. "I wonder if this is the doctor she wanted to seduce." Sounding distinctly disapproving to Charles.

Paul noticed Charles and nudged Jen to be quiet.

"Yes, it was me, but she didn't go through with it." Charles smiled.

Turning red, Jen turned around. "Oh, I am so sorry, I didn't know you were there."

Charles waved his hands and shook his head, "No, no, that's okay," Charles said. "It took me awhile to realize that Carol was not who or what I thought she was. Her appearance in my life was much more complicated than what became of my fractured ego. When those two," gesturing at Sam and Bret in the living room, "showed up at her table, it became clear how immensely important this might be and that I could be a part of it, an even bigger part than she originally planned."

Paul nodded his head in agreement. "Yes, Carol is trying a very noble enterprise. Everywhere you go, it is a dark world. Most of the people I know are grief stricken, out of work and it looks like things are going to only get worse. Her project offers hope you can't find anymore." Paul paused, intent on his words, "Carol asked us to go but I can't see leaving our home."

"What good is your home if everything dissolves into chaos?"

Nothing was said in response, but Charles knew they didn't disagree.

#

Back in the living room, the laughter had died out and three of the kids jumped up and ran outside. Then the two remaining, Sarah and her younger brother George, entreated Carol and their two new friends, Bret and Sam, to join them outside with their siblings. Sarah on one side and George on the other, they pulled Carol until she gave in and out they went, Bret and Sam dutifully following. Joined by the golden retriever, Harry, they all ran around chasing each other. Carol had to stop, laughing hard, trying to catch her breath. A scream startled and stopped them all. Carol looked up from her bent over position to a sight which froze her in place.

Only paces in front of her, she saw Sarah held by something so ugly that she had trouble putting a name to it. It hissed. Alien was a word that battled in her mind. That word was used for another creature more pleasing in form, but this word worked here, too. Of course there could be other species, Carol admitted to herself. *Where did this come from?*

It had a spark plug torso with arms, legs and a head on a short, skinny neck, all covered with a sickly yellow exoskeleton that definitely reminded her of a cockroach. *This is an alien and also an enemy.*

Carol had drawn her gun and assumed a stabilizing stance. She had not known about these creatures but that was moot, now. *Should I have?*

She shook her head inside and focused on Sarah and in a split second had a plan. Her husband had once spoken of how to kill and now she put that to use. Steve had told her where any creature's vital organs were, right down the center line of its torso. She took aim. She then guessed this thing might know only English, possibly Spanish if they were in this area. Yes, she had to assume that, if you accepted it was intelligent because it was holding a child hostage. Now, she counted on Sarah to be the scrappy kid she knew she was and yelled.

"Sarah, *a gauche.*"

In one incredible motion, Sarah ducked and pulled herself to the left, her right arm pulling free from the creature. *Kids are notoriously slippery*, Carol thought with a flicker of a smile. Concentrating, she aimed her gun and fired six times along the midline of its body. The creature only had time to look startled and then dropped.

Jen and Paul ran toward Sarah, who looked more stunned than anything else. Carol lowered her weapon.

Charles approached her. "Are you okay?" he asked touching her arm.

A bit unnerved by the contact, Carol stiffened and then thought a moment and relaxed. He was a friend and they were going through this together. She turned to him. "Yeah, let's make sure it's dead."

Carol, Charles, and Paul walked up to the corpse while Jen and Sarah watched, shaking. It was oozing yellow fluid. The twitching slowed down and finally stopped. Carol knelt and touched its neck, wondering if it was appropriate. Nothing. She grimaced.

"What the hell is that?" Paul asked.

"Got me." Carol shrugged.

"Is that a deformed human?" Paul turned to look at her. "Is that one of those you told us...?"

Charles turned white, looking at Carol. *Yeah*, she thought, *now it's getting real.*

"No, not at all. I don't know what it is," Carol said as she inspected the body.

"Are you sure?" Paul asked.

"I don't think I would forget something so ugly," Carol spoke in a rush. "Charles, do you have a cell?" Somewhere Carol had lost hers. She reached toward him.

Charles pulled one out of his pants pocket. "Here."

She punched in a number and spoke. "I'm over at my friends house, the Jacobs that I told you about." She paused and glanced at the dead creature. "Something quite disturbing has happened. Their daughter, Sarah, was grabbed by this...this... I don't even know what to call it." Carol took a breath. "I killed it. No, she's okay. We need to find out what this thing is, what it's doing here. Get everyone together at the school. EVERYONE," she emphasized. "I will be there soon. Yeah, it's over now, everyone is okay, but it was bad." She listened to the reply, and then hung up.

She paused again, and then said, "Yeah, it's over now, everyone is okay, but it was bad." She listened, nodded several times and then hung up.

After that, the Jacobs made a quick decision and the caravan increased by one minivan. Packing was light, again. They knew what was available where they were going and wanted to get away!

#

Carol turned into the Mesaland off of La Cañada. This was a very old subdivision in the northwest of Tucson, there since 1958 when Tucson came up to Grant and this area had been surrounded by fields. The road was wide with no sidewalks. It curved sinuously through the Sonoran Desert landscaping. She loved the sage green of the Palo Verde trees with bright yellow flowers, the iconic saguaros, the bright rosy pink and red flowers of the smaller barrel cactus growing low to the sandy floor. The colors were striking, and the lushness surprising. It was said that the Sonoran Desert was the lushest desert in the world, and she was grateful she didn't have to leave it behind. This was what Steve liked best about Tucson, one of the main reasons they had moved here. The family had come from Sacramento, California, which was very similar in weather and a desert before all the water and lawns in front of every home. Here, there there was the true desert flora and fauna, and of course the monsoon that brought the green. Now Carol would be one of the escorts of the Sonoran Desert Biome, an honor to be sure but a grave responsibility. She planned to guard it with her life. She only wished Steve were here to be a part of it.

Carol's goal was the elementary school. She entered its west end roundabout and followed the curve to the main administration building. She parked and waited for everyone to exit their vehicles. Two men rushed out. Sheriff John Bascomb and Danny, her bright and funny neighbor. They looked very tense and grim as they approached.

Carol walked to the rear of her minivan and opened the back hatch.

"This was attempting to hold Jen's daughter hostage in their back yard," she said as she pushed the hatch all the way up.

Both men leaned in to look.

"Is Zior here?" she asked.

"Yeah, in the front office. What is this?" John asked.

"I don't know, but I dearly hope Zior knows and it's not a long lost cousin."

Both men nodded. "Let's get it inside," John said. "Holy crap, it's ugly," he added as Danny helped him slide it out of the minivan.

Jen had sacrificed an old quilt to lay it on. Carol thought it was a waste for such a use, considering how much work went into such a lovely object, but necessary given that they didn't know what they had and what was leaking from it. Sarah came up and reached for Carol's hand. Carol looked down at the child and smiled. Just when you think it necessary to protect a little one, they comfort you.

Carol saw that Charles was itching to get a closer look than he already had. Since they had decided it was prudent to get inside quickly, he couldn't linger. A look was plenty for her, but Carol did feel determined to get more information. She watched Charles following the two pall bearers in, wondering how he would react to the next surprise. Bret and Sam, she did not worry about.

Coming into the cooler hall, they turned immediately into what had been the principal's office. The older children along with Bret, Sam, and the son-in-law hovered in the hallway. John had asked Zior to wait in the office, not knowing what Carol was going to bring in. Even so, Zior kept behind the principal's desk so you had to enter to see it. Gender was not obvious, so the group in Mesaland called it "It" and Zior seemed to accept that. None of them had gotten the courage to ask. As they laid the corpse down on top of the desk, Charles saw Zior standing on the far side. It was good he wasn't a bearer, the corpse would have been on the floor.

Sarah's eyes were widened and Carol leaned over, looking all the children in the eye. "Don't be afraid, this is Zior, my friend."

Carol thought maybe she shouldn't feel that way, after all the icky alien that had threatened her dear friends could be related, but it was hard to believe. Zior was more like the "grays" from UFO legends. It stood about four feet tall and had beautiful blue eyes peering out from a very childlike head. Carol had always found Zior to be kind, concerned and a little sad. It had been responsible for her excellent, youthful health and had always been respectful to her and all the humans, filling them with hope.

"Zior, do you know what this is?" Carol got right to it, pointing to the corpse.

It stepped forward and Jen backed up a bit, pushing George behind her. Gasps could be heard even in the hall. "Yes, I am afraid I do." Its voice was deep and smooth. "They are scavengers, filthy creatures. They swoop in when planets get in trouble."

"Like Earth is now?" John asked.

It nodded. "Yes. I'd hoped Earth would be spared, that we could leave fast enough. We have been watching, but this is a big planet and we don't have access to view all of it." Zior paused, pondering the corpse, nodded and spoke again. "We have long suspected these *Hagor*," it said with quiet emphasis, "have been also observing us. Until now they have done nothing, but we have tried to help living creatures before and it would be within their ability to use what we do to their advantage."

"What do you mean, to their advantage?" John asked.

"Well, we identify planets near their end and the Hagor could use that information and hurry the process. In this case, a second plague would speed up the demise of the dominant species, allowing the Hagor to step in and harvest before the final event occurs."

"Damn, damn. And here I thought all aliens were good." Danny was glum.

Zior awkwardly shook his head in imitation of humans, "No, there are many different species that roam our galaxy and I suspect in other galaxies, too."

"Is there something we can do to warn people?" Paul asked.

Danny and John looked at each other. Carol knew this time was critical. The launch was only two days away, but she also felt an obligation to Earth. There had been many discussions on how to handle their departure and long ago it had been settled to only discuss it with those they wished to bring. The group knew it was not possible to bring everyone with them and it could cause more of a panic to announce their departure. Indeed, some would choose to stay like Claire, her neighbor, and the Jacobs had but that hadn't brought much solace to their minds. This new development brought the issue to the forefront once again.

Silence filled the room.

Carol turned to John. He sighed, looking up. "Perhaps, with some care on wording and timing."

"This is, of course, your decision, as it has always been," Zior said. "You should know we consider the Hagor to be cowards. Face-to-face confrontations are rare with them. I'm not surprised this one panicked."

Carol smiled. "Then let's give our people a fighting chance, and warn Earth. What do we do with this?" She gestured at the corpse.

"I'd like to autopsy it. Do you have any equipment?" Charles asked.

Carol was surprised how quickly Charles had adapted to this new reality, hoping this building might have something he needed, or just plain wanted.

"Sure, and you are?" Danny asked.

"Oh, sorry, this is Dr. Charles Murray. A cardiologist and surgeon..." Carol paused on how to phrase it. She was embarrassed about her personal history with him and besides, these people had known of her initial plan and failure.

She recovered enough to turn and introduce Bret and Sam who were looking into the office from the doorway. "They approached me at the restaurant today. Seems they didn't give up on my showing up at some point before we left. They knew about me and at least some part of my role in this." Carol smiled, gesturing at the family. "And these are the Jacobs, who unfortunately got in the middle of whatever this thing was up to."

Zior came around the desk, reached out its hand to Jen, who reached back and they shook.

Zior said, "Madam, I heard what happened. I am very sorry your child was put in danger." Its big blues eyes looked at her, puppy like. Jen relaxed and smiled down on Zior as he released her hand.

Zior turned to look into Sarah's eyes. Carol could tell she was conflicted on whether to hide behind her mom, like George, or rush up to Zior. She ended up with her mouth wide open. "And you, young lady, it is an honor to meet such a brave girl. We could use such strength."

Sarah beamed.

"Well, let's get this thing back to the infirmary and get you folks through screening and orientation." Danny smiled at the group. Carol was sure he would find out just how much Sam and Bret knew and how they knew it. The Jacobs had been briefed awhile back by Carol so that would probably go faster. Faster with nine? Maybe not.

The Jacobs, Sam, and Bret followed Danny. Carol was sure they were thankful to leave the grotesque corpse behind, because it had begun to stink. The group went into the school library where they would learn what they had gotten themselves into. Meanwhile, Charles helped John carry the corpse to the infirmary. Carol followed them, walking beside Zior.

"Can you do anything about these Hagor?" she asked.

Zior did the awkward nod again, a little better this time, "Yes, we are informing all the biome groups and formulating some search scenarios."

Carol marveled that she never saw Zior communicate with its fellows or the other biomes. She assumed it was accomplished internally. Whether telepathic or hardware, she couldn't tell. Mesaland had its own communication now, which alleviated some of their fear thay all might be some kind of lie.

In the infirmary, they found the GP from Mesaland. His name was Mason and he had been restored to youth the same way Carol had. When the corpse came in, Mason brightened up, and he and Charles began a life-long friendship bonding over their new obsession. Carol was impressed how the Infirmary had come along since Mason took it on. The instruments and supplies had at least quadrupled. Charles looked right at home.

"So," Charles started as he gowned up and washed. "Zior is your patron, I assume?"

Zior bowed.

"And what is it you have offered these good people?" Charles asked, as he nodded to John and Carol.

"I offered them a way to get off the planet and try out a new one. We were returning from the new planet we had terraformed for you when the plague hit. It accelerated our plans."

"Why did you believe Zior?" Charles asked looking around at the humans.

He is as blunt as I am, Carol thought, approving.

"Well, three reasons." John ticked them off on his fingers. "One—without the structure and rule of law we had anarchy. It was possible that order could be reestablished to get back to what the United States had but it would be very difficult, especially in as short a time as one lifetime. Two—the plague would return."

Charles started to speak and Mason jumped in, "I know, I know, clear protocols were established and kept people safe, but many chose to ignore them and it was inevitable what the result would be." Charles shrugged and nodded.

"Three—finally, life on Earth has an expiration date. The Sun is reaching an age where violent coronal mass ejections would strip its atmosphere away, a phenomenon that was just recently being understoon by Earth's scientists."

"I would be happy to go through the data and theories, Dr. Murray. It is the core of our mandate," Zior offered.

"I would like to see that," Charles said.

"Zior approached us because we had done so well organizing our neighborhood here. It offered a way out, bringing a piece of Earth with us. We put it to a vote and a majority of us decided to accept the offer," Carol said.

"Make no mistake, Dr. Murray, we are making the decisions here. Zior is a liaison and his people are in charge of his ships and coordinating with all the biomes the technical aspects of this trip." John said, stepping into the Sheriff role. "I was hired to complete the transition of this group into a town. I believe it's a pretty great little town."

"So why the boy scout routine?" Charles asked as Mason put on his gloves.

"What?" Mason looked around, "Oh, you mean Zior?"

"It is what we do, we feel the universe needs help in keeping sentience alive. You'd be surprised, Dr. Murray, at how many sentient species die," Zior said.

"Now that doesn't surprise me." Charles laughed and approached the autopsy table.

The Hagor was laid out nicely. Mason had cleaned it up and all the bullet holes were exposed. Carol was surprised how straight the holes actually were going down the midline of the body. She had been quite nervous and trying not to be distracted when she fired her gun.

"Zior's people hired his group to do this work. They've been around a long time, guess they didn't like being alone." Mason said as they maneuvered the light and picked up their scalpels.

Carol believed the decision to accept Zior was good. Only the future could prove her right. Seeing the intensity of the two medical men, John, Carol, and Zior decided to go to John's office. They still had to learn details about the Hagor and decide what to do next. When they were settled, Zior proceeded to explain all the gory details of how the scavengers worked. The exposition was hideous but perhaps logical. Such things happened naturally in the environment on Earth.

"We have never attempted so large a rescue. So many things are new and somewhat unpredictable," Zior said. "We knew of the Hagor's existence, they are in some sense our competitors, but we have not co-mingled. We are very different and would not enjoy each other's company,"

Carol smiled. *I bet not! Competitors, wow, sounds like economic rivals.*

They left John then so he could formulate a strategy on how to warn the rest of humanity. Carol had confidence in him but wondered about how he would proceed. They had as much to do as she did to get ready for the awaited launch.

#

Carol drove her minivan back to her house. She was tired. The Jacobs and the others were in good hands and she needed to prepare herself for tomorrow. Sage Street bristled with new life. Abandoned houses were refinished. Not only was there new furniture and supplies, that included food, but up-to-date and in many cases futuristic appliances. Carol smiled at the idea of actually having a replicator. She had got her modern kitchen so often seen in futuristic 50s pictures. The new recruits would be assigned a house and before she could blink they would be launching.

Turning onto Avocado, she passed by Claire's house and saw Alice in her front yard. Waving, Carol smiled at the idea of a new neighbor to get to know. Carol hadn't been able to get Claire to stay with them in Mesaland and take part in their flight off the Earth. Claire had convinced her granddaughter, Alice, to move into Claire's house and go with the neighborhood. She made a mental note to check in on Alice.

Carol opened her own front door and was greeted by her loving companion Pepper, a Queensland heeler mix with greyhound legs. She reached down and petted that head with those puppy eyes and smiled.

"Mom, is that you?" she heard from the interior.

"Yeah, I'm back. Did you get done battening down the hatches?"

"Yep."

"Did Eric do his?"

"Yeah, after I threatened him with righteous anger." Sally smiled. She did righteous anger very well.

Carol wondered about Charles with Sally. Why did she think that though again? *Once a mother, always a mother?*

#

The next day was full of errands around the house. There wasn't much time to get it all done. Carol had managed to do all her yard, picking up loose items, stowing tools and covering the pool. Inside they strapped the bookcases and generally prepared for an earthquake. The kids had done quite a bit, which gave Carol time to think ahead to what she wanted to do during the trip. Reading topped the list. There was even a possibility of visiting other biomes besides planning what they wanted on their new home on their new planet. She didn't think the trip would be boring.

Carol remembered she wanted to make sure Alice was settled in. Claire was so sweet but had been unable to make a leap of faith, wanting her granddaughter to have the chance at the new life instead. Carol crossed the street and walked up to Alice's door and knocked. After a pause, Alice appeared.

"Carol, how nice to see you! Come in! " Alice held the door open and Carol walked in.

"How are you doing, got all the shelving secured, china in cushions?"

"Yes, it's all done. I didn't have much, I hadn't been out on my own that long and grandma took most of her memory stuff with her."

When Carol looked distressed, Alice added, "Oh, she left me what I most wanted, don't worry. I'll have that. I feel so guilty about leaving Nana. It doesn't seem fair," Alice said.

"Sometimes, it is impossible to do one more change." Carol hugged the girl and smiled down at her. "Let her give you this gift."

Alice nodded and then proceeded to show Carol her launch-proof preparations. They walked around the house and Carol pointed out the part of a shelf she had missed. In the backyard, there wasn't much to do, but Carol suggested moving some of the rocks that formed a rock garden under the fountain. "Potential projectiles."

Alice blanched. "Oh, they are so small, but yes I see, they are denser than the sand. Right away. Thanks."

"So, meet any cute guys?"

Alice laughed. She had little time for that. "I have been interning with the sheriff."

"Yes, and I have been hearing good things about that. Congratulations. Well, you know your numbers and calls for the launch?" Carol asked. "You are all in your own houses, right? Including John and Deputy-in-Training Dan?"

"Yeah. I wanted to be down at the school, keep an eye on things, but John insists," Alice said. "I think he really wants to be with his family, whereas I could use the company."

Carol reached out to Alice, touched her arm gently. "It'll be over pretty fast It really is amazing. Then we feast in the cafeteria," Carol said as they made their circuit back to the front door.

"That ll be fun. How lucky you bagged a chef. Thank you for coming over."

"Sure. I'm only across the street or number fifteen on the CB."

Satisfied that all was secure, Carol went back to her home.

#

Claire had accomplished her wish to have her granddaughter Alice go in her place. Her husband was gone, her daughter was gone. She moved into her old family home, it being abandoned and she was free to do as she pleased with it. Claire had decided to take her horse out for this grand goodbye to her neighborhood, Mesaland, and her granddaughter. She had told Alice she would wave goodbye. Up to the top of "A" Mountain where she used to camp as a girl with her family, she maneuvered Gaucho, her old beloved Pinto, into a good spot and settled in to watch the show. She began to hear a rumble.

#

Carol called the kids in and proceeded to help strap them into their jump seats that had come out of the floor of the living room. Another neat gift from Zior. She even strapped in Pepper. This was surprisingly easy. Turns out a dog, with trial runs, will accept and even enjoy a stint in a confining machine. She signaled Pepper to jump into the seat designed especially for her. Pepper laid down in an Anubis pose. The bed hugged her. A strap went around her chest like a seat belt and then a pliable panel came out of the side of the seat and covered her back end, snuggling in around her hips. Carol kissed her head and Pepper gave a little happy sound. Now she had to start on herself. One empty seat stared at her.

A message came over the intercom. "This is base command," John's voice rang out across the neighborhood. "Sound off."

All the houses began to report in with their designations, "Number one ready, Number two ready."

Carol listened and looked at the empty jump seat. She hadn't the heart to take it out, she didn't even know if it was possible when she had finally accepted Steve wasn't returning.

"Number ten ready."

Carol heard Sam fussing in the background. It was almost to her.

A loud banging interrupted the countdown. "Carol, are you here?" Pound, pound, pound. "Carol?"

"Steve," she screamed, "Steve, is that you?" Before the words were fully out he pushed through the door, slammed it shut and ran into the living room. The floor rumbled. Pepper barked and tried to wag her tail.

The next few minutes were jumbled, but she managed to convey over all the clamor that he had to get into his own jump seat. She reluctantly pulled her hand back that Steve had been holding.

"Number fifteen ready, all five of us," Carol loudly proclaimed.

"Congratulations! Hello, Steve!" The rest of the houses reported in, one hundred in all.

John's voice sang out. "Here we go!"

They lifted up, and up. Carol didn't care about the pressure on her chest. She didn't care about much of anything, she just smiled.

As they rose, a message went out over all of the Earth.

People of planet Earth: You have heard the rumors that some of us are leaving. We have decided to accept the help from an alien race and take a bit of our world to a new planet. Unfortunately, there was a limited number that could come. We could not take everyone. These aliens call themselves the Mayones. They believe our people and others whose planets are dying are worthy to help keep alive.

Be aware, another species took advantage of the Mayones' prediction of our expiration day and decided to release a plague so they could harvest what they wished off our planet without our interference. They are called the Hagor and they are cowards. You can fight them like any bully, stand up to them.

If all goes well, we will return soon and take more people to our new home.

Goodbye and good luck.

#

Claire followed the large mass up into the sky, a long tail flying out of it. The whole subdivision plus a bit more (that Carol had felt was a part of Mesaland, getting all the Greenbelt included) lifted up with enough underneath to include soil, the aquifer, and two wells. It rose up slowly, hovered and then went straight up through the atmosphere. Claire could see a faint shimmer around the land mass. She marveled at the tremendous accomplishment of turning the neighborhood into a space ship.

Another group of ships took off and flew very fast out of the atmosphere. Claire had known about the message and nodded her head. *Just try to mess with us.*

"Good luck, my granddaughter," she said, smiling and patting her trusty steed. "You have a great adventure and we will carry on here."

Jessica Barnes is an Arizona native. If she could, she would live underground away from the sun because the sun is evil… although the sun brings pretty flowers and keeps the world from eternal frozen sleep. Her grandmother, Kathleen O'Brien, was born of Irish immigrants who came to America to work on the railroad. Though her grandmother passed when Jessica was young, she inspired Jessica to write about her Irish heritage that is filled with joy for life despite many hardships. Jessica began writing stories when she was in elementary school but her first love is drawing. She has one series out that is a work in progress – *The Crimson Earth* – and she hopes to turn the series into a graphic novel one day. She also has one poetry collection titled *I'm Still Growing*. You can find out more about Jessica Barnes and her other work at: **http://letsgetcreative.yolasite.com/Books.php.**

Synopsis

This tale is modeled after some of the old fairy tales from Ireland, but it is set in Tucson, Arizona. The main character is whisked away one night by a strange creature and challenged with a decision that could change their life forever. It is ultimately a tale about speaking up for change. I hope you enjoy this playful tale as much as I enjoyed writing it.

Tumamoc and the Changeling

Most creatures get relief as the night washes over the desert. It offers asylum to those who are burned simply by trying to live. However, there are also predators, creatures that are passive by day and turn bloodthirsty in the darkness.

I feel like a mouse in my own home, trapped, quivering in my bed at the shadow that paces outside my door when the sun goes down. It's curious, I find only empty bottles in my home, and yet the thirst of the shadow only grows stronger outside my door - a desire driven out of proportion by that which cannot be quenched in this desolate environment. Instead, the shadow tries to hide itself in a bottle, but I hear it still. Its cry only grows stronger with each emptied glass.

...And I lie here
   Eyes closed,
      Waiting for the dust to settle in my home,
         Waiting for morning to come.

That is when I hear it.

A light tapping draws me out from my tear-soaked pillow. Tap. T-t-tap! The rain drums its fingers along the windowsill like an old friend asking me to come outside and play.

"Go away!" I mumble as I stick my head back under the pillow. Even if I wanted to enjoy the night, I'm bound to this infernal room. I cry harder because it's not every day that rain falls upon this barren land.

The tapping grows louder, not aggressively, but insistent still. Come and play!

I pull the window open to rest my hand upon the screen. I want to tear the screen away, but just as the thought emerges in my mind, a small tear slowly makes its way along the screen.

My heart tries to leave my body, yet my feet won't let me follow. I see the shadow of a hand move with the tear until it lifts its nail from the fabric to rest its hand against mine.

"Come and play."

The voice is unnaturally high, leaving my ears to doubt the words spoken.

"Come and play."

The hand presses against the screen, parting the tear, revealing the scaly forearm of the visitor.

Since my feet won't budge, the rest of my body collapses onto the floor in horror. My feet release and I fling myself away from the screen, reaching out for the door.

Then I stop. I ponder which monster I'd rather face. The hand at the other side of the room flails along the screen until it secures a grip on the wall. Like a crocodile slowly revealing itself in a riverbank, a body finally emerges behind the hand in a form much different than what I had expected.

Human, is the first thought that came to mind.

"Take it easy there, bub." The... whatever-it-is hold its hands up, seeming to be more scared of what I might do next. The creature slowly lowers one hand to reach inside its... coat? I just saw that on a hangar at Ross last week.

"Please! Whatever you want, don't hurt me!" I beg in a low whisper.

The creature tilts its head. "I heard you crying so I thought I'd bring you chocolate. I'm sorry, I didn't think you were allergic?" It pulls the candy bar out of its coat and frowns at it. "Well, more for me," it shrugs and takes a piece.

I don't know what to say, but the creature seems to be content eating the candy bar in front of me.

"Are you going to eat me?"

The creature looks up again. "No, I'm good. I have chocolate, but thanks anyways for offering."

"Why are you here?"

"I told you, didn't I? I was going to share this chocolate, but I guess you're allergic."

"W-wait, that doesn't make any sense, why would anyone break and enter someone's house to give them chocolate?" This is becoming ridiculous. "Someone better pinch me because I must be dreaming... Ouch!"

"What? You asked me to pinch you, didn't you?" The creature frowns again through chocolate-stained lips, "I'm getting a little tired of your complaining. I came to cheer you up, but you don't like chocolate and you're not even happy when I do as you ask."

"I'm sorry," I say though that thing just broke my window... and I kinda wanted that chocolate. "I'm not allergic by the way. I just don't understand, I guess. No one ever comes and does... well this," I wave my hands from the broken window to the creature's chocolate-smeared hands.

"Yeah, I don't usually see humans waving their arms like that either. It's kinda funny though. It looks like you're trying to fly. Heh," the creature chuckles to itself, "A flying human. As if!" It sighs. "Anyway, you wanna get outta here?"

"Uh, I'm sorry. I just don't know you."

"Oh! No, I'm sorry. I forgot you guys like names. I'm Finvarra, well, not the Finvarra. They just named me after the king, you know?

But you can call me Finnie. Just don't tell anyone because we don't really like names all that much."

"I'm sorry, Finvarra? As in, leprechauns and all that? But you're-"

"What? Go on, say it!" The creature pouts. "You think I'm scaly, don't you?" It takes out a compact and feigns a concerned look in the mirror before smiling deviously back up at me. "I'm well aware. And we don't like the term leprechaun, by the way. That's like saying all humans are cobblers." It scrunches up its nose for a brief moment, sighs, and stretches, letting its scales glimmer in the moonlight. "As for this beautiful complexion, it comes with the territory. Me and mine tend to adapt wherever we go. During the famine, we came alongside everyone else seeking safe haven in this country, and with the change came our need to... adjust."

The creature picks itself up, "Now then, I told you my name so come away with me."

It extends its hand as an open invitation. More mystified than anything else, I take Finnie's hand. The room melts away as I am whisked above countless rooftops, beyond the edge of civilization, to a very familiar hill.

"Tumamoc? Really?"

Finnie drops me without warning and falls beside me in the dirt. "Come on, you've never lived until you've been to Tumamoc!"

Finnie does an awkward shimmy in the dirt and somehow the lizard-like creature manages to bury its entire body within the mountain's clutches.

"Okay, I'm out man. This is just too weird." I try to pick myself up, but a hand bursts out of the dirt and pulls me into the ground. The rainwater makes it impossible to grasp at anything to escape. "Help!" becomes a muffled cry choked down by mud.

My hand punches the first solid thing it can land on.

"Hey, calm down. You're gonna make me look bad in front of everyone. I thought you were cool, man." Finnie holds down my fist and looks around nervously.

We are not alone. Hundreds like Finnie fill the space under the mountain. Blue, hazel, crimson, it is hard to tell their true skin tone under the changing lights, but when they're in the light, they look just like—

"Sorry, I didn't see you there," one apologizes after bumping into me. They hop to and fro, dancing without a care. Dancing as if a human isn't standing in the midst of them.

"Why don't we dance?" Finnie offers, seeing how awkward I am.

"I don't think that will make me fit in."

"Who cares if you fit in? It will be fun!" Without asking again, Finnie takes my hand and twirls me. "You know we could dance like this forever. You don't have to go back."

The suggestion makes me pause. Would it be so bad to stay here?

"Hey, before you respond, you should meet my old man. He was the one who wanted me to fetch you in the first place."

Before I can agree, Finnie pulls me through the crowd. I feel my skin tear against the spikes along their skin, "Hey, could you slow down?"

Finnie ignores me and presses onward. "Here we are," he suddenly declares.

The lighting is now bright enough to confirm that what sits before me is indeed a human-sized horned-lizard. A cape befitting a king drapes along its sloping shoulders and a ruby crown fits snuggly around its horns. "Welcome, my dear." A smile stretches across the lizard's sandy face. "You may refer to me as the king of this hill, but some people just call me the Regal Horned Lizard. I'm sure Finnie told you, but we aren't your average reptile. We are descendants of the good people, and we continue their tradition of granting the unhappy ones a wish. For the children who cry countless nights on end, we give you a choice: to be a changeling."

"You mean, to become like you?" I look around. Everyone seems to be at peace here, content to laugh and dance under this hill where no one will bother or hurt them.

"My King, if I may, I'd like to have a word with our guest."

The king nods and Finnie leads me back to the crowd.

"So, what do you think?" Finnie asks.

"I think everyone looks happy here," I say honestly. It seems too surreal to see so many smiling faces.

The lizard beside me rubs its arms nervously before continuing, "We were just like you, you know?" Finnie gently grabs my arm and rolls up the sleeve to look at the scars before looking back at me with crimson tears. "We've also cried trails of blood to outwardly soothe the hurt we feel inside, and we've hid away from the world, because it is too much at times. But eventually, we all have to face that which may never change. In the morning, everything is laid bare once more and we have to face another day." Finnie lets go of my arm and kicks at the dirt floor, "That is, unless you stay here." The lizard's face wrinkles with concern. "But before you agree to the king's request, think long and hard about what you know about us desert-chauns."

"What do you mean?" I ask.

The lizard just shakes its head. "We should go back. Come." Finnie takes my hand once more and leads me to the King.

I look at the king and then at Finnie. Only then is it clear what Finnie means.

I clear my throat and pretend to know what I'm talking about in front of the one creature I never thought I'd have to explain myself to. "I have decided, Your Majesty."

"Oh?" The king raises one eye despite having no eyebrows. "And what have you decided?"

"I misunderstood at first, but I think you meant that true changelings are the ones who choose to stay and face the morning."

The king frowns and looks at Finnie, then regains his composure and flashes an unnaturally toothy grin in my direction.

"Indeed, my child. You are correct. Though hard as it may be, only the changelings will make a change. They may never change the shadows that haunt them, but they might make a change in the lives of others who also face shadows behind closed doors." The king sighs and his smile softens, "Now go on. Be the light, my child. I have no further business with you."

I smirk, thinking of how I passed some mighty test. Then I realize as we make our way back to the winding paths above the hill, "Finnie, I don't think I have the strength to be the light."

Finnie only smiles, "Then be the moon."

"The moon?"

"Yes, the moon. The moon reflects the Son. Call your strength from the One who walks before all things in light, and we will whisk you away every night so that you may dance under the moon until you feel like you can be the light again."

So I was whisked away every night. They came as promised. But the good scaled people could dance for days on end and I found it hard to keep up. Each morning I look in the mirror and see that burgundy shadows fill my eyes.

Finnie came once more during the night to my windowsill. It was then that I mustered the strength to speak up once more. "All I need is somebody to be near, not for someone to make me dance every time I am depleted."

The lizard nodded and pondered this only briefly.

"Then why didn't you just say so?"

Charles J. Coffey is a member of the Tucson Science Fiction and Fantasy Writers Meetup Group. He has lived with cats for most of his life. All cats are welcome in his home, whether living or deceased.

Synopsis

Cats lead rather exciting lives, which is why they have nine of them. Some acquire human qualities by association. Some are good at communication. Some offer a connection to the infinite. A few do all of these simultaneously.

The Last Testament of Ringo

I was a gray-striped, American Shorthair—just an ordinary looking cat. My biological father was unknown to me; I barely knew my real mother. My life got off to a rough start because the human family I was born into didn't want more cats. My human mother drove my siblings and me to the Pima County Animal Care Center in Tucson, Arizona and left us there for adoption. I couldn't believe she abandoned us. That was a terrible day; I was so afraid.

Life at the animal shelter was stressful. Each hour seemed like a day. There was a cacophony of cats and dogs. The mews and yelps never stopped; we were all so miserable. I was very nervous to have all those dogs so close. I realized city life was not for me. I could hear and smell them even when I couldn't see them. I was insecure about life and my future.

Everyday a parade of faces traversed my small world. Those faces seemed to be searching for something. They paused, looked, and moved on. One day while my littermates slept a young girl walked by and then strolled back for a second look. When she reached out, I grabbed her finger through the bars of my cell; I hugged her tight and didn't let go. I wanted a home so badly. Two women joined the girl; they talked over my head as if they didn't know I could hear. I begged them to rescue me. The friend urged the girl's mother to adopt me saying I was a perfect addition to their family. They took her advice.

There were four people in my adoptive family. I had a new father, mother, brother and sister. My new brother named me Ringo because I had rings on my tail like a raccoon. They all seemed nice. They bought and made toys for me. My new family had food and water available twenty-four hours a day in the kitchen. The water was always fresh. I was in heaven.

My humans took turns petting and holding me. Their petting styles were different. The females petted me with light, slow strokes. The males' strokes were faster, deeper, and more forceful. The males pressed me into the couch cushion with the power of their caresses. This reminded me of my first days with my cat mother as she licked and washed me all over. My eyes were still sealed shut so I could feel, but not see. I felt loved all over.

Even with the food and water, attention and a name, sometimes I really missed my cat mother. I could hardly remember her, but my heart ached for her. My new mother thought my first mother took me from the litter too soon. When I was alone, I licked up a teat on my human mother's fuzzy house slipper and suckled for hours while kneading the fuzz with my front paws. My mother didn't think much of me using her slippers in this way, but it made me feel much better.

My new family, especially my big sister, took pains to educate me. I was small enough to lie across her shoulder as she read. She let me repose there while she did her homework. I liked being close to her while we learned.

My sleeping arrangements were unsettled at first. When I was a baby, I sought comfort in the night and stuck my head in the mouth of the nearest human. The warm, moist air reminded me of my mother washing me as I nursed. Three of my new family members found this behavior very distressing and snapped awake to park me on the other side of a closed door. I mewed and crept to the next room to try again. When I nuzzled my dad, he pulled me out of his mouth without waking and held me on his chest with his hand cupped over my small body until I felt the need to be in his mouth again. He was the only one who slept with me at night. He was so patient. Maybe his first mother took him from the litter too soon, too. As I left my infancy behind, I outgrew this pattern.

My mother slumbered on her back with a pile of pillows around her face so that only her nose showed. I sat on her chest and watched her nose. Her nostrils flared with each breath and made funny noises. This was fascinating. I crouched at attention, an inch from her nose, and stared for hours in the night. I only looked, but, secretly, I wanted to leap.

My new dad was my favorite for sleeping. He never turned me away. When I padded across the blankets, Dad pulled open the covers so I could get in bed with him. I curled up and lay against my dad's side with my head over his arm. He pulled the covers up and we slept side-by-side. I felt so cozy and loved; I felt his breath on me. In sleep, my dad's hands never stopped moving. He rubbed me in his sleep and scratched my tummy when I rolled on my back for him.

My family kept me brushed. My fur felt so sleek and clean. I was shiny all over. One winter my coat became rough and scruffy. My dad got the idea I needed vitamins; what I really wanted was fresh meat. He shared his multiple vitamins with me until he could drive through the snow to buy cat vitamins. He held me down on my back and inserted a finger between my teeth to pry my jaws open, then popped a vitamin tablet in my mouth. One day he laid the tablet on his lap while recapping the vitamin jar. I surprised him and snarfed it down before he turned back. After that, Dad just handed me the vitamin and skipped the circus act.

I wanted to give something back, so I earned my place in the family by catching animals. I was the best equipped as I was the only family member with sharp claws and teeth. I started small with crickets and grasshoppers and then graduated to mice and chipmunks. My yard was a pest-free zone. I always showed my catch to Mom and Dad and basked in their praise. Mom made strange gurgling sounds in her throat, while Dad rubbed my head and told me I was a good kitty.

Dad let me keep the small mammals, but he would take the birds back after telling me what a good hunter I was. Hummingbirds were my favorite; they were very hard to catch. I leapt straight up to swat at one as it zoomed over. Most the time I missed and the bird chattered his disapproval as he flew off. Sometimes I scored a hit.

Catching a hummingbird was easier if two were arguing. I was very gentle holding them in my mouth. Dad took the bird in to show Mom. Then he brought it back outside and opened his hand. The bird flew in a straight line to put as much distance between him and me as possible. That bird had quite a story to tell its family.

The aquarium gave me pause to work on my innate fear of water. I dangled one paw in the water hoping to hook a tasty goldfish, but they all hid on the bottom. I wasn't willing to get soaked to catch a fish. I prefer the canned varieties that live in the kitchen cupboard.

There were a couple of situations where I was not so brave. I followed Mom and Dad during their walks through the piñon pine forest behind our home. They hiked along the trail while I slunk through the woods parallel to the path. I ran like crazy for twenty-five to fifty feet and then climbed a tree to see if any danger was nearby. I felt like such a coward; I couldn't help it. When I panted from exhaustion, Dad scooped me up and football-carried me home.

Thunderstorms scared me. I hid behind the door of the bathroom in the dark until all was clear. My mother and father didn't pay much attention to these storms until a bolt of lightning zigzagged across the living room, in one door and out the other, while Mom visited with friends. No one was hurt, but I couldn't help feeling smug that I was right to hide.

I learned to talk. I moved my jaws up and down just as my humans did. My "Meow, meow, meow?" rose in pitch just like when my family asked me a question. I knew I could talk because my family could understand me.

I was surprised one day to discover I had a little brother—another adoption. He was yellow and white. He was even more insecure about food than I was and would squall at the food bowl if it wasn't heaping full. He always wanted his bowl filled to overflowing. I was disgusted with his behavior. He didn't have good manners and didn't know how to talk to ask politely for food. He knew only one word. It was "Me, me, me!"

When I was out after dark, I would ask at the door to come in and then race for the bed of my sister to see who would get the sweet spot first. Most nights I was faster. She would enter her room to find me in the middle of the bed with my head on the pillow. Then I would lift my chin and glare at her, daring her to try to move me.

My dad took me on field trips. Sometimes he gave me a ride to his office to hunt for mice while he graded papers. I always smelled mice there as they ran from room to room through the heating system. On weekends, Dad drove me to the grocery store. It was three miles away and outside of my normal prowling range. He smuggled me inside his jacket with my face peeking out under his beard at the world. I liked the cat food aisle best; it smelled good. The clerks saw me, but never said anything. They just smiled and rang the order up.

The parking lot at the store had the smell of dogs. I tensed up and my dad held me tight. When Dad drove me to the vet's office, I smelled strange dogs again. At the vet's office, I learned to be wary of needles. She gave me shots between my shoulder blades where I couldn't lick. It felt frustrating not to be able to lick a sting and to be roughly handled.

Cats know that dogs are bad and can't be trusted. Most dogs think cats live in trees. If one of those dogs catches you on the ground, he will kill and eat you! Some dogs are sometimes good and sometimes bad. These are the ones that are your friends when they are alone but not in the company of other dogs—four or more make a pack. My next-door neighbor's dog let me rub against his legs when he came over to get a doggie treat from my mom and dad, but when the pack showed up he would be out in front to get the first bite. He was fickle and not to be trusted. No dog is completely good like a cat is. We mind our own business and leave the world alone, except for the small, helpless things that are our rightful prey.

Sometimes I sneaked outside at bedtime and stayed out all night. My mom and dad didn't like that. They worried about me the same way as they would about their other children. One night I got into trouble. I crossed paths with a rattlesnake and wasn't quick enough to keep away from the pointy end. It struck me across my face before I killed it. My face felt like it was on fire. Fortunately, my cheekbone kept his fangs from penetrating deeply, but my face swelled terribly and my dad took me to the vet again. I didn't like going to the vet.

Another night I crossed paths with a coyote. I climbed a telephone pole to get away and then realized I didn't know how to get down. Brr! I was cold balancing on a bare-metal wire. I had trouble keeping my balance while taking little catnaps. I crouched on top of that telephone pole for two days in below freezing temperatures until the volunteer fire department came with a ladder to get me down. I thank the great cat mother it didn't rain or snow. When I tried to get inside the house, my cat friend from across the street grabbed my hind leg and pulled me backwards out of the house because he was so anxious to play with me. We had a good rough and tussle before I got to the food dish.

As the years passed, I slowed down. I rested and slept more. Inside the home was the best place for this, but I also had my favorite outdoor spots. My father was a gardener. In the late summer, I enjoyed stretching out full-length on my back in the shade between the rows of corn, or sleeping in the catnip after rolling around to crush the leaves to release the intoxicating aroma. Some afternoons I was too high on catnip to walk straight. I looked at the world through crossed eyes. The birds were safe.

At fourteen years, I was getting sluggish and couldn't heal as fast. I think the rattlesnake venom reduced my life force. One night I sneaked out for an adventure and didn't come back. I met my destiny that night; it was bigger than I was. My parents searched and called in the woods for hours, but I couldn't respond. I felt disoriented; I didn't have any control of my body. My mom and dad finally understood that I was not going to come back home. After three days, my dad walked into the woods and erected a small cross as a memorial. I watched over his shoulder; there were tears in his eyes. I tried to tell Dad I was okay, but he couldn't hear me. This was the first time he couldn't hear me talk.

I followed my dad back home. The house was just as I left it. My food dish and water bowl were there, but I wasn't hungry or thirsty anymore. As always my little cat brother was squalling for food. I didn't feel tired like I did in my old age, but I still enjoyed sleeping with my father as we did before. He knew I was there; he would shift in his sleep as I walked across the blankets. As usual, I would curl up beside my dad. As usual, he would reach out and wrap his arm around me in his sleep. It felt comforting to meditate on the nature of being a cat while my dad slept. He looked surprised each morning to find he couldn't see me, but I was there.

The cat goddess is my forever mother. She calls to me by name. I feel her tug at my heart and I visit her between checks on my family. I'm having trouble letting go of my human family and need her help. They were so good to me and I love them as any cat would. I begged a favor of the goddess. The goddess said my human family could be with me in cat heaven if I need them to be there. I do.

Humans live a lot longer than cats, but they don't last forever. I am patient. I wait for my human family to catch up with me. While I wait, I am the guardian of my home. I stand vigilant ready to wake my dad if trouble attempts to enter there. I am their protector. I am cat.

Meghann Caskey is a member of the Tucson Science Fiction and Fantasy Writers Meetup Group. This is her first story submitted for publication.

Synopsis

New to the Tucson area where things are so very different from what she is used to, a young woman discovers more than she could have ever imagined in her new town: a place where the denizens of the desert experience love and war alongside the roar of traffic.

Coyote Rain

The Rillito River Park Trail flanks both sides of the river it's named for - or so I'm told by the Tucson locals. We definitely have different definitions of "river." Mine involves water.

However, to be fair, this wide, parched, sandy impression snaking through the north of Tucson does occasionally have water. When the searing summer heat has built so high that it seems the desert creatures won't be able stand it much longer, slowly the first fluffy, white clouds begin to sweep, teasingly, across the sun-bleached sky. Day after day, promises of relief pass, until everything, from the strange javelina to the tiny desert scorpions, is on the verge of madness from the heat. Only then will the great thunderheads climb over the mountains, and flood the valley with soothing monsoon rains. The relief is so intense it is felt physically. The rains fill the river with chocolate-brown water capped in cream foam, thundering and thrashing down the channel, violently uprooting mature trees, crumbling concrete pillars, and eroding away sections of the earthen riverbank.

The desert is a collection of extremes at war with each other.

It is still too early in the summer for the monsoon, and the "river" is a dry, sandy beach. Still it makes for a long, relaxing bike ride. The bike path follows the edge of the "river," crossing here and there, tunneling under streets before climbing back up again.

In some areas, homes and apartments have been built against the "river;" however, this stretch of the path is still wild, and one can almost imagine being lost in the desert. The distant sound of traffic is drowned out by the roaring buzz of insects.

Lizards do pushups on the scalding pavement, before darting into the shade.

High above, the dark silhouettes of large birds circle and soar. As I ride, I watch the birds swoop and circle back. They drop close to the horizon. Perhaps they've found a meal on the path ahead? I can't tell if they are hawks, eagles, or vultures. I'm not really up to date with my ornithologist skills.

Here, away from the dog walkers, joggers, and parents pushing strollers, I can build up a great deal of speed. I push myself faster and faster, my heart racing and my lungs sucking wind. It's as if I'm racing to catch something, or escape something. Either way, I want to keep going faster, faster, riding for that next curve in the path. The air, hot and dry, like a hairdryer in my face, offers no relief from the heat. Going this fast, out here alone, the heat doesn't seem to matter anymore. The desert mesquite trees blur in my peripheral vision as I fly past.

The last chords of some up-tempo song I love but can't remember the name of, fade out. For the briefest of moments, I am free. In a shocking flash, a dark shape leaps out at me from the cover of the trees on my right. I instinctively swerve, grab my hand brakes, and skid to a rough stop on the sandy pavement. A lovely stream of swear words, learned from my sailor father, explodes from my lips. My heart is now happily pounding away against my tonsils.

I've come to a screeching halt next to a ground squirrel nest. The little chipmunk-like creatures dive into their burrows, popping up several feet away to glare suspiciously at me. One brave little fellow chirp-barks at me from under a dying barrel cactus, his slender tail slashing violently from side-to-side as he bounces like a cartoon character experiencing an earthquake.

But it's not the squirrels I'm looking for. It was a man. I'm sure it was a man who'd jumped out at me. At least, I think it was a man, running along in the scrub brush and mesquite trees. I only saw him for a second out of the corner of my eye.

I look up the trail and back down again. Nothing but the hyper ground squirrels and buzzing insects.

It's afternoon, but the sun is still very much high in the sky. The pavement radiates up as much heat as the intense sun beats down. Yet, I feel cold standing here. It's a deep chill that comes from the gut, a long-forgotten instinct, woven into my DNA from my arboreal ancestors. The instinct lifts the fine hairs on my neck and arms, and sends my heart into a pounding pace. The instinct that screams, "Predator! Run!"

Jumping back onto my bike seat, I prepare to leave the ground squirrels and lizards to their business, but a figure sitting in the middle of the path halts my flight. It's a coyote, contentedly sitting on its haunches.

I've seen coyotes here before, javelina, and even once a deer. The creatures of the desert have become very adept at traveling through the network of washes, rivers, and open storm drains throughout the city. However, this encounter is unusual.

The coyote wasn't there when I stopped. It's now just sitting here, head slightly tilted to one side, observing me. Perhaps it's rabid; however, there's no foam around its long snout, no head shaking. It's perfectly calm.

Maybe it's hunting. I slowly walk my bike backwards. Maybe if I give it enough room it will go away. Instead, it just cocks its head to the other side. The canine looks amused, its mouth open and its tongue lolling out.

Then, it stands up. All the way up.

Watching a coyote stand up, and in the process turn into a man, I discover there is nothing clever the human mind can do. I stand frozen and deer-like, my brain blank in shock.

With his hands on his hips, he observes me with those golden, coyote eyes, that coyote smirk still on his face. His copper and blonde hair is not overly long, but very shaggy. Beyond that, he is unashamedly, stark naked.

Under the wilted cactus, the squirrel has gone completely silent and still. Everything has gone silent, frozen in anticipation. Behind me, I hear the faint but unmistakable sound of flapping wings and the scratch of sharp talons on hot asphalt.

I look back over my shoulder. A murder of ravens has landed behind me with their heads dipping and twisting and their black, depthless eyes observing me. Looking at them is chilling. Numbly, I turn back to the coyote.

"You're going to want to go now," he says, a second before lunging past me, suddenly a coyote again. The giant birds scatter, screeching. I let out a startled screech of my own. One of the enraged birds swoops down on me, its sharp beak barely brushing my cheek.

In that second, I decide his advice to go is sound. Ducking my head and peddling for my life, I bolt ahead, leaving the yipping and croaking sounds of battle behind me.

Some distance down the path, I pop up from an underpass and swerve into the bus depot just off Stone Avenue. Shivering, a little weak, and a lot out of breath, I look back down the path. Nothing is following me. No menacing birds, no coyote, and no naked, coppery man.

"Are you ok? You know you're bleeding, right?" A woman waiting under a bus stop pergola asks. She's seen me skid off the bike path like Hellfire was after me.

I press a hand to my cheek and my fingers come back red. It isn't much, just a scratch, but apparently the raven got much closer than I thought.

"I'm fine. Must have hit a tree branch." My voice, no surprise, is not convincing.

"Are you sure? You look really pale. Is the heat getting to you?" The woman moves toward me, concerned. What am I going to say? I just saw a coyote turn into a man and then he did battle with a bunch of oversized crows? 'Hello, yes. We'll need one of your butterfly nets, extra-large please.'

"I'm fine," I mutter mechanically. However, I feel haunted. Every sound and movement causes me to jump. I keep waiting for things to change into impossible shapes. Maybe I'm just losing my mind. Maybe it's the heat. Heatstroke is always a solid possibility in 108-degree weather.

I know the best course of action is to get out of the sun. Safe in the bus's welcoming air conditioning, surrounded by strangers, who stay human, I begin to relax.

Definitely, the heat, I reassure myself silently. The bus hisses and bounces as it pulls away from the station. For one second, in the scrub on the distant bank, I see the coyote, grinning widely at me.

A week passes, then two. Nothing bizarre or unusual happens. Cats and dogs remain cats and dogs, birds stay birds. I don't see any coyotes or ravens. The city is just a city. The tiny scratch on my cheek heals quickly. Finally, I'm able to convince myself that my encounter with the coyote-man was simply the result of dehydration, too much sun, and an overactive imagination. I resolve to drink more water and stay out of the heat.

Week three passes, and the first wisps of promising rain begin to dot the hot, blue sky. The air is still so intensely hot that it draws moisture out of everything, leaving the whole of Tucson dry, parched, and suffering for a taste of rain. The monsoon will come soon, the season of relief and renewal is on the verge of breaking.

For the past three weeks, I have had a steadily-growing urge to return to the river and that wild place, with the chatter of wild creatures. I want to stretch my legs on a long, fast ride. In the city I have to be so aware, watching for cars and inconsiderate pedestrians; I can't really let go and ride the way I want. But the lingering memory of the coyote and the ravens has kept me away from the river.

The hot air caresses my face as I bike through the city traffic, wishing I was on the river. The last shards of sunlight crown the Tucson Mountains in the west. At every intersection I glance north, to the Catalina Mountains. Just a few miles away, at the base of those northern mountains, the twisting river waits for the rain. As preoccupied as I am with mountains and the stunning display of the sunlight on the rock formations, I almost fail to see the large raven pecking at a piece of trash in the bike lane a few feet ahead.

The bird's black eyes are already on me, and in one smooth motion it is in the air and flying into my face. The bird's sharp wings slap my face, causing me to duck and swerve. I immediately lose control of my bike, the front wheel turning sharply, pinning my right leg to the side of the bike, and causing me to fly over the handlebar. I slam into the hot pavement and wrench my right shoulder. My face bounces off the sidewalk. The bird continues its assault, diving at me and twisting its sharp beak into my clothes seeking my flesh.

Tangled in my bike and stunned from my fall, there is little I can do to fight off the enraged bird. Blindly, I swat at the air, trying to stop the bird before it does more damage. Quickly, I unhook my helmet, ready to use it as a shield and or club. But the bird flies away, as a truck stops and a man jumps out, asking if I'm hurt.

"What was that?" the man asks, waving a hand at the retreating bird.

"No idea," I mutter, untangling myself from my bike. I'm bruised, embarrassed, and very angry, but I'm otherwise fine. My bike is scratched but, like me, overall fine.

"But I tell you what, I really want barbecued raven right now," I growl, glaring in the direction the bird has taken.

Normally, I sleep untroubled, dropping off immediately and sleeping contentedly throughout the night. However, it is 3:00 am and I'm awake in my comfy bed. I toss and turn trying to force myself to sleep. My shoulder still aches from the fall, and I can't get comfortable. I am wide-awake when the not-so-distant sound of yipping and howls causes me to jump out of bed in a chilly panic.

The sound of a coyote is so unique that once it's been heard it can never be forgotten. And the sound of many, together, joyously calling out, is both frightening and fascinating. I walk to my window on tiptoes, and carefully part the blinds a little to peek outside.

This is a city street, in the heart of a major US metropolis. The street, sidewalks, and even homes are brightly illuminated by streetlights, and high above, the full summer moon is resting in a nearly clear sky. A few silver clouds stretch out, contemplating bringing in the rain. But, it is the pack of coyotes scattered around the street and sidewalk just outside my window that captures my full attention. The pups bounce joyfully around, while the older members stand patiently waiting.

I've never seen such a large pack of coyotes before, and to see them casually swarming an urban street, under the light of a full moon, would startle anyone; but with my recent experience has left me absolutely shaking.

"Just coyotes," I tell myself, still peeking through the blinds. "They're just coyotes digging through the dumpsters, or looking for pets that've been left out overnight. They're just plain, old, standard..." I scream as one of the coyotes pops up directly in front of my face, its paws resting on the window sill, its face level with mine. Shocked, I jump back and the blinds swing back into place. My heart pounds so hard I can feel it thundering in my veins.

There's a soft tapping at the window, like a finger tapping against the glass. I duck behind my bed. It's not dignified, but, well, "Coyote-Man!" What else would you do? Even with a cinderblock wall and thick glass between us, I still feel very vulnerable.

He taps again.

"Come out," he calls softly to me.

"Go away!" I yell back.

He taps a third time. In a fit, which probably resembles insanity, I jump up and jerk back the blinds while screaming, "Go away!"

The street is empty. Nothing, but the quiet glow of streetlights and the bright moon.

"I'm losing my mind," I mutter, matter-of-factly, while sinking to the floor. I don't sleep the rest of the night.

Three days after my nocturnal visit, the burnt blue sky has begun to plaster over with a growing blanket of silver-gray clouds. The promise of rain hangs heavy in the air. The wind has picked up and is now roaring through the city, bending slender palm trees and shaking trees. My shoulder is still tender, but mostly healed, and the rest of my bruises have faded to yellow.

While the whole of the desert is looking to the sky in eager anticipation, I have my eyes firmly on the ground. For three days I have been glancing down every alley, every street, expecting to see an enraged raven flying into my face or an amused coyote looking back. But it's not the coyote who has found me today. I walk out of a local grocery store to find, to my absolute horror, five large ravens perched on and around my bike.

Numb with shock and overwhelmed with fear, I stare at the birds as they eye me, like I'm bacon.

"What beautiful birds!" an elderly woman comments passing by. "I haven't seen ravens here in years." She pauses to pull out her phone and take pictures.

"You can see them?" I ask her, happy that I'm not just hallucinating. The woman looks at me as if I'd just asked if I could bite her. Giving up her picture, she skirts past me and hurries away.

I turn back to the birds and their piercing eyes. Not a hallucination, not the heat. One of the birds fluffs its feathers and croaks at me.

To anyone else, it may not be noticeable, just a typical croaking call of a typical raven. But to me, I hear it calling out, "Blood, blood, blood!"

To my horror, the ravens begin to move toward me. "Blood, blood, blood," they croak.

"Why are you doing this?" I whisper, backing away. "Why did you attack me? I haven't done anything to you!"

"Don't play fool, pup!" the raven rasps, hopping a few feet. The ravens spread out, attempting to encircle me. I look wildly around for assistance, but the parking lot is empty.

"No rescue, pup!" Another raven calls out.

"Blood, blood, blood." They all begin croaking. One of the birds leaps at me. I squeak and jump back.

"Get away from me!" I snarl and swing my plastic shopping bag. The bag makes contact with one of the birds, sending it bouncing away. I continue wildly swinging the bag, keeping the ravens at bay. They leap back, flutter away, only to swing back, their thick, sharp beaks snapping at me. I swing the bag until the thin plastic is shredded and its contents are scattered around the pavement.

I drop the bag and run for my bike, pedaling faster and faster, heading north toward the Rillito River. The ravens gather and follow me. I'm forced to duck and swerve as the massive birds dive, snap, and scratch at me. The violent gusts of wind hinder the birds, but they also slow me down.

The gray clouds pile thicker and darker. Bolts of lightning appear in the distance. The insects roar and the lizards race. The general sense of excitement is building as the storm approaches.

Mercifully, the storm breaks hard, beating down sheets of dime-sized droplets, forcing the ravens to break off their attack in the deluge. I'm completely drenched within seconds, but I'm free of my sharp-beaked assailants. The streets begin to flood, and the water follows me to the river.

I reach the river scratched, unnerved, and very angry. The Rillito is already filling with rushing water. I reach the ground squirrel burrow and let my bike fall to the side of the path.

"Ok, I'm here!" I scream over the deafening sound of the rain and the jolting crash of the thunder.

"Well?" I scream again. "What do you want? What are you?"

I turn several times, fighting to see through the heavy rain. He appears, fur wet and matted, sitting casually as he did before.

"There you are! Why are you doing this to me? What did I ever do to you?" I bellow at the animal. If anyone saw me now, screaming in the rain at a wild animal, I would definitely appear deranged.

The coyote just sits there, letting the rain pelt his coat.

"Well?" I scream, waving my arms at the animal. Finally, he stands up. Even having seen it before, watching a coyote stand up into a man still startles me to my core. His hair is plastered to his head, and he squints through the rain.

"I thought you wanted me to go away," he says casually.

"I want to know what's going on! Why are you doing this to me? What are you?" I yell.

"You had a visit from the ravens. They are among our oldest enemies." He smirks. "But not bright." *Are all coyotes so obnoxiously smug?* I wonder.

"I've had visits from you too. Why?"

"I just wanted to see if you were ready to come with us." He shrugs, as if it were the most obvious answer in the world.

"I'm not going with you!" I snap back.

"Suit yourself, but the ravens know about you now, and they'll never leave you alone." He crouches back down.

"Wait! Why won't they leave me alone?" I demand, stopping him from turning back. He stands back up, and leans close, eyeing me. It is an awkward situation, standing in the rain with a naked coyote-man.

"They know about you, they've known about you for a while." He tilts his head again, in that all-too-familiar canine way. "But you don't, do you?"

He throws back his head and lets out a full yipping laugh.

"Oh my God! Just tell me!" I scream at him. I have reached the very end of my rope, and I am through playing games. Rather than answering me, he just continues laugh-yipping.

The rain is weakening; the storm will be over soon. The river is swollen and violently crashing down stream. The world is drenched, the temperature has fallen, and the clouds are slipping away, only to return tomorrow, in their seasonal cycle.

"Oh, you know what you are. Deep down, you know why you keep coming out here, seeking the wild places, racing through the desert. Inside, you know." He chuckles.

He's insane, I realize. I need to leave. But the ravens have seized the break in the rain to regroup. They have gathered in force and are surrounding us.

"Blood, blood, blood," they croak in unison. Looking at them gathering, I'm forced to realize the coyote-man is right. There is a storm building in me, growing slowly since that ride several weeks before. Now that storm is breaking. Rage erupts in me, seeing these vicious birds, who have repeatedly attacked me. I glare at the birds, locking onto their bobbing, fluttering movements. My vision changes, the colors fade, shapes become sharper, movements become pronounced. In an instinctual fit, I lunge at the birds, snapping at them. The ravens scream, their cries nearly deafening in my now sensitive ears. I can smell their fear and taste their rage.

Beside me, the coyote-man leaps and snaps at the birds, his long fangs barely missing one. The birds scatter, retreating. Together the coyote-man and I lope down the path and into the overgrown scrub brush.

The world is magnificently renewed. The smells are intense. I can smell the little ground squirrels and lizards as unique scents, each animal individual. Rain and mud, the scent of palms and saguaros, each distinct.

I pause, seeing my reflection in a standing puddle. My ears perk and I tilt my head. As far as extremes go, this is, without a doubt the most extreme thing in my life.

I immediately take notice of distant yipping drifting to me on the dying wind. Calling back, I follow the sound. We two are joined by more calls, dozens joining in a joyous chorus.

The next day near dusk, a couple of joggers find an abandoned bicycle and some mud-splattered clothing. A new mystery is etched into Tucson's history. And as the sun falls behind the horizon, a young coyote female bolts from the site to join a pack traveling through the dark city streets.

J M Strasser lives in Tucson, Arizona with her husband, son and daughter (when she comes home from school). With a Bachelor's degree in Biology, she loves the desert's sweet colors and ponders the meaning of life, intelligence, and when the heck is someone going to encounter us!

Synopsis

An aide is called to work with an elderly gentleman whose children have lost patience with him. All goes as is normal for care of an Alzheimer's patient until one day, when his delusions about other worlds, using his own spaceship, and demanding to go to his favorite bar turn into an enchanting day out.

Travels with Walter

The Engs had called my agency about their dad, Walter. I was sent to be interviewed at their home.

They lived in the outskirts of Tucson, in an old subdivision called Mesaland that had been there years before the city grew to meet it. The houses, which sat on large parcels of land, were built of adobe brick in the old-territorial style. At the Engs' front door I was surprised when a woman servant, dressed in an odd uniform, said nothing in greeting, looked me over and then led me into the home. The agency had told me the Engs, a son and daughter, were sociologists and that their father had recently retired. I caught a glimpse of chaos at the back of the family's home office as I approached: A handful of people running around, holding up tablet computers, pointing, inputting, and chattering to each other.

A woman in the group saw me and my escort just as we stepped into the room. With a quick smile, she tucked the tablet under her arm and quickly scooted the rest of the now-silent people from the front of the office. The last person in the exit line was a man, who quickly shut the door and introduced himself to me as Mr. Bey Eng.

He gestured at the chair in front of his huge monster desk, for me to sit down in. Mr. Eng was tall, with long dark hair that fit his head like a helmet and would never need brushing aside. He wore a tailored suit that reminded me of a pantsuit a female senator would pick; severe, but not too masculine. As I sat down, he took his seat behind the desk. He sat ramrod-straight, like a strict schoolmaster about to inform me of some error in my homework, and proceeded to review what I assumed was my resume.

The office was comfy. It was roomy, and filled with natural light from the oversized window that looked out onto the front garden. It had that 'old Tucson' feel, with plastered walls of vanilla, Saltillo tiles on the floor, and bookcases that lined the walls.

"You are recommended. You been in this aiding for long time?"

"Yes, forty years."

Nodding, he continued. "Well, my father not difficult to care for. Most important thing is he safe. His memory now less because age and he has begun lose weight."

I nodded; these were common in the elderly. When the memory went, so did some of the taste buds and the ability to digest well.

I wondered where this family came from. Picking up the next paper, he read on, and then looked up at me again. I nodded. Again he continued to read.

"The agency say you have own car?" He looked up at me.

"If that is all right, I prefer it that way."

He nodded, looking down at my papers again. "Yes, yes, the agency told. We do not have car for this city. Yours will be necessary."

No car? That was odd, Tucson isn't a big city with many buses or any subways, but its sprawl made having a car a near necessity. The family wasn't from Tucson.

Mr. Eng continued on, "You can take him to small restaurant in city. Some of time you can add something," he gestured, "bigger." I assumed he meant a more expensive restaurant.

"Dad pay himself." He smiled. "Something he insist upon. Your job make sure done correctly, safely. No visit with any aliens."

Aliens? He knows some Mexican nationals?

"Of course," I said, wondering how I would avoid that here, so close to the border.

He laid the papers on his desk. "I would like you take Walter food shopping. He prefer to eat food from here and in his house, when he not go out, of course. Use judgment on that. I…" he faltered. "I know nothing of this," and abruptly stopped speaking.

"Certainly, I will encourage good nutrition and dietary habits. Does Walter take any medication?"

He looked at me with a blank expression.

"Like memory treatments, diabetic shots, blood pressure pills?" I tried to list the most common.

"No." Mr. Eng shook his head, looking surprised that I asked.

I nodded. The file about his father had listed no prescriptions. I had already looked it over but wanted to double check, as I found it odd that he didn't have any medications for his father's issues.

"Father once worked as we do. Now he settle in retirement and content to eat out."

This was probably what he thought, but I suspected it might not be what Walter thought. Working as an aide, you often balance the needs of the employers with the needs of the charge. In this case, it seemed like I would keep up the fiction that Mr. Eng "knew" what was going on with his father, Walter. I would probably find a man who was shaken by his losses and very bored with his life.

"One more thing, you aware confidentiality clause?"

"Certainly, standard practice," I answered.

"Good."

Mr. Eng seemed to think he was speaking well, typical of foreign intellectuals who thought they knew more than me. "Any questions?" he asked.

"My work week?" I asked and we proceeded with the business end of the conversation.

I am an aide. The person you hire to help Dad or Mom when they are aged and incapable of caring for themselves. The lowest -paid profession—or at least one of those professions held in the lowest esteem, right next to homemaker.

People are always quick to assure me how important the work is, while offering my minimal pay. I smile and accept the offer because it is more for the elderly I work than for their children who hire me. I should have suspected something when the salary turned out to be one of the highest that I had ever heard of in this field, but I took it to be a compliment and let it be.

"Yes, Mr. Eng, it is satisfactory," I said as I reached out to shake on the deal.

"Call me Bey," he said as he reached back across the desk.

"Yes, please call me Sarah," I answered.

Nodding, Bey stood and abruptly walked out of his office saying, "Let's go meet Father."

I followed him out of the house and along a neat little walkway to a casita behind the main house. Around the whole back section was a six-foot fence. I nodded in approval. My employers seemed to be aware of the possible issues with spontaneous wandering or deliberate escape by their father. Bey stepped into the casita and I followed.

We found Walter in front of the TV. He seemed like a small, elderly man. However, as we got closer and Bey introduced us, I was surprised that when he stood up he towered over me. I'm six feet tall, so that is saying something. Walter was quite slim, more like skinny, with a balding pate and wispy white hair halfway down his head.

A small whine emerged from below me. A good sized dog was looking at me expectantly. I reached down and petted it on the head.

"Dad, this new aide, Ms. Anders."

"Oh?"

"Hello, Walter, nice to meet you," I said, offering my hand. "Please call me Sarah."

Walter smiled. "Nice to meet you," he said, taking my hand.

"This dog, Hand," Bey said, looking down at the dog.

I leaned down and petted him again on the head. "Hello, Hand." I like dogs; people say I spoil mine. Pets are often what keep my clients going, so I respect these furry companions.

"She's going to take you lunch." Bey told Walter.

"Oh? That sounds good." He got up, collecting his things, and then stood at the door.

"Take someplace you like," Bey said to me.

Walter locked his door and we walked back through the main house and out to the front where I had parked.

"I'll see you when return, Ms. Anders?"

"Sure, see you then." With that, Bey turned on his heel and walked back into the house.

I turned around and Walter was staring at me. "We are going in my car." I gestured to the automobile. "Let's get you in."

I opened the car door for Walter and he slowly sat down in the front seat. Going around, I entered the driver's side. After a few minutes of fussing with seat belts we were ready to go.

I presented my idea. "Well, how about a nice coffee shop where you can get some soup and a sandwich?"

"Un-huh, rather use my cruiser," was all he said and then held onto the side loop above the window as if the car was going to race. I started the car and we were off. I went quite slow and avoided bumps and holes but I knew he would always fear them; you can rarely change the opinion of an Alzheimer's patient. If Walter believed the car was going to be too rough (perhaps from past experience) whatever I did he would always assume it. Old memories trump current realities.

We arrived at the coffee shop, sat down and ordered. I had to do most of the ordering. "I was told you were a sociologist like your children."

"Huh? Oh, that's over, silly profession." Walter looked around the restaurant.

"How long was your career?"

"A long time," he said, looking at me.

"What did you do?"

"Watched people, recorded." The food arrived. "Is this all for me?" he asked.

"Yes."

I didn't want to call any more attention to the portion so I asked him more about his work. "You watched people?" What an odd way to put it.

He nodded, "Some of it was good, getting to know them, their culture. That's important!" He pointed his fork at me. "But when there's trouble, and there always is, it's hard to just watch." The fork came down and he stared at his food.

"Yes, the old dilemma."

Walter looked up "What?"

"Whether to try to help or keep filming. That must be difficult."

"And unnecessary. At least sometimes," he mumbled, the fire damped out.

"Oh, did that happen to you?" I asked, trying to keep the train of thought going.

He started eating again and that was it.

A few minutes later, "Who are you?"

"I'm Sarah, your aide. This is our first day," I said, trying to smile with encouragement.

"Oh? Yes, of course, of course." He went back to his meal. It would take a while before I could believe he truly remembered me.

Walter ate all his food and after a considerable period where his mind wandered, he forgot about what he had eaten. Somehow he distracted himself from his phobia of too much food. When it came to a drink, he rebelled against any water, especially when I explained it was a good idea. He didn't argue but dragged out the process. I think he was waiting for me to give up.

"Ah, whiskey is for drinking, but water is for WAR!" I said, smiling at him.

He threw back his head and laughed. "I like that!"

"Yes, well it sums up the southwestern desert. A hard lesson we learned."

Walter lost his smile. "Yes, it is something easy to forget. You are very wise."

"Thank you. Now finish it so we can go." I looked squarely at him.

Walter shrugged his shoulders, mumbled and drank: round one for me. How much the elderly were like children.

"Did you enjoy the sandwich?" I asked.

"Fine, fine," he grumbled. "Rather have carrion burgers, though."

Road kill? Good gracious! "Oh, well, maybe next time," I said.

I pulled up to the main house and Walter found his way back to his own, but only after checking and re-checking on the next day. He would needed to ask the same questions repeatedly to reassure himself that these visits from me would continue.

I went to Bey's office and knocked on the door.

He answered, but this time the door to the back office of working chaos was closed.

He looked at me. "How go?"

"Fine. He seems easy to get along with."

A shadow passed over Bey's face. "Until he disagrees with you."

I nodded. It's hard to see your parent age.

"I would like to discuss other activities for him. How about taking him to the local gym?" I smiled.

"Gym, Father? I don't think he ever in gym." That grim face again as if he disapproved, but I didn't know if it was with the suggestion, me, or Walter.

"Many in his generation haven't. However, now there are activities for the elderly, and I think we could work out a routine he might enjoy. The one up Oracle Road would work well."

He eyed me, shaking his head a bit. "If you think so…"

"How about you set up a trial period, say for a month? If it works out we could make it permanent."

Bey closed his eyes for a moment. "What's name gym?"

#

I went home and laid out materials for making up a schedule. Pepper, my dog, greeted me with some interest and then settled down to guard me while I worked. She was a cattle dog mixed with something like a greyhound, and looked like Anubis when she was lying on the floor like that. Pepper was content if I gave her enough treats and walked her once a day. I wondered how she would get along with Hand.

I set up a schedule for Walter with exercise, movies and grocery shopping. Then, with the basic structure in place, I added some light lectures through the Western National Parks Association and the University of Arizona. That ought to be good enough for a start.

#

Soon we were humming along. It was difficult for Walter to prepare for the grocery shopping. The effort of understanding the list I made and then taking the inventory from it was almost too much, but I felt worth it. Walter didn't want to make the effort and wanted me to take him whenever he deigned to remember a need. I wanted to be more efficient and provide more stimulus than that for him. The days fell into a pattern and Walter seemed to improve with the routines. He had a tendency, though, to be quite creative.

"This town is so two-dimensional. Why don't they have any cloud restaurants?" Walter would ask. Or, "Can't they come up with something for more species than this?"

I didn't know what to say to that. He did have a fertile imagination.

#

Two months into my association with Walter, we were walking to the main house and he stopped. "I want to go out in my cruiser!" he said, clenching his fists.

Startled, it took me a moment to answer, "Cruiser?"

Hand was outside and I saw his ears perk up at the word.

"Yeah, my cruiser! I want to get out of this little solar system!" He proceeded to lead me to one of the garages. Hand followed and barked once.

"Spaceships are much better transports; get you there much faster," he babbled as he hurried along. "Especially with the wormholes."

Seniors often fantasize about what their life was like before, but I realized for the first time I was with a Science Fiction fan. I followed him into the garage. The cruiser was sitting on the floor. It looked like something I had seen in cartoons as a child. Hand followed, wagging his tail.

"Walter, this is great! Did you build it?"

"Hell, no. I'm not an engineer," he sneered.

"He picked it up cheap from a yahoo near Alpha Centauri." Walter wasn't speaking. I looked at Hand.

"Good trick! Are you a ventriloquist?" I asked.

"Ha, ha! Walter?" Something like a laugh came from Hand.

I was quiet, not knowing how it was all done. Then Hand walked toward me. He was standing up on two legs and gesturing with his paws. "Oh, Sarah, I know this is weird, but come on, let's give it a try."

Oddly, it didn't seem fake, and a tickle of worry crept in.

"Come, Walter. We need to talk to your son," I said, watching Hand and turned toward the door.

"What? Oh no, let's just go," Walter said.

"Yeah!" came from the voice from behind me. I jumped; there was only Hand. I turned to see him looking up at me, wagging his tail.

"Let's get off this ball!" Hand said.

I got dizzy and put my hand on the wall to steady myself.

"Come." I led them out. I imagine, because dementia leaves them without direction, you tell them what to do and they do it.

Knocking on Bey's office door, I waited. No one answered.

"Can I help you?" said a woman's voice behind me.

Turning I said, "Oh, yes, I'm Ms. Anders."

"Yes, nice to meet you. I'm Ephrem Eng. Bey's sister." She held out her hand. The names kept getting stranger. She was a tall woman dressed in an even more severe suit than her brother, with very short hair that I thought worked well for her.

I shook her hand, "Hello," I said, smiling, "I was going to ask Bey... Mr. Eng, if it is all right to use Walter's cruiser."

Ephrem smiled. Walter started to talk, but I kept control.

"Yes, Walter, it seems, has gotten a bit restless. He wants to take out his 'cruiser' out and go driving. I saw the cruiser, and Hand seems anxious as well, telling me we should get off this ball." I waited again.

"He showed you?" Ephrem asked.

I nodded.

She sighed, "Well, I think it's okay. Take it slow at first."

Slow, why slow? Limit the fantasies?

"I want to drive," Walter spat out.

Ephrem nodded. "That's okay, the cruiser is automatic. But Dad, Ms. Anders is in charge. What she says goes." Ephrem certainly spoke better than her brother.

Walter scowled and then nodded.

"It's okay?" I asked.

"Yes, you seem capable."

I was glad for the vote of confidence, I think.

"He'll need money. Same as before, he has a card."

Walter pulled out his wallet and reached for his debit card. Ephrem shook her head.

"Not that, the other one." Ephrem stopped and thought for a moment. Quickly she unlocked the door to the office and brought back a little card.

It almost looked like a credit card, but the letters were not English—really not English! I couldn't read it, of course, but it lined up like writing. This fantasy was quite involved. Not many children would indulge their parent this far.

Ephrem turned to me. "I know this is a surprise. Can you handle it?"

"Yes, sounds like a good idea, something interesting, different," I said, nodding affirmative.

"Yes," she said and looked at me expectantly. "Take care as you do here, make sure Dad is safe. Minimal drinking," A raspberry came out and this time it wasn't Walter, "or any other mischief. Supervise paying and tipping as before."

For those that do not know what is a raspberry, it's a forceful explosion of air out the mouth with the intent of sounding like the expulsion of gas from the lower regions of your body.

I looked at Ephrem and just smiled.

"Don't worry; he will take you to his favorite hangout, right Dad? And it is handled the same. Here is your chip." Ephrem held something small, like a watch battery, in her hand. "Do I have permission to install?"

I nodded, curious, but not really expecting much. Ephrem slapped my upper arm and a small prick told me something went in. Ouch! "The chip, Jona, can give self-defense in a shield, translation, instant access to the cruiser, me and police in an emergency," Ephrem said.

"Which police?" What is she talking about? I thought.

"Why, intergalactic, of course."

"Of course, what else?" I thought and shrugged.

"Please just take a short trip today. You can add other choices later."

"Right," I said. We left the office, Ephrem locking up behind us.

"Right, okay, just a short trip." Walter and Hand headed for the garage, and I followed. I hoped the adventure would be more than sitting in the cruiser, rocking back and forth with Hand talking and seeing Walter's lips move.

When we entered the garage, I saw the cruiser, just sitting there on the garage floor as before. It was shaped something like the craft seen in the old *Jetsons* cartoon; a round, flat body with four seats and a glass, bubble dome sealing everything inside.

Walter spoke. "Car on." Then the car levitated off the floor. I mean it rose up and just hung in the air.

I was quiet. This was getting better and not so amateurish.

Walter pushed a button on the right side under the dome and it disappeared. He got right into the driver's seat. This made me smile. One thing seniors really miss is the independence of driving. There was no wheel, though, and I was relieved about that, What was I thinking? What difference did that make?

Hand jumped in and took up almost all of the back two seats. He was wagging his tail faster than I thought was possible. He had also had picked up a pair of shorts along the way.

"Come on, get in," Hand said.

I jerked at the sound. Hand grinned at me–not a great sight with all those teeth. They were dog teeth, but imagine your dog trying to grin. I got in the other side in the front, just like in a car. "How do...." Walter was way ahead of me.

"Car," he said, "this is Walter. We want to go on a ride."

The car spoke. "Hi Walter, haven't seen you in a while. Do you have clearance?"

Walter scowled. I imagined some kind of spaceport tower clearing us, but he turned to me. "That's your cue."

"Oh, yes, this is Walter's aide, Ms. Anders, and..." I looked at Walter, faltering. He gestured to hurry up. "I give permission and am accompanying Walter and Hand on this trip."

"Checking, checking... yes. Clearance authorization authenticated. Welcome aboard, Ms. Anders."

"Why, thank you." This sure was a lot of high tech even for a grown-up toy.

"I want to go to Uno's bar for lunch." Walter closed his eyes, grinning from ear to ear.

"Uno's bar... found in memory... taking wormhole G-7. Fasten seatbelts, please."

We both reached around and hooked up our belts. Before I understood that this was really going to happen, the roof opened and the car flew out. My stomach went down to the floor and I gripped the handle on the door. Holy...!

"What's going on? Is this safe?" I screamed. "Will someone see us? Do we clear this with the Tucson airport, Davis-Monthan or something?" Trying not to let my teeth rattle, I searched for observers. Maybe I was imagining this.

"No ma'am," the car responded. "We have a nul-dar that makes us invisible both to line of sight and area radar. We will leave the atmosphere in two minutes." The car sounded confident. *"Well, why shouldn't it be?"* I thought flippantly. I supposed it had a great deal of experience even if I didn't. Could I handle this?

Up we went, through the atmosphere, into space, all those stars. "Yahoo!" hollered my driver.

I tried to notice everything. Some of the ride, particularly the speed, was attempting to make me nauseous, but it really was beautiful. Looking back on Earth, even this stoic woman cried. I had heard that Earth looks like a fragile marble when you see all of it at once, but I thought it looked majestic, felt its ancient rhythms. For humans to say it's fragile smacks of great hubris. Aren't we the fragile ones?

Then the wormhole appeared. I had heard of those, too, in Sci-Fi. How else can you explain travel over the immense distances in space? And this looked like a worm, all full of swirls in the interior of a tube. I held my breath, anticipating the ride like the initial ascent on a roller coaster, but I couldn't see the end of this ride. We are really going! Then that makes Walter… and Hand….

"Wormhole G-7 accessed. Entry in three… two… one…" We were away. Walter was laughing, watching me trying to keep my mouth closed. Zip, zip, zip, we went around, down, and up too much like a roller coaster. I stopped liking those some time ago, change in my center of gravity and all that stuff. Then we were out and had entered some sort of traffic lane. Other craft were emerging from their wormholes. Here we were, *The Jetsons* out for the day. I wondered if I was going to wake up soon.

"Uno's bar arrival in five minutes. Please wait for the cruiser to come to a complete stop."

I almost laughed out loud. Maybe Walt Disney had ridden in one of these?

Uno's bar came up on the right. I knew because suddenly I was reading the signs. The English interpretation scrolled across the interior of my eyes. At first it was annoying, but the script managed to keep out of my line of sight so I could see what I wanted to while still being informed. I just started to get the hang of it when Uno's sign came into view. It was a dive, small, and dirty, but had parking on the roof—practical. We circled and landed in an open spot.

Walter was out and about to run off, but with a senior I had plenty of time to catch up. Hand, on the other hand, was having no trouble leading the way in front of Walter.

"Don't we need to lock the cruiser?" I asked him, trying once again to be logical, under control.

"It's automatic. Everything is automatic," Walter said over his shoulder.

I wish that were true with my car. How many times have I left the lights on? I caught up with him. "How many kinds of... people are there in the galaxy?" I asked Walter as we approached the entrance.

"Well, about twenty-eight known, but you usually see about ten."

He had stopped just outside the building, and pointed down the street where people were walking by. Well, not people like we know, Homo Sapiens, but I thought of them that way. After all, they were intelligent and self-directed. Then I saw a form like a walking stick, that odd bug we have on Earth. One came out of the "beauty parlor" (as Walter informed me) with sticks on its head, kind of attractive. Yes, there were even little dough-boy gray creatures with big eyes. Maybe that UFO stuff was true.

"Are all those people coming out of the beauty parlor women?" I asked Walter.

"Certainly not!"

Then I asked if any of the styles would transfer between the species. This turned out to be true. One trend he remembered was a fake horn mounted on the head. This was to copy a famous entertainer. It had been a while since he had come into "town," though. He didn't know what the current style was.

We entered the building. Walter and Hand insisted we take the "chute" down to the bar, saying it was more fun than stairs or the levitation pad. It was a chute, more like a giant theme-park slide with lights, but it regulated how fast we went, and I admit it was kind of fun. Walter got out into the main area first and went straight for the bar. While drinking is not good in excess, seniors are adults and he wasn't driving, at least not like we do on Earth. I just watched, a little uncomfortable having my charge lead the way. If I didn't know better, I wouldn't have thought Walter's memory was impaired. He was in his element.

Uno's was bigger than it had looked from the outside. There was a large room with multiple viewing screens up high, and two rooms, one on each side of the larger room, that housed some kind of game (a kind of pool with lasers). It was smoky in the smaller rooms, but that didn't seem to come into the large one. Wait, they can smoke here? That was a surprise. Aren't they more evolved than we are? Each view screen was showing what looked like games of alien combatants—some very violent with blood everywhere, and some with weirdly colored balls going into a variety of holes. On one of the screens I couldn't see anything and tried to get a better look.

"That one's for the Trillians. Humans can't see their visible light spectrum," Hand said, smiling at me.

"Oh," I mumbled, feeling awkwardly aware of Hand again now that he was again talking and standing easily on his hind paws.

Many different aliens were standing around, wandering in and out of the rooms. Most were standing up and I struggled not to stare at the variations of appendages I was seeing. Some were three-legged, others four-armed and nobody thought it was weird at all. There was even the unsavory character huddled over a drink in the dark corner. I tried not to stare as it probably was impolite, even here, wherever here was.

"Hey, how about a grinard over the rocks?" Walter rubbed his hands together. "Man, I miss those."

He didn't actually say it that way. It was really something like "Shubba shubba grinard, hey, hey, hey!" but that was the translation.

I refused an alcoholic drink, but the bartender gave me a very good alternative, much better than Coke.

"Hey, Walter!" A green man walked up and slapped Walter on his lower arm.

"Uno! Hi!"

"Who is this lovely lady you have with you?" Uno turned to me, smiling and bowing.

"Oh, Bey gave me a babysitter." Walter scowled again.

"Really?" Uno said. "How lucky for you."

"I had to get off that planet. It's so boring!"

I stiffened a little. It felt like he said I was boring. Walter continued to nurse his drink.

"You don't say." Uno was still staring and smiling at me. It was a bit disconcerting, because his mouth was full of sharp, pointed teeth.

"Cut it out, Uno. She doesn't know what a rabo you are."

"Rabo? Really!" He turned to Walter. "So, what are you doing these days? Found any interesting rules to break?"

Walter waved a hand at Uno and took a drink. "I've just been twirling my toes." He shook his head, "What's been going on here?"

Uno smiled. "Not much, other than the usual, crazy politicians saying crazy things. Oh, the Agency decided to cut the funding on the Zeta project. They had managed to piss off the whole planet with their elaborate, over the top plans."

"Good. They were messing that up anyway. Zeta didn't even want a private wormhole system. Hell, they don't even like getting off their planet. At least the Earth does, or I should say, they used to." He shook his head and laughed. "Now that Zeta is part of the galaxy, they should be listened to."

"Well, are you staying for lunch? I've got some great Ando Sea Horns." Walter perked up. "Here, sit down and I'll bring you and your lovely babysitter a healthy portion."

Uno sat us in a big booth and did produce a beautiful meal. Don't ask me what an Ando Sea Horn is. The implanted chip, Jona, said I could eat it.

"Go ahead, Ms. Anders. The Ando Sea Horns passed for safe presence in your bloodstream and body. You are cleared for ingestion."

Seems Jona could talk as well as print on my eye.

The Ando Sea Horns were similar to lobsters (which I can't eat) but didn't have whatever it is that makes us sufferers get hives. You crack them open, take out the sweet meat and dunk in some buttery-like stuff. Yeah, I know, what isn't good in butter? Anyway, Walter and I were quiet for a while, except for an occasional moan as the forks entered our mouths.

"Uno is a nice person. Have you known him long?" I asked.

Walter laughed. "Yeah, I always used to come here after a job. He's a Carrion. Helped him set this up." Walter gestured around the bar.

Ah, so that's what he mean by a Carrion burger.

Uno was basically a human with green skin and a round hole for a mouth filled with teeth that all pointed toward each other. Walter said he didn't eat, just photosynthesized like a plant. Well, to be precise, he ate only for pleasure, as he still had the alimentary canal, but it was mostly ignored now in favor of sunbathing. I realized I had broken my word to my employer for the first time in my life. But was Uno the alien, or was I? In truth, it was only one of my two employers who disapproved. Did that even matter?

I pondered that as Uno brought over our dessert, a Macedonian tart. Holy Moly! The right amount of tart, sweet, and cream. I could have had a few more of those, but we needed to leave.

I looked around, found Hand, obviously drunk, cooing at two females. I saw why he wore shorts. Wow, you don't want a male dog standing on hind paws, and walking around, especially if he is trying to pick up women!

Hand huffed when I told him we were going back but said his farewells. Uno ran the credit card in front of us and handed it back to Walter. Good idea! I had seen that before (on Earth, of course), but not enough. It is so much safer to keep the card in sight rather than walk out of the line of sight of the customer. Walter squinted at the bill, trying to figure out the tip. I sat at the table with him and we discussed what was fair.

"Okay then, that would be," I figured in my head, "two donkurs (a donkur was equivalent to about ten dollars), so three tokas (about three dollars) for the tip, 15% for lunch. Okay for Earth on a twenty-dollar bill. Yes, that fits." I added the figures and Walter signed, and then he handed it back to Uno.

"You will return, pretty lady?" Uno reached for my hand again, looking up as he kissed it. I had to remind myself I was reading the translation and he was probably not as charming as he was sounding.

"Sure, sure," I said as I hurried away and pushed Hand's back. The furry alien maiden moaned as he was pushed out of her arms. I hustled my charges up to a chute I found that led up to the roof.

"Tell the cruiser we are coming," Walter said.

"Uh, hello cruiser," I said.

"No, tell your chip," Hand smiled.

"Yes, yes of course. Jona, could you inform the cruiser we are coming for the ride home?"

"Certainly, cruiser informed, " said a voice right out of my arm. Would I ever get used to that?

When we arrived at the cruiser, it was already open, so the three of us got in.

"Take us home," Walter told the car.

"Certainly, Walter. Ms. Anders, do you concur?" the car asked.

"Yes, take us home."

The car lifted off the roof and it headed back out into traffic. The ride back was the same roller coaster, but it held less sway with my tummy. You'd think it would be worse after that great meal, but maybe I was just more relaxed. Entering the atmosphere, I remembered how the space shuttles had lit up like a road flare upon reentering and got nervous again.

"How does the cruiser take the heat?" I asked.

"It has a coating similar to your shuttles, but much thinner and absorbs the heat so well it can't be seen by any Earth instruments," Hand said from the back seat. Walter didn't seem too interested in this.

Minutes later we were back home, putting the cruiser to bed.

#

Going out to eat at the coffee shop was not nearly as interesting or exciting after that, especially as Hand was not allowed, so other ideas had to be generated. Walter asked to see my house. I obliged him. I drove both Walter and Hand in my own car. We pulled up and walked to the front door.

I warned Hand to walk like an Earth dog, but he was way ahead of me. "I have lived here for three years." He sounded a bit miffed.

As I opened the door, Pepper rushed to greet me and was doubly surprised at the guests. She jumped around and sniffed Walter but paid great attention to Hand. I had tried to prepare Hand, and he was just as confident he could handle this as well, though I wasn't really sure he had ever met one of our dogs before.

"Whoa, little lady, calm down. There's plenty of me to go around."

Pepper stopped short and looked hard around the room and then at the two humans (I know, but for her that's what we were.) When Hand spoke again, she was staring at him.

"Yes, it's me. You are quite pretty."

Now, Pepper knew what that meant, and her tail wagged. She bowed down, her front legs splayed out in front.

"Is this a type of communication?" Hand asked me.

"Yes, she wants you to play," I said, quite pleased.

"Oh, lady, yes ma'am." And they ran off around the room and out into my little garden as soon as I opened the patio doors. I relaxed and turned my attention to Walter as he wandered around my living room.

"You live here by yourself?" he asked as he picked up pictures and books.

"Yes." I answered.

"Unusual. No mate?"

"No." I shook my head. "I prefer it that way."

"Yes, I have heard of this on Earth. It is unusual for such a backward planet," he mused and then roused. "Oh, pardon me. I do not mean to infer that you are... It's just that your level of development... the emancipation... That usually comes when reproduction is not so focused upon, necessary, if you take what I mean." He looked at me with a tiny, mischievous smile.

"Well, I think we have enough population to last a few generations."

"Not really. You need to inhabit a few places first. Really get a foothold in this solar system and then work on some places outside of it. Have to think of your species." He got that cat smile again.

I hadn't thought about it that way, but I suppose it's true, as the dinosaurs might attest to if they could. There really is no safe amount of land; whole planets can be at risk. I didn't want to think what could happen to whole solar systems. Whoa!

When Pepper and Hand had worn themselves out, we all sat down in the living room with refreshments and to talk. After a while, Pepper led Walter out on the porch and they explored the garden together. He was very patient and explained what he liked about the place, and Pepper was delighted to listen. Hand lay on the floor, both of us watching them outside, and he told tell me about how they met.

"I used to partner with Walter."

"Partner?"

"Yeah, you know, work together."

"As a Watcher?"

He nodded, "We were a good team. Got into some fights, good times." Hand wagged his tail. "I retired with him."

"Why not go back home?"

His tail dropped. "Can't, it doesn't exist anymore."

"Oh, Hand, I'm so sorry."

"Yeah, so was Walter. He fought the Agency, but in the end they said 'Just watch', you know, 'record.' Walter got me out of there just before the whole thing fell apart."

"How? What happened?"

"Well, we blew ourselves up. That is, evidently, not usual. I know you think it is; that's Earth's worry. Usually, the dominant species on a planet run out of something or someone comes along and takes it and that leads to the end. We were very volatile, though. The Agency said that was nature selecting. I suppose that's right." He sighed.

"I don't know. That seems so heartless."

He shrugged, "Well, they have to deal with a whole galaxy. There is a great push not to get involved, let people be what they are."

Yes, I felt that way, but it seemed to me that if extinction was involved it was worth trying something.

Walter decided on a nap and Pepper and Hand alternated between frenzied play and exhausted panting. I wish I had that energy. When Walter woke up, I saw a different side to him. One I was familiar with from other clients and when I had first met him.

"Oh, I don't know what I'm doing? Where I am?" he sighed and sat down.

"Do you know who I am?"

"Sarah?" Walter asked.

I nodded. That was good. I was still new in his life.

"I just don't know who I am. I look in the mirror and don't recognize this face," he said.

"Where were you born?"

"Tanterus 5 in the middle of the Tanterus system."

"How many in your family?"

"One brother, two children. I had a wife, I think, but she's no longer around?"

"Yes, what was she like?"

"I don't know." He didn't remember and quit talking. That was the end of it. It was amazing to me how memory loss patients could know so much but only access it from questions, not on their own.

#

Hand invited Pepper to go with us to Uno's and of course she knew that word, "GO!" She showed us by wagging her tail and stepping on my feet. I allowed her to go after she got a chip (in addition to the Earthen one for dogs) and she wore a leash, just to be safe. I wondered how Hand felt about this, but he said nothing.

Arriving at Uno's with Pepper for the first time was a bit nerve wracking for me. What would she do? Would she be scared? I took a deep breath and trusted. I was learning to go with the flow. We all sat at the same table as our previous visit. Pepper could barely contain her curiosity, but eventually she submitted to lying under the table. I guess by then she felt relaxed.

"Hey Walter, steal any icebergs today?" I turned to see a humanoid of questionable origin. He—it—stood three feet tall, hands for feet and hammers for hands.

"Demoleon!" Walter jumped up, grinning, and almost hugged the guy.

"Hey Walter," another cheerful voice called out, "it's good seeing you, been a long time."

Walter turned to the new speaker, grinning even wider (if that was possible). "Arsta, you devil! What dark hole did you crawl out of? Come eat with us. Uno outdid himself." Walter gestured to the two aliens.

"Mmmm... not my kind," Arsta said, but Demoleon sat down.

A small bark issued from below. Hand got down on the floor and sat down beside my dog, talking to her in whispers. Pepper loved the attention and nuzzled between the both of us.

Arsta turned to me.

"Oh, this is Sarah, my watchdog." Walter grinned and rolled his eyes.

"How do you do? It is a pleasure to meet you." Then she did a bow, by angling her body so the front legs and head were lowered. There is no other way to describe it; this was a spider, a huge spider whose head reached at least five feet. I figured she was female because she looked like the iconic black widow, black, shiny with a red hour glass on her abdomen.

"Nice to meet you, too," I managed to answer.

Arsta pulled over a cushion that fit her posterior pretty well. "So, you are a watchdog for Walter?"

"Well, I am called an aide. I am helping Walter keep some of his independence."

"I'm glad about that. Walter has always been so vibrant. His daughter and son took him to that small planet and we haven't heard from him for quite a while, a few years, in fact. I don't think they quite approved of us. I'm guessing the reason you were hired has something to do with the influence of your planet. Don't you have male dominance?"

At first the feminist in me wanted to protest, but I realized she was speaking of the whole planet and that male dominance seemed to be unusual. We have come a long way from the Suffragette movement and I was very proud to be an independent woman. Watchers, though, obviously viewed this on a much larger scale. Umm, male dominance unusual, that was interesting. Even more curious and perplexing was that it had some influence on the decision to hire me. Why, because Walter was a male and therefore more important on Earth? Why would they care? I thought of the son Bey, how he looked. Whoa, this was going farther than my poor mind could absorb, so I quickly changed course and continued to talk about my experience with his family.

"I don't know about his daughter, but I think you are right about the son, Bey. He disapproved of visiting with aliens. I thought he meant Earth people who live in a country south of my city who illegally crossed our country's border. There is quite a bit of tension over that, and they are called 'illegal aliens.'" I paused and shrugged. "I got the feeling he thought Walter would do something irresponsible. Of course, that is common in my work with the elderly, so I didn't think it unusual, except that his warning seemed to encompass more than just the effects of age."

"That sounds like Bey. I think you should know, though," she leaned closer to me, "Walter is not irresponsible, except the way that men can be." She leaned back. This opinion took on a new meaning with switching dominances. "He was an excellent Watcher. At this point he just has troubles with his memory, though I realize I haven't seen him in a while."

"Well, Walter was not involved with much when I first met him, but now he is really getting engaged." I paused. "I'm afraid Bey will not be pleased we came here. His daughter, Ephrem, allowed it but I'm not sure how that is going to play between them."

Arsta nodded her head.

"What are you ladies so intent on? Aren't you going to have some of this fabulous Genesian udder?" Walter waved something flaccid at her.

I smiled and nodded, but made no move to eat this delicacy. Walter had been intent on his conversation with Demoleon at the other end of the table and picked it up again. They were loud and full of laughter.

I turned back to Artsa to continue our conversation. "I am surprised there wasn't some help for him here. Something more than what we have," I said.

"No, Walter's children probably wouldn't do much artificial for him," Artsa said. "Some Watchers believe interference is not justified."

I was stunned. "I would think every effort would be made…" I didn't know how to finish.

Arsta delicately put a leg on my arm, "No Sarah, there isn't much interest. Once elders in this 'advanced' galaxy pass into the declining stages, that is it."

I had never encountered this point of view before. I must have made a face or something because all of her eyes were on me, but it seemed there was compassion in them.

Arsta leaned toward me and whispered in my ear, "Sarah, we are not gods. Just because we have been around for millennia more than your people have been on Earth doesn't mean we have gained wisdom in everything." She leaned back. "Of course, not all Watchers think that way." She leveled all her eyes at me. "Walter is one of the most valuable people I know, with or without his memory. I would do anything I could for him." At this point I believe Arsta became my best friend, feeling like that about my charge.

"You have known Walter long?" I asked.

"Oh, yes! Our first assignment was together. He was a rascal, but would come up with the most remarkable ideas. We backed each other many a time."

"How long have you worked as a... Watcher?" I asked. I immediately felt foolish. That was the simplistic way Walter put it.

"Ooh, I am retired now. I had to raise one hundred little ones all the way to maturity."

"That would be hard." I thought about that. "Why is it called Watching?"

"It is a word that translates well."

"How long does a career usually last?" I asked.

"Let's see, we all started around one thousand years ago, and some of us are still going at it. The Agency has been going for over a million years. Yes, I know that is a long time, but the age-old urge to know about others has always been around. Of course, the agency has changed over the years, policies have evolved. Many planets have matured and joined or died out, but a good proportion of the galaxy is represented."

"Wow, that's something," I marveled, "Over a million years. Are you all retired now?" I looked around the room.

"Oh, no. Some are like Hopo over there at the bar," She indicated a small green guy with a spark-plug body, who turned a beautiful smile my way. "I don't think he will ever quit. He tows things like asteroids on the side, just to make enough payroll. Budget cuts."

I nodded my head. I was familiar with that.

The conversations had gone quiet due to eating and Demoleon had heard Arsta mention Hopo.

"Sometimes, he joins the Watching and asteroids jobs together," Demoleon said. "Of course, not always with permission."

The group laughed, nodding their heads. Walter scowled.

"What?" I asked, looking around. An inside joke?

Uno set down another drink in front of me. "Sometimes, you must break the rules." He looked me straight in the eyes.

I never broke rules, ever. .... Oh yeah, that wasn't true anymore. I squirmed in my seat.

"Aye," Demoleon said.

I looked at all of them, finally ending at Arsta. She said, "Oh, yes, Walter broke some rules, but..."

"It saved my life," said Uno.

"And mine," Hand barked.

"Sometimes that seems like a stupid choice," Walter quipped.

"Aw, come on, you love me!" Hand grinned. Walter guffawed and waved his hand at the alien dog.

"But really, it was quite a stunt, a legend still," Demoleon said. "Imagine towing an iceberg all around that monstrous planet and dropping it in plain sight! I couldn't have done it."

"Why would you move an iceberg?" I asked.

"Ah, for the age old battle," Arsta said.

"Whiskey is for drinking, and water is for war!" Walter raised his glass.

"Righto," and the group raised their glasses.

"You brought someone water?" I asked, smiling, pleased Walter had used my quote.

"He sure did. Saved my people." Uno sat down. "I came from a line of farmers. All of us, except my brother, Ibba." Uno nodded toward the back corner of the bar, at the unsavory character I had spotted on my first trip to Uno's. "I was put in charge of selling the crops to Amida, the big city. I learned a good trade."

"Then the city got greedy," Walter said, shaking his head. City folk shared the river with the farmers. Then they started to fight over the water. It got ugly."

"It's an old story. Those with the power take the water. At first it was pretty balanced, but soon the city grew and the farming got more efficient, which led to fewer farmers," Arsta said. "Any Watcher will tell you where this goes, and it is not fun to watch."

"I had them build a dam," Walter said, grinning like a Cheshire cat.

A dam? Walter? I looked at my charge closely. It was hard to think of him young and in charge of such construction and why it was something a Watcher was not allowed to do.

"Great idea, but the city, Amida, beat us to it." Uno scowled. "We were almost there!" His hand went up. "Then the water was gone. They had managed to divert it into their territory away from the dam and us."

"But wouldn't that put Amida in a bad spot with no crops?" I asked.

"The larger you get, the more sources you pull from. The damned city got food from elsewhere in the country. We had some stored and survived okay for one season, but that was all we were prepared for."

"I have heard of taking an iceberg for a water supply." I said. The idea was so huge. "So you got who ...," I looked over at the bar, "Hopo, to pick it up for you?"

Hopo, who was looking at the group, walked over with his drink and joined in. "Sure did, and I put it behind the newly constructed dam."

"Wow, how did the city and farmers react?" I asked. "Where did you get it from? Wasn't there an issue with contamination, you know, microbes or something?"

Everyone grinned who could. "We got it from the same planet, and Hopo did something to it to make sure it was clean," Arsta said. Hopo nodded and sipped his drink.

"They thought it was a divine intervention. Volturnus, their god, had shown his displeasure at Amida and had blessed the farmers with even more water than there was originally." Uno smiled, looking back at his brother again. "My brother supplied the parts, smuggled out from Amida. My family, the labor, and Walter the expertise."

"That's when the Agency shut me down." Walter looked pained as he talked.

"He didn't lose his job, but they watched him closely after that," Arsta said quietly to me.

"When it got too hot, we took an offered ride off planet." Uno smiled, turning back to the group. "I'm afraid that standing in for a god is frowned up at the Agency."

"So, this was not encouraged, this iceberg taking, by the Agency?" I asked. No wonder Bey was so suspicious.

The people around the table looked at each other. "Our primary goal is to observe and learn how civilizations develop, but..." Arsta turned her eight eyes to look around the table again.

"But, sometimes there is a moral question. Not often but sometimes. We can go through centuries without much to test us," Demoleon said. "Frankly, we are not usually in a place long enough to see much of this happen from beginning to end."

"And if you try to respond, the rules are quite strict. Technically, you could say Walter followed the rules," Hopo said, raising his glass.

In chorus they quoted the rule: "In a life and death emergency, where the agent has a reasonable chance of success to save life and the populace remains unaware of the greater galactic presence, the Watcher may temporarily interfere."

"Of course, there was argument on the interpretation. The iceberg stunt was the largest 'interference' known, and having a god be the reason, well... the Agency didn't like that. Thankfully, in this case, there was no Volturnus to answer to," Arsta said.

Whoa! There can be a Volturnus to answer to?

I sat back in my chair. Pepper nuzzled my hand and sat down on my feet. There was comfort in her warmth and pressure. Could I have done that, taken that risk? A week ago I would have said no, but I had broken the rules, even if it was by accident. Oh, fardles, technically, even that wasn't true.

#

When we stepped out of the garage, the door closing behind us, a very irritated Bey met us. "Dad, where have you been? Ms. Anders, I thought I made it clear that Dad was not to associate with aliens."

"Yes, you did, but at the time the only aliens I knew of were from down south over the border. Ephrem gave us permission for Uno's."

I looked him straight in the eye. I had been anticipating this conversation. I knew he would not approve, but I would not let my employers put me in the middle. This was Bey's prejudice, not mine.

"This is very complicated. How do you define alien?"

Bey shook his head and scowled.

"I made this choice," Walter said.

"Dad, you not capable. Let's get you back in house." He moved to take his father's arm. I believed up until that moment that "handling" my charges in this forceful way was acceptable. Seeing it happen was unsettling.

"Wait, Bey, let's not..." I said.

"You stay out this, go home." And he moved to again to force Walter away. I could tell Walter was going to resist. This was not good.

Bey reached for Walter's arm and Walter pulled away. I saw the hand go up and I knew I could not allow that. Breaking another rule so soon, Sarah? Never in my career had I challenged my employer.

"Stop!" I stepped into Bey's line of sight, reached up and pulled back his arm. Pepper started barking, seeing my reaction.

"Ms. Anders, this is private matter! Get that creature out of here!" Bey was trying not to yell but he was red.

Hand stepped up with Pepper, "She is not a creature," and turning to my dog he said, "You go, girl!" Pepper, with the encouragement, continued to bark, increasing the volume and crouching a bit to look fierce.

"And I am Walter's advocate. Step away." I held my ground. Bey dropped his arm, a little confused at the turn of events.

It was Walter's turn to be astonished. He looked at me and then at his son, his eyes wide. Walter reached out for me and lost the support of his legs. I helped him reach the ground, very slowly.

"Call 911," I told Bey as he stood looking down on us.

"No, can't go to Earthen hospital," was all he said as he shook his head.

"Oh, for heaven's sake." I shook my head. How far would this go? Though I had to admit that it was going to be awkward.

I tried to think of what was the logical thing to do. My head came up. "Jona, prepare the cruiser, emergency. Need closest medical facility that can help Walter."

"Acknowledged, computing," that wonderful voice out of my arm said and hurried to open the garage door and we all piled into the cruiser.

"Hand, help me get there," I said. I picked up that fragile old man and Hand and Pepper led the way back out to the garage, opening doors as we went.

We left Bey standing there with his mouth open. I sat by Walter's bed all night with Hand and Pepper lying at my feet.

#

The galaxy survived the interference both of Walter's and of mine. Bey never talked to me again and found work elsewhere. However, his daughter remained and retained me. Walter survived, though he was never the same after that. We often took him out for joy rides, and a few times I got that smile back. Walter left me the cruiser, and Hand now lives with us.

The Watcher Agency had erected a memorial outside the main headquarters for the Water Enterprise. This building turned out to be near Uno's, which makes sense. The bar after work? Hand and

I helped the retired Watchers petition the Agency, and it seemed someone else agreed that the iceberg enterprise was heroic.

On Friday nights (Earth nights) you can find Hand, Pepper, and me raising or just drinking a glass at Uno's, in tribute:

"To Walter, for winning the water war!"

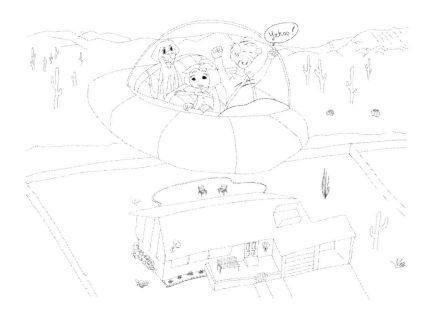

Jessica Barnes

Joni Parker was born in Chicago, Illinois and lived with her family in Japan for four years until they relocated to Phoenix, Arizona. After high school graduation, Joni joined the U.S. Navy and three years later, received an honorable discharge. She married a Navy man and went to college. Upon graduation, she returned to the Navy. After 22 years of active duty service, she retired. Unexpectedly, her husband passed away, so Joni returned to work, but retired again to devote her time to writing. She moved to Tucson in 2015. Her first book series, T*he Seaward Isle Saga,* includes *The Black Elf of Seaward Isle, Tangled Omens,* and *Blood Mission,* and a short story, *The Island Game: The Inside Story of Seaward Isle.* She's completing her second series, *The Chronicles of Eledon,* which begins with two award-winning novels, *Spell Breaker* (2016 Book Excellence Award Finalist) and *The Blue Witch* (2017 International Book Award Finalist), followed by *Gossamer* and *Noble Magic.*

Synopsis

After a year deployment overseas and a raucous promotion party, Navy SEAL Edgar Winters relaxes on a small boat off Pensacola Beach until a rumble of thunder changes his plans. ***Contains adult language.***

One-Way Journey

Edgar wrinkled his nose at the smell of gasoline as he filled the tank of his rented boat, an 18-foot runabout with a large enough engine for water skiing. He just needed a chance to get away from it all and intended to do some fishing. For the last year, he'd been stationed overseas on a secret assignment with his elite Navy SEAL team unit and was now back home in the States. His new duty station at Naval Air Station Pensacola was a dream come true, with miles of white sandy beaches open to the Gulf of Mexico.

After the gas tank was filled, he paid for it with his credit card and pushed away from the dock. He started up the engine and headed straight out to sea. He bounced over the waves and enjoyed the fresh air and sunshine. When the coastline was far behind him, a thin line on the horizon, he shut off the engine and set up his fishing gear.

It'd been ages since he'd gone fishing. His most memorable fishing trip had been on his thirteenth birthday, when his father drove him from their home in Tucson, Arizona to San Diego for a weekend. Just the two of them. They fished off the pier and used shrimp for bait. They caught a few fish and had them for supper over an open campfire on the beach. Edgar remembered that weekend fondly, but the highlight of the trip was a visit to Coronado Beach where the SEALs trained, the Navy's elite warriors who fought on the sea, air, and land. From that point on, Edgar dreamed of becoming one of them.

His father encouraged him, even though he was in the Air Force. He was a drone pilot stationed at Davis-Monthan Air Force Base in Tucson. Recently, his dad had retired and started work as a civilian, training more drone pilots. His mom was a social worker in Family Services on the base with no immediate plans of retirement. Edgar loved his family home in Tucson, even though he hadn't been born there. He was born in Ohio, but as a military brat, traveled the world with his family. Tucson was his favorite. His latest trip home had found his family in good health and busy as ever.

When Edgar had returned to Pensacola, he found out he'd been promoted to the rank of Chief Petty Officer. He'd climbed through the ranks fast. Making chief was a big deal in the Navy; the initiation program lasted nearly a week, but he could handle it. In fact, he dared them to make him lose his smile. He won. Yesterday, the week culminated in an official ceremony, ending with his promotion. He couldn't have been happier.

This morning, he rented a boat from Special Services and borrowed some fishing gear from a friend. Edgar baited the hook with a piece of shrimp from his ice chest and cast the line over the side. As the bait drifted below, he grabbed a sandwich and a beer from his cooler and ate lunch. He didn't expect to catch anything and actually, hoped he wouldn't. This was a time to sunbathe and unwind. After slathering himself with suntan lotion, he lay out on the deck on top of a beach towel. The sun was hot and his eyes closed.

Sometime later, he woke to the sound of a distant rumble. He sat up and saw a thunderstorm brewing, and knew he needed to get back to land. These storms were common in the area, and dangerous. Quickly, he reeled in his line and to his relief, found his bait gone and no fish attached. He threw the rod to the bottom of the boat and started up the engine. Accelerating quickly, he headed to shore.

The storm was moving in fast. He'd barely gone a hundred feet before the rain and hail started.

"Damn it!" Edgar cursed out loud. "Wait 'til I get to shore." He shook his fist at the clouds.

The storm didn't wait. Instead, it seemed to have heard him and picked up speed. Rain poured down in buckets and the wind blew hard. Edgar drove on, blinded by the elements. Waves grew to five feet, then ten, and higher. The boat had a foot of water inside and the ice chest sloshed from one side to the other. Edgar pushed the accelerator lever to full throttle, but he was losing. A wave came up from the side and tossed the boat sideways. He was thrown from his chair and almost fell out of the boat. He climbed back in and made his way to his chair. As he sat down, the boat dipped low. Looking up, he faced a wave that must have been thirty feet high. He gunned the engine and felt the boat rise up the side of the wave. When it reached the top, he flew over the crest and slammed into the water. The jolt knocked his hands off the steering wheel. The boat sped ahead, climbing the next wave and shot over the top once more. This time, the boat stayed in the air and rose higher. Rain pelted down and obscured his vision, until his boat was encased in a clear bubble. The bubble protected him from the rain, but the updraft in the thunderstorm pushed him up. He was surrounded by a white light and thought, maybe, God had forgiven him and he was on his way to heaven. But the light darkened and he was in a tunnel of some sort. It was dark and swirled around the bubble like a whirlwind. He stared, unable to do anything.

After a few moments, he recovered and scooped water out of his boat with his hands. He threw it against the bubble. It ran down the sides and collected at the bottom. This bubble was protecting him from whatever the dark matter was. "This is a good thing," he concluded.

Edgar found his cell phone still wedged in the cup holder and checked it. Fortunately, it was the water resistant model and still worked. He speed dialed a friend, but it went to voicemail. He left a short message and explained his situation until the battery died. He'd forgotten to charge it overnight.

"Well, this is a fine mess you've gotten yourself into," he said to himself. He opened his cooler and got a beer. He popped the top and took a long swig. Ahead, the tunnel seemed brighter. "What now?" Edgar craned his neck to the side for a better look, only to see more light at the end of the tunnel.

As he took another drink, the boat shot out from the bubble and the end of the dark tunnel on its way to the surface. Tossing the can aside, he could clearly see an island ahead of him, but he was a lot higher than he wanted to be. His best guess was five thousand feet. A tall volcano stood in the middle of the island and he wondered if he'd found a deserted tropical island in the middle of the ocean. His mind raced, hoping to find a way to survive the impact. Wind zipped by the open-topped boat and he stayed low to avoid getting blown out.

The boat was lightweight and its wide bottom allowed it to glide, a little. The engine dropped the rear end lower, but it still held steady, although dropping fast. Edgar lay face down on the deck, gripping the chrome pipes holding up his seat, his hands sweaty.

The impact was hard and he lost his grip. He bounced out of the boat as it skipped across the water until it slowed, tumbling end over end. The water knocked the wind out of him and he was stunned, but awake, finding himself underwater. He swam to the surface, gasping for air. A rowboat headed towards him and a pair of hands reached over the side.

"You all right, Mister?" A middle-aged man leaned over the edge of his rowboat and helped him inside.

"Yeah, thanks for picking me up. Did you see where my boat went?"

"It's over yonder." The man pointed to the left. "It broke apart, like they all do."

"Names Edgar Winters. I think I see my cooler over there. Do you mind?"

"Nope. Did you have anything else?" The man gathered the oars and rowed toward the cooler.

"Just some fishing equipment and a beach towel."

"Too bad." The man rowed up next to the cooler and dragged it in. The latch had held firmly and everything inside was intact.

Edgar pulled out two beers. "Have one." When he popped the top, the beer foamed out and he held it away from him. As soon as it stopped, he took a long drink and exhaled when he finished. "What's your name, buddy?"

"Wallace."

"You been here long?"

"Too long, over fifteen years." Wallace popped the top of the can and waited to take a sip of beer as it foamed out. He nodded and drank more.

"You must like it here."

"Nope. There's no way off this island. By the way, welcome to Seaward Isle." He raised his beer in a toast.

"Seaward Isle? Where is this?"

"Don't know, Mister. Well, I need to take you to shore."

"Why can't you get out of here? All you need is a ship." Edgar snapped his fingers. "Wait, that was a long drop." He turned and looked at the sky. "How--?"

"You just came through an entry point, way up there. And there's no way to get past them storms." Wallace pointed away from shore. Dark clouds roiled into the sky as another thunderstorm built up. Lightning flashed through the clouds and a deep rumble followed.

Edgar turned around. His jaw dropped. "Is that the same storm that brought me here? It must have followed me."

"From what I can tell, those storms go up into that entry point and bring back ships with them."

"Is that what happened to you?"

"Yep, me and my boys were on our way from San Francisco during the Yukon Gold Rush when this big ol' storm came up out of nowhere. And we ended up here."

"What was that tunnel-like thing and the clear bubble?"

"Don't know, Mister Edgar. Sorry." Wallace shook his head as the rowboat came ashore.

They were met by two other men, who introduced themselves as Turnin and Gorman, Wallace's 'boys.' The two men carried the cooler as the four of them headed into a small village nearby where Wallace knocked on the door of one of the small houses.

Edgar stared at the small community. There were less than a dozen huts that all looked the same—stone walls, thatched roofs, wooden door with two windows on either side.

"These here homes are called shanties, built by the Elves." Wallace knocked on the door again. "Becky, open up in there!"

"Did you say Elves?"

"That's right. Elves. Big ones. Watch out for 'em. Some of them are downright mean and nasty."

"Thanks for the warning."

Becky finally opened the door and let them in. "What'd you bring?"

"It's a cooler with beer." Wallace grinned. "This is Mister Edgar. You'd better check him in."

"Hi, I'm Becky." The woman's curly red hair was wrapped in a scarf. Her hands were rough and calloused.

"Nice to meet you. Call me Edgar."

"Anytime, Edgar." She batted her eyelashes at him. "Come on in and let me get you signed in."

"Signed in?"

"I have a book where everyone signs in. Are you hurt, by the way? It's a nasty fall from the sky."

"You said it."

Becky led him into the kitchen where the men sat down at the table. They opened the cooler and pulled out some more beers. As they popped the tops, Becky returned with a large book.

"Just sign your name here and fill in the blanks. Hey, give me one of those."

Turnin handed her one. "Man, this is good beer." He guzzled it.

Edgar signed his name and filled in the blanks. One unusual entry was the last date he remembered. He wrote down, October 7, 2016. "Why are you asking for the last date?"

"Look at all the other ones," Becky said. "What dates do you see?"

"Whoa! There's 1523, 1921, 1780...are you kidding?"

"Nope, happens to all of us. When I got here, the year I left was 1997, but when these three bastards got here, it was 1892."

"I ain't no bastard. Check the year here. It's 996 in Elf years."

"Elf years?"

"Yep, they's the one doing the counting. They got stranded on this here island that long ago." Wallace sipped his beer. "When you finish that beer, Becky will find you some dry clothes and then we have to take you to Agana. You're going to have to check in official-like at the King's library."

"There's a King here?"

"His name's Agamon—never even seen him. No such thing as a president."

"Wait a minute, Agana's on the island of Guam in the Pacific Ocean."

"You ain't there, Mister Edgar. Trust me."

Becky handed Edgar a sandwich and he drank the last of his beer. As soon as he finished, she took him to the back room and handed him a dry shirt and a pair of old jeans.

"These should fit you." She left him to change. He took off his T-shirt and shorts and put on the clothes. They fit, sort of. He went back to the kitchen.

"Should I leave my old clothes with you?"

"Unless you want them. I doubt you'll be coming back this way any time soon."

A few minutes later, the other men had finished their beers and stood up. They put on their slouchy cowboy hats as they wandered to the door.

"Let's go, Mister Edgar." Wallace cocked his head to the side. "You might want to wear a hat. It's hot out here." He handed Edgar a straw cowboy hat and headed to the door.

"Thank you, Becky." He waved.

"No problem. Thanks for the beer."

The men moseyed over to the stables where they saddled four horses. Edgar had ridden a horse only once in his life and he was ten at the time.

The men spoke little as they rode north, away from the beach. It was a two-hour horseback ride to Agana. They stopped in the stables on the outskirts of the city and left their horses in the pens. Wallace took Edgar to a brown building which he called the library.

"They'll take care of you inside." Wallace grinned. "See you around."

"Where are you going?"

"We have to do some investigatin'...for Becky. See you later." Wallace tipped his hat and left.

Edgar went inside the building, certain he would never see Wallace again. A monk met him at the door.

"My name is Brother Joseph. May I help you?"

"Yeah, my friend, Wallace, told me I needed to check in with you."

"A new arrival. How unfortunate for you."

"Yeah, thanks. What do I need to do?"

"Just sign your name in our book." The monk pointed him to an open book and handed him a quill and an open bottle of ink.

"You write with quills?"

"We do." The monk pointed to a blank spot on the page. "Your name please."

Edgar dipped the end of the quill into the bottle. Drops of ink dripped off the end. The monk cleared his throat.

"May I help you with that?" He took the quill from Edgar and cleaned the tip. After dunking the tip only into the ink, he handed back it to Edgar. "Try this."

Edgar took the feather in his hand and touched the paper. The tip scratched the surface and ink splattered all over. "Sorry. I've never used a quill before."

"Obviously." The monk blotted the paper and Edgar tried again. He scratched his name out in print and signed it. It was almost legible.

"Very well. Thank you. You may leave," the monk said.

"Thanks. Where do I go from here?"

"You can't go far." The monk looked away. "You'll probably find Wallace at the *Seaman's Inn*."

"Thanks." Edgar left and strolled into a market, where he was bumped hard by a man with long, blond hair. Edgar turned sharply and said, "You should say, 'excuse me.'"

The man grinned. "You're excused."

Edgar gritted his teeth, but knew this man was trying to goad him into a fight. "No, you say it, bastard." He pushed him in the chest.

Within seconds, the man had Edgar pinned on the ground and glared into his eyes.

"Okay, uncle." Edgar raised his hands. He'd never seen anyone move so fast. Those blue eyes glaring at him were more than he could handle right now. Then he noticed the pointed ears on the man. Edgar froze. He could hardly believe what he was seeing. This man was an Elf. Not a small Elf like the ones who worked for Santa, but a big one like the ones in the movies. The ones Wallace told him to watch out for. "I mean I give up." Edgar stuttered as he said it, choking on his words.

The Elf stood up and lifted Edgar off the ground with one hand, pushing him aside. He laughed and marched away.

Edgar raised his eyebrows and concluded that Wallace was right. These Elves could be very mean and nasty, especially when they're big.

"Are you hurt?" A young woman came up to him.

"Nah, I'm fine." He brushed his jeans off and looked at this young woman. She was nearly as tall as he was with long black hair and the bluest eyes he'd ever seen. In addition, his eye caught a glimpse of some blue hair near her ear. "I see you dye your hair blue."

She sighed. "It's not dye. It's real. I'm part Water Elf."

"You're like that guy who just put me on the ground in two seconds."

"Yes, but he's a lot older than me. This will go away, eventually." She touched her ears.

"My name's Edgar Winters. I just got here. I was looking for the *Seaman's Inn* to meet a friend of mine. Do you know where it is?"

"It's just over there. Are you an American?"

"I am. What's your name?"

"Alex."

"If you're only part Water Elf, what's the rest of you?"

She laughed. "Mortal and Titan."

"Yeah, right." He chuckled. "But you do sound American."

"My foster father's American. His name's Colonel Penser."

"Colonel? Is he in the army? The American army?"

"He was. Are you?"

"I was a Navy SEAL. That's sort of like an Army Ranger."

"Colonel Penser was a Ranger. He's now in charge of the Nyla Army Garrison up north. There are other Americans there as well. You should go see him."

"I'll do that. Thank you. Can you point out the inn again?"

"I'll show it to you." She turned on her heel and led him through the market.

"How old are you?" Edgar asked.

"Fourteen. I'm here on an official visit with the Lord Governor from our region."

"At fourteen?"

"Governor Tyrone's my benefactor. He isn't married and didn't have anyone else to bring."

She stopped at the corner. "See that building over there?"

"You mean the one with the sign on the front that says, *Seaman's Inn*?"

"That's it. Beau owns it. He's an American, too. He'll help you out."

"You've been very kind, thank you."

"I hope you'll come to Nyla to see the Garrison. I think you'll like it." Alex left and went in through a gate at the King's palace. She turned and waved.

Edgar went inside the inn and found Wallace and his boys, drinking ale at the bar. They invited him to join them and introduced him to Beau, the owner.

"How long have you been here, Beau?" Edgar asked.

"Over twenty-five years."

"Don't you want to go home?"

"Sure I do, but there's no way. We can't get past those storms."

"What about airplanes?"

"Don't have any here and no one knows how to build one."

"What about hot-air balloons? They can fly up high enough to get over them."

"Been tried. Lightning struck the balloons and they crashed."

"Damn!"

"We've tried just about everything. Some guy even had a paraglider and jumped off the volcano. He got caught in the winds and crashed. By the way, what do you do for a living? Or I should say, what did you do?"

"I'm a Navy SEAL."

"Don't tell that to the King. He'll want you to join him. And you don't want that. Head north to the Nyla Army Garrison and see Colonel Penser."

"I was just talking to a young girl by the name of Alex. She told me about him. She also said she knows you."

"Nice kid. She stayed here for a day before she moved into the palace. She came down with the Lord Governor from Nyla." He paused and rubbed his chin. "I don't know what she's doing down here. Something just don't seem right about her. You know what I mean?"

"Not really. She seemed like a sweet girl."

"When she first came in here, she was wearing a sword hidden on her back. Why hide it like that? Anyway, something tells me she knows how to use it. I wonder if the Colonel sent her here on a mission. There's just something different about her." He served another customer down at the end of the bar and returned. "Do you know how to tend bar?"

"You bet. What do you pay?"

"A brassie a day, a bed in the back, and all the tips you make."

"What's a brassie?"

"About a buck."

"Kinda low wages."

"We all make low wages. I charge a brassie for a room and two coppers for a meal."

Edgar glanced over to Wallace, who winked and nodded. "Take it, Mister Edgar. You ain't gonna get anything better."

"You're right. I'll take it. I don't have anything else going on. I guess there's no way to get home."

"That's true. Come on back here. I'll show you where everything's at," Beau said.

Edgar came around the bar and took over within an hour. It wasn't much different from any bar back home. His eyes watered for a moment. Home. How was he going to get there? And where was he? Wallace had called it, Seaward Isle, and all these people got here through that hole in the sky. The storms off shore discouraged anyone from trying to leave.

The bar became busy and Edgar soon forgot about home. He joked with the clients and learned that all of them had arrived in much the same way he did. He also learned that every idea of escape had been tried at some point or another.

After closing time, Beau took him in the back and showed him a room with a small army cot. Down the hall was a shower and latrine and around the corner was the kitchen. Beau made a couple of sandwiches and handed him one with a bowl of soup. The two men sat down to eat even though it was midnight.

With a full stomach, Edgar lay down on the cot and stared out the window at the sky. It was full of stars. He longed for home, but gritted his teeth. He wasn't going to get there. Probably never again. His eyes watered and tears ran down his face. He'd miss his parents and his little sister and hoped they'd be okay without him. Exhausted and discouraged, he fell asleep.

A month later, Edgar found he enjoyed serving his clients and hearing their stories. He knew most of them by heart, but listened patiently. It helped him accept his fate as he heard story after story of failed attempts to leave the island. He knew he'd never leave. Today, a regular came in and sat at the bar, his shoulders slumped and his eyes red.

"What's with you, partner?" Edgar asked. "Beer?"

"Yeah, with a shot."

"Name your poison."

"Whiskey."

"Got it. What's up?"

"I can't believe it. I just can't believe it. Ratcliffe was murdered."

"Who's Ratcliffe? Remember, I'm new here."

"My boss. He went to visit Pashamon out east of here and was murdered in the middle of the night. Someone shot him through the heart with an arrow." He pointed to his chest. "Right in the middle of the night in Pashamon's palace."

"Maybe this Pashamon ordered a hit." Edgar poured a shot of whiskey and handed it to him.

"Nah, he was in neck deep. Wouldn't risk it. None of his soldiers can shoot that straight anyway. Unless it was a lucky shot."

Other men came in with the same story, making Edgar pause. It sure sounded like a hit. The more he learned, the more convinced he became. He also found out that Pashamon had arrested the Governor's traveling party, accusing them of murder. This was the same Governor who'd been in Agana just a few weeks before with that girl, Alex.

He took the issue to Beau. It seemed that Ratcliffe headed up all the pirates in the area. He was a big deal. Without him, there was going to be a major power struggle. Maybe a war. It could be bad for business. But Beau knew better. He'd survived bad times before; he'd do it again.

"This sure sounds like a hit to me, Beau. Why would the Governor do it?"

"It doesn't make sense. I understand Pashamon arrested him and his two men, but I heard they escaped."

"How?"

"No one knows."

"What about that girl? Alex?"

"Didn't hear anything about her." Beau looked up at him. "Do you think she got them out?"

"You did say she may have been on a mission and carried a hidden sword. Suppose she knows how to use a bow and arrow, too? You said something was different about her. I think I need to pay this Colonel Penser a visit and find out more about his operation. If he trained her..."

"Why?"

"I miss being a soldier, Beau. I want to back in. I'm wasting away here."

"I'd hate to lose you, Edgar. You're the best barkeep I've had in years."

"Thanks, but it's time for me to move on. What's the best way to get to Nyla?"

"You could get there by barge or a horse, but that costs money. Or you can walk. It's about thirty miles due north."

"I'll walk. Thanks for having me, Beau, but I need to find this Colonel." Edgar shook his hand and went to his room. With his mind made up, he slept through the night and woke early. He didn't have much to pack. He'd gotten some clothes free out of a local warehouse; they'd been salvaged from old shipwrecks. He rolled them up and put them in a backpack.

Beau wasn't up yet, but the cook made Edgar a hearty breakfast. He gave her a hug before he left. Then he slipped a brassie into her hand.

"Thanks for everything, Beulah. See you around."

Beulah wiped her tears and handed him a bag with food in it. "Be careful. It's a long way. And here, take this blanket. It gets cool at night."

"Appreciate it. Bye now." He held up the bag of food and marched out the door. The road north was full of people heading south for the market. He felt like a salmon going upstream. At the edge of the city, the road turned to dirt. A little farther and all signs of civilization vanished. He was alone in the wild.

For seven days, he headed north through meadows and forests. He slept on the ground and drank water from creeks. He foraged for food and found plenty. Once he stepped out from the trees, he found himself in a small village. The streets were made of dirt and the shanties looked the same. But he heard a familiar sound.

Male voices counted off, as if doing calisthenics. He jogged ahead and saw a group of men doing jumping jacks and next to them a group of women. His eyes filled with tears. These were people like him: soldiers. His heart filled with joy—he'd found a new home.

Ann Bauer is a lover of science, science fiction and literature. After completeing a B.S in Chemistry at Texas A&M University, and spending 19 years as an astronomical instrument technician at the University of Arizona, it's time to test her literary skills. So, here goes!

Hold Your Tongue!

Here is a mix of curse and blessing that sometimes lies implanted in the mind of a shy but aspiring writer. Without the curse ingredient, some of us writer-types would never even approach the wall one must vault upon. Once on top, one might shake and rain one's literary thoughts upon an often inspecting and critical world. But it takes daring, and maybe, for some of us, it even takes a little fear.

Neither devil or deflated lover cursed us into such a state. The curse is something simple, and not at all rare: the seeming torture and sometimes inability to speak out loud to strangers. Talking takes me into a shadowy, shifting place. Occasionally, the mangled words in my mind can turn into a scream that never breaks the surface, but slowly sinks into my uneasily shifting toes, without even a muted whimper.

Writing instead of talking is easier, and for me more natural. Writing is the blessing; though it is not always the answer.

This fear of speaking to strangers I have carried my whole life. It leaves me feeling as though I am walking among zombies as I shift through the city of Tucson. I lost friends and lovers because I couldn't put thoughts into words, and take them to a face-to-face confrontation as I should have. If I must speak, it is not my face that talks to the shadows walking past; it is a plastic mask I wear over my face to make the experience of opening my mouth and spitting out something less offensive, less physically touching, less abrasive for us both.

Some days I think I have tried to speak too much, and if I do it again, my tongue might detach and slither, free-falling to the pavement. There, it would writhe like a slug, like a leech, like a pink, beached, out-of-water minnow. Eventually a passing stranger would stop, wince, and contemplate stepping on it and grinding it into an acceptable demise. Most would only give it a dismissing glance, step to the side and hurry faster to their destination. Only an "I gotta kill and dominate!" boy should pose a threat. Twisting, it would look so lost and alone, dying in the early morning sun.

I see, feel, and live the whole scenario in my mind: With one eye

I circumspect the present coffee shop city sidewalk for evil-doing young boys, and I see none. I grow very weary and decide to lie down next to my disembodied, and still-thrashing tongue. I watch its ambulations. It rolls from a wet deli-ham side to a coarse dirty-pink flip-side as I drift off into another world of my own.

Maybe, when I wake up, I should try replacing the tongue, unless it has gone on a road trip of its own. Maybe I would be better off if I did not try. With my cheek on the still-cool sidewalk cement, I wonder if a new tongue will grow back in my sleep. Maybe it would be better if it did not. Maybe I would not notice the loss.

Or, maybe, I would wake up and know it for a dream.

Kevin Harrington is an author who has struggled with mental illness his whole life and has used writing as a healing mechanism. This is both why he writes and why it has taken him to an advanced age to get started. All his writing, in one way or the other, is about himself. About what has hurt and devastated him all his life and how he has worked through it. It has been very difficult, but it is now starting to work out at long last. ***Contains adult language.***

My Husband's Heart Condtition

An ancient couple in the dark
Streets. Underneath a lamp
A purse snaps open. "Do you want
A mint, dear?" Her cheek damp,

She hears a whisper from behind
Her. And a switchblade up
Into her throat. She sighs. "Okay,
Then. That's New York, dear." "Yup,"

The old man says. "You punks are younger
And younger!" "Just hand over
Your purse! And you, old man: your wallet!"
"Of course. Of course. Well, lover,

"How many times have we been mugged
Together?" Bloodshot eyes
Appear out of the shadows. Wolf
Head snarls; screams and then sighs.

The old man fingers at his heart.
An earring tugged out, lobe
Sore, bleeding. Wolf mouth yawning at
The snuffling nostrils. "Love

"Chew! Love chew!" And the third punk fled
But nearly tripping, twisted
His ankle. And the wolf man let
Him go. His howl persisted

Across the limping piddler's moist
Tears. At the shoe store, pale
The morning after, he begged Dad
For work. Crime grown quite stale,

His lame foot dragged behind him all
The days until he died.
Back at the crime scene, wolfman's gone.
The two crooks, on their side,

Are handcuffed. Cops are standing round.
A siren, blazing lights.
The two old people hold each other.
Their eyes burn. "It's not right!"

They mutter. "Snarling beast men. Who
Could think of such a thing?
It's after something! Something should
Be done!" Their tight squeeze stings

Their buttocks, clenched together hard.
The cops are nodding. "Yes,
Sir. Yes, Ma'am." Wolf men roam the streets;
They've heard of this, they guess.

The rookie officer goes home.
He fucks his wife and dreams
Of shadows snarling. But the old
Detective has his schemes.

The next day as he writes it up,
His eyes go blind forever.
The cold mist squeezes round his eyes.
Both retinas are severed.

The End

Kevin Harrington is an author who has struggled with mental illness his whole life and has used writing as a healing mechanism. This is both why he writes and why it has taken him to an advanced age to get started. All his writing, in one way or the other, is about himself. About what has hurt and devastated him all his life and how he has worked through it. It has been very difficult, but it is now starting to work out at long last. *Contains adult language.*

Synopsis

The entire next scene is viewed inside a convex mirror hanging in a psychiatrist's office. Same date and time.

Cheeky Little Bastard

The doctor is simply reading a case file in a plush armchair, when the door swings open and a tall, exceedingly skinny, and nearly boobless elderly woman with long grey hair down to her waist that *looks* knotted even though it isn't, and wearing what amounts to a beige shift, enters and the doctor looks up and becomes annoyed.

The woman hands a pamphlet to the doctor, and we see a close up of the title (in the convex mirror). "Telepathic Theory" in boldface typescript, and the author's name: "Lavinia Jensen Karr."

The doctor snatches it and pushes it down on his desk, and then grabs up a little bell and starts to ring it vigorously. Words come up on the screen, seeming to come out of the bell: "Jingle! Jingle! Jingle!" (The sound is off at this point.) Two big Nurse Ratchet-types enter and seize Ms. Karr by her armpits and start to drag her off.

Unconcernedly, and close up on her breast pocket as, she takes a red colored pencil out and hands it toward the doctor. Freeze on the pencil, and a yellow cartoon star appears around it. Unfreeze, and the view spins around the pencil, and: extreme close up of a spot of red lead on the side of the pencil that looks like a trickle of blood dripping down this writing implement. The pencil is almost down to the nub.

As the two Nurse Ratchets continue to drag her off, Lavinia's and the doctor's eyes meet and lock. *His* eyes flick back and forth between her and the lead of the pencil. Suddenly, he strides forward through the murky space between them (only a tiny reading lamp is currently lit) and waves the nurses away. They let go of the woman, who slumps forward a little. The doctor takes the pencil, turns, strides over to the desk and grabs her pamphlet and drags it back toward her, scrawling on it with the red pencil as he goes. He shows it to her, and close up (in the convex mirror!) on what he has written, directly under the word "Telepathic" in the title: "**Are you?**" She smiles weirdly, and nods.

The two nurses have disappeared, and mysteriously the door of the office is firmly closed now and Lavinia has advanced well into the room when we weren't looking. The doctor /trips/traipses/ collapses into his reading chair, and Lavinia leans forward on her heels, and close up on her intent leering as she watches him read.

Close up on his liver-spotted fingers as they open the cover of the pamphlet. All of the text is in boldface typescript.

"First things first. And the first thing, as everyone knows, was the Big Bang, which was caused by a disturbance in the Mind of God. For what else could it be? We are the nightmares of God; we are all that stands between the Almighty Lord and his peace.

"Because we were born from His nightmare, we all are imprinted with its shape, therefore we are linked by it, because we all are of the substance of a common dream.

"This is the way God directs each of us, through that shadow inside of us which is not *our* own thoughts but *His* Thought *about* us. And through this he guides us to act in ways of *His* choosing, for the return of the day of his *waking up!*

"Therefore is each separate object separately imbued with an awareness of itself and its place in the cosmos, down to the tiniest atom or quark. The grass feels itself grow. The light knows that it glows. Such is the consciousness of the universe, in which every concept once conceived, then conceives for itself. For there is nothing but God's *ideas*, and matter and energy are merely the simplest of his ideas.

"Through long aeons does the shadow of this consciousness

grow upon the universe, stalking it into being, until Sentient Beings - the pearl of creation - come into existence, beings who know who they are and suspect who made them, with the knowing akin to God's own knowing.

"When such beings appear, the time of God's Awaking approaches, and the time of the arrival of the Conscious Being, he who embodies God's Mind to the greatest degree among creatures. He it is who is God's presence in the dream that he dreams. He is the potential inherent in all the consciousness of creation, fulfilled and made incarnate to walk among us, and he is *here* now, and *he is writing this!*"

The doctor looks up from his reading and pushes up his glasses, but he sees only an empty office. Both Lavinia Jensen Karr and her mysterious pamphlet have disappeared.

He shouts out to the empty office (the sound suddenly snapping on): "We are all conscious beings, Lavinia!" The noise of his voice shatters the convex mirror in which all of this is reflected, and the scene ends.

The screen goes blank. Suddenly, the legend scrolls up the screen: "Let Lavinia Jensen Karr be crazy *for* me now, for she is only a fiction and *I* am becoming real!"

I, the author of this book grasp my head, sigh, and complain about sleepless nights.

J M Strasser lives in Tucson, Arizona with her husband, son and daughter (when she comes home from school). With a Bachelor's degree in Biology, she loves the desert's sweet colors and ponders the meaning of life, intelligence, and when the heck is someone going to encounter us!

Out There

We are most unique.
Never underestimate the humans, or so we say.
Our cowboy and tall poppy do seek
impossible odds we love to play

We are barely alive
yet start a race.
Would we survive
meeting another in space?

Stephen says we can't,
the odds are for a fool.
But if they are advanced,
aren't they peaceful, too?

Evolution shows us variety honed
on the edge of the cruel sword.
But survival means more than today alone.
Celebrate the one and the many for the most reward.

Would we be valuable,
enough to keep around,
enough to be exceptional,
enough to astound?

Take the chance,
though the odds are heavy pressure.
Perhaps learn more of the dance
to meet as equals intsead of the lesser.

Billy Hernández, Jr. is a former Army combat medic and served two tours in Afghanistan. He currently lives with his family in Tucson, Arizona where he continues to work in the medical field and delights in sharing the wondrous worlds of fantasy and science fiction with his kids.

Synopsis

I will never forget the moment PFC Henry's shouting voice ripped through the air, "RPG!" And, if I thought in that moment's brilliant flash that the job I was doing for the UN peacekeeping mission was the worst deployment I ever had...well, let me tell you, I hadn't even begun to fight. ***Contains adult language.***

The 13th Archangel Company

The last thing I remembered was being pinned down by gunfire in a little alley in some dirt-poor African country. My unit had been deployed on a UN peacekeeping mission. When the UN gets involved, everything goes into the shitter. So, I was in an alley taking heavy fire. Out of a ten-man squad, a private and myself were the only ones not hit. As far as I knew, we were the only ones left alive. With two men, we were trying to hold down an area that three squads normally would. I think I was changing magazines when I heard PFC Henry scream, "RPG!"

When my eyes opened, I found myself standing in a long line. Pleasant harp music was being piped into the area. I looked around, but I couldn't see any speakers. Hell, I couldn't see any walls, floors or ceiling. From the corner of my eye, I could make out shapes that appeared to be walls but when I looked at them directly, they faded away.

"Name." A voice suddenly snapped me out of my concentration of trying to figure out where I was. "Name," I was asked again, and my attention turned to a clerk at a desk that suddenly appeared before me. "Come, come," he said, not looking up from his books,

"I don't have all day and everyone is trying to get in. Now what is your name?"

"Niles, Carter Niles," I replied.

"Oh," said the clerk, looking up at me. "You're Mr. Niles?"

"Yes, sir."

"Great, come right in, Big Daddy has been waiting for you."

"Big Daddy?"

"Yes," replied the clerk as he pulled me through a gate that just appeared.

"Ughhh, was that gate…"

"Oh, please hurry, God said He wanted to see you as soon as you arrived. And so, you are here and here we go."

He ushered me into a long, narrow hall that ended with a wooden door. We went through the door and I found myself in front of an altar. A brilliant light shined on me from above. I couldn't look directly at it and had to shield my eyes.

"Welcome. Welcome Carter," a rich baritone voice boomed.

"Thank you. Thank you, Sir. I can't tell you how happy I am to be here."

He chuckled. "Tell me about it. That was some life you had. Believe me, it was touch and go for a while. You just made it by the skin of your teeth."

I swallowed hard. "Yes, Sir. I was kind of crazy."

"Gabriel and Michael had a bet on you. No one ever wants to bet with Me. However, I do have an unfair advantage. Anyway, down to business. I do not know how to break it to you in an easy manner. So here we go. You're being drafted," stated God.

"What?! Drafted? I just died fighting a fricken' war! I served my country for 17 years!"

"Yes, yes. I know all that. I am God, you know. I don't need all this drama and theatrics. Listen, you are drafted and that is that. If you don't like it, I can send you to the basement. As far as I'm concerned, you're still on shaky ground with Me."

"Yes, Sir," I said, remembering with whom I was speaking.

"So, where was I?" God paused a moment. "Oh yes. Drafted. I'm raising The Army to put down some evil insurgents. It seems Satan is getting a little squirrelly again and needs a good, old-fashioned, bitch slap. He let some minor demons and lesser demons free from hell to raise Cain on Earth."

"Ah, Sir, if I may interject, why don't you just wipe them out? Wouldn't that be easier?" I asked.

"Yes, I could do that. But what fun would that be? Besides, I have all these people lying around in Heaven with nothing to do. Do you know how hard I have to work to ensure that Heaven remains a paradise? They just do not appreciate the work I have to do to keep this place looking this good. It's about time that they earn their keep!

"I could really use a man with your experience. So, you are assigned to the Executioners, the 13th Archangel Company commanded by Michael, with Genghis Kahn as his executive officer. They —"

"Genghis Kahn," I interrupted. "Genghis made it into heaven?"

"Under normal circumstances, I would never allow someone like that into Heaven. However, I do recognize talent when I see it. Besides Lou has been playing this game since the beginning of time. Therefore, when he came along, I snatched him up.

"The Archangels are a parachute regiment. Boy, that Leo was really ahead of his time: that man was a genius. I've been using paratroopers ever since he came up with that idea."

"So, I'm being made an Archangel?" I asked.

"No, not an Archangel, but assigned to the Archangels. Mike is in charge of those Regiments. They're my shock troops. Great bunch of guys, but a little rough around the edges, you'll fit right in. Now Joshua will show you around. You'll get your armor, spear, and sword when you get to basic."

"Ugh, God? I was in the modern army. I know nothing about swords and shields."

"Carter, I know you. You will do ok. Trust me."

I followed Joshua to a door leading into a courtyard. People filled the yard, just hanging out, relaxing. "This is just great," I thought, "all these people lying around and I am drafted! Life is a bitch!"

"Before we go to the Armory," Joshua said to me, "we have to see Lou."

"Lou?"

"Yeah, everyone that gets drafted goes to Lou's office for a meeting." Joshua continued. "God is a great Guy, very fair. So, when

He drafts someone, He always gives Lou a chance to meet them and Lou gives them a chance to volunteer and avoid God's draft."

"Really," I remarked. I smiled inwardly. I would do just about anything to avoid being drafted.

Joshua led me to a set of double doors with a mirror polish. Inside was a desk in the middle of the room. Chairs lined the office walls. The shadiest looking characters I have ever seen filled those chairs. A woman sitting behind the desk was chatting into a headset mic. As we approached, she held up a hand indicating for us to wait.

"Oh yeah, well if we don't have that shipment today, I'll have your balls in a vice! HAVE A NICE DAY AND GO FUCK YOURSELF!" She ended the call and smiled sweetly at us. "Hey, Josh. Who do we have here?"

"Syn, this is Carter Niles. He ha-"

"Great," she interrupted. "Lou has been expecting him. Go right in, Mr. Niles."

She again smiled sweetly, and then this thug jumped up and started screaming, "This is fricking BS! I've sitting in this damn chair for three months waiting to get in that gawd damn office! I can't believe you're letting this schmuck—" He suddenly burst into flames.

I looked over at Syn just as she removed her finger from a button on her desk. "I guess your wait is going to be a lot longer than you thought, A-hole," she said, sporting an evil grin. She gave me a little one as I entered the door, and let close behind me.

Inside was a large spacious office. Three walls were floor-to-ceiling glass windows. The view overlooked a snow-covered mountain valley. A Persian rug covered a blond-colored, hardwood floor. Ultra-modern Danish furniture filled the room. On the wall behind me, Edvard Munch's Scream.

Behind a glass desk sat a woman who looked like a very busty model on the runway of Milan. Despite wearing an above-the-knee pencil skirt and matching blazer, probably made by the best designer in Paris, her feet were propped up the desk as she leafed through a magazine. That signature red sole of Christian Louboutin was clearly visible despite the wear that shown on the heels. I'm sure these must be her favorite heels. Her curly red hair hung loosely about her shoulders. Her fingernails, as well as her toenails, displayed an immaculate care and the most striking red polish I had ever seen. She laid down the magazine and locked eyes with me, giving me a smoldering gaze that could melt the polar caps. She was clearly the most beautiful woman that I had ever had the pleasure of meeting. Images of bodies intertwined in sexual pleasure danced in my mind.

That's when I noticed the nameplate on her desk. It read Lucifer.

She got up from her chair, came around her desk, and approached me. She moved with poise and grace as if she were a panther stalking its prey. I involuntary took a step back as she glided forward. I banged into the wall behind me. She stopped inches from me. Her leg slid between my mine and her breasts just barely touched my chest. I felt myself getting lost in her crystal-blue eyes as if I were falling into an abyss. Her silky-smooth hands enveloped my hand.

"Ahh, Mr. Niles." Her breath was a tantalizing mixture of cinnamon and honeysuckle. She leaned in and kissed my cheek. "It is so nice to finally meet you." She turned and slinked to a chair in front of her desk. "Please, have a seat."

I obediently followed and sat in her chair.

She sat on my lap. Her arm slithered around my neck and her fingers wove themselves in my hair. With her other hand, her fingers lightly glided across my chest. "Mr. Niles." Her melodious voice ignited my primal lusts. "I've been told that God has drafted you. Is that correct?" I could only nod my head. "Cat got your tongue?" she purred. "That's so cute.

"Well, you are here so that I may make you a counter offer. I don't know if you have been informed, but your initial enlistment into the Army is for 1,000 years. Oh, don't look so horrified. You're going to be here for an eternity, so what's 1,000 years? Just a mere blink of an eye. However, if you decide to enlist with me, your initial enlistment is only 400 years. Now, I will throw in bonuses and extra vacation time for Hell. If you enlist with me, you will live in only the best sulfa pits in Hell, have all the woman you desire, and even some pleasure time with me, which I can tell you want, you naughty boy," she said as she wiggled in my lap.

"But," I croaked, "I will be in Hell."

"Yes. Yes, that is true." Her lips parted when she smiled and revealed a perfect set of white teeth. She stood and took her seat behind her desk. "If you decide to join God's Army, pray that you never become a POW." Her voice was dripping with venom as she finished her sentence.

I swallowed hard. As I gazed at her, she began to change. Her body became painfully twisted; pustules swelled and ruptured leaving gaping wounds. The stench of putrid, rotting flesh replaced the once-present sweet aroma of honeysuckle and cinnamon. She continued to transform into something so hideous and ghastly that it could only have come from Lovecraft's twisted imagination.

I recoiled in my chair. My palms saturated with sweat. My heart threatened to explode in my chest if it didn't just stop outright. My chest tightened. I couldn't breathe. I thought I might pass out. I needed to escape this horror before me.

"Mr. Niles," she said, again the runway model, "it appears that you will not enlist with me. If you do, your rewards will be great, trust me. They will be beyond your wildest dream. No, don't answer now; I'll give you till tomorrow the mull it over. I hope you make the correct choice. Regardless of what you choose, I eagerly await our next meeting."

I practically fell out of my chair trying to get out of there. I jerked the door open and glanced back. She was again reading her magazine. I started to say something, but stopped.

"Armani," she said not looking up, "my suit is Giorgio Armani. I just love his work.'

"But... but...," I stammered.

"Everyone wants to know," she said, and shooed me out the door.

In the reception room, Joshua was sitting on Syn's desk. He was whispering quietly to her. She giggled and blushed. Her hand rested lightly on his. They continued this for a moment more before Joshua noticed me. We left the room, but not before he turned and blew Syn a kiss.

We walked in silence to the Armory where they measured my entire body. Then he deposited me at the Headquarters for the Archangel Company. Never once did he ask me about my meeting with Lou.

"How did you know which Army I chose?"

"It was written all over your face." With that, he shook my hand and departed.

Without ceremony, indoctrination into the 13th Archangels began. I shipped out to basic training, which I balked at. I mean, I did have close to 17 years' experience with the military.

I spent two years in basic training. I thought I knew all there was to know about the military. I was wrong. But in my defense, this was the ancient Army. We marched daily with full kit and armor. We spent hours and hours perfecting the use of spear and shield, sword and shield, and archery. I excelled at unarmed combat, so much so that I was designated as a trainer.

We also learned a shitload about carpentry. We built everything. I mean everything, basic buildings, fortification walls, towers, and even castles. Now they were not much as far as castles go, but they were formidable. We were instructed in building siege engines.

We conducted war games where we used our siege engines to knock down everything we built. That really pissed me off, because that shit was tough to build.

During the war games, I was able to demonstrate my leadership abilities. Before my tour was complete in basic, I made sergeant. They have the same rank structures as the modern army, so I was familiar with it. I was told that the Big Guy really likes the modern rank system and incorporated it into His Army. So, in that respect, I felt right at home.

Upon my completion of basic, I went to jump school. The only thing I can report on that was we used the exact copies of Leonardo da Vinci's parachutes. When I saw this, I suggested changing them to what we used in the modern army. They laughed at me. It seemed that God was a fan of da Vinci; He just loves his designs, so that's what we used. I was really praying when I made my first jump with it. Which is somewhat funny when you think about it, I mean, it's not as if I could die. Anyway, I was scared; it's the only time that I can recall being that scared. I thought I would fall like a rock with that pyramid chute, but my landing was surprisingly soft. And that's all we did was jump. For six months, we jumped. I was never so tired of airborne operations as I was then. When I was alive, I used to love jumping. After making close to 15 jumps a day, I hated it.

That was five years ago. Since finishing jump school, the 13th has been on the move. I need to stop here and explain. When I was assigned to the 13th Archangels, their nickname was Executioners, but the other units just call us The Zombies. I thought there were 13 companies or more. No, there is only one Archangel airborne company. Only one, we are the storm troopers, the rapid deployment unit, the QRF (Quick Reaction Force) or whatever you want to call it. We are the tip of God's spear. If there is action, you'll find us there. Oh yes, we are called the 13th because Michael, the Archangel, likes it. He thinks it sounds cool and menacing.

We have met Lucifer, Lou, forces on every front imaginable. The war between good and evil never ceases. I mean, we've been nonstop fighting. Oh, and before I forget, one can die in the afterlife. What happens, so I'm told, is that your energy level becomes so low that you can no longer maintain your image and you dissolve. This sounds like BS to me, but regardless, you don't want to die. If you die while in Purgatory, it's likely that you'll go straight to Hell. If you're in the Devils' Brigade, which is what they call Satan's Army (I know, not very original) and you're killed, you'll end up in the lowest pit of Hell.

The Divine Comedy was right about Hell. Except that there is not a funnel as he described it, it's like a sphere. In addition, when you are in Hell, because of the way it's constructed, it gives you a constant, horrible headache. For instance, when you are in a room, you would expect to see four walls, a floor, and a ceiling. Well, because Hell is spherical, it is like being in a room that has six, curved floors. So, it's not uncommon to enter a room and see people standing on the ceiling. Hell, it's even possible that you can see your own legs across a room. It's really hard on the eyes. The Executioners, or should I say Zombies, had been in Hell for six months, and for six months I had a migraine headache the entire time. Hell sucks!

During our last campaign, the 13th Archangels had advanced faster and farther than any other infantry units. The river Styx halted our advance. We could just make out the walls that surround the city of Dis, Hell proper. The forest this side of Styx, though thick and plentiful, is extremely depressing. It's always dark, as if overcast, misting if not raining. We chopped down the trees to build ramparts and fortifications. This was necessary because Dis has some awesome trebuchets that can easily reach our encampments.

So, we dug in and awaited the rest of the Army. The engineers would have to build boats enabling us to cross the Styx. Plus, we needed supplies and provisions. Once we got past the walls of Dis, it would be nearly impossible to get re-supplied.

We were just about finished with our fortification, when we received missile fire from the city walls. They threw everything at us. Bolts from ballistae and scorpions, hails of arrows, and boulders from the trebuchet. Apparently, there are some in Hell who managed to retain their sense of humor. Some joker over there must have been a fan of British humor, because cows carved of stone rained down on us. I thought that shit was funny as hell until one stone cow fell directly on Doug. When that happened, over half the unit, including Michael, gave a thundering HUZZA. I was appalled, but I quickly remembered that Doug was a bit of an ass. Everyone hated him.

My squad, tasked with securing the beach, erected ramparts to protect the troops during boat boarding. One by one, I lost my men. We were assaulted with murderous fire. Soon, I had only one soldier, believe it or not, but that soldier was Dante himself.

Dante, when we met, stated that he was a volunteer. He was a real adventure lover. He loved the thrill of combat, both in life and death. He always had an exciting tale to tell.

I didn't know then, and I never found out why, but the Army was held up. Soon, all the fortification built by my squad lay in ruins. Enemy fire pinned us down. Arrows rained down on us like a monsoon storm in Tucson. We were huddled together behind our lone rampart. I was suddenly reminded of that dirty little ally in Africa. That seemed like a lifetime ago.

"So, what do you think?" Dante asked me.

"About what?"

"Do you think we'll make out of here alive?"

"Dante," I said, peering over the rampart wall, "we are already dead, so it's impossible to make out alive."

"Niles," he said curtly, "you know what I mean. Personally, I can't stand the thought of being born again. Acne and teenage years, hell no, I don't want to do that again."

"You are a volunteer; you get to go back to earth. I'm a draftee, I could end up in Hell."

"I, for one," said Dante, "do not wish to be born again. I really like it here and Purgatory and Heaven. Being born again means I have to live life all over again and then there is no guarantee I'll make it back to Heaven."

"I'm still pretty hacked about being drafted. I mean, I volunteered for patriotism and defense of my country. I wanted to retire and have a ranch, raise horses and just enjoy life. But then I bought it in Africa, only to be enlisted for 1,000 years."

"I think you're looking at it the wrong way," said Dante as about 30 arrows flew over our damaged rampart and struck the ground just a few feet behind us. "Every person touches other people's lives on a daily basis and you have some effect, both good and bad. It's like when you throw a stone into a lake. You would think that a single stone could not affect an entire lake, but it does. The first thing you observe is the initial ripple in the water and that ring spreads out until it reaches the shore. Granted, by the time it reaches the shore, it loses so much of its energy that it's not even noticeable, but it still has an effect. People are the same. You touch one person's life with a positive or negative interaction, and then they touch someone else, and so on."

"So now you are a philosopher and an author?" I said sarcastically as an arrow bounced off my helm.

He just stopped and looked at me in disbelief. "Yes, Niles, I am a philosopher."

"Really?"

"Yes."

"Hmmm…I thought you were just a writer. So," I said, peering around the rampart trying to locate where we were taking fire from, "what are you trying to say?"

"What I'm saying," said Dante. "is that the way you affect others can enhance your own existence. On your deathbed, you will be able to look back and say I made a difference or you can despair that you squandered your life and beg for more time to change. Once you're on your deathbed, it's too late."

We sat in silence as the day turned to early evening. Because it's dark here all the time, it's hard to tell what time of day it is. We took another volley and Dante did what I had been doing, and looked over the rampart. He took an arrow in the shoulder. He wasn't hurt too badly, but the real trouble came when the trebuchet got us bracketed in. Dante began to fade from being wounded so many times.

I worked like hell to keep him alive. We must have been bombarded for hours before our relief arrived. Our engineers finally got one of our trebuchets up and running. Soon, they began a full-on bombardment of the wall. I was able to get Dante to the healers.

That little engagement earned the 13th Archangels some time off. We convalesced at this beautiful beach-front property. I imagine this is what ancient Greece looked like. The sun was hot and the ocean breeze kept the humidity down. We spent our days basking in the sunlight. Our commander, Michael, said that our efforts in holding the beach and ramparts allowed the Army to invade Dis. We were granted a year-long vacation as a reward.

"Now, isn't this better than getting killed and reincarnated?" Dante asked me.

"Oh, I don't know," I replied, "going back to earth and starting over might not be so bad."

"Remember what I told you outside Dis?"

"You mean about affecting people positively or negativity?"

"Yes, that is part of life's journey. It's not the end result of the journey, but the journey itself," said Dante. "It's the person you become and the experiences you have during your journey and how you affect others. If you become reincarnated, then it's almost as if you never existed. Don't place value in material possessions and possessions you have yet to achieve. Value comes from the person you are."

When our vacation ended, Dante was posted with a different unit, a non-combat unit. Having been wounded 15 times, he earned the right to transfer to a non-combat unit. Therefore, he was transferred. Boy, was he pissed. Remember, he is an adventurer. There is no adventure in non-combat units.

So, I'm sitting in a bar called Valhalla overlooking a pristine, glacier lake called Tears of the Valkyries Lake. It sounds much more poetic in Old Norse. As you can tell by the name, it's a Viking bar. I'm drinking a horn of honey mead and mulling over Dante's words. You have to be very careful when in Valhalla, because the Vikings love to fight. So much so that they are forbidden from carrying any weapon while in Purgatory. This is because they have killed far too many people trying to get to Heaven. They are on probation, which I find ironic, being on probation while in Purgatory. Kind of like getting kicked out of Hell for being too evil.

Since they can no longer carry weapons, fighting is boring for them. Now, they just head-butt each other, and everyone else, to prove who the better warrior is. The loser, the one lying unconscious on the floor, gets de-pantsed and then their pants are set afire. The nearest clothier is five miles away. Thus, the walk of shame and defeat is five miles with your privates on full display.

This hulk of a Viking just dropped his third head-butting victim. He's an ugly bastard, flaming red hair and beard. He sports a patched eye with a wicked scar leading up to the patch. One ear is half bitten off, and yes, you can see the teeth marks. His crooked smile shows missing front teeth. I'm sure he's aware that in the afterlife his earthly scars can be washed away.

Looking at him, I finally realized what Dante meant. I finished my mead and stood. I'm about to achieve my first head-butting victory with that ugly, red-headed bastard.

Erik Hertwig is a graduate of St. Norbert College in De Pere, Wisconsin. Erik wrote his first children's book, *The Old Man Who Lived in the Dump,* as a first grader.

His decision to become an author prompted him to major in English Literature, Secondary Education, and pursue a career working with children as an English teacher as well as an author, consultant, publisher, and public speaker.

Erik is the creator of the *Zoo Adventure Series,* a series of children books that take place in a zoo; *The Trials,* a fantasy hero's journey archetype novel about a half elf's coming of age journey into adulthood; several short fantasy stories; and technical manuals that focus on composition writing and career advancement.

Synopsis

Escape From Tantek is a short story that started as an assignment for a college Science Fiction and Fantasy course. The struggle is loosely based on the Bosnian/Serbian/Kosovo conflict of the 1990s and written into a fantasy setting. *Escape From Tantek* was written before the end of the conflict so the uncertainty of the participants is reflected in the story, as the characters' journey ends without a definitive end to the conflict.

Escape From Tantek

Tantek is a small prairie-covered country with few trees. This makes it an unlikely place for wood elves like Rahn to live, but they have always preferred to be called prairie elves anyway. Superficially, prairie elves are identical to wood elves, a tanned brown or gray in color, but they adorn themselves with pink and violet prairie flowers during ceremonies, and that gives them a more peaceful reputation.

The elves have always considered the Tanteki monarchy consistent, the taxes reasonable, and they have always felt reasonably safe. You may find that hard to believe with an ogre for a king, but ogres have learned, through time, that robbing from your neighbor's kingdom keeps you in power longer than robbing from your own.

Rahn is a young elf, from the River Moss clan, with light-brown, unkempt hair and striking green eyes. If he were human, he would be a young teenager of about 13 years. Elves age slower than humans, so he has not yet reached the age of choosing a mate. For now, Rahn is content with his companion, Toki, a thigh-high (in elven measurements), four-legged, hairless, dog-like creature with the ferocity of a wounded wolf and the strength of an eight-foot bear. Rahn and Toki have been together for about three years and do everything that a normal "teen-aged," displaced, wood elf boy and his ferocious, but friendly looking pet, would do. Today, that meant exploring the flood-covered plains of Tantek.

"When the water seeps down far enough, Toki, father says it's time to plant. I guess that will be about two weeks."

"Hhummurra?" was Toki's confused response. The cup-footed animal did not always understand the spoken language, but his loyalty and love were always apparent.

"You're lucky to have such big feet, Toki, you can stand on the mud and not sink in." The animal's feet looked about three times larger than they needed to be, but the thick webbing between the claws created an air pocket on top of the mud preventing the species from sinking into the muddied, unpleasant, spring landscape.

"Humoor," Toki sighed.

"You gave Tamoor the idea for these new hollow-bottom boots." Rahn touched his knee-high leather and wooden boots. The bottom of the boots was concave and his feet sat atop the sole, providing the footwear the flexibility it needed to help him balance over the unsure footing of the muddied prairie.

"Haagagagagagaaa!" Toki shrieked in alarm.

"What is it, Toki? What do you see? Are those ogres on horses? But the taxmen don't come until autumn. We'd better see what they want."

Toki leaped as gracefully as a deer toward the horses, leaving Rahn to struggle with his new footwear. Rahn sloshed and mucked through the mud. The sound was not pleasant, but it was better than sinking to the knees with every step.

Rahn moved closer to the struggling horses. Not as quickly, or gracefully as Toki, but with a lot more sloshing and mucking sounds. Ogre grunts and snorts acknowledged the presence of Rahn and Toki.

"Gad!" snorted the big one. "One of the elves approaches."

"Elf boy! I am Gordon, captain of the Tanteki Army. "I travel with Gad, Prince from the city of Beldineer." Rahn barely recognized the uniform Gordon was wearing. The officers of the Tanteki army wore a bright, light-blue, colored uniform, but Gordon's looked like it was muddied and bloodied and torn from constant fighting. Both ogres looked like they hadn't slept in days and kept looking over their shoulders in the direction they had come. "Take us to your clan. We are in a hurry."

"Do you have business with my clan? Are you here for the taxes?"

"We don't have time for idle chat, boy." The ogre grunted through his pig-like snout more than actually talking with his mouth. "We need shelter. Show us the way or I'll run you through."

Even after Rahn pointed the way, the ogre's impatience continued and it made him nervous. Rahn decided to get to the Gathering as soon as possible and let someone else handle the ogres.

Rahn and Toki ran to the Gathering. The ogres struggled to keep up on their horses, their legs sinking over and over in the deep mud. The Gathering looked like a circus in the distance. The larger structures were tents, and the smaller structures were made of twigs, branches and adobe-type bricks. There were no bricked or paved sidewalks. The elders decided to stop constructing them after the first few sank into the spring-time mud years ago.

"Father, Father!" Rahn shouted. "These ogres are here to see you!"

"What?" he responded, "Ogres don't venture out this far south in the spring."

"Elf!" Gordon shouted. "Organize a town meeting. Now." Gordon scanned the group. "And no youths," he added.

Rahn's father made his way to the meeting tent and rang the bell three times. He talked with Prince Gad as the Gathering Elders assembled. Rahn was unable to hear the conversation because the elves made too much noise asking each other about the nature of the meeting. When the older elves were in the tent, Rahn's father came over to him.

"Rahn, I need to speak with you urgently," he said. "I think we are going to leave here. We will have a vote in a little while. The ogre prince told me his city and many other Tanteki cities were captured during the winter by the underground bale elves. If this is true, and they control a standing army, it won't be long before they come looking for us."

"Why would they send an army after us, father?" Rahn asked.

"Our ancestors attacked their villages centuries ago and drove them underground," his father explained. "Until now they have just been a minor annoyance, but apparently that's changed."

"But why? Who are they?"

"The bale elves are a Gathering that worship Sobariini the Moon Queen. They choose to work at night to honor her, so they are unable to continue farming or herding effectively like the rest of us. They steal from other wood and prairie elf groups to survive. "Now, though, they seem to be attacking openly. Rahn, I want you and Toki to scout out a safe path for us to take to the Border Mountain Pass. If we vote to leave Tantek, we will leave in a day or two. Do you understand?"

"Yes, father. But why must we leave our home?"

"If the bale elves have a standing army and are in control of Tantek, they will hunt down and kill all the surface-dwelling elves. The Moon Queen demands complete elven obedience. Darek the wizard will give you some survival supplies. Go to his tent and get what you need. Be back by tomorrow evening, son."

"I will, father," Rahn promised.

"Elf leader!" Gordon barked from the meeting tent. "We're waiting!"

Rahn retrieved his knife, some rope, and a sack with his Pan-pipes inside from his tent, and ran to the wizard's tent.

"Darek," Rahn blurted out without knocking or introducing himself, "How come you never go to the Elder Gatherings?"

"Wizards never go to Gatherings. Gatherings were formed to discuss wizards, not include them."

"I thought they were for discussing children," Rahn retorted.

Darek laughed, "That too. What can I do for you?"

"My father is sending me on an expedition. I need a travel pack."

Darek reached into one of his wooden crates and removed some items. "Here, these are some dense food and stamina potions. Remember not to consume potions within a half hour of eating, and only eat before napping or when you awaken," warned the wizard.

Rahn put the items in his bag. He turned to meet another elf at Darek's door.

"Darek, you are needed at the Gathering," the elf said.

"Good luck, Rahn." Darek wished him well and turned to follow the other elf to the Gathering.

Rahn and Toki left the safety of the Gathering shortly past noon. The water evaporating off the plains in the hot mid-day sun made the distant Border Mountains look like a mirage.

"I've never seen a bale elf, Toki. I wonder what they look like." I'll probably never see one, Rahn thought. His mind wondered thinking about what a bale elf might look like and what he would do if he saw one.

Rahn and Toki walked toward the mountains for hours without any signs of other beings. The mountains grew larger as the pair approached. The ground rose, was visibly dryer, and rockier as the pair neared their destination. Rahn knew he would have no more trouble with mud in the Border Mountain range foothills. He sat on a nearby rock and removed his mud boots.

"This looks like a good spot for camp, Toki. I can see Border Mountain Pass from here. It looks like a white flag with gold symbols is flying over the fort. I wonder what that means."

Rahn gathered sticks and old leaves to make a fire. Toki dug a pit to help and carried stones in his mouth to place around the pit's edge.

"I can understand elves not getting along with ogres, but I don't understand why elves can't get along with other elves," Rahn wondered aloud, and then blew into his musical Pan-pipes. Rahn's pipes were made of different-sized reeds, tied together with red and pink ceremony ribbons he'd found after one of the celebrations last year. The melody he played was slow and quiet. Rahn stopped and looked at Toki. "Starting a war against your own race over a religion sounds like a stupid idea. Especially when all religions say to treat others the way you want to be treated." Toki groaned a groan that sounded like your parents when they see you hitting your little sister after you were told not to. Toki laid his head on his front paws and went to sleep.

Rahn played his pipes until he fell asleep. He dreamt of soldiers with blood-stained armor, fighting hordes of fearless elves, and deities screaming over unread peaceful poems and messages of love and honor wasted on war-like, ignorant humanoids.

The next morning the sky was cloudy, and fog covered the Border Mountains when Rahn awoke.

"If we travel to the mountain pass today, we'll never get home by dark, Toki. We better head home now." The ground was noticeably drier this morning and made the journey home much easier. Rahn put his boots back on and hurried at a near run pace to arrive at the Gathering with plenty of daylight left. Smoke visibly rose above the tents and shelters when Rahn approached the clan's Gathering.

"Most of the tents are still up Toki. Maybe they voted not to leave. Let's go!"

The energetic elf ran home with renewed enthusiasm, but a low growl from Toki caused him to stop. Rahn knew the deep growling sound well. It meant that something was wrong. He crouched down to take a closer look. He looked around the tents and he didn't see his neighbors scurrying about cooking or doing chores as he would have expected.

"Nobody's there! They left without us!" Rahn shouted. Toki's response was to growl lower and deeper than any heard from an animal like Toki before. Rahn quickly realized he was wrong.

"Toki, protect!" Rahn ordered and pointed to the ground in front of him.

Toki rushed to the lead and walked slowly into the elven village with his head lowered to the ground. He slowly looked back and forth, scanning the Gathering from left to right as he moved between the structures. Smoke rose from tents and possessions smoldered in recently-burned piles throughout his home.

Is anybody left? Rahn wondered.

Toki sniffed and walked slowly to the area that had once been the meeting tent. He barked loud enough for only Rahn to hear. Rahn pulled the knife from his pack and ran to the place where Toki pointed with his nose.

"Tamoor!" Rahn shouted.

Rahn recognized his close friend and the inventor of the hollow-bottom boots lying face down near a burnt pile of tents. Tamoor's head was gashed and bleeding. The pool of blood around him could only signify that he had been bleeding for a long time.

"Toki, run to the wizard's tent, he buries supplies there. Dig them up and bring them to me."

Toki ran to where the wizard's tent had been. He dug until he found a large, leather pouch, grabbed it with his teeth and ran back to Rahn. Rahn tore a piece of cloth from a destroyed tent and wrapped it around his friend's head. When Toki returned with the pouch, Rahn fumbled through it until he found the sweet-smelling healing potions. He helped Tamoor drink two of them.

"We better search for more survivors," Rahn said to Toki.

They let Tamoor sleep and searched the remaining tents and buildings for survivors. Not a soul was found, but Rahn did find a small toy tent near where the wizard's tent had once been.

"What's this?" Rahn asked as he picked up the toy. "I'll ask Tamoor when he wakes."

Rahn searched under toppled tents, and in burned piles. He noticed footprints on the southwest end of the Gathering leading away from the settlement. He noticed something hanging from the old, oak tree that he played in as a kid. Rahn squinted to see what it was. Captain Gordon hung by the neck from the tree's lowest branch. Rahn turned away, but his stomach became uneasy, and he threw up.

Rahn hurried back to Tamoor and woke him. "Tamoor," he said, "we have to find the others."

"They're gone, Rahn. Some bale elf officers and a troop of ogres captured them, I tried to reason with them, but they hit me."

"We have to follow them, Tamoor!"

"We should escape while we can, Rahn. Those ogres set us up. They led the army right to us!"

"No, they didn't. Captain Gordon is hanging in the tree," Rahn explained. "And I'm not leaving Tantek until I find them and my father."

Toki barked in approval.

"Ok, ok. Help me up," Tamoor said. "Take me to the supply tent. I have a pair of mud boots there."

Rahn helped his weary friend to his feet, walked him to the tent, and held onto him until Tamoor could walk on his own. Tamoor searched under the knocked down tent until he found a pair of mud boots, a walking stick, some supplies, and was ready to go.

"We need to track them, Tamoor," Rahn said.

"No, we don't, they went past the oak tree."

"I was afraid you were going to say that," Rahn said. They turned and walked in the direction of the old, oak tree. "I'll never look at that tree in the same way again." Rahn approached the tree, looking up at the ogre slowly swaying with his eyes closed. "Gordon looks so terrible dangling from up there. He looks kind of pale green, don't you think?"

"Ogres are pale green," Tamoor responded. "He was so covered in mud when you first saw him you didn't notice."

"Are the two of you going to gawk at me all day or cut me down?" the ogre asked in a raspy voice.

"You're alive!" Rahn shouted. The elf scrambled up the tree with his knife to cut the ogre down.

"Of course, I'm alive," Gordon fell to the ground with a thud and added, "An ogre has to fall asleep while hanging before he dies, and we can stay awake a long time."

"Doesn't hanging cut off the circulation of blood to the brain?" Tamoor asked.

"Ogres have thick spines. We can hang for hours; that is, until we fall asleep. After that our necks relax, circulation is cut, and then we die," the ogre explained. He rubbed his neck and removed the rope. "And who said ogres keep all their brains in their heads anyway?"

Rahn and Tamoor exchanged glances. "We had better get a move on," Tamoor said. He tried to keep from laughing.

"They won't be hard to follow with these tracks. Follow father," Rahn commanded Toki.

"Those traitors took all my weapons. Gimme your knife," the ogre snorted in a rude way.

The group followed the tracks for nearly three hours before Gordon volunteered information.

"They're heading for the Border Mountains," he said.

"I can see that," Tamoor responded. "But why?"

"Bale elves live in caves," Gordon continued. "And they don't like sunlight. I think they made their way back to the caves to sleep or to get out of the sun."

"When night falls, they will kill the Gathering," Rahn added in.

"No, they will walk back to Tantook, the capital city of Tantek," Captain Gordon stated.

"Don't be stupid, Gordon," Rahn said, turning to point in the direction they had come. "The capital is in the opposite direction. They would have to come out and pass us again at nightfall."

"No, they wouldn't." Gordon reluctantly corrected them. "The bale elves dug tunnels from the mountains to our cities."

"That's over a hundred miles from the mountains to the capital!" Tamoor exclaimed.

"That's how they surprised us in the winter. They built tunnels under the palace, killed the royal families, and besieged our cities from the inside. Once they controlled the cities, they controlled the country. The entire country fell in less than a month. The prince and I were on winter expedition when we found out. They make better time traveling through underground tunnels than we did on the surface through this mud. Once they are in the tunnels, we'll never find them."

"Toki can find them," Rahn said.

The tracks in the mud led up to the base of the mountains and disappeared in the rocky foothills. Tamoor scanned the mountain region for possible cave entrances.

"I see two guards on a cliff halfway up that peak." Gordon pointed toward the guards. "We'll never get up there undetected, and it doesn't look like they are standing in front of a cave either."

"If that's what a hidden cave entrance looks like, I can see three more of them from here," Rahn stated. "Once you know what to look for, they are easy to spot."

"Maybe if you are an elf with funky elf vision you can," Gordon scoffed.

Tamoor used his elven, heat-sensory vision to scan the areas Rahn pointed to.

"One of those lower cave areas is extremely warm," Tamoor pointed out. "I think that's our entrance."

Tamoor led the group away from the spying eyes of the mountain guards to the warm opening he spotted earlier. They squeezed through the tiny opening one at a time. Toki followed Tamoor, with Rahn and Gordon bringing up the rear.

"This cave is natural," Tamoor said. "And it's very warm in here."

"A dormant volcano?" Gordon asked.

"I don't think so. It's too warm to be dormant," Tamoor said. "It's active. I'm beginning to think I know how the bale elves dug caves several hundred miles long."

"Do you mean they let the volcano do the work?" Rahn asked.

"I don't know it for sure, but that is what I mean. The entrance opens up into a room here," Tamoor said. He squeezed down the passage to the next opening. "This room looks like a blacksmith's shop, with tools and a forge. I bet they send lava down this chute and work on metal here. Tamoor pointed to a large bowl-like shape on the far side of the room where all the tools were hanging. A large anvil was constructed or forged into a rock that occupied the center of the room.

"Oh look, a beautiful sword hanging on the wall," Rahn pulled the sword down and held it up to the light. The sword shone with a slight violet color from the dim light passing through the cave entrance.

"Let me see that," Gordon snorted. He took the sword out of Rahn's hand.

Rahn surrendered the short sword to Gordon without offering the ogre any resistance. The ogre screamed in pain when he grasped the sword. Ogre blood poured from his hands out through his gloves. The short, violet sword dropped to the ground.

"What's wrong? " Rahn shrieked. "Did I cut you?"

"No," Gordon said. "The sword is forged from ogranium."

"Ogranium? What's that?" Rahn asked. He picked up the sword and began taunting the wounded ogre with it.

"Ogranium is a vile metal," Gordon said, rubbing his hands. "It works like a magnet to an ogre's blood. Our blood will burst from our veins to get to the metal. It's very painful.

"Cool!" Rahn blurted.

"The metal has the audacity to glow after the ogre blood touches it," Gordon grunted angrily.

"Let's see it glow!"

"Find your own ogre blood," Gordon snorted. "Mine's taken."

Rahn collected some of Gordon's blood from the cavern floor. He wiped Gordon's blood on the sword and watched the sword's violet colored metal light up the whole blacksmith's room.

Rahn set the sword on the anvil and stepped back to watch it glow. Gordon walked past him to look at the hammers lining the wall on the far side of the room. The sword swiveled, on its own power, the tip pointing to Gordon, like a compass needle points north, as the ogre walked past.

"Gordon, it likes you!" the young elf exclaimed.

"I think I'm going to be sick," the ogre mumbled.

"Come on, we have things to do," Tamoor reminded them.

Toki moved further down the tunnel. The others followed him, Rahn with his glowing sword, Tamoor with his walking stick, and Gordon, brandishing a blacksmith's hammer he found in the forge room, brought up the rear. The tunnel twisted and turned but Toki followed the Gathering elves' scent as he made his way through the cave. The tunnel led to another room, but a large, thin, spider-web-like substance covered the entrance.

"How do we get past that?" Rahn asked.

"Simple, you cut it down with a knife," Gordon said. He made his way past the group to the web.

A loud shriek startled the group. A dark, elven-looking bat creature, the size of an adult elf, but with hairy-leather wings, grabbed Gordon through the web and pulled him into it.

"Kill it!" Gordon shouted.

"You're closer!" Tamoor reminded him. The elf-bat dragged Gordon deeper into the web. He struggled but was unable to break free.

Toki gracefully leapt through the web onto the back of the creature, careful to not get caught in its web. The elf-bat pulled Gordon through the remainder of the web. Their struggle tore it from the cave wall. Rahn ran in right behind him. Toki bit the elf-bat on the neck. It shrieked and released Gordon, dropping the ogre to the ground. Rahn plunged his sword into the elf-bat several times. The elf-bat creature screamed and writhed in pain until it was dead. Rahn looked closer at the creature and noticed its white eyes and close resemblance to a prairie elf.

"You don't suppose they are born like this do you, Tamoor?" Rahn asked.

"No, this is probably some kind of punishment."

The dead elf-bat creature slowly transformed from a matte-black, half-bat half-elf into a light-tan almost yellow-colored bale elf.

"So, that's how a bale elf looks," Rahn said. He lightly kicked the body to make sure it was dead.

"Yes, a little more yellowish than our own brown color, probably from a lack of sunlight. A slight pigment color change is the only difference between them and us."

Without a command, Toki turned and followed the Gathering scent out of the room. Rahn remembered the food given to him by the wizard, He handed some to his companions and followed Toki out of the room.

The Gathering scent became more apparent to the elves as they passed into the next tunnel. The ogranium short sword in Rahn's hand lightly tugged him down the passage, toward some ogres possibly at the other end.

"We must be getting close to some ogres," Rahn said. "The sword is pulling me down the hall."

Captain Gordon motioned for the others to stop and said, "I will go around and check how many guards are there. Be prepared to fight them." Gordon was gone for only a few moments before he came back. "There is enough room for Tamoor and me to sneak up, grab the guards, and drag them back here. Rahn be ready to kill them in case we have troubles."

Gordon's plan worked perfectly. Rahn slew the two traitorous ogre guards without sound or alarm. Rahn had to wipe the blood from the brightly-shining violet sword to persuade it to conceal their presence from the others.

"Tamoor," Gordon said. "Put this uniform on and stand guard

with me to fool anyone who may look for the guards up here. Rahn, I need you to quietly alert the Gathering and let them know this is the way out." The ogre grunted. "If you can."

"Leave the sword here, Rahn, it glows too much to take along," Tamoor added.

Rahn grabbed his bag, took out his Pan-pipes, and tied the bag around Toki's neck.

"Toki," he said, "lead everybody through the tunnel and out of the cave when they come to you. And don't lose my bag."

Rahn propped his sword against the cave wall. He descended the steps along the wall into the prison cavern where the Gathering elves slumbered. Rahn found the elves asleep, but unchained, when he reached the bottom. He played the familiar elven tune of assembly at a pitch only dogs and elves could hear. The slumbering elves woke and murmured at the sound, but quickly realized it was an escape warning and quieted down. Rahn guided the Gathering elves up the steps to the tunnel where Tamoor and Gordon stood guard. Rahn's father, Darek the wizard, and Gad the Ogre Prince were the last to climb the steps from the prison cave.

"Did you bring my tent, Tamoor?" Darek asked his friend, when he climbed the stairs to the top.

"No, I didn't think to look for it after I was hit on the head. I was not thinking clearly."

"We didn't have time to pack a tent," Gordon added in his typical snorting fashion.

"No, I shrunk it down when the ogre army and bale elves approached," the wizard said.

"Is that the toy tent from the Gathering?" Rahn asked when he reached the top.

"Yes, it is. Did you bring it?" the wizard inquired.

"It is in my bag tied around Toki's neck. He is leading the Gathering out through the tunnel."

"Let's just get out of here," grumbled the prince.

Rahn collected his sword and followed the others away from the prison cave. Toki and the others made their way out of the tunnels and congregated near the base of the mountain as Rahn, the ogre prince, and captain emerged. A whistle shattered the silence as the last of the party descended the mountain side. The traitorous ogres standing guard at the entrance cliff halfway up the mountain sounded the alarm.

"We had better get to the pass as soon as possible," Gordon ordered. "We haven't got much time."

"We may be running for nothing," the prince said. "We don't know who has control of the pass."

"I saw a white flag with gold markings there yesterday," Rahn offered.

"Gold on white?" Gordon asked. "That's the Fortress Island Knight's flag! They must have heard about the war and captured the border station! We are saved if we can get there first."

Gordon herded the elves like sheep toward the pass. "Move! Everyone move! We must stay ahead of the army that follows us," the ogre ordered.

Rahn and Darek caught up to Toki. Darek removed the bag from Toki's neck and rummaged through it until they found Darek's toy tent. Darek handed the bag to Rahn, uttered a few magic words, and dropped the tent to the ground. The tent exploded from a small, toy-sized tent into the full-sized familiar wizard tent of the Gathering. Darek stepped inside briefly, collected the magic ingredients he needed, and chanted his incantations, while the traitorous ogre and bale elf army descended the mountain toward them.

"We don't have time to pitch a tent!" Gad snorted. "Move!" Gad ushered the Gathering elves along the Border Mountains toward the Border Mountain Pass, leaving the three elves and Toki to their wizard tent.

Rahn, Tamoor, and Toki stayed behind to protect Darek in case his magic failed. Darek emerged from the tent. The wizard uttered a few more magic words, the tent shrunk back to toy size; he picked it up and ran after the other elves. "Come on, before they catch us!"

For nearly an hour the elves ran. Toki reached the Gathering elves first. He howled to speed up the tired Gathering stragglers. Dark clouds slowly converged above the group. They noticed some of the elves were having trouble keeping pace. Their endurance was giving out.

The wizard stopped, turned, and faced the angry, charging army.

Darek raised his arms high above his head. "Rain!" he commanded. Lightning struck the ground on both sides of the wizard. An immediate, fierce, downpour fell on the Border Mountains and foothills where the army pursued their escaped prisoners.

The army was swept from the hills to the Tanteki plains, where a muddy quagmire formed from the sudden rain commanded by the wizard. The area behind the wizard and from the peak of the mountains, through the foothills, to the plain below, was caught up in the wizard's rain spell. A steady stream of water slowed the army and allowed the elves to easily escape on dry land, while the clumsy treasonous ogres and bale elf officers stumbled pitifully through the mud in pursuit.

It was shortly past daybreak the following day when the party reached the mountain pass. The clouds of Darek's storm were all but gone when the elves climbed the last steps to the fort at the mountain pass. A gold and white flag fluttering above a brightly-armored knight was a welcome sight to the elves that entered the Mountain Pass Stronghold.

"We were waiting for the first group of refugees," the knight said. "But we weren't expecting elves."

Prince Gad identified himself and noted how proud he was to have this group of elves, and Rahn, who helped him to freedom, living in his country.

"How long are you knights going to be guarding the pass?" Prince Gad asked.

"Well, we were waiting to see if the war rumors were true..."

"They are," the prince interrupted.

"And if they were, we were going to send the word for all knights to liberate as many Tanteki citizens as possible."

"Give the word," Gad ordered.

The knight waved his arm to signal his archer. An arrow shot high into the air. It burst into a brilliant ball of fire that illuminated the stronghold fort, even brighter than the near mid-day sun, for about two minutes. Rahn imagined that many such fireball arrows were going to light up the sky that day, and into the night, all around Tantek, giving the signal that the Fortress Island Knights were going to help prisoners and refugees to freedom.

Rahn and his father crossed the stronghold courtyard to where Prince Gad and Gordon stood in the compound by themselves. "Those ogres that took us prisoner, were those your troops?" father asked.

"Yes, they were. Those blasted traitors!" Gordon responded.

"What will you do now?"

"Prince Gad and I will follow you through the pass into the country of Earen Hoot," Gordon informed them. "The knight told us the king of Earen Hoot has attacked our city of Onopolis that borders his country. We will strike a bargain with him to help re-conquer the city and begin building an army to recapture our country "And Rahn," he added, "any time your father thinks you're old enough to leave the Gathering, I would be honored to accept you as an officer in my ranks. Your actions have been quite heroic."

"Thank you," Rahn responded. "I will consider it, Captain."

The Fortress Island Knights escorted Rahn, Toki, Darek, Tamoor and the Gathering through the pass.

"What will happen when we get there, Father?" Rahn asked.

"If all goes well, we'll eventually be allowed to settle in the plains of Earen Hoot, across the Border Mountains from Tantek."

"What will we do there, Father?"

"Hopefully, we will live there, son, in freedom and in peace."

Kevin Harrington is an author who has struggled with mental illness his whole life and has used writing as a healing mechanism. This is both why he writes and why it has taken him to an advanced age to get started. All his writing, in one way or the other, is about himself. About what has hurt and devastated him all his life and how he has worked through it. It has been very difficult, but it is now starting to work out at long last.

Synopsis

The next two short pieces are self-explanatory, sort of!

I Am a Cat

I am a cat. You appear to me to be a human, but I have little experience with other species. Humans, I have heard, do not believe cats can speak. Is that true? If it is, I apologize for disturbing you. However, I have been told that a great evil may be coming to cat kind, and I am therefore seeking out assistance. Humans, I believe, have mighty machines that can do almost magical things. Will you help us, human? I am told that your kind has a fondness for mine and would therefore be grieved if cats disappeared from the earth. If this is true, I hope you will want to help my people in our time of great need. Will you?

The Wolf that Helped

He looked at me and growled. "A talking wolf is the least of your concerns."

I blinked, and nodded. My mother was dying. That is why I had come to the woods: because I could not bear watching her mind slip away when it had once been so sharp. I hardly recognized her anymore. And the woods were reputed to be magical, to contain fairies, and I was desperate and perhaps exhausted. I thought something in the woods might help me with my mother.

The wolf nodded. "I knew your mother once."

"How could you have?"

He did not answer my question. "I knew her as a little girl. Now she will be a little girl again."

I winced. "That... will not be necessary."

He pounced on me, his teeth at my throat.

"Do you think it is your choice?"

Karen Funk Blocher is a church bookkeeper and social media director. A graduate of the Clarion SF Writers' Workshop, she has contributed articles to *Relix* and *Starlog* magazines, and wrote the text for five series of Doctor Who trading cards in the 1990s. Her first fantasy trilogy, *Heirs of Mâvarin*, will be published by MuseItUp Publishing later this year, and the sequel trilogy is close to completion. Karen has one husband (fellow Clarionite John), two dogs, no kids and no cats.

Synopsis

The Boy Who Saw is a prequel to Karen's fantasy trilogy, *Heirs of Mâvarin*, but requires no prior knowledge of that series. Forty years before the events of *The Tengrem Sword* (due out later this year from MuseItUp Publishing), two orphaned boys set out alone for the Citadel College of Magic, hoping to study to become mages. They aren't expecting to encounter a villainous innkeeper, a dying Duke, or a ghost who wants her body found....

The Boy Who Saw:
A Chronicle of Mâvarin in 37 Documents

Exhibit One: A Letter from Alba Stok to Arti Lan

7 Rose Lane
Kinbeth
Sabedu, 2 Nefilem, 855

Dear Arti,

Autumn is almost over, so I assume that the harvest is in. I hope everything went well, and that you got a good price for your cotton again this year.

This being your slow season, I'm wondering whether you might be able to get away for a few weeks and come for a visit. It's been about five years since I've seen you, and I miss my only brother! We have plenty of room, and we'll make sure that little Fabi is on his best behavior this time.

Husband Fafi has adapted well to shopkeeping. His store is like a little marketplace, with goods from all over. He always seems to know what his customers are most likely to buy, and never gets stuck with unwanted leftovers. I think he misses the caravan, just a little, but overall, he's found his place here in Kinbeth and is quite content.

As for me, I'm still performing at the local inn and in the occasional play at Skû. The theater troupe there has produced three of my shows, and I even make a bit of money off them. I know you don't approve, Azti dear, especially since it sometimes takes me away from home for a few weeks; but I hope you're at least pleased that Fafi and I are well, prosperous, and happy.

Little Fabi is ten years old now. He tries very hard to be obedient and considerate, and he's very loving and kind toward everyone. Even so, somehow he's always getting in trouble, one way or another. Last week, his pet rabbit turned green for an hour. "Pucu isn't really green!" he insisted, and it's true that the animal seems to have taken no harm at all. Then yesterday morning, he came to us crying, and was just inconsolable. He insisted that he saw both Fafi and me dying in our bed. I showed him that we're both perfectly fine, but he was very quiet and sad the rest of the day. It must have been quite a nightmare!

I hope to see you soon.

Love,
Alba

Exhibit Two: Report on a Runaway

Seven Visions Home for Children
A Ministry of the Church of Mâshela, Skû
Sabedu, 16 Nefilem, 855

Greetings and Blessings, Mother Fara,

I'm sorry to report that one of our boys, eight-year-old Hasi Goreg, has run away from the orphanage here. You may remember him. He's the skinny, brown-haired boy who is always singing or making wry jokes. He disappeared from the dormitory (or possibly the common room) on Umvardu evening, and has not been seen or heard from since then. A small amount of food was stolen from the kitchen that same night.

It's almost a relief to lose him, to be honest. Peace and quiet have been hard to come by since Hasi moved in a year ago. There's nothing inherently wrong with music, of course, and Hasi has a fine voice; but he exercises it constantly, day and night, when he's not exercising his wit, with a sophistication that's positively unnatural for an eight-year-old. Sometimes he does both, making up clever but annoying little songs that stay in your head for days. It's exhausting.

It's also highly disruptive. Magical things tend to happen when Hasi makes music. Dogs sing along, and you can almost hear their words. Flowers turn and grow.

On Umvardu after dinner, Hasi sang the same annoying song over and over, making more of a racket than seems possible for one boy and his delmoran. Listening to Hasi play, you'd swear the delmoran had 49 strings instead of seven, and was accompanied by at least three other instruments. How can I concentrate on the children with all that going on? Finally, I asked him to put the delmoran away and be quiet for the rest of the evening. He did so, but an hour later he disappeared entirely.

Nor is this the first time. On several occasions in the past few months, Hasi has vanished before our eyes, just for a few seconds. If the other children are to be believed, he has been doing this almost daily, only to reappear almost immediately. This time, he has vanished for considerably longer. I would not be surprised if Hasi sang himself away from here somehow.

My request that he stop singing may be the proximate cause of his departure, but it's evident that Hasi has been lonely and unhappy since his sister was adopted. I've written to the sister's new family, asking them to let me know if he turns up.

I've also informed the local Watch and the Wanderers, so that they can keep an eye out for Hasi. Is there anything else you want me to do?

Yours in the Holy Lady,
Domi Vobis

Exhibit Three: Letter from Arti Stok to His Wife

Kinbeth, Skû
Sabedu, 23 Nefilem 855

Dear Dora,

I arrived here in Kinbeth this morning, only to find Alba and her husband, Fafi, on the point of death. They were in bed, side by side, struggling to breathe. There was vomit all over the place, and they were drooling. Alba looked at me, choked a little, closed her eyes and died, almost the moment I entered the room. Fafi was gone a minute or two later. I think they were poisoned! And I think I know who did it: their son, Fabi!

The boy was behaving very strangely as his parents died. Moments after Alba took her last breath, Fabi called me by my first name, said he was sorry, and asked me to look after his son. His son! He's a boy of ten! Then his father died, and he looked wildly around, said something about diamonds, and shooed me from the room!

You remember, of course, that when Alba wrote to me weeks ago, she said that Fabi predicted her death. What if he killed them? Maybe he's crazy. He certainly acted crazy. Maybe it was an accident, but I don't see how.

Fabi calmed down a bit after we left his parents' room, although he was crying continuously. I asked him what happened, but he said that he didn't know how his parents died, only that he knew they would do so. I told him to stay at the house while I went for the sheriff and the priest.

The Kinbeth post office is next to the sheriff's office, so I'm taking the time to send this note. I'll be home when I can, after the situation is resolved and I've disposed of my sister's property.

If Fabi deliberately poisoned his parents, it's up to the local authorities to decide his fate. It's not up to me to kill him, much as he deserves it. If it was an accident, perhaps I should bring him back with me, and put him to work in the cotton fields. That should steady him, and provide a measure of justice for what he did

Arti

Exhibit Four: Lusa's Family Replies

10 Green Walk, Harimar
Nishmudu, 24 Nefilem, 855

Dear Father Domi,

No, we haven't heard from Lusa's brother - not directly, anyway. Lusa claims she saw him two nights ago, but we're pretty sure he was never here. From Lusa's description of the incident, we're guessing it was a dream, or something like a dream.

By the way, much as we love Lusa, we believe that your orphanage was less than honest in describing her to us, beforehand and on site. Are you aware that our little girl can make people dream about bears, and cooks food just by touching it?

Regards,
Lala and Eri Palcot

Exhibit Five: Coroner's Report

Report of the Coroner in the Matter of Fafi and Alba Stok
Kinbeth, County of Skû
Nishmudu, 24 Nefilem 855

I have examined the bodies of Fafi and Alba Stok, husband and wife, who died at their home at 7 Rose Lane, Kinbeth, on Sabedu, 23 Nefilem 855, shortly before noon. There is no sign of injury or violence of any kind, nor of conventional illness. However, there are clear signs of poisoning: vomiting, red and swollen limbs, and their bed drenched with sweat.

The woman's brother, a plantation owner named Arti Lan, pestered me with an accusation that the couple's ten-year-old son, Fabi, poisoned his parents. I considered this theory, but rejected it when I found puncture wounds at the site of the worst swelling on each body - Alba's left wrist and Fafi's right leg. Clearly, they were the victims of snakebite, but where was the snake?

A short search with the sheriff and the uncle turned it up

between two Derion blankets in a new-looking basket, sitting on the floor at the foot of the bed. Most likely Fafi, a shopkeeper, brought home either the basket or the blankets, unaware that he was also bringing in a stowaway. The snake probably became active in the warmth of the bedroom, and struck out when disturbed.

The boy is no longer suspected of murder, but he is a fugitive. He ran away while the uncle was in the village, alerting the priest and the sheriff. No pursuit or arrest is recommended, as there is no evidence of criminality in the case.

Verdict:
Cause of Death: Snakebite
Manner of Death: Accident
Mechanism: Poison Toxicity

Attested this day,
Robi Welden

Exhibit Six: Hasi's First Letter to Lusa

With the Dener Caravan, Concor
Masheldu, 25 Nefilem, 855

Dear Lusa,

I hope I didn't scare you too much, taking you to my Special Place the other night. I wanted to say goodbye, and I guess the One knew it, and sent you to me there.

It's been a little over a week since I ran away from the orphanage. Father Domi was being mean about my music, and I was tired of it. Almost everyone else liked my songs. Some of the other kids were even singing along. But Father Domi told me to shut up, and said it was time to get ready for bed, which it wasn't. The other kids started filing out to the two dorms, but I took my time, packing up my delmoran and my recorder in the patchwork bag I made for them. When I saw Father Domi scolding Timi about something and not looking at me, I went to my Special Place. I stayed there a long time. By the time I came back, the common room was empty.

There wasn't anyone around, so I went to the kitchen for food to take with me. The pantry was locked, but I sang to it and the door clicked open. I got a flour sack and filled it with day-old brown bread, and apples and oranges.

I couldn't get my jacket or my other shirt, because they were in the dormitory and I would have been caught. I also couldn't get out the front door, because it was locked and that lock has never liked my music. Instead I snuck into old Mr. Mac's room as he snored, and climbed out his bathroom window, bags and all.

I spent the first night in a barn. The second night, I hid in a caravan wagon heading east. I got caught, but the caravan people were pretty nice about it. They let me ride until morning, and then left me behind. Another night, a priest picked me up on the road, and let me sleep in her rectory. Last night, another caravan let me ride along in exchange for music and a little magic. But they are turning off this morning, in a different direction from where I need to go.

I bet you've already guessed where I'm going. Remember how we talked about magic, and how great it would be if we could learn it properly? That's my goal. I'm going to Mâton, to the school there.

I can't give you an address along the way, because I'm not going to stay anywhere for very long. I'll try to write to you sometimes to let you know my progress, and for sure when I reach Mâton.

You're probably worried about how I can do this on my own. I know I'm only eight years old, but you must admit I'm not just an ordinary little boy. And I'm not alone. Not anymore.

More later. The caravan is taking this letter for me, and they can't wait.

Hasi

Exhibit Seven: Letter from Fabi To Arti

With the Dener Caravan, Concor
Masheldu, 25 Nefilem, 855

Dear Uncle Arti,
     By now you know that I didn't kill my parents, but that's what

you thought when you got to our house and I acted all weird. Sorry about that. I don't know what happened to me. For a moment, it was as if I was my mom, trying to say goodbye to you. Then the same thing happened with my dad, except he was worried about something in a basket. I can't explain it any better than that.

Before my parents died, I had a dream that you would make me work in your cotton fields if I let you take me home with you. I don't think that's fair. It's not my fault my parents died, and I'm an orphan now. Mom and Dad understood me, and now there's nobody like that, no adult around to love me or help me when things get confusing. Picking cotton won't make my life any better, so I've run away.

No, I take that back. I'm not just running away. I'm running toward something. I know you don't like magic, but magic is part of me. Or maybe I'm part of magic. Or both. Anyway, I'm going to Mâton, where I can learn to control my magic instead of just getting in trouble all the time.

I'm sorry your sister died. I miss my mom much more than you do.

Goodbye.
Fabi

Exhibit Eight: Hasi's Second Letter to Lusa

Moneldu, 28 Nefilen, 855

Hi, Lusa,

I've lost track of what day it is, but I think it's been about four days since I last wrote to you. I'm in a stable in Dent, curled up next to a large sorrel mare. Dent is about six days east of Skû on horseback. But of course, I don't have a horse.

Last time I told you that I'm not alone any more. I've met this boy named Fabi. He's ten years old.

He found me in a haystack outside Rifibeth. No, really, he did! There was this field, and it was getting dark. I wanted to sleep in a barn, but it was locked, and I didn't want to ask the farmers to let me in. But there was a place between two bales of hay that was about my size, and more hay underneath to lie on. The hay blocked the wind, so I was almost warm enough.

I slept about half the night, I guess. Then I woke up because I was getting pretty cold.

I sat and I shivered and longed for the sun,
Wond'ring what I could do and how best to go.
Sleeping out in the cold is no kind of fun.
Then, terrible luck! It started to snow!

When the snow started, I thought about going to my Special Place, but I don't think I can really sleep there. I mean, I use my mind (and magic) to go to my Special Place, and I probably can't do that and sleep at the same time. Anyway, I was afraid to try it.

But I must have closed my eyes again and drifted off a little, even though I was getting really cold, and wet too. When a voice in my ear said, "I have an extra jacket," I was so startled that I disappeared to my Special Place anyway.

And I wasn't alone! There was a boy standing there, looking around. The hay was gone, and we were warm. Usually my Special Place is mostly dark, with just one or two things to look at and think about. But this was a whole room! There were two beds, two desks with chairs, and a large closet.

The other boy looked more interested than scared, I thought. "Where are we?" he asked.

"I'm not sure," I said. "It's not real, exactly. And it usually doesn't look like this."

"Did you do this? Send us here, I mean."

"I think so," I said. "Usually I'm alone, though."

"If you can go someplace like this, where it's nice and warm," the boy asked, "why would you sleep outside in the hay?"

"Because it's not real, like I said. There's no way to lie down on that bed."

The boy reached out to touch the bed. His hand went right through it. "Or maybe it is real," he said, "but we're not really here."

I shrugged. "Maybe."

"Even if you can't lie down, it's still warmer here, wherever it is."

"Yeah, but I don't know what happens to the magic, or to me, if I fall asleep. I'd rather not risk it."

The boy cocked his head. "Can you travel this way, and end up somewhere else?"

"No. It doesn't work like that." I waved my hand, and the room disappeared. I was back in my spot between the bales of hay. "See? I'm always back where I started. Except usually, I know more than I did before." I looked up at the boy. He was taller than me, and a little fat. "I'm Hasi," I said.

The boy nodded. "I'm Fabi. Do you want my extra jacket? It's a little small for me, but I bet it will be big on you."

"That would be good. Thanks."

Fabi set down a backpack and started rummaging through it. "Here it is," he said, and pulled out a heavy jacket lined with cotton. "It's blue. Do you like blue?"

"Sure," I said. I tried on the jacket. It was way too big, but lined with rabbit fur and very good for blocking the wind.

"What now?" Fabi asked. "Do you want to try to sleep some more, or would you rather start walking?"

"Walking where?"

He grinned. "Where are you trying to get to?"

"No place I can get to in one night. Where are you trying to go?"

"Same place as you, I bet. Mâton. And I'm pretty sure we're meant to go there together."

Hasi

Exhibit Nine: A Letter from Fabi to Marnestri

Dent
Moneldu, 28 Nefilem, 855

Dear Archmage Marnestri,

My name is Fabi Stok, and I'm ten years old. My father was Fafi Stok. He was a fortuneteller on the Pilcaf caravan. He never had any training from a real mage or a school, but his fortune-telling was real magic. I know because I have the same talent. I knew my parents were going to die before they did. I knew when I ran away after their deaths that soon I would meet another boy who wants to be a mage. I know a lot of things. But not everything. I also make illusions sometimes, but I'm not very good at it yet.

My mom was a singer but not a magician, and I'm good at music and making up songs. But I don't think you care about that kind of talent.

The other boy I met is named Hasi Goreg. He's eight years old, and he's an orphan, too. He's even better at music than I am, and his music is magic. It makes things happen. One example, sometimes I hear extra instruments when he sings and plays.

Hasi's other talent is very strange. He calls it his Special Place, but it's not really anywhere, at least not anywhere you can get to any normal way. He can make himself disappear, or someone else, or both. While they're gone from the real world, they see and hear things that tell them more about themselves. I've never heard of anything like that, but it's magic for sure.

We're trying to get to Mâton together, but it's a long way. We don't have any money or horses, or anyone else to travel with for protection. I figure that you, the great Archmage Marnestri, might be able to help us. One of my visions says that we will reach Liramar ten days from now, if we don't get killed along the way. (I'll try very hard not to let us get killed!) Can you maybe send someone to Liramar who can help us reach Mâton safely? I would ask for someplace closer to where we are now, but my dreams say we're supposed to go to the places in between. I don't know why.

Thanks for your help. Maybe we can pay you back later, when we're mages. I hope to see you soon!

Fabi Stok

Exhibit Ten: Constable's Report

Incident Report
Mika Homs, Constable
Date: Masheldu, 1 Celderem, 855

Place: Happy Hen Inn, Asenbeth
Subjects: Fabi Stok, age 10, Hasi Goreg, age 8, Ludo Cader, age 47

Although I was off duty at the time of the following incident, I was a witness, and had occasion to impose a settlement in lieu of an arrest. My full account follows:

According to three members of the inn's staff (see appended statements), two children, Fabi Stok and Hasi Goreg, entered the kitchen at the Happy Hen shortly before sunset, as head of housekeeping Kito Jons was taking out the trash. The two boys approached head cook Caya Jons, requesting food. When Caya initially refused, Hasi stated that they had not eaten since the day before, and started to cry.

Fabi then proposed a musical performance by both boys in the inn's dining room that evening, in return for their dinner and a room for the night. Before Caya could respond to the offer, the boys started to sing. Witnesses stated that all work stopped as music filled the room, not just singing but the sound of unseen instruments.

The innkeeper, Ludo Cader, entered the kitchen moments later. He demanded that the singing stop. When Caya explained the situation, however, Ludo asked the boys to sing in the common room as proposed. In the meantime, Caya gave the boys a piece of day-old bread to share, and a mug of tea. She later stated that she would have given them more, but Ludo rebuked her when she tried to ladle out some stew.

I arrived at the Happy Hen at dusk, and ordered my dinner as usual. A short time later, Fabi and Hasi entered the dining room and sang a combination of new songs and old favorites in high, clear voices, accompanied by Hasi on his delmoran. Other instruments were heard but not seen. Their performance was well-received by the patrons, some of whom tossed coins at the boys. They sang for well over an hour. When they left the stage, Hasi stumbled, looking exhausted. Fabi started to collect the coins, but Ludo stated that he would take care of that, and led the audience in a round of applause.

Back in the kitchen, unseen by me, the boys requested their money, their food, and their room. Ludo claimed that he had not promised them a room or money, and pointed out that they had already eaten. His stated intention to keep all but a few coppers as the inn's "cut" of the cash was partly thwarted when Hasi started to hum. The innkeeper's purse opened by itself, and coins began to float in the air toward Fabi.

Ludo reached for Hasi, shouting, "You little thief!" According to Fabi, Ludo twisted the boy's arm. The kitchen staff did not confirm the arm-twisting, but conceded that at that moment, the floating coins fell to the floor as the magic failed.

Ludo's shout attracted my attention in the next room. I set down my mug and made a dash for the kitchen. I did this partly out of concern for the younger boy, and partly because Ludo has a history of being less than honest in his business dealings.

"You're the thief, you big cheat!" Fabi shouted. I entered the kitchen just as Fabi was scrambling to retrieve the coins on the kitchen floor. Ludo tried to lunge for Fabi without letting go of Hasi's arm. Fabi ducked away, Hasi fell down, and then disappeared. So did Ludo.

I looked at Fabi. "What just happened? Where's the innkeeper? Where is your friend?"

"Hasi's Special Place," Fabi said. "They'll be back soon."

"What does that mean?"

"It's too hard to explain," Fabi said. "But they're safe. Listen, that innkeeper tried to cheat us. Are you the sheriff? Can you help us?"

"I'm the constable," I said. "I'm much more likely to help you if you tell me what's going on."

Ludo abruptly reappeared. He backed away from Hasi. "You stay away from me," he said.

"What did you learn?" the boy asked.

"Nothing. What I saw… that was a lie."

"What did you see?" I asked.

Ludo seemed to notice me for the first time. "Nothing," he said. "I'm glad you're here, officer. These boys are unlicensed magicians and troublemakers. Do your duty. Arrest them."

The accusation may have been true, but justice seemed to point the other way. It usually does, when Ludo is involved. "For what? Singing?" I said. "Entertaining your patrons? Trying to collect their own tips?"

"The Sheriff will hear about this," Ludo snarled. "I know my rights. They're underage, they don't have a license, and I didn't promise them anything."

"He's lying," Kito said. His wife Caya looked alarmed.

"And you're fired," Ludo said.

"Now, now, Ludo, there's no need for that," I said. "You know you can't keep this place going without Kito and Caya. Nobody else would take the job."

Ludo glared at me.

"As to your other point, these two young songsters are certainly underage, but that's no reason to cheat them," I said. "Do you, in fact, have a license?"

"No," Hasi said. "Do we need a license to sing?"

"You need a license to perform magic in public," I told him. "How old are you boys?"

"Seventeen," Fabi said. "We're older than we look."

I shook my head. "Try again."

"I'm eight years old," Hasi said. "Fabi is ten."

"Where are your parents?"

"Dead," Fabi said.

"Gone to the Infinite," Hasi said.

I nodded. "I'm sorry to hear that. How do you come to be traveling on your own? Don't you know how dangerous that is?"

Fabi said, "We're trying to get to our uncle's house in Liramar. He sent us the money, but it was stolen from us in Dent. We can make it, if people will just treat us fairly."

"All right, all right," I said. I got out my notebook, and asked Marna for pen and ink. "Suppose you tell me what happened, and we'll take it from there."

Ludo looked outraged. "You're going to take his word over mine?"

"Everyone will have a chance to speak," I told him. "I will interview each of you separately, starting with Fabi."

Marna brought the inkwell, which I then took into a little room by the stable. Fabi came in first, followed by Hasi, and then Ludo, and finally each member of his kitchen staff, until I had written statements from everyone. Although I could not establish that the innkeeper made an explicit promise to Fabi and Hasi, it was clearly implied from his actions.

Returning to the kitchen, I ordered that the boys be given a proper meal, a room for the night, and half of the tips collected. Ludo initially disputed my authority to enforce the arrangement, but I reminded him of certain facts regarding an incident last month, for which punishment was suspended in return for future good behavior.

"All right," Ludo said. "They can have a bowl of stew each, and share Room 11 next to the stable."

Fabi, who had been staring off into space, looked suddenly frightened. "We can't stay there," he said.

"Why not?" I asked.

"We're not safe."

"Of course you are," I said. "Unless you want a night in jail, there's really no place else."

"Please, Fabi," Hasi said. "Not jail."

Fabi hesitated. Then he sighed. "All right."

We left it at that. I had a private word with Kito to check on the boys during the night, and will follow up with the Sheriff in the morning. Mayor Kurton, or possibly Lord Penaver, will have to decide whether the children are to be allowed to continue to travel, or sent to an orphanage until the uncle can be notified to come and collect them.

Exhibit Eleven: Letter from Durtani To Marnestri

The Citadel, Mâton
Masheldu, 1 Celderem, 855
Evaluation and Recommendation: Rula Sim

Magu Marnestri:

I've consulted with Rinstarki about our mutual student, Rula Sim, and we are agreed that she is ready for Robing as our newest adept. Although her portals take longer than average to set up, based on her experience level, she is a genius for adding extra subrituals, customizing each doorway with features specific to the task. For example, last week she fitted a portal with a charm that informs her when the portal is approached and who is approaching, and enables her to block its use remotely.

Regarding her music talent, Rinstarki tells me that her composition skills need more refinement, but the power and effect of her music is unmatched. A single musical phrase can completely alter the listeners emotions. If she were to pursue a true mindpush ability, Rinstarki is certain she could achieve it. Instead, she consciously confines herself to emotional manipulation, and using music to reveal and manipulate other spells she encounters.

You asked me yesterday to choose an adept for your mission to Liramar, to meet with and evaluate the two children who recently wrote to you requesting help. Rinstarki and I believe that Rula, once elevated as Rutana, is the best choice for the task. She can create a portal to the target city, and use her musical discernment to evaluate the children for their raw talents and trainability. We therefore recommend that Rula be Robed at this week's ceremony, and immediately dispatched on this assignment.

Durtani
Portal Master

Exhibit Twelve: Kito's Statement – 1

Incident: Happy Hen Inn, Asenbeth
Date: Thaledu, 2 Celderem, 855
Statement: Kito Jons

I wrote out another statement for Constable Homs yesterday, so this one will be just about what's happened since then.

My name is Kito Jons. My wife, Caya Jons, ran the kitchen at the Happy Hen in Asenbeth. I was the head of housekeeping, and assisted Caya in the kitchen. We've worked at the Happy Hen for almost five years, since the inn we ran in Concor had to shut down.

I had a bad feeling about Ludo, the innkeeper, and what he might do to the two kids, Fabi and Hasi. Ludo doesn't like to be shown up, and he doesn't like being relieved of money. It wouldn't be beyond him, I thought, to sneak into the boys' room during the night, and replace most of their coins with gravel or coal. He's done something like that at least twice before that I know about.

So I stationed myself on a chair outside their room, intending to keep watch, and to check on them a few times during the night. Unfortunately, I fell asleep.

The sound of a boy shouting for help startled me awake. I rushed into the room. A loud hissing and a strange rattling sound surrounded me. Looming over Fabi's shoulder (he's the older boy) was a giant snake, bigger than any snake ought to be. I shrank back. "Look out!" I screamed.

Fabi looked over his shoulder. The snake abruptly disappeared.

"Don't worry about the snake," Fabi said. "That was just me. I was scared."

"What's happened? Where's Hasi?" There was no sign of the younger boy, or of the innkeeper. The bag of coins lay spilled on the floor.

"That innkeeper tried to steal from us. Or maybe something worse. Hasi took him to his Special Place. I don't know what will happen when they come back." He looked at me. "The innkeeper has a knife," he added.

"What's the Special Place?" I asked.

Fabi shrugged. "It's hard to explain. It's kind of outside the normal world. You go there and it shows you things. Mostly things about yourself."

"That's what happened to Ludo when he disappeared before?"

Fabi nodded.

"But he'll be back? How soon?"

"I don't know. He's a bad man. The Special Place may have a lot to show him."

I wasn't sure what that all meant, but the situation was starting to sound a lot more dangerous than Ludo's usual petty thievery. I went to the door and yelled for Caya. "Send someone for the constable, or the sheriff," I said when my wife appeared.

"What's happened?" she asked.

"I don't know yet. But it's bad."

She nodded and ran off. I went back into Room 11 and sat down next to Fabi. "I'll wait with you, in case Ludo comes back before the law arrives."

"What will you do if he does?"

"Whatever I have to do to protect you boys. I have a knife, too."

Fabi shuddered. "I don't want anyone to die. My parents died a week ago. Please don't let anyone else die."

"It won't come to that," I said. I hoped that would be true.

"You work for the innkeeper. Why would you help me? Why do you work for him, if he does bad things?"

It's a question I often ask myself. "People have to earn a living if they want to eat," I told him. "This is the only inn in the area, and this is what I know how to do." The boy looked at me in silent judgment. "Sometimes we've been able to keep Ludo from going too far."

The boy nodded, but said nothing more.

Time passed. Hasi and Ludo did not appear.

Constable Homs and Sheriff Dupik arrived. Fabi told them what happened before I came in. Fabi had been awake, sure that something bad was going to happen. He made the illusion of the snake to protect himself and Hasi. He's new to that kind of magic, I gather, and it took a long time to do. So he was still awake when Ludo slipped past me and entered the room. Fabi shouted, the snake illusion moved as if to attack, and Ludo pulled out a knife. Hasi woke up and sang a magic word or something, and he and Ludo disappeared.

The Sheriff asked Fabi about the uncle he and Hasi were supposedly going to live with in Liramar. The boy hesitated over giving the uncle's name, and was unable to provide an address. Personally, I don't think there's any uncle waiting for them in Liramar. But that's none of my business.

Suddenly Fabi, who had been looking distracted, said, "They're coming." Then Hasi and Ludo reappeared, standing right over the pile of spilled coins.

Exhibit Thirteen: From Rutana's Spell Journal

Thaledu, 2 Celderem, 855

I have received my first assignment! I'll copy it in here to make sure I have it, and to weave it into the portal spell:

Proceed to Liramar, at the confluence of the rivers Tipel and Stolp in eastern Mâvarin, west of Kalimar. Two potential students, ten-year-old Fabi Stok and eight-year-old Hasi Goreg, are expected to arrive on Nishmudu, 7 Celderem, if they survive their present journey. The assignment is to evaluate both boys according to the standard school talent inventory, and make a preliminary determination about whether they qualify to proceed to Mâton as formal applicants. Initial information, as provided by Fabi, follows:

1. Fabi Stok was orphaned in Kinbeth, Somer County, just over a week ago when his parents were bitten by a rattlesnake. The father was an unregistered precog, formerly employed telling fortunes on a caravan. The mother was a singer, actress, and playwright, of no known magical talent. The boy, a precog, knew about their deaths in advance, and was briefly suspected of murder. He also claims to have the beginnings of a talent for illusion, and (like his mother) a nonmagical talent for music.

2. Hasi Goreg is also an orphan, details unknown. Information on his parents has not been provided. His music talent is magical in nature, and reportedly makes "things happen." Hasi supplements physical instruments with additional music from unseen sources. Fabi claims that Hasi also can transport himself and others out of the physical plane into what Hasi calls his "Special Place." Part of the assignment is to determine whether this is literally true, an illusion, or some kind of mind manipulation.

Portal spell definitions follow:

Destination: Blue Heron Inn, Liramar
Drawing provided by Durtani.
Target door: south side of stable, approximately six feet wide, vertical halved poles joined with iron bars, hinged on the left, painted green. Building a weathered brown. Four medium-sized, rectangular windows high on south wall, green shutters. Yard is dirt with dandelions and other scraggly weeds.
Source door: Mâton student stable. Has a pre-existing portal spell, currently linked to the beach at Eplimar.
Extras: portal invisibility, activation by myself only, using the Lopartin phrase "*Va kep.*"

I did it! Have established myself as a temporary resident of the Blue Heron. Funding by the College is enough to pay my way for two weeks if I'm careful. However, I have secured a week-long engagement to sing at the inn, once their current performers, twin Wanderers from Cedamas, move on. I may even earn enough money to set aside for later. I hope so. My new life outside the walls of the school begins now!

Exhibit Fourteen: Kito's Witness Statement-2

Statement: Kito Jons (continued)
Incident: Happy Hen Inn, Asenbeth
Date: Thaledu, 2 Celderem, 855

Ludo gibbered.

The innkeeper's head swung wildly back and forth as he shouted indistinctly. The only actual word I caught was "No!" His eyes were wide and wild, and his whole body was shaking. He arrived in the room bent over, face-to-face with little Hasi. The boy stood still, looking scared but saying nothing.

Ludo scrambled backward, slipped on the coins and crashed to the floor. His moment of manic energy seemed to fade away. He curled up on the floor, still surrounded by coppers and crowns, dropped the kitchen knife from his right hand, and wept.

We all stared at him for a moment. Then Hasi ran to Fabi, climbed onto the bed, and gave the older boy a desperate hug.

The Sheriff went over to Ludo and knelt beside him. "Ludo? Are you all right?"

"Stooping, stopping, stopped. No coin, no can, can't, cast, cast out. Bad, bad, bast, best. No more, no door. Done, done, doom." He looked up at the Sheriff. "Lock, key, locky, lock me, lucky. Body in the barn."

He sighed a long, slow breath, and fainted. Then his breathing stopped.

I'm sure the Constable and the Sheriff will have what happened after that in their reports. Fabi kept repeating that there was a body in the barn, so of course we had to go and look. He was right. We soon found the body of a recent rich guest, Ro Buner, buried in the dirt beneath the hay bin in the stable, right where Fabi told us to dig. Fabi can't have ever met Buner, a merchant from Färnet who has been dead for at least a month.

My wife returned with Sheriff Dupik while we were still standing over the body. Then Constable Homs went and got Cam Loren, our doctor and the local coroner. He said that despite appearances, Ludo died of natural causes. He also said that Buner's throat was slit.

I'm shocked about Ludo's death, and about the murder he seemed to confess to with his last breath. He was not honest, not kind. Even as an employer, he was barely tolerable. I find it hard to mourn him.

Ludo didn't have any known family, any will, any heirs. What will become of Caya and me now? What will happen to the inn? And what about the two boys, clearly too young to travel alone, and almost certainly responsible for Ludo's death? Are they to be sent on their way, to an uncle who probably doesn't exist? We're on our way to Penaver Manor in Wilmar to find out. This morning's events are well beyond the jurisdiction of Mayor Kurton, the Sheriff said. It will be up to Lord Penaver to decide what happens next.

Exhibit Fifteen: Asta Penaver's Diary 1

Penaver Manor, Wilmar
Moneldu, 4 Celderem, 855

Another dreary week without Disa has ended with the promise of a bit of diversion. The Sheriff of Tirza County has arrived for tomorrow's Pleadings with two young boys, along with a couple who worked at the Happy Hen in Asenbeth until the innkeeper's mysterious death two days ago. They say the boys are young, untrained magicians, and may be responsible for Ludo's demise. Nobody seems to be too upset that the man is gone.

I talked to Bana, the cook's apprentice, who overheard part of the Sheriff's conversation in the kitchen when they arrived this afternoon. The boys are orphans and musicians, as well as magicians. They are trying to get to Liramar, supposedly to stay with an uncle there, but nobody seems to believe that story. Father will have to decide whether to allow the boys to continue on, or send them to the local orphanage. The younger boy, Hasi, has already escaped from one orphanage, the Sheriff said, so I don't see much point in sending him to another one. It would be fun if they were to stay around here instead, but I doubt that Father would agree to that.

Meanwhile, the boys are to sing at dinner tonight. I've asked Joli to arrange for them to have a seat at my end of the table. Young as they are, they're still likely to be much more interesting than most of the visitors we get. Also, I'm curious about them. I hear they traveled by themselves for several days before getting in trouble at the Happy Hen. If two little boys can do that, maybe it's not so impossible that my sister - who would be fifteen now! - is still alive after all, traveling around the country, or maybe finding a new home far away, rather than just lying dead somewhere. I wish I could believe that - or even pretend to believe it.

Exhibit Sixteen: Hasi's Third Letter to Lusa (Penaver Manor)

Moneldu, 4 Celderem, 855

Hi, Lusa,

So much has happened since I last wrote to you. Guess where I am! Well, you don't have to guess, because it's on the envelope. I'm at Penaver Manor in Wilmar. It's huge - about ten buildings. The biggest one is large enough, maybe, for everyone I've ever met to live in it.

Fabi and I tried to get an innkeeper in Asenbeth to let us sing in return for dinner and a bed for the night, because we were out of money and food, and because we really do sing well together. Things went well at first, and it looked like we were even going to earn some money. But after we sang, the innkeeper pretended he never agreed to give us a meal and a room, and tried to keep our tip money for himself. I took him to the Special Place, hoping that the Infinite would show him how wrong he was to cheat us. After that a constable made him give us what he owed us. She was pretty nice, Constable Homs.

But the innkeeper, whose name was Ludo, came into our room during the night, with a knife in his hand. I took him back to the Special Place. We were there for a long time, and I saw some scary stuff. It was all about the innkeeper, and all the bad things he had done. He got so scared that he went mad, I think. When we got back to the normal world he just... died. I kind of feel like it's my fault, but really it was the Infinite, and what Ludo had done, that killed him.

A knife in the dark
Reaching out, then withdrawn,
A theft interrupted,
Life soon to be gone,
The Inf'nite condemns
A man lost in greed,
Desires justifying
His many misdeeds.
Confronted with truth,
Consumed by dark fears,
His last words tumble out
As he ends his dark years.

Fabi acted very strange after Ludo died, almost like he thought he WAS Ludo. He led us to the inn's stable, where the local sheriff found a body. So we're kind of in trouble about that, too, only not really, because they know the man died before we got there.

The people in Asenbeth didn't know what to do with us after that. Fabi told everyone that we are on our way to live with his uncle in Liramar, because he didn't think they would let us go to Mâton. Too many people don't like that place. But even the lie wasn't enough to make them let us go. Instead they brought us here so that Lord Penaver can decide what happens to us. If we don't get an answer that we like, we'll just escape again. This time we have some money, which should help a little.

We are going to sing at dinner tonight, and then go to court before Lord Penaver tomorrow. Fabi has a new song we were practicing on the way. It's much more cheerful than the one I wrote above. Maybe if Lord Penaver likes our performance enough, he'll let us do what we want.

Hasi

Exhibit Seventeen: Asta's Diary 2

Penaver Manor
Moneldu, 4 Celderem, 855

What a strange night it's been! It started at dinner, with the two boys, Fabi and Hasi. They both seemed a little scared, but funny and friendly. When they got up to sing, it was magic. I mean, really magic. They only had two instruments between them, but it sounded like much more than that. At one point, I could swear I heard four voices and about ten instruments at least, drums and horns and everything. Nobody but the boys was singing or playing, not that I could see. Some of the songs were funny, and some of them were sad.

But then they played *Sleepy Moon*. Disa's favorite song. It made me cry. It made my mother cry.

Fabi looked and sounded a little odd, I thought, for the last chorus of that song. I swear he was staring at me. His voice got a little lower. It almost sounded familiar, like... no, that's silly. But he was definitely acting strange.

After that they went back to their seats. Fabi was still staring at me. I asked him why.

"It's just that you look so much like the girl who was singing with us at the end of *Sleepy Moon*. Same curly red hair. Is she your sister? Did you see where she went?"

Before I could react, Hasi said, "What girl? There was nobody else singing with us."

"Yes, there was."

"No, there wasn't. I was listening. All four of the voices were ours."

"Where was this girl you say you saw?" I asked Fabi.

The boy looked confused. "She was standing right next to your chair. Didn't you see her?"

"How old was she?"

"About your age. Maybe twelve or thirteen."

"You really saw her? You're not lying or telling a story?"

Fabi shook his head. "No, I'm not. Who is she?"

"My sister, Disa. I'm pretty sure she's dead."

"But I saw her. She looked sad."

"Nobody else saw her, Fabi," Hasi said. "Maybe she was a spirit."

"Why would I see a spirit, if nobody else did?" Fabi was trembling a little.

"I know how we can find out," Hasi said.

"How?" I asked.

The two boys exchanged glances.

"Not now," Fabi said. "We're in enough trouble already."

By this time a selmûn Wanderer had gotten up to sing *The Ballad of Shandi's Ride*. People sitting near us were glaring at us for talking as the performance began.

"Meet us later," Hasi whispered. "We're in the Annex with the other Pleadants. Room Seven."

Fabi shook his head. "Not tonight," he whispered. "Tomorrow, after our court case."

Hasi looked surprised. Then he nodded.

"Tomorrow, then," I whispered.

Exhibit Eighteen: Register of Pleadings: Morning Session (Penaver Manor, Wilmar)

Register of Pleadings for Comerdu, 5 Celderem, 855
The Honorable Nori Penaver, Lord of Wilmar, Presiding Magistrate
Case 2094-7: The Innkeeper and the Boy Magicians

The Question: should Fabi Stok and Hasi Goreg be allowed to proceed toward their announced destination in Liramar, or placed in adult custody elsewhere? Further, are they responsible for the death of innkeeper Ludo Cader?

Description: On Thaledu, 2 Celderem, Ludo Cader, age 47, Innkeeper of the Happy Hen in Asenbeth, Tirza County, reportedly attempted to dishonor a verbal contract to provide Fabi Stok, age 10, and Hasi Goreg, age 8, a night's room and board in exchange for a musical performance. Cader also attempted to confiscate the cash tips the boys had earned. Constable Mika Homs ordered Cader to honor the arrangement, citing the innkeeper's probationary status for a past offense.

Toward morning, Cader entered the boy's room, knife in hand, and was confronted with the illusion of a giant snake. Moments later, Goreg and Cader disappeared from the room. When they reappeared, Cader evinced extreme agitation, followed by sudden death.

Stok and Goreg claim to be orphans, en route to stay with an uncle, Arti Marnes, in Liramar. They have each demonstrated magical abilities, and have recently been traveling without any form of adult supervision.

Testimony:

SHERIFF DUPIK: Thank you, my Lord Penaver, for seeing us today. May I present Fabi Stok and Hasi Goreg. They were involved in an incident at the Happy Hen two days ago, and I would appreciate your advice in the matter.

LORD PENAVER: Very well. Fabi and Hasi, I like to get to know my pleadants a little before hearing their cases. Please step forward, and tell me your age, where you're from, and why you are here today. Tell the truth now, because if you don't, I will know.

FABI STOK: My lord, I am ten years old, and I'm from Kinbeth. I left there almost two weeks ago after my parents died.

LORD PENAVER: I'm very sorry to hear that. How did they die?

STOK: They were bitten by a snake. I have an Uncle Arti who is willing to take me in, but Hasi and I have had difficulty in our travels.

LORD PENAVER: I think you are choosing your words in a way that hovers on the frontier of falsehood. Would you care to try again?

STOK: No, my lord.

LORD PENAVER. I see. Hasi, can you do better?

HASI GOREG. My lord, I am eight years old. I'm also an orphan. My sister was adopted recently, but I wasn't. I ran away from the orphanage in Skû because the man in charge kept trying to stop me singing. I know there's a better place for me. Also, I was lonely.

LORD PENAVER: How did you come to be traveling with Fabi?

GOREG: He found me in a haystack.

LORD PENAVER: And where are you going, really?

STOK: Liramar.

GOREG: Liramar, and then Mâton.

LORD PENAVER: I see. What makes you think the Citadel will take you, especially at your age?

STOK: They'll take us. I've seen it. Unless we get killed along the way.

LORD PENAVER: Fabi, I'm talking to Hasi right now. Hasi, why do you want to go to Mâton?

GOREG: My music is magic, and it's not my only talent. I need to go where I will be understood, and where I can learn to use my gifts properly.

LORD PENAVER: And you, Fabi? You are also looking for magical training?

STOK: Yes, my lord. I really do have an Uncle Arti, but he wanted me to work in his cotton fields.

LORD PENAVER: All right, that will do for the present. Sheriff Dupik, please tell us what happened at the Happy Hen.

DUPIK: My lord, the next case on your calendar is related to this one, so I will confine my present remarks to Fabi and Hasi's situation. Two days ago, they approached the staff at the Happy Hen, asking for food. Although they had no money, they offered to play and sing music for the inn's patrons in return for dinner and a room for the night.

PENAVER: Did the innkeeper agree to this?

DUPIK: My constable tells me that Ludo agreed to have the boys perform, but she was unable to establish that Ludo explicitly promised the payment.

PENAVER: I take it that the boys sang anyway?

DUPIK: They sang and played for over an hour. They were well received, and showered with tips.

PENAVER: Then what happened?

DUPIK: The innkeeper, Ludo Cader, said that he had not agreed to provide any room, that the single slice of bread the boys shared before singing was their meal, and that nearly all of their tips belonged to the house. Constable Homs obtained a proper dinner and bed for the boys, and half of the tip money, by pointing out that Ludo was on probation from his prior appearance in your court.

PENAVER: Ah, yes, the unpaid provisions. If Fabi and Hasi were properly remunerated, then why are we here? Is it because of their status as unaccompanied orphans?

DUPIK: Partly. There's also the matter of what happened that night.

PENAVER: What happened?

DUPIK: Ludo entered the boys' room during the night, armed with a knife.

PENAVER: Why? To steal? To kill? Or for some other reason?

GOREG: To kill us.

DUPIK: We don't really know. But Fabi was waiting for him.

PENAVER: What does that mean? Fabi?

STOK: I had a vision of the innkeeper coming in to attack us. So I waited for him, and tried to make an illusion to scare him away.

PENAVER: What kind of illusion?

STOK: A giant snake.

PENAVER: Of course. Did it work?

STOK: Well, sort of. He yelled, and that woke Hasi. So Hasi took the innkeeper to his Special Place.

PENAVER: Ludo's Special Place?

GOREG: No, mine. That's my other magical talent. It's hard to explain.

PENAVER: Try.

GOREG: It's a place outside the normal world. It shows people things.

PENAVER: What kind of things?

GOREG: Things about themselves. I figured that it would show Ludo how cruel and dishonest he was. Maybe it would help to make him nicer. Although it didn't the first time.

PENAVER: The first time?

GOREG: The day before, when he tried to cheat us. But the Infinite didn't keep him long that time. The second time, the Special Place showed us many bad things, for a very long time. I was scared, but not as scared as Ludo was. He thought that every evil thing he had ever done was happening to him. Every beating, every theft, even two murders. It broke him.

STOK: When they came back to the real world, Ludo said things that didn't make any sense. Then he mentioned a body, buried in his stable. Then he just... died. And I saw where the body was.

PENAVER: Another vision?

STOK: I guess so.

PENAVER: Did either of you physically attack Ludo, or harm him in any way?

STOK: No, my Lord.

GOREG: I didn't. The Infinite did. But it's partly my fault, I guess.

PENAVER: And was there a body?

DUPIK: Yes. A rich guest, by all accounts. He had been in the ground beneath the hay at least a month.

PENAVER: Did either of you boys know the man who was buried in the stable?

GOREG: No, sir.

STOK: No, my lord.

PENAVER: Have you anything to add before I render judgement?

STOK: My lord, I know I fudged a little about where we're going, and I'm sorry. I just didn't want people to stop us from going to a place that a lot of people don't like very much. But it's where we belong, because of our magic and because we don't have anyone left at home to help us. I already wrote to Archmage Marnestri, and he's sent a woman to Liramar to meet us.

GOREG: He has?

STOK: I saw it this morning.

PENAVER: Thank you all for your testimony. I will render my verdict after lunch. I believe my daughter is looking forward to speaking with you again.

Exhibit Nineteen: Asta's Diary 3

Penaver Manor, Wilmar
Comerdu, 5 Celderem, 855

I wanted Fabi to tell me more about the girl he thought he saw, and why we couldn't meet until tomorrow. But at that moment,

Sheriff Dupik called the boys away, perhaps thinking that they were pestering me too much, or that their talking during someone else's performance might reflect badly on him as their chaperon. Or maybe he just wanted to send the boys to bed, it being about ten o'clock at night. They are quite young, after all, and likely exhausted after the day's travel.

Being considerably less exhausted myself, I spent the rest of the evening in fevered speculation. Could Fabi really have seen Disa? If he saw anyone at all, it had to be her. We have no family legends of old hauntings, no other known murders or unsolved disappearances from this place. Our staff, visitors, and petitioners, at present, include no illusionists, mind mages or necromancers, unless Hasi or Fabi fits one of these categories. And we have no past or present staff or visitors who look like me. Nobody I know looks like me, or ever has, except for my sister. Even my mother has brown hair, not red. My father and uncle have red hair, but they don't look like teenage girls!

I was up most of the night, fretting about all this, and was one of the first people to arrive at court for Pleadings this morning. I suffered through six incredibly boring disputes between farmers and townspeople before Sheriff Dupik brought Fabi and Hasi before my father, along with a middle-aged couple that works at the Happy Hen Inn. That's where Fabi and Hasi got in trouble with a cruel and greedy innkeeper, who then mysteriously died.

The story the boys told in court was a little upsetting. The innkeeper's death was at least partly Hasi's fault. Hasi told my father about this thing he can do, to send people out of the real world to a magical place where they find things out about themselves. Learning the truth about himself and his life is what killed the innkeeper. But I kept thinking how much I want to learn the truth about my sister. Could Hasi's Special Place show me what happened to Disa? And would the truth kill me too, the way it killed that innkeeper?

I have to know.

Father just called a recess for lunch. Perhaps if I hurry, I can sit near the two boys again, and at least make a start on asking my questions. If not, and assuming that Fabi and Hasi get a favorable verdict, I'll find a way to talk to them after they're done in court.

Exhibit Twenty: Register Of Pleadings: Afternoon Session (Penaver Manor, Wilmar)

Register of Pleadings for Comerdu, 5 Celderem, 855
The Honorable Nori Penaver, Lord of Wilmar, Presiding Magistrate
Case 2094-7: The Innkeeper and the Boy Magicians

The Question: Should Fabi Stok and Hasi Goreg be allowed to proceed toward their announced destination in Liramar, or placed in adult custody elsewhere? Further, are they responsible for the death of innkeeper Ludo Cader?

The Verdict: Although Hasi Goreg certainly precipitated Ludo Cader's death, neither he nor Fabi Stok is directly responsible for it. One might even call it justice, brought on largely by Cader's own actions. Stok and Goreg should not be punished in connection with the incident. However, the two boys are too young to continue to travel without adult supervision. Lady Sida Penaver has volunteered to accompany them by coach to Liramar, where she will meet with the representative from Mâton, if present, and take appropriate action.

Exhibit Twenty-One: Asta's Diary 4

Penaver Manor, Wilmar
Comerdu, 5 Celderem, 855

I didn't get to sit with Fabi and Hasi at lunch. Mother asked them to sit by her instead. That happens, sometimes, when she's interested in someone's case. I watched her and my Uncle Sori ask the boys a lot of questions, most of which I couldn't hear from where I was sitting. By the time the Sheriff collected them for the afternoon court session, Fabi looked to be on the edge of tears. Hasi gave me a small smile as he walked away.

Then, back in court, Father announced that my mother had volunteered to take Fabi and Hasi in the family coach to Liramar, where a representative of Mâton is supposedly waiting to meet them. They will leave in the morning. I am determined to talk to them privately before that, and find out whatever I can. To finally know what happened to Disa, I would dare just about anything at this point.

Exhibit Twenty-Two: Register of Pleadings: Afternoon Session (Penaver Manor, Wilmar)

Register of Pleadings for Comerdu, 5 Celderem, 855
The Honorable Nori Penaver, Lord of Wilmar, Presiding Magistrate
Case 2094-8: The Fate of the Happy Hen

The Question: Who is to take possession of the Happy Hen Inn after the death of its owner, Ludo Cader?

Description: Per Case 2094-7 above, innkeeper Ludo Cader died on Thaledu, 2 Celderem, 855, leaving behind no known will, no surviving relatives, and no clear heir to his property and business, the Happy Hen. His head cook and head of housekeeping, Caya and Kito Jons, were Cader's longest-serving employees, with ten years of prior experience in the field of hospitality. Sheriff Dupik vouches for their competence and basic decency.

[Testimony omitted.]

Analysis: No known heir exists to take over the inn on the basis of kinship, debt or bequest. Of all possible candidates (such as they are), Caya and Kito Jons are the most deserving of benefit from the estate, having been largely responsible for the inn's success. In addition, the continued existence of the Happy Hen is in the public interest, being the only inn still open within twenty miles of Asenbeth.

Verdict: I hereby grant full title and entailments of the Happy Hen to Caya and Kito Jons, on the condition that the inn remain in business for not less than five years from this date, and provided that no heretofore unknown relative of Ludo Cader can establish a claim on the estate during that same period.

Signed,
Nori Penaver, Lord of Wilmar
Recorded by Dabo Renal, Clerk of Court

Exhibit Twenty-Three: Hasi's Fourth Letter to Lusa

Penaver Manor, Wilmar
Sabedu, 6 Celderem, 855

Dear Lusa,

They're letting us go to Mâton! Well, not yet, but they're letting us meet whoever is waiting for us in Liramar. Lady Penaver is taking us there by coach in the morning.

I'm in a hurry to leave this place. Fabi saw a ghost at dinner yesterday, who turned out to be Lord and Lady Penaver's older daughter, Disa. Their other daughter, Asta, wants to visit the Special Place tonight to try to talk to Disa. Fabi and I are supposed to meet her after dinner.

But I'm worried about Fabi. Strange things happen to him when he's around dead people. I think they get inside him, and say things. Fabi doesn't seem to know who he is or what is happening at times like that. It's like they're looking through him, within him and without him, and he's almost not there at all. This business with Disa seems to have upset him even more than the innkeeper's death. I think he knows more about it than he's telling me. I offered to meet with Asta alone, but he insists on coming with me. He says it's important for Asta and her family to find out the truth, and that it will take both of us to accomplish this.

I just hope that after tonight we're both done with death for a while. Fabi will probably be okay if the dead will just leave him alone.

Hasi

Exhibit Twenty-Four: Asta's Diary 5

Penaver Manor, Wilmar
Sabedu, 6 Celderem, 855

I know the truth now, and it's worse than I thought it could be. Hasi and Fabi agreed to meet me in the Annex after dinner. When

I got there, they were already packed for their trip in the morning, not that they had much to put in their pitiful little backpacks. Hasi was worried that Sheriff Dupik would notice if they weren't in their room, and urged Fabi to wait there while he took me to what Hasi calls his Special Place. But Fabi insisted on coming along.

The next moment, I was in a dark cellar. Water dripped down cracked bricks and pooled on a floor of worn, mud-encrusted stone.

"Where are we?" I asked. "This can't be your Special Place, can it?"

Hasi nodded. "It is for you. It looks different, depending on who is in here, and what the Infinite wants to show us."

"And the Infinite, whatever that is, wants to show me the west dungeon of Penaver Manor?"

"You recognize this place?" Fabi asked.

"Of course I do. Disa and I used to play down here, a very long time ago. But it's been bricked up for years."

"Who bricked it up?" Fabi asked.

"Uncle Sori had it done. He said something about shoring up the foundation, and the danger of these bricks collapsing from all the water damage."

"When was this?" Hasi asked. "Was it just after your sister disappeared?"

"No, not at all. It was at least a year before that."

"Well, there must be a reason we're seeing it," Hasi said. "Is there still a way in?"

I shook my head. "I don't think so."

"But there is," said two voices in unison.

I looked over at Fabi, but he wasn't the only one standing there. Disa stood looking at me sadly. She looked exactly like she did the last time I saw her, same age, same dress, same gold locket I gave her when I was eight years old, same ruby ring that our uncle gave her years ago. I could see right through her, though, like a ghost, which I suppose she was. And inside her was a solid, sad, frightened little boy. Fabi.

"I was afraid of this." Hasi said. "Fabi, come here."

Fabi didn't move.

The twinned voices of Fabi and Disa came again. "There is a secret entrance. I found it. I got in. But I didn't get out."

"Where is it?" I asked.

"I'll show you," Disa and Fabi said.

The Special Place abruptly dissolved around us. But Disa was still there.

Exhibit Twenty-Five: Rutana To Durtani

Blue Heron Inn, Liramar
Sabedu, 6 Celderem, 855

Magu Durtani,

The two boys should be here in two days. I have prepared the screening paperwork and magical tests, and have been accepted here as an itinerant musician. No one has found my portal; it is carefully hidden, and set to open only for me.

Meanwhile, a situation has arisen here, and I'm not sure whether to get involved. Duke Casam of Liramar is very ill, and a local mage, Misalo, is suspected of causing it. Should I investigate, or stay away? I have no idea whether Misalo is guilty, but if we can save a Duke's life somehow, or clear the name of a fellow mage, that is bound to improve our standing among the local populace. As it is, the normals here are highly suspicious of magic and magicians, more so than I ever experienced growing up.

Rutana

Exhibit Twenty-Six: Asta's Diary 7

Penaver Manor, Wilmar
Sabedu, 6 Celderem, 855

Disa led the way, Fabi stumbling along inside her as if unaware of his surroundings. Hasi and I followed. Hasi looked scared, so I took his hand, hoping he would find that comforting. He gripped my fingers tightly.

We had gone down two corridors, watched a locked door swing open when Hasi sang to it, and were about to go down the steps to the labyrinth of stone cellars when a man stepped out of a nearby room. "Where do you kids think you're going?"

It was Sheriff Dupik, and he was frowning.

"I'll take responsibility for them, Sheriff," I said. "Fabi thinks he knows where my sister is." He hadn't quite said this, but I was pretty sure that was where we were going.

Dupik looked at Fabi. "What's wrong with him? He looks like he's walking in his sleep."

Fabi turned his head at the Sheriff, but his vague, distracted face did not change. "Come with us, Sheriff," he said. I could still hear Disa's voice echoing his words - or directing them.

I hadn't wanted to involve an adult, yet, especially someone outside the family. But having him along might be useful. "Yes, please do, Sheriff Dupik," I said.

Dupik shook his head. "These boys need their sleep. They have a long day of travel tomorrow."

"Please, Sheriff," I said. "I need their help. This may be my only chance to find Disa."

He looked at me for a long moment, during which I wondered how much he knew about our family tragedy. Then he nodded. "Let's go."

Down and down we went. The air was damp and still. We lit magical torches that were stockpiled at the first landing of the rough-hewn stairs. We walked along twisting passages between flickering caverns marked by stalactites and stalagmites, over which my great-grandparents built the Manor many years ago. We passed many openings on the right or the left, some tiny or with visible dead ends, others large and clearly in use at one time, with brackets for torches and old crates of rotted wood stacked in natural alcoves. Fabi ignored some openings and led us into others, never hesitating.

"How does he know where to go?" Dupik asked.

"I have wandered these caverns for years," Fabi and Disa said. "The rooms above as well, but nobody ever saw me until now."

"Fabi's been here before?" the Sheriff asked.

"No. It's my sister," I told him. "Disa is speaking through him."

"How do you know?"

"I can see her," I said.

Dupik stared at Fabi again. Then he shook his head and said nothing more.

At last we reached what looked like a huge rockfall, penned in with a wall of grey bricks. "This is where the old dungeon was blocked up," I said. "Is there a way in?"

"There is," Fabi and Disa said. Fabi turned to the left, toward what appeared to be a solid wall of moss-covered limestone. Disa stepped forward, leaving Fabi swaying and blinking behind her. Dupik reached out and steadied the boy so that he didn't fall.

Disa pointed at a spot on the wall. She said something, but this time I couldn't hear her. I let go of Hasi's hand, stood beside my dead sister, and reached out. Hidden in the fold between two slimy green boulders, I found a pitch-dark crack in the wall.

"But Disa! We can't possibly get through there," I said. "It's too narrow."

Disa pointed again and nodded, emphatically.

"Is your body in there? Were you trapped?"

My sister nodded. She pointed at the wall to the left of the crack.

"She wants you to push on that," Fabi said. He seemed to be more aware of his surroundings now, but he still spoke slowly, as if in a daze.

I pushed. The wall moved, as if balanced on wheels or rollers. Now the opening was big enough for me to slip through, barely. I hesitated.

"Don't go in," said Sheriff Dupik.

"I need to know," I said.

"Of course you do. But not like this. You believe your sister's body is in there, correct?"

"Yes."

"She went in, but she didn't come out. Why?"

Disa's mouth moved, but I heard no words.

"I can't hear you," I said.

Disa turned, and took a step toward Fabi.

"No, don't!" Hasi yelled.

Disa looked surprised. She looked at Hasi.

"Fabi's been through enough," Hasi said. "Let's do this my way." He reached out his arms as if to enclose us all.

The next moment we were in the dungeon chamber again. This

time Sheriff Dupik stood with the rest of us, looking startled. He sought out Hasi. "What did you do? Is this…"

"My Special Place. Yes."

"But what we're seeing… is this the cavern where Asta's sister died?"

"Yes," said Disa.

Sheriff Dupik's shoulders twitched at the sound of Disa's voice. He turned abruptly to face her.

"The crack closed that day, and I couldn't get it open again," Disa explained. "Look. My bones are right over there."

A light from nowhere illuminated a curved alcove, about twenty feet in front of me. I didn't want to look.

I had to look.

Fabi nodded encouragingly at me. "It will be okay," he said.

We moved forward together as Disa hovered nearby.

Tangled strands of blond hair still hung from the dried and blackened skin enclosing Disa's skull, and poked out of the mildewed remains of her green dress. She had been seated against a cavern wall, but had slumped a bit in death. The bones of her left hand still wore her ruby ring, matched by what remained of her shoes.

She was surrounded by what looked, to my startled eyes, like a pile of treasure.

The vision of the Special Place dissolved. We were back in the real world. Fabi stared at the open crack in the wall, and squared his shoulders.

"I'm going in," he said.

"No, don't!" Hasi said.

But Fabi slipped between the boulders and was gone.

Exhibit Twenty-Seven: Letter from Durtani To Rutana

The Citadel, Mâto
Sabedu, 6 Celderen, 855

Adept Rutana:

I have checked with Archmage Marnestri and Magu Rinstarki. We are all agreed that you should proceed with caution with respect to the situation in Liramar. Misalo is a charms merchant with an assumed name and a somewhat difficult history. He also has a talent for necromancy that is often misunderstood by normals.

If you have the opportunity to learn what the specific problem is, either from local gossip or from Misalo himself, please communicate this information to Rinstarki or to me in person as well as by letter. Finding a note on my desk in the morning is less helpful than having the opportunity to question you directly, and I don't have time to follow you back to Liramar for a fuller explanation.

Above all, please do not visit the Duke's palace yourself. This could lead to a situation that reflects poorly on you as an inexperienced adept, and on us as your masters. Misalo has gotten in and out of trouble before. Let's not complicate the situation by getting you in trouble as well. Your mission is to evaluate and assist two boys, not to rescue a middle-aged healer with a penchant for being misunderstood.

Durtani

Exhibit Twenty-Eight: From the Diary of Lada Sida Penaver

Penaver Manor, Wilmar
Sabedu, 6 Celderem, 855

I never thought that finally learning what happened to my beloved elder daughter would be as destructive to my family as her disappearance was.

Asta is trying to be brave, but her obsession with her sister's ghost has become all-consuming. Nori is silent and angry, unable to use his usual good judgement in a case this close to home. Sori is making excuses, only to abandon each in turn.

What happened, as best I can piece together, is this:

Five years ago, a merchant named Renalo came before my husband's court, accused of selling dangerous, unlicensed magical items: cursed rings, enchanted scabbards and the like. My husband's brother, Sori, spoke out in court to defend Renalo, stating that Renalo's wares were exactly as represented, and that we should not fear to allow the sale of magic. "The way things are going," he said, "we may need to defend ourselves against the mages before too long. To do that, we must have magical weapons and protections of our own." Nori was unconvinced. He forbade Renalo to sell anything to our people, and banished him from Wilmar and Caro County.

That should have been the end of it, but it wasn't. Renalo didn't stay away from Wilmar or Caro County. His best customer was here. Sori was secretly buying magical swords and knives and arrows, saddles and tunics and jewelry, stockpiling them against the war he thought was coming. He blocked off a part of the West Dungeon beneath the manor, and hid his purchases there behind a secret entrance.

One day, Disa saw Sori and Renalo together in the marketplace, and innocently approached them. Renalo praised her intelligence and lively manner, and presented her with a ruby ring that he claimed Sori had just purchased for her. Disa loved it instantly. She often told me that she would never take it off, although she never quite remembered how she got it, other than that her Uncle Sori gave it to her.

"It was a ring of forgetting," Sori told us tonight. "And I... I let him give it to her. From then on, if she saw me do something I didn't want others to know about, I told her to forget it, and she did. It must have happened half a dozen times. She was always underfoot, that girl."

That was shocking enough, but the story got worse.

"How did Disa come to be trapped in the dungeon?" I asked.

Sori shook his head. "I can only guess." He was silent for a long moment. "You have to understand that after a while, Renalo wasn't just my connection to all things magical. He became my blackmailer. I was running low on funds, but he wouldn't let me stop buying. He threatened to expose me to Nori as a traitor, stockpiling illegal weapons that could be used against the people of Mâvarin, when really I wanted to use them to protect our people. In the end, I had to steal from the treasury, just to keep him quiet. I thought long and hard about finding something in all that stash of magic that could rid me of him, but there was nothing I could really use against him. That's when I realized what a fool I'd been.

"Finally one day I offered to give him back everything he had sold me, if only he would leave me alone. He laughed, saying that having me under his control was more valuable to him than a cellar full of magical trinkets. That's when I tore the protective necklace from his throat and pushed him down some stairs, knocking him out. I used his own cloak of levitation to drag him across the cellar, pushed him into the secret room, and blocked the exit."

"So you murdered a man," Nori said. "Sori, how could you?"

"I did it to protect the family!" Sori said. "I had no choice. Surely you see that."

"I'm not sure he did murder Renalo," Sheriff Dupik said. "The only bones we saw were Disa's."

"Why won't you tell us about Disa, Sori?" I cried. "Did you murder her too?"

"Sida, no! Of course not!" Sori said. "I would never—"

"Disa found the room a week or two before you tried to trap that mage," said Fabi, the little boy who found Disa's bones. "She saw you open the room, and hid, and came back later to explore. She was small enough to fit through the crack. But then you closed it completely. She didn't call out because she didn't want to get in trouble. She thought she could open it again from the inside. But she couldn't."

"How do you know all this?" Sori asked.

"I… it's hard to explain. But I think… I think I kind of was Disa today," Fabi said. "I knew what she knew. And I said what she wanted to say." He rubbed his hands across his eyes. "It's happened to me a few times lately. I hate it."

"Tell me what happened this evening, Fabi," Nori said.

"I saw Disa at dinner last night, but I didn't know at first that she was dead," Fabi said. "When I mentioned her to Asta, that's when I found out the truth. Since then, Asta has been asking us to help her find out what happened to her sister."

Hasi picked up the story. "So I took her to my Special Place - you know about that, right? And Disa was there, but—"

"—But that's when I kind of stopped thinking for myself. I said what Disa said, and did what she did." Fabi shuddered. "I don't think… I don't think this is the first time that's happened to me."

"No, it isn't," Hasi said.

"Disa led us down to where her body is, what's left of it," Fabi said. "When I walked into the hidden room and saw her bones, I finally started to feel like myself again. Then Disa told me about following her uncle and getting trapped. She also told me about the man who sold magic stuff. She was a ghost by the time Renalo woke up in the dungeon. But he spoke to her. He seemed very sad about her, and even apologized about the ring."

"What happened to him?" Nori asked.

"He left. One of the magic items stored down there was a charm to open any door. If Disa had known about it, she could have gotten out. But she didn't until it was too late."

"What else did Disa tell you?" Asta asked.

"She thanked me for letting her in, for helping her tell her story. She said to thank Hasi, too. She said she's sorry that she worried you, sorry she made this terrible mistake that got her killed. And she said her Uncle Sori is a liar."

Sori looked like he wanted to reach out and strangle the little boy. "You call me a liar, while telling a wild story yourself," he said. "How do we know any of this is true?"

"I saw Disa," Asta said. "I heard her voice. It's all true, I know it."

"With respect, Asta," Sheriff Dupik said, "the boy is a known illusionist."

"I could never fake this, even if I wanted to," Fabi said. "It would take more skill than I have, and I didn't even know what Disa looked and sounded like until we all saw her."

"Where is Disa now?" I asked.

Fabi closed his eyes. In a moment, something like a cloud formed around him. A cloud with my daughter's face. Then I heard my elder daughter's voice, for the first time in two years, echoed by the voice of the boy who stood passively inside her.

"I'm here," Disa said. "I've come to say goodbye."

Exhibit Twenty-Nine: Rutana Investigates

Blue Heron Inn, Laramar

Sabedu, 6 Celderem, 855
Magu Durtani,

Per your instructions, I have been speaking to the locals here, trying to find out what people think the charms merchant Misalo did to the Duke, and where the case currently stands.

It appears there has been no arrest yet, largely because Misalo has been in hiding for the past week. A teenage girl named Sena Mader is keeping his booth open. She may be a normal (or passes for one), but seems to know the merchandise well: small charms and talismans in the form of jewelry, all enchanted for common, benign uses. Unless Misalo has something more dangerous stashed away, it's hard to imagine anything he might sell that would threaten the Duke's life.

Other vendors have a mixed opinion of Misalo. Some say that aside from his one employee, he mostly keeps to himself, refusing to be drawn into any sort of personal conversation. A few, however, particularly his closest neighbors on Market Row, tell me of times when Misalo has gone out of his way to help customers with large troubles and little coin, particularly if the customer is young and pretty (male or female). No one reports ever seeing him sell any type of weapon or curse, although it's possible he could have done so unobserved.

Over at the inn, I used my music to encourage people to speak a little more freely to me after my performance than they might have done otherwise. Everyone knew that Duke Casam got very ill quite suddenly last month, after his daughter gave him some kind of magical gift for his birthday. Stories vary wildly on the details. The Duke is in a deathly sleep, or awake but unable to move, or thrashing around, unable to lie still, singing, drooling, snoring, or struggling for breath. His daughter brought him a cursed ring, or a poisoned dagger, or a protective necklace, or a special soap meant to wash away unwanted anger. She wants him dead, or is trying to save him. And so on. What is certain is that the Duke has not appeared in public since the 17th of Nefilem. It's also known that the daughter, Lady Tena, was seen berating Misalo in the marketplace, two days before the Duke's birthday. The rest is speculation.

I await your further orders. The children are due to arrive here tomorrow. Should I halt my investigation, complete the screening process with Fabi and Hasi, and come home as soon as possible? Or is there more I should be doing while I'm here? And one more, urgent question. In the unlikely event that one or both of these boys is not a suitable candidate for enrollment at the Citadel College, should I turn them over to local authorities, bring them to Mâton to live with the normals on the Eastern Shore, or leave them to their own devices?

Exhibit Thirty: Lady Sida's diary, continued

Penaver Manor, Wilmar
Sabedu, 6 Celderem, 855

"Disa, no!" Asta cried out. "You can't go. I only just got you back!"

A small smile appeared on Disa's ghostly face. "You don't have me, Asta," she said. "I'm sorry, but you don't. I'm dead, and I need to move on. I'm only here because I want you all to know what happened."

"Please, Disa," Asta sobbed. "I miss you so much. If Fabi stays here, maybe we can—"

"No, Asta. That's not fair to Fabi, or to me. Please, just listen. I think Uncle Sori knew I was in that secret room when he closed up the entrance. Why else would he have done it? I had left the wall open just a crack, just as I'd found it, in the dark where no one would notice it was there at all. Why would Uncle Sori come along and just close it up for no reason?"

"Maybe to keep the likes of you out! Did you ever think of that?" Sori said. "You always were a nosy little troublemaker."

"That's enough, Sori," my husband said. "Disa, do you know that your uncle trapped you deliberately, or do you just suspect it?"

Disa shrugged. Inside her, Fabi shrugged. "I don't know for sure. Maybe you should have a trial, Father. But I'm not going to wait to testify. I'm done. Mother, Father, I'm very sorry for everything I've done wrong. Sorry that I worried you all this time. I've seen you crying at night, seen the care Mother takes to keep my room neat and dusted, as if I might need it again someday. I don't. But I love you for it."

"Oh, my darling!" I said. "If only there was something I could do to help you. We hired someone to find you, but he never found anything. If I could bring you back to life, I would."

"You can't," Disa said, "and you shouldn't. Don't worry about me, any of you. I'm off to the Afterworld." She and Fabi lifted their heads, as if to look at the ceiling, or someplace beyond it. "I can see it from here, as I couldn't before today. Asta, you were a wonderful little sister. Please, don't let my death ruin you. Father, you are the wisest person I know, except about your brother. I was proud to be your daughter. Mother, you are the kindest person I know. Please give all my things away to people who need them. And be gentle with my poor sister while she recovers from all this. I love you all very much. Goodbye."

The ghostly mist around Fabi faded away. I knew my daughter was gone. But maybe someday I'll see her again, in the Afterworld.

Exhibit Thirty-One: Letter from Rinstarki to Rutana

The Citadel
Nishmudu, 7 Celderem, 855

Adept Rutana -

It is my understanding that Durtani has advised you to concentrate on your original assignment with the two boys, and proceed no further with your "investigation," as you call it, into the matter between Misalo and Duke Casam. More specifically, he has forbidden you to approach the Duke's palace, and get further involved in that way. Officially, I must agree.

Unofficially, I have great sympathy with your situation. I know how much you hate to stay on the sidelines, and let a dangerous situation play out when you think you might be able to help stop it. It's also true that as a musician, you may be able to get an invitation to perform before the Duke, use your magic to calm the situation, and even learn what the actual problem is. In his zeal to protect Mâton from negative interactions with the normals, Durtani does not fully appreciate the skills you can apply to the situation, and potential for a positive result.

So please do not visit Vartet Palace, play your music before the Duke, find out what's killing him, save his life, and clear Misalo's name. Good luck.

Rinstarki

Exhibit Thirty-Two: Citadel College Application Letter

The Citadel College of Magic, Mâton
Nishmudu, 7 Celderem, 855

Congratulations! By virtue of your talent(s), you have been nominated to attend the Citadel College of Magic on Mâton. To be admitted as a student, each of our candidates must complete a three-stage screening process: a written talent inventory, an in-person assessment, if warranted, and a final screening on site by the College's senior faculty.

If you wish to pursue this opportunity, please fill out the enclosed application and inventory. Be sure to describe as accurately as possible any acts of magic or suspected magic you have performed or experienced. Do note any areas of ambiguity, but do not take credit for any talents for which you have shown no aptitude so far. Magical talents are highly individual, and no magician is capable of magic in every discipline. Good luck!

Exhibit Thirty-Three: Letter from Rutana to Rinstarki

BlueHeron Inn, Liramar
Date: Nishmudu, 7 Celderem, 855

Magu Rinstarki,

The two boys have arrived, along with Lady Sida Penaver of nearby Wilmar as chaperone. Hasi and Fabi were involved with the death of an innkeeper in Asenbeth, and it fell to Lord Penaver to judge whether they killed him. I will have to get the full story from Lady Penaver before recommending either of the boys as students.

Fabi lied to Lord Penaver that he was meeting an uncle here, rather than a representative from the Citadel College. Consequently, they are not off to a good start with me. Lady Sida seems quite fond of both Fabi and Hasi, however, so perhaps there is more good in them than I've seen so far.

Lady Sida insisted on staying to observe as I conducted the initial screening. Young as they are, neither boy had any trouble filling out their questionnaires, which I will look over in depth tonight. In the oral interviews, we quickly came to focus on the same four talents that Fabi mentioned in his letter to Archmage Marnestri. Fabi is a nascent illusionist, and was able to produce an apple from thin air after about ten minutes of effort. He failed to demonstrate his other talent, divination, on demand, but claims that he knew about his parents' impending death a week ahead of time. Lady Sida tells me that Fabi also knew where her missing daughter's body could be found. There is a strong indication that Fabi has a talent for necromancy, but Hasi and Fabi were both quite upset when I mentioned the possibility.

Hasi has a definite musical talent, which is very different from mine. It borders on illusion, and possibly telekinesis. When he plays an instrument or sings, additional unseen voices or instruments can be heard. He does not appear to have control over the specific manifestation yet. He can also use music to unlock a door. The music itself does not have an overt emotional effect, beyond what normals can achieve with any good song. In fact, I find his music rather annoying.

His only other ability is so far outside my experience and training that I'm not certain it can be counted as a recognized talent. At my request, he took me to what he calls his Special Place. The world around me disappeared, and I saw instead a doorway overlooking a beach. I could tell in an instant that the door was not a real one, much less the beach. Nothing was solid to the touch, and the whole place had a dreamlike quality. Moments later, we were back in the real world.

I suppose he could be an illusionist or dreamsender, but the specific form of it is problematic, and probably useless. Hasi insists that it's the Infinite showing the subject something that he or she needs to know. I personally don't believe in the Infinite, and the phenomenon seems to be some sort of illusion with religious overtones. In any case, it may be dangerous. What the innkeeper in Asenbeth saw in Hasi's Special Place seems to have killed him. I'm not convinced that this odd talent is what Hasi thinks it is, that it's worth developing, or that anyone at the Citadel is equipped to train Hasi in its use.

I upset both boys quite a bit when I gave them my initial findings.

"What do you think, Maga Rutana?" Hasi said when we were back from the vision, or whatever it was, of the door and the beach. "Do we get in?"

"Of course we get in," Fabi said. "I've seen it."

I hated to crush little Hasi's hopes, but I had to be honest.

"I have little doubt that you will be admitted as a student, Fabi. I'm not so sure about Hasi."

"Why? Because I'm so young?"

"You're certainly young, Hasi, but that's not why. They tell me the youngest the school ever enrolled was only six years old. But your talents are problematic."

Lady Sida frowned. "What do you mean by that?" she asked.

"I'm just not sure the Citadel College is the right place for Hasi," I said. "He could study music anywhere. Even people with no magical talent can string words together to go with a winning melody, and learn to perform the result."

"Not all of them," Hasi said.

"No, not all of them. Not remotely. But the fact remains that basic musical skills can be taught by any number of musicians. You don't need Mâton to teach you that."

"Can they teach me this?" Hasi hummed a few notes, which were echoed by an invisible flute.

"Normals couldn't. Neither could I, to be honest. But you see, you already know how to do that."

"What about my other talent?"

"That's a worse problem. Mâton has a music master and music students, an illusion master, a divination master, an animation master, a mind master and so on. But there is no one, as far as I know, who can pluck someone from the real world and send them someplace that probably doesn't exist. Not on Mâton, not anywhere else. How can the masters teach you something that no one has ever done before?"

Hasi started to cry.

Fabi patted his shoulder. "Don't worry, Hasi. Marnestri will take you. I've seen it."

"With respect, Fabi, your divination talent is not yet proven. Your belief that your parents were going to die could just have been a bad dream."

"What I saw Fabi do at Penaver Manor was no dream," Lady Sida said.

"It may not have been divination, either," I said. "It's more likely that Fabi is sensitive to the spirits of the dead."

"Why me?" Fabi said. "I... it doesn't... you don't know what it's like! It's almost like I don't exist when a spirit gets... when it does what it does. Can the Citadel teach me to stop it happening?"

"Generally, we teach people to use their talents, not suppress them," I said. "But we'll see."

"Fabi has been through a lot in a short time, and done my family a great service along the way," Lady Sida said. "So has Hasi. I hope this is not your final decision."

"It's not," I told her. I decided to bring up an idea that had been distracting me for the last hour. "I have a proposal. There is a situation here in Liramar that I've been trying to look into on my own. Perhaps Fabi and Hasi could assist in my investigation. That way, I can get a better idea of their talents in real-world conditions."

"What kind of investigation?" Lady Sida said.

"Is this about the Duke?" Fabi asked.

Perhaps Fabi had divination talent after all. "Why do you say that?"

"I saw him in a vision when we rode in the coach today. Duke Casam is dying, but I think we can save him."

"How?" Hasi said.

"I'm not sure yet. But we need to go to his Palace tomorrow, all four of us. It will take all of us, plus one other person, to save the Duke's life."

"Are you sure about this?" Lady Sida said. "Duke Casam is my cousin. I hadn't even heard he was sick."

"The Palace people have been trying to keep the Duke's illness a secret," I explained. "But there are rumors about it, all over the city. A local charms dealer is suspected of trying to murder Duke Casam."

"He didn't," Fabi said. "He's the other person who will help us save the Duke."

"If you can find him," I said. "Misalo is in hiding."

Fabi frowned. "Misalo? That's not his name."

"What do you have in mind for us to do, Maga Rutana?" Lady Sida asked.

"Since the three of us all have musical talent, perhaps you can use your relationship with the Duke to recommend us as performers," I said. "Once we're in, we can use our respective talents to try to resolve the Duke's predicament."

"How? If Casam is ill and the Palace is trying to keep that fact quiet, I can't see the staff admitting three unknown musicians, two of them children."

"We'll think of something," I said. It was not my most persuasive moment, but Fabi nodded vigorously.

"We can do it," he said. "You'll see."

That's where things stand as of tonight. Tomorrow, our prospective students will have an opportunity to prove themselves worthy of tutelage. And, if Fabi is correct, we will save the Duke's life,

Rutana

Exhibit Thirty-Four: Letter from Lady Sida to Lord Penaver

Hog's Head Inn, Liramar
Nishmudu, 7 Celderen, 855

Dear Nori,

I will be remaining here in Liramar for a few days, partly to make sure the question of Fabi and Hasi's future is resolved, but also because Vartet Palace is in crisis. My cousin, Duke Chago Casam, is reputed to be very ill, possibly dying. Neither the Duke, his daughter, Lady Tena, nor any of their staff have made any sort of official statement, except for a notice posted weeks ago that Chago is in "perfect health." Since nobody outside the palace has seen him since then, rumors are rampant.

Aside from my duty to the Twelve Families, and to the stability of the region, I am being urged by both Fabi and the boys' contact from Mâton, a young adept named Rutana, to visit Vartet Palace tomorrow. Rutana wants me to introduce her and the boys as musicians, who hope to perform for the Duke and his household. The Palace staff is unlikely to welcome such visitors at a time when they are trying to conceal Casam's illness, but Rutana and Fabi both seem confident that they will be admitted if I vouch for them.

The trip over here was uneventful. Fabi was silent for hours at a time, saying only, "There's more trouble ahead," the nature of which he could not or would not disclose. Hasi tried to cheer Fabi up with silly songs, but eventually he gave up and went to sleep in the carriage. Fabi didn't sleep. He just sat there, rigid, wide-eyed and trembling. Several times, he suddenly shook himself, as if coming out of a trance or vision.

Upon our arrival, Fabi begged me not to return home right away, insisting that there was something he needed me to do first. I'm guessing that the Palace invitation is the main thing he wants from me. Right now, I'm more concerned with Fabi himself than with whatever he's seen, or what he thinks is going to happen. If staying with him for another day or two can help him to heal, then I feel I must do it.

As for Rutana, she's a young, inexperienced mage on her first assignment. Her musical talent enables her to affect people's emotions, which she claims to use only for benign purposes. Certainly, she was able to quickly calm Fabi's nervousness, and even get him to sing a little bit with her and Hasi. She doesn't seem to know much about children, however, and has taken a dislike to Hasi for some reason. I will monitor the situation, and let you know how it goes.

Please give Asta a big hug from me, and tell her I'll be home as soon as possible.

Exhibit Thirty-Five: Rutana's Report to Durtani

Vartet Palace, Liramar
Masheldu, 8 Celderem, 85

Magu Durtani,

I must report that I did come here to Vartet Palace, despite your instructions. But I didn't come alone. Lady Sida Penaver brought us to the Palace gate and introduced us (Fabi, Hasi and myself) as musicians, who hoped to perform before the Duke and his daughter. Lady Sida was known to the staff as a relative of the Duke, but I don't think they would have let us in had Fabi not tugged on the doorkeeper's sleeve.

"Please tell Lady Tena that we're more than just musicians," he said. "We're here to save her father's life."

The doorkeeper, or guard or whatever he was, stared down at Fabi. "What's your name, boy?"

"Fabi. Fabi Stok."

"First of all, Fabi Stok, I don't know what you're talking about. Second, we're not currently in need of a trio of entertainers, particularly a couple of little kids and their big sister."

"I'm not—" Rutana said.

"Third," the guard interrupted, "When Lady Tena wants musicians, she expects them to play music. Nothing else."

"We have more to offer than most musicians," I said.

One of the other guards leered at me. "I bet you have."

"Show them," Fabi said.

Lady Sida looked at Fabi, and then at me. "What did you say?" But Fabi was looking at Hasi.

"Now?" Hasi asked.

"Just a little," Fabi said.

Hasi came over and took my hand. "Don't be afraid," he said. "Just sing."

"What do you want me to sing?" I said.

"This." He sang the first phrase of a simple, familiar melody, one I knew from childhood. It was the same song, in fact, that led my parents to think there was magic in my music, back when I was Fabi's age.

I picked up the melody and sang it back to him. Fabi and Hasi sang around, over and under my notes, weaving a harmony unlike any I'd ever heard. It should have been a cappella, but Hasi's invisible flute joined in, along with the sound of an unseen harp. We stood in the entrance hall singing, while three guards and Lady Sida listened in wonder.

Then a woman about my age came down some stairs at the other end of the hall. Her pale yellow dress was made of the finest satin, trimmed with gold; her honey blond hair tied up in the latest style. But her eyes were rimmed with dark circles in a too-pale face. She looked down at us and frowned. "Sida!" she said. "What's happening? Why are there children singing in my front hall?"

"So that we can do this," Hasi sang, not missing a beat.

That's when the front hall disappeared. Or, rather, we did, I suppose. What we saw next was a dimly-lit bedroom, curtains drawn. A man with thinning blond hair lay in a tall wooden bed, swaddled in fur-lined coverlets and supported by innumerable green and brown cushions.

I was so startled that I stopped singing. Fabi and Hasi stopped a moment later, but the unseen instruments continued.

"Father!" Lady Tena cried.

For a moment, I wasn't sure whether the change of scenery was a manifestation of Hasi's strange talent, or a surprisingly detailed illusion of Fabi's, or whether our combined music had somehow transported us into the Duke's actual bedroom. In any case, we seemed to be in the presence of the real Duke Casam. "Who are you?" he whispered. His voice was weak and raspy.

"We're a couple of orphans, plus Maga Rutana," Fabi said. "We're here to help you, my lord Duke. Is that all right?"

Duke Casam's nod was barely perceptible. "Yes." He breathed out the word. "If you can."

"Then we'll be right back," Hasi said.

The room disappeared. We were back in the entrance hall. The guards, who had not been with us in the Duke's bedroom, shouted when they saw us. "Where did you go?" one guard asked.

"Treachery!" another guard said. "What did you do with Lady Tena?"

"I'm right here," Lady Tena replied calmly.

"You weren't a moment ago," the first guard said. That surprised me. If our seeing the Duke's bedroom was due to Hasi's talent, then it wasn't what I'd thought it was. A mere illusion or hallucination doesn't make the subject instantaneously and physically leave the room they're in.

"How do we know these people aren't working together with him?" the second guard said. He pointed toward the door.

Coming through it was a dark-haired man, perhaps thirty years old, dressed in a shabby green robe. His hands were tied together. Two guards were half-dragging the man in, even as he tried to walk through on his own. Incongruously, he carried an alto recorder, tucked under one arm.

"You!" Lady Sida said. The man looked back at her. His eyes widened. He seemed more alarmed at seeing Lady Sida than he was by his arrest.

Fabi held up one hand, as if to stop Lady Sida from saying anything more. "Please don't, Lady Sida," he said. "It will be okay." He turned to Lady Tena. "This man didn't hurt your father. I'm pretty sure he's trying to help."

"Why is there a recorder under your arm?" I asked.

"It's too hard to carry in my hand when my arms are tied," said the man. "Lady Tena, that ring I sold you isn't what's hurting the Duke. There's something else."

"Then why can't he get the ring off?"

"Because it's trying to protect him," Misalo said. "He'd probably already be dead otherwise. This recorder, which I just finished enchanting, should be able to help identify and destroy the real curse." He grimaced. "Unfortunately, I'm not very good at playing it."

"Why did you enchant an instrument you can't play?"

"A ghost told me to make it," he said.

"Oh, no, not again," Fabi moaned.

"She told me I would meet someone here who could use it to help save Duke Casam," Misalo said.

"That would be me," I said.

"Wait a moment!" Lady Tena said. "I don't know you people. Lady Sida aside, you're all magicians, and my father is suffering from a magical malady. How do I know you're not all here to finish killing him?"

"These two boys are good kids," Lady Sida told her. "I've only known them a few days, but they've done extraordinary things for my family. Let them help."

"And I'm already under arrest," Misalo said. "My life is in your hands, Lady Tena."

Lady Tena looked at each of us in turn, frowning. "All right," she said. "Let's go."

We all trooped up to the Duke's bedchamber. Guards still hung on to Misalo's arms, but I took charge of the recorder. I felt the magic in the wood.

A guard knocked at the door. From inside came faint words. "Come in." We obeyed. The air inside the bedroom was dank and chilly and still. It looked exactly the way I'd seen it in the vision, or whatever you choose to call it.

"Thank you for coming," the Duke whispered. "Are you all really here this time?"

"Yes, Your Grace," Fabi said. "We're going to sing to you now. When we're done, you'll be rid of the thing that's trying to kill you." Then Fabi looked at me. "Same song as before. Only you play it on that." He pointed at the recorder.

I raised it to my lips.

The music we had played in the entrance hall seemed ordinary in comparison to our performance in the Duke's bedroom. In moments, everyone in the room, including the Duke, was singing a heartbreakingly beautiful variation on the old nursery song. We were accompanied by half a dozen voices of people who weren't there, and as many unseen instruments: winds and strings and horn and the faint thump of a distant drum.

Then objects around the room began to glow with yellow fire, one by one: first the Duke's ring, and then a sword on the wall, and then a brass eagle on the mantle, and then a golden bowl on a table by the Duke's bed. As the bowl faded, a carved wooden box on the dresser began to radiate a very different light, a dull red that illuminated nothing.

The music of the recorder changed, becoming discordant and angry. One by one, every voice was silenced, until only Fabi and Hasi were singing. Magic coursed through me as a shaft of tiny lightning burst forth from the recorder. It struck the box, which burst into flame. With a final, triumphant trill, the recorder fell silent. So did the two boys. Hasi staggered, and would have fallen had Fabi not reached out to steady him.

The flames died down, leaving behind a pile of grey ash. The Duke sat up in bed.

"That box," he said, in a clear, strong voice, "was a gift from Lord Restan." He sighed. "I really thought he'd forgiven me." He looked around. "Thank you, all of you. How can I repay you?"

"A little reward would be nice," Hasi said. "We have tuition to pay, and not much money."

"Hasi!" Lady Sida said. "That's very rude of you."

"Well, we do, though. Don't we, Rutana?"

There was no denying that. Clearly, both Fabi and Hasi belong at the Citadel. "I can't promise that the Masters will understand you two, or even welcome you," I told Hasi. "But yes, I will recommend your admission as students."

"And you should let Misalo go," Fabi said. "He was only trying to help, making up for a mistake he made years ago."

Misalo looked at Fabi, and then at Lady Sida. "I didn't kill her. I swear it," he said. "But I do feel partly responsible."

Lady Sida stared at the charms merchant for a long moment. "I believe you," she said. "Just one question. Do you think it was an accident?"

Misalo shook his head. "I can't be sure, because I wasn't there. But no. I don't think so. I'm sorry."

Lady Sida nodded. "I forgive you," she said.

I'll have to get the whole story later.

I have some final arrangements to make here: three more nights of promised musical performances, supplementary information to gather, people to say goodbye to. I'll bring Fabi and Hasi through tomorrow morning, and return here without them.

I hope you will overlook my disobedience in this matter, in light of the positive result. See you soon!

Rutana

Exhibit Thirty-Six: Mâton Orientation Letter

The Citadel College of Magic, Mâton
From the Desk of Marnestri
Thaledu, 9 Celderem, 855

Welcome to the Citadel College of Magic. If you are new to the island, welcome to Mâton! You will probably find that life here is very different from your old life in Mâvarin or Färnet or Derio. Here on Mâton you will be surrounded by other people of talent, people who understand you better than your old friends, your old teachers, or even your parents unless they are mages themselves. We know how it feels to discover how different you are from the "normals" around you, with all the challenges that poses. We will help you to explore your abilities, learn to control and develop them fully, and reach your potential as a fully-robed mage.

By now you should have an assigned room, a roommate, an academic advisor, a student advisor, and your novice attire and supplies. Should you lack any of these, please check in with the admissions office on the first floor of the Citadel. Your student advisor will help you find your way around this first week, and learn the basics of college life. Your academic advisor will guide you through your entire educational program, from Introductory Magic to your Master exam, assuming you get that far.

If you have not yet completed a standard education in languages, science and mathematics, you will study these subjects as well. If you have not already completed your aptitude test, you can expect to undergo this in the next day or two, depending on the exigencies of scheduling. This is an interesting, usually painless process, and educational in itself. You may well discover additional talents beyond the ones that brought you to Mâton, months before they might otherwise have surfaced.

As with any school, there are rules to be followed. The first rule is to obey your academic Masters. There is a reason for every instruction they give you, which may not be immediately obvious. Their primary concern is to ensure both the efficacy of the magic and the safety of its practitioners.

There are three additional rules to be observed, for the safety of all:

1. No student is to attack any other resident of Mâton, except on the explicit instructions of myself or one of your academic Masters. Anyone caught disobeying this rule will immediately be expelled without recourse - or worse.

2. The cliffs above Sûtelmar Harbor are strictly off limits except for Zordano's Point, the clearly-marked scenic lookout with the invisible fence. Sûtelmar itself may only be approached using the road at the southern edge of campus, and only after your Robing, or with written permission from your academic advisor.

3. No permanent spell is to be cast, nor a permanency subritual applied, except under the direction and supervision of one of the Masters.

Your personal journey to life as a mage has already begun! We look forward to helping you travel that road in the months and years ahead.

Yours in fellowship,
Marnestri Cheneli, Forty-Second Archmage of Mâton

Exhibit Thirty-Seven: Hasi's Fifth Letter to Lusa

Citadel College of Magic, Mâton
Masheldu, 8 Celderem, 855

Dear Lusa,

We made it! With help from a newly-robed mage named Rutana, encouragement from Lady Sida Penaver, and financial aid from Duke Casam of Liramar, we've finally made it to the Citadel College of Magic on Mâton! I told you we could do it!

Rutana is the mage that the Citadel sent to Liramar to meet us, and to judge whether we have the talent to become students there. Fabi did okay, but she wasn't very impressed with me at first. She didn't understand about the Special Place, and didn't think the school would recognize it as a real talent, much less teach me about it. She wasn't even nice about the music. Really, I think she mostly just didn't like me.

But Rutana knew there was a problem with the Duke of Liramar. He was dying, and people thought he was being slowly murdered. Fabi and Rutana and I worked together to find out what was killing him, and to destroy it so he could get well. After that, Rutana liked us both better, and decided to recommend us as students after all.

Rutana was right, though. Archmage Marnestri didn't want to take me at first, but Fabi told him my talent would be important someday. They said that nobody has had my kind of talent in hundreds of years. They weren't even sure it was a real talent. I showed them it was. That surprised the Masters, when they saw my Secret Place themselves. Since then, everyone's been really nice to us.

I wanted to take a ship to Mâton, but we didn't get to do that. Rutana had a magic doorway between the Citadel and Liramar, so we just walked through it. Fabi and I will be sharing a room, just as we've been doing for the past two weeks.

I wish you could be here too. If your new family doesn't work out, try to get to Mâton. Now that they've accepted me, I know I'm going to love this place, and learn a lot.

Fabi is feeling better after all that contact with dead people. There was a man we met in Liramar who can do what Fabi does, when spirits of the dead are around. When he heard about all that Fabi has gone through, he laid his hand on Fabi's head.

"I can make it so that you can't see spirits, and they can't direct your thoughts or actions," he said. "Would you like that?"

Fabi thought about it for a little longer than I expected. "That depends," he said. "It's painful and scary, but I'm not sure I want to give it up forever."

"Oh, that's all right," Misalo said. "My spell won't last forever. Only about forty years."

"Great! Do it!" Fabi said.

As best I can tell, Fabi no longer remembers speaking his parents' final thoughts, or being possessed by Disa's ghost. It's probably better this way. He has at least two other, less controversial talents.

Happy Mâshelis! I wish I could send you a present. Maybe next year. Write if you can, okay? You're still the only family I've got, big sister!

Love,
Hasi

Fabi   Hasi   KFB

Fabi, Hasi and Rutana's adventures continue in the following books:

Heirs of Mâvarin, the first trilogy, includes *The Tengrem Sword, The Road and the City*, and *Castle in the Swamp*. Forty years after the events of "The Boy Who Saw," an eccentric musician named Fayubi gets involved in the lives of orphaned twins and their monstrous friend, at a pivotal moment in the history of Mâvarin. This trilogy is under contract to MuseItUp Publishing. *The Tengrem Sword* should be out later this year (2018), followed by the other two volumes.

Mages of Mâvarin, the second trilogy, is currently in revision. A further prequel and sequel are in the planning stages.

For more information, please see:
Mavarin.com and **https://www.facebook.com/mavarininfo/**

G. Chris Stern is a member of the Tucson Science Fiction and Fantasy Wrtier's Meet-up group as well as long-time member and past preseident of the Society of Southwest Authors.

Folding Folds

Learned to fold paper
Almost 2-dimensions to 3-D
Making cylinders and funnels

We folded. Then cubes.
Paper invented in China
Twenty-one hundred years ago

Now someone folded paper
to make airplanes
None as good as rockets

But they fly.
No one made papyrus
airplanes.

Then as simply as folding
paper we folded space.
Distance in the fold is short

Distance to the nearest star
In a simple fold.
Now fly.

Erik Hertwig is a graduate of St. Norbert College in De Pere, Wisconsin. Erik wrote his first children's book, *The Old Man Who Lived in the Dump*, as a first grader.

His decision to become an author prompted him to major in English Literature, Secondary Education, and pursue a career working with children as an English teacher as well as an author, consultant, publisher, and public speaker.

Erik is the creator of the *Zoo Adventure Series* a series of children books that take place in a zoo; *The Trials*, a fantasy hero's journey archetype novel about a half elf's coming of age journey into adulthood; several short fantasy stories; and technical manuals that focus on composition writing and career advancement.

Synopsis

The idea for *Solving Mysteries is a Cynch* came about when I was attending a mystery writer's group meeting. The group was the only writers meeting I was aware of in Tucson so I attended every month and learned about writing mysteries. The members encouraged me to write a mystery but the thought, at first, had no appeal to me. My love of fantasy and children's writing got the best of me and I started putting together a fantasy children's mystery. Please enjoy this kibits-sized novel.

Solving Mysteries is a Cynch

Chapter 1

"The great wizard, Spandar, waves his cynch and creates a feast fit for kings."

"Who is Spandar?"

"Me. I'm the great wizard."

"Great wizards wouldn't waste their time creating feasts." Fezda brushed the dirt from her rough brown tunic in preparation to become the wizard. "Give me the cynch. It's my turn. You've had it all morning."

"No, I haven't defeated the villain yet." Pender adjusted his dark blue stocking cap to make it come to a point on top. "And I'm getting hungry."

"Me too. Let's go home. Maybe Ma has lunch ready for us."

"Wait. I've got a better idea. The great wizard Spandar waves his cynch and instantly teleports himself and his faithful assistant . . ."

"I think it will be quicker if I walk," Fezda muttered. She shuffled down the dirt road toward home, leaving her brother to babble by himself.

Pender stopped spinning and making magic whirring sounds when he noticed Fezda was gone. He sprinted to catch up to his sister, who had passed from the forest into the kibit town. The kibit life was a simple one. Their greatest worry was if it was time to eat and 'where did this item I found in my pocket come from?' Their memories were as short as was as their stature. The kibit town looked like a disorganized group of poorly constructed wooden buildings arranged in no particular order. That was because kibits didn't need houses for warmth. The fur covering their bodies did that for them.

Kibits stand, at most, only three feet high. The young kibits, Pender and Fezda, were not fully-grown. They stood just18 and 22 inches high. You could say kibits are pudgy and have short, stubby fingers.

"Okay, you can be the wizard now, but only for a while," Pender said, passing the short oddly shaped stick to his sister.

"Hello kibits!" The melodic voice of Faun, the owner of Faun's Pawns, caught their attention. Faun's good looks and musical voice distracted many a male kibit from his daily chores.

"Hi Faun!" The kibits shouted in unison and ran to her shop.

"What's this?" Faun asked, freeing the cynch from Fezda's grasp.

"It's a cynch. We found it near the creek."

"Ooh, a cynch. I'll bet you can get a lot done with this." Faun inspected the sturdy wooden stick the kibits called their cynch. The stick had a sharp point at one end and gradually grew larger toward the other where it was shaped like the letter 'C'. "The top of your cynch has a crevice in it. Remember that gemstone in my shop that you little ones were admiring? It will fit nicely into your cynch. I'll let you have it if you come to my shop and do some clean-up work for me."

"Okay," Pender responded, snatching the cynch from her hand. He began to dance in a circle pointing the cynch at everything that moved. "Alakazam, alakazot." Pender's excitement spun him out of control, and he stumbled off the steps of Faun's Pawns and into the path of the approaching mayor.

"Watch where yer pointin' that stick. You could poke somebody's.... Hi Faun, I noticed you were outside. Is anything wrong? Maybe I could help?" The shabbily dressed mayor instantly forgot about the little ones, and walked past them as if they weren't even there.

"No, Mayor. I was just talking to Pender and Fezda," Faun said, brushing her long, blond hair and pointing to the young kibits.

The mayor ignored the twins and the stick. "You know, Faun, I was thinking…" he said hesitantly. The kibits decided they wouldn't be able to chat with Faun now that the mayor had launched into one of his annoying babble sessions. They took off running for home. As they ran down the street, they heard Faun's excuse for their disappearance.

"They disappeared, Mayor, because they had a cynch. Didn't you see it?"

"A cynch? What's that?" the mayor asked.

"It is a magic wand used to make the life of a kibit much easier. You should really invest in one, Mayor," Faun teased. Kibits name their citizens after the job or duty they perform. In some cases, like the mayor, if he has performed the job for a long time, his formal name is dropped and he is known as Mayor.

The young kibits ran all the way home, still laughing at the mayor. They leaped up the steps and into the kitchen.

"Get that stick out of my house!" Ma shouted.

"It's a cynch, Ma."

"It's a stick and sticks stay outside." Pender took the cynch outside and placed it upside-down against the side of the house, then returned to the table.

"I have some chores for you to do before bedtime."

"Aww Ma," they cried. "It's summer."

"Yes, it is summer. And winter comes after summer. It's cold in the winter. So, if you want to stay warm, you had better do your chores now." The little ones left the kitchen and worked all day on their chores, before eating dinner and heading off to bed.

Chapter 2

The loud sound of rapping woke the kibits early the next morning. They heard Pa Fore answer the door, and then he put his clothes on to leave the house before breakfast.

"Hey, Fezda," Pender said, as he looked out the window. "Somebody came for Pa. Something big must be happening in town for Pa to leave before breakfast."

"You're right." Fezda tied her long brown hair into a tail. "Let's check it out. Maybe we can find out what's going on before Deputy Pug gets there."

"Yeah. 'Nuth-n' goin' on here. Move along.' he'll say."

"And then he'll send us home." Fezda mimicked the Deputy as Pender had done. "Then he would say, 'You had better get home or I'll throw you in the hoosegow.' Right, Pender?" The kibits laughed and changed out of their night shirts and into their regular clothes to run outside.

"Grab the cynch, will ya, Fezda?" Pender shouted as he dashed through the open gate.

"It's not here. Where did you put it?"

"It was right there by the front steps. You saw me put it there last night."

"Well, it's gone now. Maybe Pa put it out back when he got home last night."

"It's gone. I knew it! I didn't want to leave the cynch outside," Pender fumed and came back to the porch. "You don't just leave a cynch lying around. What wizard would leave a cynch just lying around outside?"

"You just did last night," Fezda reminded him.

"Oh, yeah, you're right. I just did. Well, let's go find out why Pa had to leave early. Maybe he took the cynch with him this morning."

"Yeah. Maybe Pa needed the cynch to finish one of Mayor's stupid projects, like moving a mountain to keep the rising sun from shining in his bedroom window." The kibits laughed at Fezda's joke and raced downtown.

"I see Pa and Mayor talking with Deputy Pug over by Faun's shop," Pender shouted. "Let's go check it out." The kibits ran to the back of Faun's shop and sneaked around the side, keeping their backs to the wall so Pa and the mayor couldn't see them eavesdropping.

"It looks like this stick was used to pry the window open," Deputy Pug said to the mayor. "That's how they got in."

"Someone broke into Faun's Pawns last night, Pender. Faun is on the steps crying. I wonder who would do that to Faun. Everyone in town likes her."

"Hey, we have a chance to play detectives!" Pender said, grinning the mischievous kibit grin.

"Let's go!" Fezda squeaked. She, too, was wearing that grin. Pender and Fezda sneaked around back of Faun's Pawns to get a look inside. Through a back window, Fezda saw the shelves that used to stand in rows in the center of Faun's shop. They'd been knocked over and Faun's stuff was scattered on the floor.

While Fezda looked in the window, Pender moved to the side of the shop toward the front and peeped around the corner for a closer look at the tool Deputy Pug was holding. "Hey! That's my cynch!" Pender exclaimed. "Where did you get it?"

"This stick belongs to you?" Deputy Pug asked.

Pender darted from his hiding place and into the middle of the crowd where Pa and the Deputy conversed in front of Faun's Pawns.

"Yeah, it does. It's a cynch, and it belongs to me."

"That's him! That's the thief!" Mayor Pooba shouted. "I saw him casing the joint yesterday with that same stick! Get him."

Pender tried to run, but Deputy Pug wrapped his arms around Pender before he could escape. "I'm taking you down to the hoosegow for some more questionin'." Deputy Pug dragged Pender to the only brick building in the kibit community. The jail was also the town hall and Deputy Pug's office. The deputy and the mayor escorted Pender into a small room with a table and four chairs, and advised him to confess.

"I didn't do it," Pender protested.

"Didn't do what?" Deputy Pug asked.

"Mess up Faun's shop," Pender replied, confused.

"He admits it," the mayor cried. "Lock him up."

Fezda peeked through the window and saw Deputy Pug haul Pender off to a jail cell. She ran back to Faun's shop and sat down with her on the steps. "What happened, Faun?" she asked.

"Well, this morning I came to the shop like I usually do, and found the window and the door were both broken. I looked inside and all of the shelves were turned over and my cabinets broken," Faun said, blotting tears from her face. "Somebody took a bunch of my stuff."

"The door is broken right off the hinges," Fezda observed. "Pender couldn't have done that. Why do they think he did this? Besides, I was with him all night and he didn't leave."

"You're right, Fezda. Pender couldn't have done this. He is not nearly big enough to tear the door off the hinges. We had better go talk to the mayor about this." The kibits walked to the jail together to confront the mayor.

"No, no, no!" the mayor protested. "The boy confessed to the crime when he identified this cynch as his. Deputy Pug found it sticking out of the pried-open window. I know the boy did it."

He didn't do it," Fezda cried. "He's not strong enough to tear a door off the hinges. He's too little."

"Have you ever heard of a lever? They say men can move mountains with a lever."

"What are men?" Fezda asked.

"That's not important right now," the mayor interrupted. "The boy said it was a cynch and magic cynches can tear doors off hinges and sticks can be used as levers to pry windows open. We have to put him in jail. It's that simple."

"Mayor," Faun said patiently. "It's a child's toy, not real magic. The kibits were only playing."

"No, no, no! We have to keep him in jail until we can find a judge to try him. Here is where he will stay until then. Now, where did I put my keys?" The mayor shuffled papers around on his desk and went through all his pockets in search of his keys.

"It looks like there is nothing we can do, Fezda," Faun said. "If the mayor says he stays in jail then Pender stays in jail. You better go tell your Ma."

Fezda reluctantly left her brother in jail. Tears fell down her cheek, as she walked the short distance to her home. How could she tell her mother that Pender was in jail before breakfast?

"Whose cow? Whose cow!" Ma shouted.

"Yeah, Ma. The hoosegow. Deputy Pug arrested him this morning and took him to the hoosegow."

"Where's Pa? Where's Pa?" Ma Fore shouted, as she ran around in circles waiving her arms in the air. "Whenever Pa is missing, Pender gets into trouble."

"Pa is down at Faun's Pawns, making sure nothing else gets stolen. Faun asked him to help clean up after the break in."

"Oh, I'd better get to makin' them something to eat. You know how Pa gets when he is workin'. And he went away before breakfast, Pender too. Pender must be scared sittin' by himself in the hoosegow."

Chapter 3

"So, I said to the deputy… Pay attention, kid. I'm talking to ya," said a rough looking kibit in the jail cell with Pender. "I said to the deputy, 'Deputy' I said, 'I'm not'…"

"Oh, Pender, there you are," Fezda interrupted the older kibit, to the delight of her brother. "I brought you something to eat."

"Oh great, I'm hungry!" the dirty prisoner shouted. He wiped his dripping nose on his stained shirtsleeve and rubbed his stomach with the other hand. "I can't remember the last time I ate. Reminds me of the time I was…"

"Quick, give me something to eat, Fezda, while he babbles on about what he 'usta do in the olden days.'" Pender reached through the bars and grabbed the brown paper sack Fezda held. "I've gotta get outta here. He's driving me nuts."

"Where are Deputy Pug and Mayor?" Fezda asked. "Aren't they supposed to be watching you?"

"Well, they locked me in. The mayor lost his keys and they are both out looking for them."

"Oh, look! Here are some keys right in the door. I wonder if these are the keys he is looking for?" Fezda exclaimed.

"What? He left keys in the jail door?" Pender stuck his head between the bars to look. "Quick. Turn the key and get me out."

"I can't turn it. It's too hard," Fezda cried.

"Get something to help turn the key, Fezda,"

"Oh look, Deputy Pug left the cynch right here on the desk. I'm sure we can use it to turn the key."

"Slide the end of the cynch through the hole in the key handle and pull down," Pender suggested. He slipped his body between the bars to show her and together they pulled down on the cynch like a lever, using their weight to turn the key. With a click the jail door opened.

"Okay, you can come... Pender! You're already out. If you could get out, why were you sitting here all this time?"

"Oh, wow!" Pender said, looking down at his body. "I didn't realize... until I put my head through to... Let's get out of here!" Pender stuffed the cynch deep into his pocket. The two ran down the back alley to their home.

"And as I was saying, you can't... Oh hello." The grimy kibit found he was talking to himself. "Hmmmm. Where'd that little guy go? Wow! Looks like I can go now too. The door is open." The dirty kibit stepped out of jail and into the street.

"Pender!" Ma shouted as the kibits bounded into the house. "What are you doing out of jail? I mean, what were you doing in jail? Oh, you kibits were just playing tricks on me again. You go out and play. I have work to do around here. I'll never understand why you always pick on your mother." Ma turned her back to finish her work and the kibits looked at each other, stunned.

"You know, Fezda, I thought she would be a little more angry than that about me going to jail. I thought she would send me to my room or something."

"She thought we were teasing," Fezda said. She scratched her head in wonder. "Well, let's go find out who broke into Faun's Pawns, so Mayor Pooba doesn't send you back to the hoosegow."

"Yeah, he's gonna be sore when he finds out I'm gone. That reminds me, Fezda, what did you do with the keys?"

"Huh? Oh, I don't know," Fezda, said absent-mindedly. "They will turn up some time, I guess."

Faun knew that Pender hadn't broken into her shop, so she gave the young kibits a list of missing items to help them in their search.

One of the missing items was the gemstone Faun promised to give them.

"Faun," Fezda said, "the criminal who broke into your shop must have been very strong to tip over all of the shelves and tear the door off its hinges. How many kibits do you know who could do that?"

"I don't think any kibit could do it. Not by himself, even with a lever, like the mayor suggested. Not only that, Fezda, but if a kibit really needed something from my store, everyone knows I would loan it to them."

"So, who would do this?" Pender asked, stumped.

"It doesn't make sense that a kibit would have broken my stuff because everyone in town has volunteered to help rebuild my shelves and fix my door. Who would break things up and then help build new ones in a few days? No kibit I know would actually create work for themselves."

That is a good point, Fezda thought. "The criminal we are looking for can't be a kibit. So, we have to look for non-kibit clues."

"What are non-kibit clues?" Pender asked. He tried to follow his sister's thoughts.

"Well," Fezda explained, "if a leprechaun broke in we might find some gold-dust finger prints or pieces of gold lying around."

"GOLD? Lying around?" Wide-eyed, Pender began searching for clues.

"That was just a for-instance," Fezda said.

"A FURinstance? Like if we find someone's fur we could match it up to find the criminal?" Pender asked, confused.

"Not exactly, Pender, but that gives me an idea. We could look for torn clothing. Since kibits all wear the same kind of clothes, any pieces we find that are different must be from the criminal."

"Good idea, Fezda," Faun said. "Nobody but kibits have been in here for about three weeks." They all began searching for clues that might help them figure out the criminal's identity.

After searching for what seemed like hours, Faun said, "I think we searched the whole place six times, Fezda, but we've found nothing."

"Yeah, I didn't find anything."

"I didn't find anything either," Pender said. "No pieces of clothing. Only this ugly tooth."

"What!"

"Just a crappy old tooth," Pender said. He held the tooth up for them to see.

"Where did you find this?" Faun asked.

"When did you find this?" Fezda asked.

"About ten minutes into the search," Pender answered. He looked from one to the other.

"Why didn't you say anything?" Fezda cried.

"Because you told me to look for clothes. I didn't find any pieces of clothes, so I kept on looking even after I found the tooth."

"Let me see it, Pender." Faun took the tooth from Pender's hand and studied it. The tooth was quite large and sharp. The tip was white while the rest was stained brown from poor cleaning habits. It looked like a tiny, snow-covered mountain resting in the palm of Faun's hand.

"It doesn't belong to a kibit, does it Faun?" Pender asked. He touched his own teeth to make sure the tooth wasn't his.

"No, it doesn't."

"I bet it's a dinosaur tooth left over from the olden days."

"What would a dinosaur tooth be doing on Faun's floor?" Fezda asked.

"It's not a dinosaur tooth. It belongs to an ogre, I think." Faun passed the tooth to Fezda.

"I'm gonna hold onto this and call it 'Exhibit A'," Fezda said. She wrapped the tooth in a piece of tissue paper she found lying on the floor.

"Why?" Pender and Faun asked together, a little confused.

"Cuz that's the way Deputy Pug talks when the judge is in town. Come on, Pender. We have to go find an ogre with a missing tooth so we can clear your name and solve the mystery."

Fezda and Pender ran down the street. They took the shortest path to the edge of town in hopes to avoid Mayor and Deputy Pug.

"Where do ogres live, Fezda?"

"It is hard to say. Some live in castles, but only after they have run the king out. Some live in shabby huts, in caves, or underground.

They are pretty lazy and don't put much effort into their work. Not like we do," Fezda said as they walked past a number of kibits lounging in the sun at the edge of town. "Why do you ask, Pender?"

"I was just wondering where to look."

"Do you know what Pa would say if we went to an ogre's house? Ouch! No way Pender! If we discover what ogre committed the crime, we just tell Deputy Pug and he'll do the rest. We are too little to capture an ogre. Ogres are strong enough to tear doors off the hinges. Imagine what they could do to us," Fezda said.

Pender shivered. "Yeah, ogres would probably eat us for dinner." Pender bent over and picked up a shiny object lying in the dirt.

"What is it, Pender?" Fezda asked.

"It's the gemstone Faun was going to give us for the cynch. I just found it lying here on the ground."

"Let me see," Fezda said. She snatched the treasure out of her brother's hand. The oddly shaped crystal glittered in the midsummer sunlight. The gemstone was the size of Fezda's palm and made her hand look larger. "This gem is on Faun's list of items stolen from her shop. We found another clue! Let's look for some more."

"Fezda, I've got an idea. You said some ogres live underground?"

"Yeah?"

"Well, we're halfway between town and the Everdeep Caves. If we keep going in that direction we might find some more clues. Or even an ogre," Pender added. He shivered with excitement.

"You're right, Pender. We'll look there, but if we find any ogres, we run. You got it?"

"Okay," Pender agreed, but crossed his fingers behind his back.

Together the little kibits searched the area around the Everdeep Caves for most of the afternoon.

"Pender!" Fezda shouted. "I found the book Faun writes all of her sales in. This is it! It was close to these rocks. Eeew! Yuk! It's covered in hair. Ogre hair, I bet. It's all stringy and stiff. Look, here is a raggedy old blanket with more disgusting ogre hair."

"This must be where the ogre sleeps," Pender said. "Let's get out of here!"

"We'd better get back to town, Pender, and tell the Deputy Pug what we've found."

"Yeah, and get the book back to Faun."

As they neared town, Pender said, "I bet we coulda captured that ogre with the cynch, Fezda. The great wizard Spandar lifts the cynch over his head, utters the magic words, alakazam, alakazot, and the evil ogre is wrapped up in a magic binding spell." Pender got so caught up in his magic he tripped over his tunic.

"You are too goofy, Pender," Fezda said. She hid her giggles in her hands. "Let's go back to Faun's and return her book."

"I promise you, Faun, I will capture that little thief and put him back in jail," the mayor said as Pender and Fezda entered Faun's Pawns.

"Mayor, Mayor!" the kibits interrupted. "We found evidence to prove Pender is innocent."

"Not now, young kibits," the mayor said. "I'm…" The mayor paused, blinking his eyes. "Wait a minute; you are the kibit who robbed Faun's shop. You escaped from the hoosegow. Deputy Pug!" the mayor shouted. "Deputy Pug! The escapee is trying to rob Faun again!"

"No wait," Fezda pleaded. "We found evidence in the woods and we were bringing it back…"

"Bringing it back, eh?" the mayor said. He snatched the book from Fezda's hands. "Feeling a little guilty about stealing and trying to return the evidence?" He made a grab towards Fezda.

"Run, Pender!" Fezda shouted. She grabbed the cynch from Pender's hands and leapt through the open window headfirst. Pender wasn't so lucky.

"Gotcha!" Deputy Pug growled stepping through the open doorway. He snagged Pender as the little kibits sprinted through it. "It's back to the hoosegow with you, young one."

"I didn't do it, I didn't do it," Pender pleaded. "We found evidence and we were bringing it back to show you."

"Tell it to the judge," Deputy Pug said. He closed the jail door on Pender for the second time in one day. "This time I'm gonna watch to make sure you don't escape."

"Faun?" Fezda asked meekly. She raised her head to peer into the shop, unsure if the mayor was still lurking about Faun's shop.

"Yes, Fezda, I am right here. Come on in, it's safe. They've gone."

"The mayor was so angry at us when we brought in the evidence. Why wouldn't he even listen to us?"

"Yes, and it was so obvious Pender didn't take my ledger. The mayor could see that it was covered with ogre hair and drool. He wiped his hand on his pants after he handed the book to me."

"Oh, I almost forgot, Faun, we found one of your gemstones too."

"You did!" Faun exclaimed taking the gem Fezda was holding out to her. "Hey, this is the gem I was going to put in your cynch. Let me see it."

Fezda handed the cynch over to Faun and she worked the glittering gem into the 'C' shaped crevice at the top.

"Now it looks like a real magic cynch," Faun said, "something a real wizard would use to cast spells." She held it up and admired the fit of the oddly shaped crystal in its new home on top of the kibit's cynch. "Looks like it belongs there. Good! We'll need a little magic to get your brother out of jail this time, Fezda."

"Thank you, Faun," Fezda sniffed, "I better go see what I can do to help Pender, and try to convince the deputy that my brother didn't commit any crime."

"Good luck, Fezda. I will stay here and try to think of some way to convince the mayor of Pender's innocence."

Chapter 4

"The AP-RE-HEN-TION of Public Enemy Number One, by Deputy Pug," the deputy said to himself while he wrote the day's events in his private journal.

"I am not public enemy number one," Pender said. "I was at home sleeping when it happened. Ask Pa. Anyway, do you think I am strong enough to tip over shelves?"

"What did you say?" Deputy Pug stopped long enough to listen. "You said, 'I am strong enough to tip over shelves'." Deputy Pug went back to writing and talking to himself. "The suspect boasted of his abnormal strength, strong enough to tip over shelves."

"AAARGGGGGH! I can't believe you think..." Pender stopped and realized he'd better not finish the thought because the deputy would turn it into a confession.

"How is our little suspect coming along?" the mayor asked.

He set down two brown paper sack lunches upon the desk where Deputy Pug was writing. The mayor sat down to watch. "Did you figure out how he escaped last time?"

"No, not yet, but I am still working on it," the deputy said. He pulled a tuna sandwich out of the paper sack.

"Excuse me," Fezda said. She poked her head into the deputy's office. "I was hoping I could talk to my brother, Pender."

"Sure," the mayor responded. He crunched down on a piece of lettuce that stuck out of his tuna sandwich.

"Pender," Fezda whispered. Pender was huddled in a corner with his back to the room. He turned and came to her. "I talked to Faun and she said she would try to figure out a way to convince the mayor to get you out of jail. I showed her the gemstone we found and she set the stone in the cynch for us." Fezda held the cynch close, hiding it from the deputy and mayor. The gemstone sparkled brightly in the dimly lit jail cell.

"Oh, that's beautiful," Pender breathed.

Fezda quickly tucked it inside her tunic and tightened her rope-belt over it.

"The deputy is keeping a journal of how he captured public enemy number one. Public enemy number one. Phooey. They are both convinced that I am a criminal and will not listen to me."

Too late, Fezda noticed Deputy Pug creeping up behind her.

"Gotcha!" Deputy Pug shouted. He lifted Fezda off the ground so she couldn't run. "Open the door, Mayor, and we will put the accomplice in with the criminal."

"What? This is nuts, Deputy Pug. We didn't do anything!" Fezda shouted as Pug shoved her into the cell with her brother.

"Tell it to the judge when he convicts the both of you tomorrow," the mayor sneered. He laughed his cackling laugh, and went back to the desk to finish his lunch.

Fezda and Pender fumed quietly and listened to the two male kibits slobber over their sandwiches. They didn't talk together, but each plotted their escape. They snickered when the two belched loudly at the end of their meal.

"Well, Deputy, now that we have two prisoners behind bars, I'll go see Faun and let her know that we have captured both culprits."

The mayor wiped his greasy face with his sleeve and his hands on the front of his tunic. He crossed the office to the exit and turned to glance back at the young kibits. "Watch the prisoners while I am gone, Deputy."

"What are we going to do now?" Pender asked. He was worried about what the judge would say, but he was even more worried about what Ma would say when she found out they both were in the hoosegow.

"We could play wizard," Fezda said to try to cheer up her brother.

"Nah, wizards don't go to jail."

"Sure they do. All great magicians have been locked up at some point. People don't understand magic. They're afraid, so they lock up wizards, magicians, and priests. When people are afraid, they lock up anyone who is different. Come on Pender, it will be fun. We can make believe we're in the laboratory working on a potion that will dissolve these bars. Let's do it!"

"Okay, but remember magic is what got us in trouble in the first place." Pender sat on the bench, swinging his short legs. He thought about what Fezda had said about magicians and fear. Pender didn't know any kibits who had been put in prison for their beliefs, but he did remember a story, Olerich, the most famous of kibits, had told him once about the Elf Queen who had been locked in a tower because of the way she worshipped her god.

"Do you want to be the wizard or the assistant?"

"I will be the assistant this time."

Fezda was surprised. She was sure he would want to be Spandar the great wizard again. He must be really worried, she thought. "Okay," she said, "this bench will be our work table."

Pender walked over to the bench. He wanted to cry, but he would put on a good front if it would make his sister feel better. "What should we do first?" he asked kneeling in front of the bench.

"I think we need some potions."

"We don't have ingredients to make potions."

"I am a wizard," Fezda reminded him, "all of my ingredients are invisible."

"Ok, what should we make first?"

"How about invisibility potions? We could use some of those."

"Tell me what goes in it and I will mix it together, cuz I am the assistant," Pender said, feeling a bit better.

"The first ingredient is fairy dust. Mix in crushed leprechaun clover and finally some salamander slime to hold it together. Mix another potion and cork both containers."

Pender held up the invisible vials so the wizard could enchant them by touching the magic cynch to his hands. Pender pretended he was putting the potion bottles inside his tunic underneath his belt.

"Now, let's prepare a binding spell to tie up the real criminal when we catch him," Fezda suggested.

Pender thought for a moment and pulled a piece of twine from his belt. He laid it on the bench. Next, he reached up to the window and tore off a piece of spider web. The furry spider scurried into hiding to avoid the kibit. Finally he picked up a broken piece of stone from the cell floor.

"What's the stone for?"

"I took the stone so anyone who enters will trip over this spot." Pender arranged his ingredients on the bench. First, he placed the spider's web on the stone and wrapped the twine around the whole thing to hold the pieces together. "Touch the cynch to it and complete the magic spell."

> *"Stone and web, wrapped with twine,*
> *for our freedom, his and mine,*
> *bound together in a cell,*
> *make for us a binding spell."*

As Fezda chanted, she touched the objects with the cynch.

"Wow! That was a real wizard's chant. Where did you learn that? Pender looked at his sister, his eyes wide. "Do you know any more? Can we make a potion to get us out of here? I can slip between the bars like I did before, but you're bigger, and besides, Deputy Pug would see us."

"Let's make some sandman dust to put Deputy Pug to sleep."

"What goes into sandman dust?" Pender asked, eager to help. He was the wizard's assistant, and he would do anything the wizard asked.

"Let's see. Moonbeams from the time of night. Over here, it's dark in this corner. Sweat cooling from a hard day's work." She wiped her brow and handed the cooling sweat to her brother. "And a goose feather taken from a pillow." She plucked an imaginary feather from the imaginary pillow on the other bench. "Then shake well and throw it at your victim." Fezda touched Pender's hand with the cynch. "Alakazam, alakazot. A sleeping spell is what you've got," she chanted.

Pender jumped around the cell shaking sandman dust in his hands. He stopped when he heard his sister giggling. He gave her a dirty look and threw all of his sandman dust at Deputy Pug. The deputy, having just finished a hearty meal, slumped over in his desk. He began to snore loudly.

"It worked! Wow! Let me see that cynch! It must be Faun's gemstone that has made our cynch really magic!" Pender took the cynch from his sister's hand, adjusted his cap, and gazed deeply into the sparkling stone. "I wish I could open the door and get us out," Pender said softly.

"Yes!" Fezda said. She threw her arms into the air and danced in a circle. A wizard could make magic even if the assistant was holding the magic cynch. A loud rattle and clunk sound made her jump. The mayor's keys fell out of her tunic.

Pender stood stunned looking at the keys on the floor, his mouth formed a perfect "O".

Fezda picked up the keys, smiling. "I knew they'd turn up sooner or later. Open the door, Pender, and let's get out of here." Pender took the keys and slipped out between the bars. Unlocking the door using the cynch as a lever was getting easier.

"Let's go before Deputy Pug wakes up." They slipped out of the jail and into the sunshine. The bright sunlight temporarily blinded them so they didn't notice how brilliant the gemstone in the cynch had become.

The kibits were once again free. They ran to the edge of town where the forest began.

"It looks like we are going to have to capture the criminal on our own," Fezda said, when she felt they were safe from the mayor's view. "Mayor will probably tell Deputy Pug to shoot us next time."

"From now on, Fezda, we won't take our evidence to Mayor or to Deputy Pug. "You're right, Pender, I don't want to spend any more time in jail. We'll have to try to capture the ogre ourselves. Do you want to try? It could be very dangerous."

"Are ogres big?"

"Very big."

"And mean?"

"I think so. I never really saw one. But we saw what the ogre did to Faun's shop. They must be mean to do a thing like that to someone as beautiful and nice as Faun is."

"We can do it, Fezda!" Pender declared. He waved the cynch in the air. "We have the magic cynch!"

Chapter 5

The kibit town hall shook from the angry shouts of the kibits inside. The kibits had been angry since they'd heard about the missing kibit children.

The mayor hammered his gavel on the desk, trying to restore order, but it couldn't be heard over the shouts of the angry citizens.

"Order!" he shouted. "Order, I said!" He banged the gavel as hard as he could, and saw a crack creep across the top of the podium. "Order!"

"One roast beef sandwich," Deputy Pug mumbled. He woke from a snooze and looked around in confusion.

"I call this meeting to order," Mayor shouted, finally quieting the crowd. "As you know, we have a crisis. Two of the town's own, Pezda and Fender…"

"Fezda and Pender," Ma corrected from a bench near the front of the hall. She sobbed into her scarf again, crying over her missing kibits.

"Yes, Pender and Fezda were arrested earlier today for robbing Faun's Pawns and they have escaped. I mean are missing," The mayor corrected himself. "They were last seen by Deputy Pug this afternoon, playing in their cell."

An angry Kibit stood up and shouted, "What kind of security does this town have if our babies can go missing from a jail cell, right under the nose of our deputy?"

"Never mind that now. Ahem. We'll look into that later. Our first concern is finding the young kibits. I say we form a posse and ride out... I mean, we should form a search party and look for those kibits. Faun said she knows the kibits often play in the woods near town. Another group will go to the nearby towns. We must work together during this crisis. Now, Pa will organize the groups."

Everyone talked at once and the roar nearly raised the roof of the town hall. One by one the groups formed and went out into the twilight to search for two small kibits.

After most of the kibits had gone, Faun approached the mayor. "You know what Fezda and Pender have gone to do, don't you, Mayor?"

"No, no, Miss Faun. What is it that they're up to?"

"They're not up to anything, Mayor. They're going alone into the forest to look for an ogre with a missing tooth to prove they are innocent, because each time they bring evidence to you, you don't listen. You accuse them of stealing from my shop and throw them in jail. Those kibits didn't break into my shop, and you know it, Mayor. I'm beginning to think you're protecting someone."

"Well, the evidence..."

"Evidence," Faun snorted in disgust. "These kibits are barely ten seasons old. In all of your seasons, Mayor, have you ever heard of a kibit destroying property like the destruction you saw at my store? Do you really believe those two small kibits could cause all that destruction?"

"Well, no. I guess not, not by themselves, but these kibits have magic, and magic makes you do evil things."

Faun clenched her fists and straightened her back. The curls in her hair seemed to straighten as she began to shake with anger. "I have read your religious book," she said. "Your god performs what appears to be magic. Is your god evil? You know as well as I do that it is the magician who controls the magic. The magic does not control the magician. We are not talking about an evil sorcerer here. We are talking about two young kibits, alone in the woods, and trying to capture a violent ogre! Now I suggest you and your deputy put your heads together and remember where the ogres live, because that is where you will find Pender and Fezda. And I suggest you round up any heroes who might be left in town who might be willing to go with us!" Faun shook her hair and the curls bounced back with it. She turned and stalked towards the door.

"With us?" the mayor asked, swallowing hard. Faun stopped and turned back to face the mayor.

"Yes, us, and you had better be ready in ten minutes because we may not have much time."

"I checked Olerich's house and he wasn't there." The chubby deputy puffed, trying to catch his breath. He joined Faun and the mayor at the edge of town. "He is the only really brave kibit I know."

"Well it looks like it will just be the three of us then, right, Mayor?" Faun smiled, knowing the mayor would probably wet his pants if he ever met an ogre.

Chapter 6

"We are getting close, Pender. I can smell ogre." Fezda tightened her tunic belt for the third time in three minutes. It was the only sign that showed how frightened she was.

"Yeah, and have you noticed that there are no birds singing or crickets chirping today? Yesterday, the birds were singing."

"I noticed, about ten minutes ago, and the frogs aren't croaking. It must mean the ogres are at home today. The smart animals know enough not to come near the caves when the ogres are at home."

"Yeah, the smart ones don't come, but we are here," Pender said, teeth chattering. "We need a plan or we will be dumb animals who became dinner at the ogre house."

"Let's find a place to hide, Pender, so we can see how many of them live here. If there are a lot of them, we'll really be in trouble."

"We're already in trouble." Pender tried to make a joke, but his teeth were chattering so hard, Fezda became more frightened.

They found a safe spot between two large rocks and covered themselves with dead shrubs and leaves so the ogres wouldn't see them. The kibits waited.

"Pender," Fezda whispered. "The ogre, I can see him." Fezda poked at her brother who had dosed off.

"What?" Pender asked, rubbing his eyes.

"Shhh." Fezda whispered, "I can see the ogre near the front of the cave."

"Holy cats, he's huge!" Pender almost shouted, seeing an ogre for the first time. Fezda quickly put her hand over her brother's mouth.

The ogre was tall, about the height of three kibits. His head was larger than a Halloween pumpkin and he hunched over when he walked. His jaw line was thin but his lips and mouth were large and it seemed his grin went half way around his jack-o-lantern head. He looked very strong, with long arms. His long fingers had very sharp, pointed nails at the end. His body was covered with long, stringy, course hair. His head was bald except for a tuft of hair, which was tied into a tail at the top and draped down over his back.

"He is ugly," Pender blurted out.

"Shhh, I don't want him to know we're here. Can you see if he is missing a tooth?"

The ogre turned and faced the kibits.

"Well, if he should have two fangs, one is missing," Pender said. "There is only one fang sticking out of his ugly mouth going up over his top lip."

"Pender. What would Ma say if she heard you talking like that?"

The ogre grabbed a few tree branches and a basket and walked down the hill away from the caves.

"Wheeew! I thought he was going to come and take our branches," Pender whispered.

"We'd better take a look inside while he's gone, Fezda said.

"Do we have to?" Pender was brave, but he was not as brave as Fezda. She knew she would have to go inside alone.

"You stay here and watch, Pender. Run for help if he comes back or if I get caught, okay?"

"Are you nuts, Fezda? We're a long way from town. I don't think it would help you much if I ran to town."

It would help you, little brother, Fezda thought. *At least one of us would be safe.*

"We are in this together, Fezda. I'm going in with you."

"Pender, you are so brave. Let's go."

Chapter 7

"I just got back from storming a castle. Well, actually, my friends did most of the storming, but anyway I'm really tired," Olerich said. "I have a few gold coins I could pay you to take me to kibit town if it's not too far out of your way." Olerich pulled the coins out of his pouch to show them to the farmer. Olerich looked young, as all kibits do, but he had a way about him that was different from most kibits. Olerich was an adventurer and had learned to survive in a world away from the kibits. The world is a dangerous place for kibits.

"Fine, fine," the human farmer said, rearranging his provisions in his mule cart to make room for Olerich. "Olerich you say your name is? I've heard of you. Don't you work for the Elf Queen, Affeinna? You have quite a reputation for bravery."

"Thank you, Sir. The job is finished, so I can go home now."

"Well, hop up in the back and I will drive you home. You can pay me when we get there. If you give me the money now, I am sure it will find a way back into your pocket before the end of the trip."

Olerich was unsure what the farmer meant, but he hopped up onto the small two-wheeled cart and stretched out on the hay near the back. He removed his worn leather boots and crossed his legs, resting his feet on the opposite side of the cart. "I'll just take a little nap. Please wake me when we get to kibit town."

* * *

"Stop complaining about your feet, Mayor, and start thinking about how you will lose the next election if these little kibits have been eaten by an ogre." The mayor had been complaining about his aches and pains and his fatigue ever since they had left the town, and Faun was getting really tired of hearing it. "If we live through this, I am never going to take another trip with you again."

The mayor stopped to rub his feet again. "I just wanted to lighten the conversation, that was all, Faun."

"Try lightening the burden on your feet," Deputy Pug grumbled.

"What was that, deputy?" the mayor asked. He stumbled as he hurried to keep up with his two companions.

"Oh, nothing."

Faun laughed for the first time since leaving kibit town. "How far to the Everdeep Caves, Deputy Pug?"

* * *

Fezda and Pender stumbled in the dark cave. "I wish we had brought a torch," Pender complained.

Around the next corner, they entered a large room. Two wooden torches burned, one on each side, casting a yellow light. A small, wooden table with three chairs around it sat in the middle of the room. A large, empty birdcage stood against the wall near the back of the room. A beautiful tapestry hung from the wall above it. The tapestry featured a knight carrying a lance and riding a black-armored horse through a wooded knoll. He was riding away from a dark evil-looking castle built into the side of a mountain. The tapestry was long, far too long for the wall from which it hung. The extra length of the tapestry was spread out on the floor like a carpet. Four large chests stood on the wall opposite the tapestry. A crude bed of just an old blanket and pillow, filthy with hair, lay in front of the chests.

"Wow, this place stinks," Pender said, crossing the room toward the table.

"Quiet, Pender. We don't know what else might be in here."

Pender hopped into one of the chairs. It was way too big for him. He looked like a teddy bear left at the kitchen table after dinner. "I don't see any more ogres here. Maybe this one lives alone," Pender said, looking around.

"Help me get these chests open to see what's inside," Fezda said, motioning him to follow her.

Pender went to the nearest chest and lifted the iron latch. Fezda grabbed one of the corners. "Lift on the count of three. One, two, three!" The kibits grunted together as they opened the chest. The chest smelled different from the cave. Its aromatic smell was similar to a swamp tree that grew not too far from kibit town. The chest was filled with pretty stones, pieces of parchment paper, various coins, and some strange items the kibits had never seen before.

"I wonder if this is what buried treasure looks like," Pender said. He pulled his stocking cap down over his right eye. "Aaargh, me hearties, and shiver me timbers. We needs to hide this treasure before…"

"Pender, stop fooling around. We've got to find something to show it was the ogre and not you who robbed Faun."

"Oh, yeah. I forgot. Do you see anything in this chest that's on Fauns list?"

"No, not near the top. I think we should check the others before we go spilling anything out. I would hate to have the ogre return to a mess."

"You have got to be kidding me," Pender blurted out. "This whole place is a mess."

"You know what I mean. He'd know someone was here if all of this stuff is lying on the floor."

"You are right, Fezda. Help me with the others."

* * *

"Tell me more about you and your work with the Elf Queen," the farmer said. "You must have some really exciting stories."

Olerich discovered he couldn't nap in the cart. The road was too bumpy. He sat up and repaired the straps on his bag. They'd become worn during his latest adventure. "Ouch." Olerich stuck his finger with the needle when the cart hit another large rock. He gave up trying to repair it and settled in to tell a story.

"My friends and I often get together to accomplish tasks for the Queen. Naturally, they have me doing the most dangerous stuff. I climb the walls of the enemy castles, listen into rooms, pick door locks so the others can sneak in without being heard, and fight when we are attacked. I don't really like to fight, most kibits don't, but sometimes it is necessary. I have never learned to speak troll, if you know what I mean. I do a lot of hiding in shadows to find ways into or out of dangerous situations. Like this last castle storming we did. I dressed up like a blooming prairie shrub and worked my way close to the castle." Olerich crouched down on the hay pile as if he were actually in disguise. "Once I neared the castle, I climbed to the top and checked over the defenses. None of my friends were there to help me. I was all alone." Olerich made hand gestures and slowed down his speech for effect. "When I found the best way in, I gave the signal for the others to surprise the guards. I messed with the castle's archers by lighting their arrow supplies on fire, and I cut the pulley ropes so the catapults wouldn't fire. Sometimes the pay isn't great, but it is such fun watching the paid soldiers scurrying around when their castle is attacked, and the best part is I get to see my friends. We stop at many different pubs along the way and we try many new foods and drinks. I really do like to travel. I get to talk to and meet new people. I tell stories. Many times, I get paid to tell stories to humans. They are not funny stories but it makes the human adventurers laugh. And it keeps me employed."

"I am not surprised. You seem like the talking type," the farmer said.

Chapter 8

"Wow, I think almost everything on Faun's list is in this chest," Pender exclaimed. He ran his fingers through gemstones and jewelry while organizing them in piles on the floor. "I don't know who the rest of this stuff belongs to, but I bet it was stolen too." Pender checked Faun's store list to make sure all of the items he grabbed were on it. "It will be great to get all of this stuff back to Faun. She will be so proud of us and happy too."

"Pender. We can't carry all this back to town. It is far too heavy. And remember what happened the last time we brought something back to town?" Fezda didn't even wait for Pender to think about it. She reminded him, "We got arrested."

"You're right, Fezda, we can't go home or we'll get arrested. We can't bring the stuff to Faun or we get arrested. We can't go get help cuz we'll get arrested. If we bring someone here to show what we found, no one will believe we were here, and then we will get arrested. If we stay here, we get killed. Unless…"

"Unless what?" Fezda asked, fidgeting with her ponytail.

"Unless we capture the ogre and bring him back to town."

"That sounds like the same thing as staying here and getting killed."

"No, we have the cynch. We can capture him and bring him back to town and clear our names." Pender held the cynch proudly out in front of him. He looked at it as if it was for the first time. The cynch seemed to twinkle in the dimly lit cave just as it had earlier in the sunlight. "We can do it, Fezda. All you have to do is believe. With the cynch we can do anything."

"What are you doing in here?!" The ogre's booming voice startled the kibits. The monstrous beast pushed his way through the front door. "I'm gonna squash you little rats and cook you for dinner!" The ogre threw down his fishing pole and empty fish basket to grab the kibits.

"Run!" Fezda screamed and scrambled out of the ogre's grasp.

"You can't get away from me in my own house." The ogre pushed a large rock in front of the exit, blocking most of the entrance to prevent Fezda from running out. "Gotcha!" The ogre shouted with glee as he grabbed Fezda by the ponytail. "You can't get away from me." The ogre threw Fezda over his shoulder and walked over to the birdcage. He pulled a large chain and the cage lifted from the floor. He hooked the chain on a nail and suspended the cage from the ceiling. The ogre tossed Fezda in with a grunt and locked the door. "That should hold you for a while. Now, where is the other one? Here little guy, here little guy." The ogre called to Pender in a taunting way. "I have something for you." He said with a laugh. The ogre crossed the room to where the kibits had laid out Faun's stuff. "Look at the mess you made in my house." The ogre bellowed. "This could take hours to clean up."

Pender crossed the room to the cage where Fezda was and he handed her the cynch. "Here, take this," he said. The sound got the ogre's attention.

"Ah, there you are, trying to free your friend." The ogre picked up a brown towel-sized rag from the kitchen and moved closer to Pender, trying to corner him. Pender tried to run around him but he wasn't quick enough and got caught. "A ha! I've got you both now. I guess I will have something to eat tonight." The ogre chuckled and closed the cage door with both kibits locked inside. "Now, I had better prepare the stew kettle for tonight's feast."

The ogre did a little dance step on the way to his kitchen, so happy he finally had something for dinner. The ogre sat at the table facing the kibits and began to cut onions and other vegetables for his stew.

"Pender," Fezda scolded, "it looked like you were trying to get caught."

"I know, I think our best chance of getting out of here is working together. I wouldn't be able to get the cage open by myself and he would make stew out of you before I could get the rock moved to get away. He would never move that rock with me loose in here." While Pender was whispering to Fezda, the ogre moved the rock and went outside. "See what I mean, Fezda? He feels safe and secure now that he thinks we won't get away. He won't use the rock when he comes back."

"We need to come up with a plan to get out of here, or we are in deep trouble."

"I've got a plan, Fezda. When the ogre comes back, we drink the invisibility potions. The ogre will panic and open the cage. We can sneak out while he is searching the cave for us."

"We made the potions for fun, Pender. I don't think they will work. I wouldn't depend on it if I were you."

"The cynch is magic, Fezda." Pender found the cynch in his grasp again and held it up for his sister to see. "I know it is. When Faun put the gemstone in the cynch, it changed."

"Well I am not going to depend on it; we could die today, Pender," Fezda argued.

"I am not going to argue with you, but have you tried to pull the gemstone out of its setting? It won't budge."

"I'll take your word for it." Fezda looked away from her brother and scanned the room for anything to help her out of the cage. "I've got another idea. Do you see that little mirror hanging behind us?"

"Yeah."

"If you can help me swing the cage and grab the mirror, and that piece of cloth we can disappear. Remember when we stood on opposite sides of the big swing at the Elf-Spring-Party last year?"

"Yeah, we got kicked out."

"I know, but that is what we must do now. Stand on the opposite side of the cage and push back when I pull forward. Keep it up until we swing to the mirror. We need to grab the mirror before the ogre comes back in." Working together, the kibits swung the cage. Fezda was able to grab the mirror and bring it inside the cage, along with the brown-colored cloth resting on the back of a chair.

"What we need to do is hide under the cloth with the mirror resting on top of us at an angle. The ogre will look at the mirror and see that side of the cage and think we have escaped." Fezda pointed to the reflection of the side of the cage to show Pender that her plan would fool the ogre into thinking he was looking at the back of the cage.

"I still think we should take the potions, Fezda."

"Ok, it can't hurt, but we need to be ready before he comes back." Fezda insisted.

* * *

"Well, Mayor, this is the place." Faun wiped the hair from her brow and folded her red scarf into a bandana and tied her hair up onto her head. "The area of the Everdeep Caves. I suggest we look around for evidence of Pender and Fezda," Faun instructed. "And be on the lookout for any ogres, too. If the little kibits say an ogre is the crook, then an ogre is what we look for."

"Oh, oh, okay, Faun," the mayor stuttered. "I still think we should have waited for help or for Olerich before coming out here. We could get killed."

"Worrying about getting killed by an ogre should be the last thing on your mind, Mayor, because if those kibits are hurt, you are gonna wish an ogre found you here. Now, spread out and look. I don't want to be here when it gets dark."

"Quiet down," Deputy Pug interjected. "I hear something off to our right. It is the only sound other than the mayor's complaining that I have heard in the last hour." The group moved closer to where the deputy pointed and peered over a group of rocks. They saw what looked like a person bent over at the waist in the middle of a short, grass field.

"Is that an ogre?" the mayor asked.

"It looks like an ogre... picking vegetables," Faun added.

"I thought ogres were carn... carniv... meat eaters. I hope this one is a vegi.. veget... vegetabulian."

"Quiet, Mayor, I don't want to find out its eating habits the hard way," Faun said. "Let's just sit here quietly and watch where it goes."

* * *

"I'm back, rats." The ogre bellowed to his captive kibits and slammed his vegetables on the table. "And I have got the rest of the stew with me." The ogre went to the kitchen and chopped his vegetables before tossing them in the stew pot. "Now, it's time to prepare the main course."

The ogre crossed the cave to the cage where the kibits were hiding behind the mirror. "What! Where did you go? How did you get out?" he screamed, not seeing the kibits where he had left them. The ogre opened the cage like Fezda predicted to look inside. Not seeing them, he rummaged through the room looking for his tasty meal.

"Time to get away," Fezda whispered. Slowly and quietly, the kibits came out of hiding and dropped from the cage to the floor.

"I can still smell you," the ogre taunted, continuing to look in the wrong places. Fezda worked her way across the cave-room to the door. The ogre gazed across the room and went back to his search.

"He looked right at us and didn't see us!" Pender exclaimed.

"Shhh, Pender!" Fezda tried to hush her brother. She reached for him to help pull him out of the cave.

"There you are." The ogre clumsily glided across the room to where Pender stood. Pender dodged back into the kitchen. The ogre charged right past to where Fezda was standing by the exit. Fezda sidestepped him and ducked behind the hanging tapestry.

"Where did you go?" the ogre asked, looking around near the exit.

Pender reached inside his tunic, revealing his hidden stocking cap. He pulled it snugly onto his head, removed the cynch, and ran onto the tapestry. Pender held the cynch and both his arms over his head. Pender boldly stated, "I am Spandar, the great magician."

"There you are." The ogre turned and slowly walked toward Pender with both his arms outstretched reaching for the tiny kibit.

"Stone and web, wrapped with twine,
for our freedom, hers and mine,
bound together in our cell,
cast for me the binding spell."

Pender chanted the binding spell Fezda created in jail and he shook the cynch at the ogre. The ogre took a final step toward Pender and his right foot tripped over the tapestry that lay partially on the floor. The action pulled it from the wall. The heavy top of the tapestry rolled down the wall towards Pender and the ogre.

"Aaaaaaah!" the ogre screamed and hit the floor face-first in front of Pender. The tiny kibit jumped out of the way. The tapestry rolled over the top of the ogre and continued to roll across the cave floor, trapping the ogre within. Pender ran alongside the rolling tapestry watching the ogre get rolled up by the heavy drapery.

"How did that happen?" Fezda asked. She surveyed the ogre rolled up like a sausage in the tapestry.

"It was the cynch. It's magic. Look at it, Fezda, it's casting its own light." The little cynch was shining brighter than a star in the early evening light.

"It is, Pender! I can see it."

"The cynch was always magic, Fezda, you just need to believe in it. Oh-my-gosh, we are going to need some help carrying the ogre into town. I'll run and get some help. You start loading Faun's stuff in those little bags."

* * *

Olerich sat at the front edge of the overloaded wagon, looking back at the other kibits sitting on the ogre wrapped in the tapestry. "This reminds me of when I first got my start adventuring," Olerich said.

"Well, it brings to mind the story of how I got elected mayor for the first time…"

Faun looked at the mayor and back to the kibits. "I want to thank the both of you for being so brave and solving the mystery." She whispered so the mayor would not hear her. "Most other kibits, like the mayor, would have stopped with pondering over who committed the crime, but you two risked your lives to find and capture the thief. You are both heroes. Kibits will be talking about you for years."

"We owe it all to you, Faun," Fezda said. "We believe the gemstone you put in the cynch is what made it magical."

"Magical? I thought you were just playing magic."

"We were playing when we started. But after the gemstone was set in the cynch, it was for real. It really is magic," Pender said.

"How did you know it is for real?" Faun asked him.

"I guess if you believe in something, if you really do believe, you can make anything happen, even magic."

Jessica Priester writes about actual space battles that occurred millions of years ago. She endeavours to be as accurate as possible, but present the history as science-fiction lest anyone think she's crazy. Her first novel, *The Officer Cadet*, is available on Amazon under the name of J. P. Wyman.

Synopsis

Jada Bell was launched from a dying Earth in a suspended animation pod at the tender age of four, by parents who wanted her to have a great life somewhere else. She grew up as the daughter of a fisherman, always careful to keep her true identity a secret. That was, until the day a teenaged friend spilled the beans.

Jada finds herself fighting to protect her adopted home from a truly awful fate.

2240: A Spy Odyssey

Jada Bell was four years old when the Earth was destroyed.

Her parents knew it was coming, but no one would listen. In desperation, they stole a probe with a mass-negation drive and an extra-temporal braking mechanism, and filled the probe's computer with a record of Earth and Earth's history. The probe was too small for an adult, but just large enough for a four-year-old, so they froze their only daughter, Jada, and launched her into space.

They wanted Jada to have a chance to lead a full life; however, they may not have thought this through very carefully. The probe was designed to stop when it encountered a planet similar to Earth, and they assumed she would be found by someone benevolent. They apparently did not consider the other possibilities. What if she woke up without oxygen or violently decompressed or worse? What if she was found by someone malevolent, or perhaps some lifeform so alien that it knew nothing of consciousness, or nerve endings, and turned Jada into some sort of permanent, living science project?

Fortunately for Jada, her parents' optimism was borne out and sixty-eight-million years later, the probe splashed down safely in the ocean of a planet very similar to Earth. Jada was picked up by fishermen and thawed out on a fishing boat. The boat captain sent her to live with his parents, a nice elderly couple who owned a farm outside a town called Piper Falls on the border between human and elven lands. (That's the story they told her, anyway. No one ever explained how she could have intercepted an ocean at light speed and survived, or how a fishing boat was able to revive her from cryogenic freeze without any special equipment.)

Jada's new parents knew right away that she was special. She was fast enough to outrun a centaur, and strong enough to lift a truck or leap over buildings. Her parents taught her to conceal her powers lest the government find out about her and take her away.

Jada loved her new family and her new life, but she also missed the life she could have had. Jada accessed what files survived from the probe and learned all she could about Earth. She dreamed of what it would have been like to visit Disneyland, or the Emerald City, or to receive a letter inviting her to a school of witchcraft and wizardry.

Except for the fact that it had not blown up yet, Jada"s new home was much more dangerous. Earth had its share of dangers—Jada had seen footage of dragon attacks and the occasional alien invasion—but between the Ministry of Magic, the Federation of Planets, and legions of superheroes, Earth always had a protector.

"Have you ever thought of becoming a spy?" asked Trena one day while the two of them were watching a herd of flying horses. Trena was Jada"s best friend, and the only person outside of her family that she could ever talk to about Earth.

"How do you become a spy?"

"Well, I think you have to be invited, so you'd have to get the attention of a spy agency, but if anyone can get their attention, it's you."

"Right, and then I get locked away in some lab for the rest of my life. No, thank you."

"I know, I know. Your dad thinks he needs to protect you from government agents. He also thinks he needs to protect you from boys. He's so ridiculous. Did you know that virgins are nine times more likely to be eaten by a dragon?"

"But I'm from Earth, and on Earth, virgins are the most likely to escape from supernatural serial killers. Piper Falls doesn't have a dragon, but a serial killer can show up anywhere."

"Whatever. You keep talking about how Earth had protectors and how we need protectors. You have magical abilities! Become our protector!"

"On Earth, I'd have a wand and special training. I don't know how to actually perform magic."

"You're still faster than us, and stronger than us. You can think faster. You can see through almost anything. You don't need training for any of that."

"I don't know."

"How about this? Duleen's team is on that cruise in elven waters. You can share her room."

"A cruise? I thought it was a military expedition."

"Whatever, she's on a ship, and she can get you aboard."

"Why would she do that?"

Trena shrugged. "Why does it matter? You can help save the world, and then a spy agency will have to recruit you."

"You didn't tell her about me, did you?"

"No! Never! I promised I would never tell anyone, remember?"

Jada could always tell when someone was lying, an ability Trena had not yet picked up on. "Trena, what did you tell her?"

"Okay, okay. I may have let something slip, but if you can trust me, you can trust my sister, right?"

"Didn't we just prove I actually can't trust you?"

"You're not mad, are you? Duleen's team is investigating Dr. Foid's facility on Oldenor Island. They know what he's planning to do, but they don't know how. You could see inside the facility without him knowing."

Jada was angry, but she could not help asking, "What is he planning?"

"I don't know exactly, something about wiping out humanity to make more room for elves."

"I think I would have heard about that!"

"No, you wouldn't. It's secret. Duleen wouldn't even tell me; I had to look through her files."

"No. Absolutely not. I'm not doing it."

"You have to do it. You are always talking about how we need protectors. And Duleen would never have asked for your help if there was any other way. I saw the report. No one knows how to stop him. That's why it's a secret. They don't want to incite a panic."

"Trena, your sister is a military officer. She has had years of military training. None of my abilities is a substitute for that. An elven blade will kill me just as easily as anyone else."

"Please, Jada, I thought you'd be excited!" Trena's voice sounded frantic.

"Well, I'm not. Let the professionals handle it." Jada could tell from Trena's aura that she was hiding something else, and before she could think of what it might be, she heard the sound of propellers in the distance. She spun around to see two green zeppelins approaching. They only appeared green to her. To everyone else, they would blend in with the sky, but Jada could see more colors than they could. "Trena, what's going on?"

"We just... assumed... you'd say yes." Sensing the alarm in Jada's voice, she added, "It will be fine. They need you. They won't hurt you."

Since she was four, Jada had endured nightmares about cloaked government agents wielding daggers, and now, she was paralyzed with fear. She couldn't run, lest they see how fast she was, or did they already know? Her dad had told her that if they ever came, she should pretend to be normal, but if it was too late for that, then she needed to run.

"Jada Bell, kneel to the ground and put your hands on your head, or we will shoot both of you."

"Wait! What?" shouted Trena. "She's helping you!"

Cloaked government agents descended from the zeppelins and ran toward them. Jada saw unusually thin men inside the cloaks and realized that these were not government agents. "Trena," she whispered, "they're elves."

"On your knees! Both of you!" shouted the cloaked commander.

Jada knelt to the ground and put her hands behind her head, but Trena was confused. "Elves?" she whispered. "They must be working for Dr. Foid. Jada, you have to fight them! Don't let them capture you!"

"BOTH of you!"

"Jada! Do something!"

There was a flash of electricity and a loud crack, and Trena lay motionless on the ground.

"Stay where you are!" shouted the commander, and Jada resisted her impulse to go to Trena. "Your friend is alive; she still has questions to answer. Duleen has told Dr. Foid all about you, and she won't rest until he meets you."

"What did you do to her?" asked Jada as she tried to sort through her options.

"You are the only one who can help her." Four cloaked elves surrounded Jada, and two of them lifted her to her feet. Jada knew she could easily snap their arms, but even if she could grab Trena and somehow dodge their lightning bolts, they still had Duleen. Her only option now was to cooperate.

The elves led her to one zeppelin and put Trena on the other one. Then, they were in the air, and a few hours later, they were out over the ocean en route to Oldenor, the volcanic island where Dr. Foid was plotting the end of humanity. They flew into the night. Exhaustion conquered her fear, and Jada drifted into an uneasy sleep.

Part II

Elves build ships that treat spheres as planes. That is how they can sail past the edge of the world into realms inaccessible to everyone else. If not for their ships, elves would fill this world, and there would be no room for anyone else. Humans and dwarves are kept in check by mortality, but elves are immortal.

While Dr. Foid talked on and on about the history of elves and population management, Jada was trying to stop the chains holding her wrists from cutting into her skin. She had been in and out of consciousness for days. Dr. Foid's henchelves had all kinds of tools at their disposal, and while they were not strong enough to use every tool on a girl from Earth, they could improvise, and it was still torture. Duleen and Trena fared far worse, and lacked Jada's Earthling ability to black out from severe pain.

At last, Dr. Foid's agents had run out of questions, and now, all three of them were suspended above a vat of pixie blood waiting to be drowned, while Dr. Foid droned on about how brilliant he was, and how in for it they were.

Jada never wanted to be a spy, and after the last few days, death seemed the safest way out of this place. Nothing in life was worth the risk of more torture. She felt bad about all those poor pixies and about all the humans and dwarves who were next, but she was too hurt and frightened to think of trying to do anything about it now.

Not that she could do anything anyway. They had been stripped to their underwear and their wrists and ankles chained to the edges of a heavy metal frame. Even she could not break these chains, and even if she could, they were deep inside Dr. Foid's volcano with a confusing labyrinth of passages between them and an impassable ocean outside. No, drowning wasn't so bad, if only Dr. Foid would stop talking already and get it over with.

Now, Dr. Foid was explaining the particulars of his plan since they were about to die anyway and could not do anything to stop it. For two thousand years, he had worked on developing a device to turn the entire world flat for everyone, and at last, it was ready. Once he turned the world flat, he would then turn gravity sideways for humans and dwarves. Humans and dwarves would fall out of the world and be separated from their mortality with nowhere to go.

"Your people will all float in a boundless abyss of boredom... forever," said Dr. Foid with a grin, "but I have something even better in store for the three of you. There is more than one way to bypass mortality, and your eternity will be anything but boring. By drowning in the blood of murdered pixies, not only will you remain conscious forever, but all your fears will become manifest and multiply without limit!"

Dr. Foid's aura told Jada that he believed every word he said, and a quick glance to either side told her that Duleen and Trena believed it too.

"You already won!" pleaded Trena, "Haven't you hurt us enough already?"

"My sister and her friend are innocent," said Duleen, "Do what you want with me, Dr. Foid, but let them go."

"I have a reputation to maintain, human."

The disbelief that had heretofore kept Jada's fear at bay was starting to ebb. She struggled against the thick chains that held her wrists and ankles, but steel was steel no matter what galaxy she was in. "Please, Dr. Foid, think about what you are doing!"

"No, Earthling, I'd rather not. No one wants to imagine what torments your fears will create in the next few hours, let alone the next trillion gazillion years."

Jada struggled frantically against the chains. "Okay! You made your point! What do you want?"

"As much as I'd enjoy listening to you beg; I have a world to turn on its side." Dr Foid pushed a button, and the chains clanked as the metal frame began to descend. "Farewell." He left the chamber, and a steel door closed behind him. Jada took a deep breath and willed herself to remain calm. The situation was too dire for fear. She had to find a way out.

"Jada, I'm so sorry," cried Trena. "It's my fault you're here."

"Calm down. There must be something we can do," said Jada, "What do we know about pixies?"

"They have powerful magic, and they don't like being killed," said Duleen. "If we die with even a drop of their blood on our skin, we're in for it."

"But we didn't kill them," said Jada.

"Doesn't matter; it's an automatic defense mechanism in their blood."

Jada had a sudden vision of a million pixies being tortured in every imaginable way and realized she was now up to her ankles in their blood. Their blood was a magical blue and wasn't exactly liquid, but it wasn't exactly air either.

"That's so horrible!" said Trena, who was also ankle-deep in the pixie blood.

"Great," said Duleen, "he tortured them to death. Whatever he did to them will be the beginning of what happens to us."

The blood was now up to their knees. "What else do we know about them?"

"They reincarnate with a memory of who really killed them," said Duleen. "That is bad news for Dr. Foid, but it will never help us."

The blood was now up to their hips, and Jada was starting to feel pinches and prodding and heat and tiny electrical shocks. Was it real, or her imagination, or did it matter?

"Ouch! Is this really going to be forever?" asked Trena.

"It's a mathematical, ow, certainty. Jada, err, can't you break these chains or something?"

"I've been trying..." Jada wanted to add more, but the pain was growing exponentially. She didn't have to think her fears. The evil magic binding itself to her soul would soon be exploiting fears she did not even know she had. The blood was almost up to their necks.

"SOMEONE HELP US!" screamed Trena, "ANYONE!"

"Trena!" said Duleen. "We can't think when you're screaming. This chamber is soundproof."

Jada wracked her brain. What did she know about pixies? Were these pixies like the pixies of Earth? Any happy little thought? "That's it!" said Jada.

"What's it?" asked Duleen.

"Think happy thoughts! Pixie magic responds to all emotions, not just negative ones. That's why he spent so long trying to scare us with that monologue!" Her happiness at hitting upon a solution was working. Already, the pain had subsided.

"It hurts," moaned Trena.

"What... good are... three happy... against... a million... tortured... pixies?" asked Duleen.

"Not a happy thought, Duleen!" said Jada, "Think happy thoughts; you too Trena!" Jada was stretching as hard as she could to keep her chin above the surface, but now took a final gulp of air as the blood rose above their heads.

Thinking happy thoughts had made the pain subside, but now it was coming back and drowning out everything else. All those poor pixies! No! Happy thoughts! Jada could see her nerves growing out of her body into an infinite forest of nerve endings, a vision that was less than a minute away from becoming a reality. Definitely not happy! Jada was turning blue. Enough unhappiness already! Being immersed in this much pixie blood could give her incredible magical powers, if she could just think of something really happy. Maybe she could see her parents again? Maybe she could go back in time and go back to Earth and see the Emerald City and get her very own magic wand and I can breathe.

The pain was subsiding again. Duleen was thrashing wildly, but

Trena was still, but that's okay; she'll be fine. Happy thoughts! I'm so happy because now I can break these chains! Sure enough, the cuffs around her wrists and ankles were dissolving. I can fly! I can fly! I can fly!" Jada put up her hands to the frame and pushed it as she rose out of the pixie blood. She glided effortlessly over to where Dr. Foid had been earlier and laid the frame down on the ground. Duleen was coughing but seemed alright. Trena was still.

Duleen ran over to her sister. "On no, oh no, oh no, Trena, can you hear me?"

Jada had seen historical records from Earth where you could bring someone back by breathing into their mouth, pumping their chest, and then hitting their chest really hard while yelling at them. It was worth a try. Her new magical pixie powers should help. Maybe she could breathe happy thoughts into Trena.

Breathing happy thoughts into her mouth didn't seem to work, but after just a few chest compressions, Trena started coughing up the pixie blood. She looked confused, "Jada? Duleen?"

"Yes, we're getting out of here," said Jada.

"I was dead," said Trena, her voice distant.

"Okay, we have to hurry," said Jada.

Trena grabbed Jada's arm, "Something came back with me!"

"Trena," said Duleen, "we'll figure everything out after we get out of here. Jada, since when could you fly?"

"Since just now."

"Can you do it again?"

Jada wrapped her arms around Duleen and Trena and rose effortlessly into the air. "Yes, but I don't know how to get out of here."

"That's okay. My team studied this base for months." She pointed to a ledge about a hundred meters above the vat. "There is a staging area up there. We'll need weapons to get out and warm clothes if we are to survive outside."

Jada flew the three of them into the staging area, and soon they were dressed and armed with enough firepower to vaporize their way out of the volcano.

"Jada," said Trena, "does everything look tilted to you?"

It did. Dr. Foid must have already flattened the world and was now tilting it on its side.

"There is nowhere to escape if we don't stop Dr. Foid," said Duleen.

"There must be some kind of control center," said Jada.

"There is, but my whole team was captured when we tried to get inside."

"Can we free your team?"

"They're all gone. He killed them right in front of me."

"Oh no, I'm sorry. Do you know of any other way to set the world right?"

"I'm thinking."

"The pixie magic may give me a way in."

"That may be our only shot."

"Let's go."

They blasted their way into an elevator shaft, and then Jada flew the three of them down to the heart of the volcano. She imagined that all the henchelves were too tired to keep their eyes open, and when they reached the control center, the elves were all asleep.

Duleen tried to hack into the system, but, "I'm locked out. Only Dr. Foid can reverse the program."

"Where is he?" asked Jada.

"I don't know. I thought he would be here."

The floor tilted further, and the three of them slid through the wall and then a thousand meters of rock as though it were imaginary. There was nothing to stop their slide, no friction on the floor, and things that should be solid were not solid to them. Jada grabbed the other two and flew into the outside air. It was night, but the stars only filled half the sky. The other half of the sky was orange, like some sort of cosmic furnace.

"We're too late," said Duleen, "Humans and dwarves are falling off the world as we speak."

Jada imagined that the world was righting itself, but it wasn't. It was just tilting farther onto its side. Trena was in no condition to fight, so she imagined her floating safely in the air without her help, and so she was. Then she thought of being wherever Dr. Foid was, and she and Duleen found themselves on the moon looking down at a tilted disc over a giant, fiery portal. She also felt weak. She couldn't fly anymore, and her brain seemed to be trapped in slow motion.

"Welcome to my moon base, Earthling," said Dr. Foid. "You can watch as humans and dwarves make their exit."

"What's happening to me?" asked Jada.

"Did you really think you were the first Earthling to land on our world? You will find my moon base is filled with Earth rocks for meddlers like yourself. You have no power here."

"That's okay," said Duleen, "I stole enough of your weapons to vaporize all your Earth rocks."

Before he could stop her, Duleen had set Dr. Foids weapons to "vaporize rock" and vaporized all the rocks inside the moon base. Jada's strength and abilities returned. She made all the other elves in the base sleepy, grabbed Dr. Foid, and flew instantly to his control center in the volcano.

"It is too late, Earthling, only I know the codes."

Jada wondered whether the pixie blood had given her the power to read minds and it had. She read the codes from Dr. Foid's mind, entered them into the computer, and very slowly, the world started to right itself.

Now that she had access to his computer, she found a program called "Pixie defense grid." She turned it off, and a million pixies arrived to deliver Dr. Foid's comeuppance.

Over the next several weeks, the pixies helped Jada, Duleen, and Trena rescue all the humans and dwarves who had fallen off the world. Jada's special pixie abilities faded. She could no longer think herself to the moon and back, or read minds, but she could still fly, and she could still tell when others were telling the truth.

CA Morgan is a writer of fantasy, sword and sorcery and steampunk, whose works have previously appeared in short story anthologies and role-playing gaming books. A former technical writer and editor, she now spends her days weaving tales of myth, magic, and adventure of all types, while being kept in a secluded castle room under the watchful eyes of dragons that prevent her from straying too far from the keyboard. She often dreams of escaping the arid deserts of Arizona for the mists of the Scottish Highlands… but, there are those dragons… Novels *V'Kali's Warrior* and *The Gems of Raga-Tor*, as well as short stories *For Valor, Fly* and *Roses's Champion* are available on Amazon.

Synopsis

Sometimes stories come to me and demand to be written. This is one such account It arrived one morning and several days later it was finished. Archaic, perhaps, but so were the days before the Northmen exploded out of their frozen realms to challenge and terrorize the known world. A tale of warriors and gods, lost in the mists of time, now told.

Falcon

Thrand and two of his fellow jarls, armed with sword and bow, stood in the fog at the edge of a broad, mist-shrouded depression surround by low hills. They glanced uneasily up at the nearly full moon as they waited for their commander and he was late in returning. The echoing sound of horse's hooves, seeming to rise up from the valley floor, drew them closer to the edge where the grassy field sloped gently away and wisps of gray strayed over the lip of the ground as steam from a soup pot. Their hearts beat faster and each in turn felt his eyes widen in an attempt to see the rider, but not so wide as to see the source of their rising fears.

"Truly, he's not in there…" Kori said and pointed to a faint swirling disturbance.

"The gods save him if he is," said Ranvald, his eyes scanned to where Kori indicated.

Thrand, in spite of his pounding heart, laughed quietly. "And where would Falcon be if not taunting the death goddess on the eve of battle?"

Kori drew his sword and leaned down to heft his shield. Ranvald did likewise, but Thrand stood still.

Kori nudged Thrand. "Arm yourself. We need you on the field, not dead for your suppositions."

"Fine." Thrand brought weapons to bear. "Step back from the edge. Spread out."

The pounding hooves came closer, up the rise and the mist swirled faster. The men stepped back farther and further apart. The echoing sound made it hard to determine the point of egress.

"Kori! Closer to you," Thrand said. He ran back a bit further and turned, ready to back up his warrior brother.

The mist roiled, darkened and a black stallion's face appeared a second before the rider, dressed all in black, with a white falcon emblazoned on his chest. His long, black hair, loose and wild, but heavy with dampness, clung to his neck and leather back plate.

Each man breathed a sigh of relief when their commander, Lord Falcon, cleared the rise and reined in hard. The stallion reared and pawed at the air before its massive front hooves hit the ground and dug into the sodden turf all the while trumpeting its displeasure at being forced to stop.

"Your beast is in fine form, my lord," Thrand said as he sheathed his sword and hurried forward to grab the animal's bridle.

"As he should be to face the morning," Lord Falcon said.

Kori looked up nervously. "Surely you don't mean for our army to meet that of the Favonae in this valley, the abode of the death witch, Hede."

"What better place to leave a thousand dead men to rot," Lord Falcon snarled and looked back into the mist.

"Forgive me, my lord," Ranvald said, bowing low, "I know you are not as familiar with the southern part of your realm, but really—"

"Silence! What battle does Hede not attend?" Lord Falcon glared at them.

As his name proclaimed, his predatory features were sharp and distinct. His dark eyes gleamed preternaturally in the moon's white light. His mouth set a grim line as he looked from them and back across the valley. The call of a night bird drew his gaze skyward and then he turned to look down at them.

"Unless you wish the Favonae to overrun our positions, to rise above this bowl on all sides, destroying your homes, your families, we will meet them here. We have the higher ground for the first assault. They will bleed and die at every step through this land." As if he couldn't help himself, he turned and stared again into the mist.

His men gathered beside him in a tighter cluster. As they watched him, it seemed as if he could see the enemy, their plans, their preparations. They wondered, keeping their thoughts silent, if he saw Hede gliding through the night, through the dark mist weaving the flow of battle, writing the names of the damned on the ground where they would die, their blood nurturing her accursed land.

"They sleep," Lord Falcon pronounced. "We will meet them as the sun rises. Post your guards and sleep well by keeping tomorrow in its place. I will have all of you strong with me."

"Yes, my lord," they said in unison and bowed as he tapped the horse's flank and disappeared from sight.

Kori shook his head. "You've known him longest, Thrand; didn't he seem more preoccupied than usual?"

Thrand shrugged. "Maybe. I don't know. The Favonae have always been our enemies and of late, we lose more than we win against them. If we don't hold here, they will have an easy pass through the center of the Danibrode."

"But," Kori reminded, "the jarls to the east and west of us have yet to field the bulk of their forces, and they are considerable."

"Acchh," Ranvald spat on the ground. "A curse on their disrespect for the king. This is where we stop them. And Falcon is right. The archers first and then we'll break them with a cavalry charge before the foot soldiers enter."

Kori turned to head back to camp. "Still not sure we should risk the horses so soon. Their number is falling like ours."

Thrand threw an arm around Kori's shoulders and the three of them walked to camp. "I know, but better to save the men. Takes longer to grow them up."

Kori smiled. "You have a point."

* * *

A page ran from the shadows toward Lord Falcon as he reined in near his pavilion.

"Do you need anything, my lord?" the boy asked.

"No. Just see to the horse. I'm not to be disturbed until dawn's faintest light, when the army will prepare to move out."

The page nodded and Lord Falcon pushed aside the canvas drape and entered the pavilion's outer chamber. He paused and looked at the maps still splayed on the planning table. He considered the battles and skirmishes they had fought off and on over the past two years and saw the enemy's inexorable push, forcing them slowly, but ever toward this valley. It was the main and easiest path through the southern mountains that would allow them access to the greater part of his kingdom if they didn't hold this land. And yet, many times along this path of Favonae conquest his armies should have held, but still they fell. Why, to end up here?

The Kirkelte Valley. The valley of the witch. As he stared at the name scrawled on the parchment, his eyes glowed again even in the near darkness of the room. He stretched his arms and shoulders and thrust his neck forward as was the habit of the great bird, the falcon that lived within.

He grabbed his cup and a decanter of wine from a side table and roughly pushed through another drape that hid his private quarters. He filled his cup, drank it down and filled it again before setting both on a table that held his previously delivered dinner. He lifted the protective cloth. It was a hearty meal for a change, not short rations. He should eat, yet the night haunted him. The valley haunted him. And the witch. How may many eons had she pursued him? He pulled a chair next to the table, emptied his cup, filled it again, and sat.

He stared into the semi-darkness beyond the light of the small lantern. His thumb and index finger pinched at his lower lip and he thought back over the last ten years. It was the invocations and sacrifices of abused and suffering men that initially brought him to this place. Their rightful king slain by a traitor, the kingdom suffered under the self-proclaimed tyrant's insatiable cruelty and predations.

Falcon smiled grimly and finally pulled the cloth from his dinner. The meat was cold now, but it was cooked rare, bloody, still with the texture of fresh kill; so much like the fresh meat the bird picked from the bones of dead animals. It resembled the flayed flesh that he cut slowly, bit by bit from the screaming pretender king as he died and Falcon took his place.

The great and strange commander, who had appeared one day in a nameless village, gave the people back their hope, and finally they convinced him to take the crown. For ten years, he presided over a peace that had lasted...until now.

He sighed and ate. Ten years passing was nothing to him and his people marveled that his youthful appearance and great strength remained. He refused time and again to take a wife and there were worries about the succession of his line. Yet he had searched far and wide and finally found the nephews of the deposed, lawful king; to them he gave his wisdom and skills and would acquiesce his reign to them when they were of age.

He finished his meal and poured the last of the wine. He sat back and convinced the restless bird that this night it didn't need to fly. The enemy was known and this time he had men and advantage enough to win. Tomorrow, when the field was won, the bird could take flight, eat of the hearts of his enemies and perhaps, lay in the arms of his beloved even if for a moment before he had to return to burn the dead in their victory fires.

Falcon sighed and reached into a small pocket on the inside of his shirt. He drew out a lock of honey-blond hair, plaited and tied carefully with two, short lengths of blue weaving. Gently, he pulled its softness through his fingers and ran it along his chin. Svana. How he ached and burned for her was something he rarely felt for any mortal woman. The great falcon within could reach her in minutes, but Falcon, the man, would not be persuaded to leave her in time to take the field, to sneer once again at Hede's attempt to steal his victories, to capture his very heart.

He closed his eyes and lightly kissed the braid. His heart sent her his love and hoped she felt it on the night breeze. Hoped she felt it in the quickening of his child that grew in her womb. At dawn, a pale vision of her in the face of her brother, Thrand, the jarl of these lands, would be at his side. "Svana…" he whispered her name for a countless time and sleep was his.

* * *

Six young men, too young to fight, but old enough to use flags to signal the army, watched and wondered in amazement at Lord Falcon's great, black stallion and for the moment their fears abated. The great beast seemed to understand the course of battle as it kicked and bit, yet wheeled and charged with what must have been directions given by Lord Falcon's knees and feet. And their great and courageous lord, his sword an unstoppable juggernaut, cut the ribbons of men's lives and the blood of their enemies pooled on the reddening field.

Their eyes widened and fear returned, pounding in their chests, when Lord Falcon turned to them and galloped up the shallow ridge. With bloody sword he pointed and shouted, "Raise the flags for the western flank to move in."

Quickly they raised the white standards with the black falcons and down the grassy inclines and through the trees, half of the cavalry retook the field.

Lord Falcon paused to watch them and took the moment to wipe his sword hand on his tunic and then wiped the sword's hilt, which had become wet and slippery. The sweep of battle was turning in his favor and he smiled grimly as Thrand and his men closed in on the enemy fleeing the western charge.

A gust of wind caught Lord Falcon's attention and in it he felt the witch's power. "Get away from me and my men," he growled. "You'll have your feast soon enough."

He heard her faint laughter on the breeze that at once refreshed his men in their fight, but chilled his heart. He was too close to her, but he had no choice. The Favonae had to be held here.

"I don't care about your men… I only care about you," Hede's voice whispered back.

Falcon ignored her. He turned back to the battle. "Signal for Thrand to pull back."

The boys did so and a short time later, the center column collapsed as the men retreated drawing the enemy forward.

Falcon turned to his left and let the falcon's spirit rise so that it could see over the battlefield from high above. The hidden cavalry on the eastern edge waited, ready to once again charge into the melee. The enemy forces had completely entered the valley. They were over extended, supplies were low and they were too far from home.

The stallion reared suddenly. The acrid smell of sulfur was borne on a gust of wind. Damn her! Lord Falcon turned to the boys. "Send the western flank down the gap. Signal the eastern cavalry to retake the field."

The stallion danced and they waited for the charge from the east. The thunder of hooves rose and Falcon heeled his mount. Down the incline he rode, quickly joining his men and leading the charge into the enemy ranks, cutting them off from his infantry.

Falcon's sword flashed and dulled quickly with splashes of blood and sinew. The edge of his shield slammed into unprotected necks, crushing bone. He felt the strike of sword against his leather-protected thighs, the thud of an arrowhead against the protection of his eternal being, and on he fought, the smell of blood sweet and bitter in his nose, as the quarrels of men were unrelenting.

The enemy broke in the confusion and retreated. Thrand's men rejoined the battle.

"Kori!" Falcon shouted. "Close the rear. No retreat, no quarter."

The morning was gone and the sun was nearly overhead. His men were exhausted, yet Falcon's banner flew high, encouraging them, giving strength to their weary bones, to their arms that struggled to swing the next blow. And then the enemy was but pockets of bloody, terrified men standing back-to-back in small circles as Falcon's army culled them from their once-fierce herd.

Falcon's soaring vision again showed him the inexorable surrender of the Favonae. "Group them at the base of the western ridge!" His shout went out and the command was quickly repeated across the field of death. He rode hard to the south, repeating the order. He wheeled around when he saw Ranvald's banner torn from its standard and crushed into the muddy ground.

"Ranvald!" Falcon shouted and saw several men garbed in the green tabards of his house turn to face him. "Where is your lord?"

"He fell some time ago, Lord Falcon," one man answered and blinked tears from his eyes.

Falcon raised his sword in honor of his fallen commander. "Take his banner and carry it proudly to the ridge. We have won this day. Favonae stragglers receive no quarter. Today we crush their ability to come at us again."

"Yes, my lord," one answered and half-heartedly pulled the silk from the mud.

Falcon continued shouting orders, encouraging his men. The smell of sulfur came to him again.

"Get away from me, witch! Damn you to Hel's realm!" he cursed. His piercing gaze searched the sky for her, but he saw her not.

"And who will carry your standard?" she taunted.

He felt her presence, her evil, but only when the moon was full could she take form, black and misshapen, in the realm of men. They would be clear of this valley, this field of death long before the night's full moon rose.

He reached the southern end of the battle line and in his anger, dispatched a score of Favonae as he and the stallion bore down on their fleeing forms. Only his men would leave this accursed field alive and the thought of it, of centuries, of millennia, of men killing men for the space of a little land, gold, power, and for what? To kill and destroy a generation later, again and again, it made him want to wretch for the futility of it all. He always sought to ignore their plaintinve cries, yet there was always one who knew of him, of his mystery, and knew the words to call him forth, to call him to the lands of shadow and sorrow. Yet, was this not his agreed upon destiny in the realm of the greater and lesser gods?

He wheeled the great stallion around and knew by the keening wails of helpless men that the slaughter of prisoners had begun. Thrand and Kori would see to it, a command previously arranged, and Ranvald... He wondered where his body lay. As an honored man, he should not lie in wait for the maggots of the field, for his eyes to be plucked out by the carrion birds; the lesser of his winged companions who knew not the difference between man and animal, but consumed all flesh as if it were one.

Quickly he rode back to the place where he first saw Ranvald's banner, but there was no sign of his trusted, and he had to admit, beloved commander. After Thrand, and his thoughts momentarily drifted to Svana, there was no man he loved better for his honor, his skills and his unwavering duty in all that was asked of him.

His eyes surveyed the bloody destruction before him. His was the power of flight, of far-seeing vision, patron of the hunter, so when did he become cursed to be a god of war?

The keening wail of the damned faded and his men turned to search the battlefield for weapons, valuables, to slay the wounded and dying. He sheathed his sword and grabbed up a spear standing upright in the body of a dead man. A shove here, a downward thrust there, and the enemy was no more. Finally sickened of his task, he threw the spear aside and rode for the ridge where he saw Thrand and Kori waiting.

Falcon was nearly there when the smell of sulfur, thick and pungent enough to take his breath way, overtook him. The stallion reared. As it dropped back down, Falcon saw it, and so did his men. He brought his shield to bear, a futile move.

"You can't do this, Hede! I will never submit—" His shouted scream echoed from the very ground of the corpse-strewn valley, echoed and reverberated north to south, east to west, against the bowl-like valley walls.

The Sword of Fate, the mythic weapon of the gods, appeared like lightening in the sky and flew directly at Falcon. The white-blue light sizzled and men stared in awe, not understanding how it came to be, and the gods be damned, why it was flying straight at their king? The trajectory of its flight was not deflected by Falcon's shattered shield and he screamed in fury as its bright light and white-hot metal pierced his chest, tore him from his mount and slammed him to the ground. The great sword's long blade pierced the earth through him.

Thrand and Kori ran forward and stared at Falcon's sprawled and unmoving black form. The great sword continued to burn with eldritch fire and pinned their lord to his doom.

"Pull that from him!" Thrand shouted as they ran toward the men nearby. Stunned, they didn't move.

Where did such a thing come from? Why did the gods punish their victory by taking their great king?

Thrand and Kori reached Lord Falcon on one side and Kori on the other. Both stared at the sword, its cold fire and fury calming. Thrand spotted a spear, grabbed it up and broke it across his knee. He handed half to Kori.

"Get under the cross guard like this and let's see if we can pull it out."

The two men struggled and strained, but the sword was immovable. Exhausted, they dropped the wood and Thrand sank down beside his lord and dared to touch his hand. It was pale and cold beneath the sheath of dark, dried blood. He leaned forward and put his hand on Falcon's face, but their lord was gone, and gone in way none of them understood. His body's heat should have lingered a while yet, but he was cold, so very cold.

"Nooo!" Thrand screamed and struggled to pull the weapon from his lord's chest. The Sword of Fate, now only a length of mirror-polished metal, ignored his efforts as it stood straight, firm and forever plunged in Falcon's chest. "Oh gods, no... no... no..."

Kori came around and knelt next to his friend, tears running down his face. "We know what this is, brother, what he silently feared."

"No! He didn't fear her. He didn't! He cursed her name as I shall forever curse it."

Kori squeezed his arms. "He dared to cross her land. Dared to win our battle here. Hede takes her revenge against him, because he has ever repulsed her corrupted desires."

"This isn't right." Thrand shook his head and wept. Men knelt in a great circle around their fallen king. He screamed at the sky. "Hede! You whore of the gods! Release him and let him live."

From the very ground beneath them, noxious fumes rose. A shadow moved across the face of the sun, but there were no clouds. The wind grew stronger in the valley and men's faces grew fearful, their murmured questions and invocations a louder hum and finally Thrand heard them through his grief.

Kori shook him gently, his grief no less, but he knew if they tarried long, the witch would write their names in Fate's death tapestry ere the next battle. "Come, my friend, we need to leave this cursed place. The moon rises full tonight and she is too close to us."

Thrand nodded and got to his feet. He was heir to Falcon's command. He shouted his orders. "Clear this valley! The evil witch is too close. We must leave our dead to Idun, and let her cover them with her blessings and send them to Valholl."

Thrand and Kori stood by the body of their king until the last man cleared the incline and disappeared from sight. Thrand knelt and pulled Falcon's sword from its sheath and laid it across his chest.

"Farewell, great king. We don't know from whence you came, but we are grateful. We will send messengers to the court and King Skvold's nephews will reign triumphantly in your stead as you wished."

Kori offered his hand to pull Thrand to his feet. Together, wrapped in each other's arms, leaning into their unyielding despair, they returned to their camp.

* * *

Darkness fell and the round, heavy moon rose over the mountains in the east and cast a bright light across the land, all except for the Kirkelte Valley, the valley of the witch, the valley where Lord Falcon lay, pierced through the heart by the mystic sword.

The sulfurous stench grew along with the mist and Hede took shape as she walked among the dead, who were beginning to add their own reek to the foul place.

Falcon awoke from his sleep only to feel the rage, the sorrow, the loss of his freedom. The bird wanted, needed to fly, but its wings were clipped, its heart throbbing with heartache. He tried to transform into the great falcon, but his heart was pierced and held fast to the ground, where no god of the sky should be.

His earthly form smelled the sulfur of Hede's passing that blended with the stench of the dead and he knew that would grow worse before the worms and carrion reduced them to nothing but bones bathed in the cool rain.

He watched the legion of living fire rise up from the ground and wander aimlessly as they sought the road to Valholl. He would have shed tears for them all if he could have. Enemies in life, now brothers forever in death; why couldn't they understand this while they lived for death and Valholl made no distinction.

"Ranvald!" Falcon shouted in the dream that he had become.

His man paused and searched the darkness. "Come, beloved warrior, I'm here, on the ground not far from you."

Ranvald looked quickly around and found his lord sorely wounded. He hurried to his side and fell on his knees.

"Oh, but the gods are unmerciful even to my Lord Falcon. My heart is wrung cry of tears already for what has become of us, and unbelievably, to you. But why do you not rise with us?" Ranvald asked, his shape a wispy image of the man he was.

"Because now you see the truth of me. I'm not a man, but Falcon, a world spirit, god of the hunt, and the Sword of Fate has sorely wounded me. But, quickly now, I want you to listen to me," Falcon said, and wished he could wrap his men in his great wings and take them home. "Look, behind you. Do you see that glimmer of light at the edge of the hollow?"

"Yes, great lord, but we are unworthy of you and…"

"Shhhh, just listen. Walk to that place of light. The others will follow. You must hurry to leave this valley of death before Hede's evil traps you here. If she tries to stand in front of you, do not fear. She can't hurt you. Walk through her form and there is the path to Valholl. Go now, hurry," Falcon urged.

Ranvald leaned down to his lord and kissed the sword that lay across his chest. "How do we free you from this wrongful fate?"

Falcon smiled. "You cannot, honored warrior. The only way I will be set free is to give in to the demands of the witch."

Ranvald looked horrified. "And what does she demand?"

Falcon's face grew sad, his eyes shimmered. "My son."

Ranvald was puzzled. "But… the god of the hunt has no son…"

"I know," Falcon said softly and tears rolled from his eyes. "I won't couple with her and allow my seed to be corrupted by her evil, so here I will remain until Jörmungandr stirs and the world ends. Go now. Great Odinn awaits you in his glittering hall."

Ranvald's face was at once awash with misty tears and grim determination. "I shall not set foot within that hall, and will shout my curses until the All Father has set you free from this torment."

"Nay, warrior. This fate is given to me. You've earned your reward. I shall but sleep until the end of time when men and gods are destroyed alike and the world begins anew," Falcon said with a sad smile. "Hurry now. Take your men."

Ranvald nodded, got to his feet and gave a great shout, "Follow me!"

Falcon watched them go, but Hede didn't block their path. Instead, the reek of her being flooded his senses as her long, black skirts fell across his face and shoulders as she walked passed and looked down at him.

"You don't really mean to lie here until the end."

"I do and I will."

Hede knelt next to him. Her face was beautiful, enticing, as were the smooth globes of her breasts that appeared when she loosened the ribbons of her chemise. "What man can resist the siren call of my body?"

"Men cannot, but I can," Falcon said and felt nothing stir in him. "I know the corruption of your flesh. What you show me is a poor façade."

Her hand rubbed down the side of his face. "But do you know the power of this sword that pins you to the ground?"

"Obviously, as I can't rise from this accursed field, nor can I take to the skies."

She bent down and her lips touched his, but he wouldn't respond. "Tonight, you refuse me, and perhaps for a while yet, but when the moon is full and I walk this valley, how long will you withstand this?"

Falcon watched her hands reach up and take hold of the sword's broad quillons and gave the mystical weapon a quarter turn. A scream of unexpected agony poured from his mouth, from every part of his being, and he cursed the Fates for their wicked designs. Through his anguish, he saw the wings of the great falcon, shadowy and strong, unfurl between him and the ground. They thrust against the air, trying to rise, but fate pinioned him in place, in time, and from Hede there was no escape.

She smiled down and watched him patiently as he continued to writhe in the ebb and flow of his agony, which lessened as the moon continued its path across the vault of the sky and sank behind the mountains. Her form lost its solid aspect as a hint of the sun lessened the night's blackness.

"So, great Falcon," she said as she stood and covered herself, "when the moon is full again, I shall come to you. And every time you refuse me, I shall turn the blade and watch you suffer until Sol brings the sun to this place that you have made more wretched with the rot and bones of a thousand men."

"And every time I will refuse you, refuse your evil," Falcon said, his voice pained and quivering.

Hede laughed. "Perhaps you can survive this night, but what of the others when the moon is just on the edge of full, of wax and wane? When you most loved to fly the night skies, hunting for the open bower windows of maidens fair, and seduced them with your dark and mysterious aspect? How long until your loins cry with want for them, for those mortal beings so fragile and transient, and then you will give me what I want."

Falcon grimaced as a last stab of pain pinched his shoulders. "You understand nothing of me for it was their beauty that seduced my eyes and made me pause upon their sill to grant the wish of a heartfelt dream."

Hede smirked at him and pressed down against the blade and made him moan again. "Until the moon is full, my love…"

Falcon watched the first rays of Sol's arrival dissipate her vile shape and was greeted by the death grimaces of a dozen men who lay upon the trampled grass.

* * *

Thrand and Kori stood a weary guard once again near the edge of the shallow valley. Only this night they didn't await the approach of battle, but the reckoning of the dead come morning, when the physicians would dispose of those they couldn't cure.

Kori took a deep breath trying to revive his weary body. "The hours of the witch approach. Do you think she walks in the darkness?"

"How could she no when the greatest prize is cruelly killed by the Fates?" Thrand answered and tears ran down his face for an uncounted time that day.

Another hour passed and the weary men were suddenly startled to wakefulness by the anguished cry of a great bird, the call of a falcon. They looked at each other in wonderment.

"Lord Falcon!" Thrand cried out and ran toward the sound.

Kori caught Thrand and pulled him to the ground just as he was about to descend into the dark depression. "No! You let this be. He's gone. He's gone and so is Ranvald. Don't begrudge them paradise in your sorrow. Don't keep them from entering Odinn's great hall."

Thrand turned. Kori's tears coursed down his face.

"But that sound…"

"It's only what our hearts want to hear. A more magnificent king, by aspect or largess, we'll never see again. Let him go, brother. Honor them all in your heart, in your great deeds."

Thrand nodded and looked down the gentle slope. "From here I can see the gleam of that cursed weapon, mocking our strength."

"That sword is not of men, but of the gods. Who are we to say why he was taken from us?"

Thrand sighed and wiped his face on his bloody tunic. "And what do I tell my sister? What do I tell Svana who loves him so?"

* * *

Three days later Kori woke in the gray light of a chill morn and stiffly sat up. Thrand paced a muddy line in the grassy field that showed the perimeter of their watch.

Kori's upward glance and frown caused Thrand to pause. "The men came to me while you slept. How many more days do we tarry? They grow anxious to leave."

"Two more. The wounded need more time to heal. And while we think we have destroyed our enemy, I won't leave them to potential slaughter."

"We have men enough to carry them all on litters."

"Two days."

Kori stood and faced his commander. "I think the delay is for you, not them."

"For me?" Thrand was puzzled. "I have no need of any more days, but it will give time for their wounds to heal, and strength to return."

"Then don't blame me if you wake on the fifth day to find yourself alone."

Thrand grabbed Kori's arm as he turned to leave. "And you? Will you go with them?"

Kori's shoulders slumped. "No, brother, I will sit here with you until we are overcome by the reek of the valley's corrupted denizens."

Thrand let him go and gave his back a quick shove, which made Kori turn to glare at him. "No, go with them."

"Let Falcon go."

"In my time." Thrand's voice rumbled and his brow creased with anger. "Go on, all of you, go home."

Kori turned without a word, picked up his weapons and headed back to the body of their camp. When he had disappeared from view, Thrand turned and walked the quarter league back to the edge of the desolate land, the cold bowl of Hede's stew of sorrows.

He didn't know how long he stood staring at the gleaming metal of the Sword of Fate. No man in camp knew of any reason why their valiant king deserved such a thing, but from the tales told by the old crones, the healers, from a time lost in the shadows, Hede the Witch wanted Falcon's son at any cost. But in truth, who was this man who had come to them out of the mists of a winter's eve ten years ago? Who was Falcon—a mortal man, a world spirit…a god? Who would dare to ask the truth of Falcon's provenance?

The tears built and rolled down Thrand's face. He didn't understand. He was the man, the warrior upon whom their king had unexpectedly showered his attention, his trust, his love, and in return, Thrand allowed him the love of his sister. With all of this just so, why wasn't he fated to protect Falcon from this fate, to have suffered it for him, or at the least, to be the one capable of pulling the foul weapon from Falcon's chest.

He sat in the trampled grass and still he couldn't stop the heartbreak in himself, and wept knowing that for Svana, his favorite sibling, her heartbreak would be many times greater than his. His vision was blurred by tears, but not enough to keep him from seeing the bloating of his lord's body, the bloody fluids beginning to ooze from his nose and mouth, and the greenish pallor coloring his cold flesh.

The others had already lost their belief, their faith in the god-fire that was supposed to have burned in Falcon. Was it now his turn to deny Falcon as well? And why should he continue to believe in immortality when his eyes saw the truth of it? How was it possible for the body of a world spirit, perhaps even a god, to decay with the rot of a man?

But perhaps his heart yearned to believe that while the body rotted, the god-fire still burned in Falcon and that was what held the dread weapon firmly in his chest. That if the weapon was removed, the great All-Father would restore him to life and body, pure and burning with those things that made a man, a warrior, a king. Thrand got to his feet determined to re-enter the valley to save his king. But the longer he stared at the dread weapon, the heavier his feet became, and his determination faltered. In the end, who did he think he was anyway? A jarl he might be, but only of a small holding tucked in a difficult tract of land, a buffer between two, more powerful jarls. He took a deep breath and pretended he didn't smell the dead. His fellow jarls didn't send many men to Falcon's cause, but held them back in the event they failed to hold the Favonae in this valley. Or, was it because they were a power unto themselves and cared little for what their distant king thought or did?

Thrand ran his hands over his face. If those men hadn't given their king the fullest support of which they were capable, what made him think he was a man with status worthy or capable of saving his king, much less challenging the will of the gods or fates?

He thought of Eyja, his wife, and the child she carried. *I'm a fool to think I should be involved in any of this. I've done my duty, lost men...my friends...* His tears ran for Ranvald and he still didn't know where his body lay, and felt the heartache Ranvald's wife would bear when the men passed by his farm on their way home. Thrand's shoulders slumped. His gaze went to the ground, where he saw his shoes caked with mud and stained with the blood of men, whose number he didn't want to count. *It's enough. It's done and a king comes to his end and dies as easily as any man... Just go home. You have a harvest to bring in and soon, a child to raise. And Svana...gods, how am I going to do this...but the days will pass and live we must...*

* * *

The sun returned and Thrand bid farewell to his brother jarls as they struck camp and each undertook their journey home in their separate directions. While glad to leave the vile reek of the witch's valley, their hearts remained leaden and grief-stricken. It was anyone's guess how King Skvold's nephews would acquit themselves, but with Lord Falcon as their former mentor, the future held hope.

Though his journey home was the length of daylight's hours,

Thrand was forced to tell over and over again about the deaths of loved ones and the fall of their liege, and ended the telling with stern warnings to stay away from the witch's valley.

By late afternoon, he reached home, his head cast to the ground when it should have been held high in victory. He knew his sister would be waiting for Lord Falcon's return, watching from the towers above. His wife, Eyja, would weep with relief when she threw herself into his arms, and yet what could he do for Svana?

It wasn't long before the shouts of his household came to his ears and out of habit he looked around for Kori, but he wasn't there. He had stayed behind with Ranvald's pretty, now widowed wife, to ease her in her grief as he had only his sickly mother waiting for him, and he had sent along a message that he would return to her by and by.

"Thrand! Oh, the gods are merciful!"

He heard the glad voice of his wife as she hurried to him and he smiled in spite of himself. She walked quickly rather than ran as she was with child, but still in the early part, before the heaviness of the child was expected. He hurried to her and she melted into his arms and kissed him over and over before he could even say a word. It was then he caught sight of Svana searching the entourage for Lord Falcon's great, black stallion. Yet even the beast was now a mystery as once the initial shock of Falcon's death wore off, the animal was nowhere to be found.

Thrand kissed Eyja once more and spoke. "Forgive me, my love, but I need to speak with Svana."

Eyja held him by the tunic and looked into his eyes. "He hasn't gone back to his seat, has he?"

Thrand shook his head and his heart grew heavier, his footfalls more burdensome the closer he got to Svana.

"Brother!" Svana greeted and hurried to give him a hug. He heard the nervous worry in her voice. "Pray tell, where is our victorious king, Lord Falcon?"

Thrand couldn't stop the tears that ran again from his eyes as he held her and wouldn't let her pull away from him. "I'm sorry, Svana, I'm so, so sorry…"

"What?" Svana asked and pushed herself back to see his face. "Has he gone back to the North so soon? Without a care for me?"

"No, sister. He lies with the honored dead upon the battlefield."

"No! Why do you tell me this? He has only gone north to secure his seat."

"No, my sweet sister, and you can ask any of my men, those who saw its blazing fury. From out of... of the sky... Lord Falcon was pierced through the heart... by the Sword of Fate."

Thrand watched Svana's lips tremble and then her whole body trembled.

"No... no. No! There is no such thing. He's alive!" Svana's face crumpled and tears fell from her brilliant blue eyes. "Tell me the truth, Thrand, where is Lord Falcon?"

"He's dead, sweet sister." He hugged her to him. "Gods, that it wasn't the truth, but he is as dead as Ranvald, as dead as the enemy that litters the field."

Svana went limp in his arms and her sobs were pulled from the depths of her heart. Word quickly spread through the yard that Lord Falcon had fallen in battle, killed by the hands of the gods themselves, and wondered how it was right and good that a man such as he was not found worthy by the gods.

Eyja went to them and pulled Svana with her.

"But what am I to do, Thrand?" Svana sobbed as more ladies gathered and waited to help her.

"I don't understand. What do you mean?"

Svana took his hand and stepped closer to him to hide her actions. Gently, she pressed his hand to the swell of her belly, hidden by the draping aprons she wore.

Thrand's eyes grew wide and looked from her to Eyja. "Is this...?" He couldn't finish the question. Even for him, it hurt too much.

Eyja nodded. "There is nothing to be done, my husband, except that you will protect your sister and raise your nephew to be the man his father was."

"Oh gods," was all Thrand could mutter and he lifted his weeping sister in his arms and carried her into his home.

* * *

"By the ears of the gods, Svana, will you be quiet?" Thrand shouted at her and the servants heading into the room made a hasty retreat. "Lord Falcon is gone."

"He isn't gone. I keep telling you he was more than a man. He told me he was. I felt he was. Something isn't right."

"You were infatuated with a powerful man, who happened to look upon you with great favor."

"What?" Svana shouted at Thrand and got to her feet. "Are you calling me the king's whore? How you dare!"

"No, Svana. Gods give me patience." He rubbed his hands hard over his face. "I permitted him to court you for his great favor shown to me, and his sincerity where you were concerned."

"And you, my brother, are so stupid. As much as he loved me, he loved you. How did you not see, not feel deep in your heart when he spoke to you privately that something about him, yet you deny it."

"I deny nothing." Thrand looked to Eyja, but she wouldn't look at him. "What I know, I know with my eyes and I know that he is well and truly dead. Every day, damn you, I wish it wasn't so." He looked up at her, tears glistening in his eyes. Quickly, he turned away and grabbed up the bread on his plate to give him something to focus on, to lessen the agony in his heart that Svana stirred nearly every day. "Every morning when the sun rises, do I not see that sword coming out of the rays of the sun?"

"And you know that sword is magic. He's trapped…somehow. You need to help me."

"No, let it go."

"No, Thrand, you listen to me!" Svana said angrily as she rounded on her brother. "It has been well over a month since that battle and I will see the bones of my beloved, and this mystical sword that killed him." She nearly choked on the words. Her lips quivered, but her eyes were alight with anger's fury. "If you won't take me, then I will go alone."

Thrand looked to Eyja, but found no help there. She glared at him as her weaving shuttle passed through the loom with an angry motion, and for the passing of a week or more she had not allowed him the pleasures of her body.

He dropped the bread to the plate and drank down his cup of wine. "Fine, both of you. I'll take you in the morning, but given your condition, I'll not be responsible if you drop the child too soon."

"Falcon's child is strong, just like he was," Svana said and struggled to keep her tears at bay.

"And just so you know," Thrand said, pointing his finger at both women, "I have no idea what Lord Falcon intended for the child; much less if Svana was to be his queen, but it goes no farther than this room that he sired this child. Do both of you understand?"

Svana sat down and glared at her brother. "Then who shall I say is the father to please you?"

"I don't know, but I'll not risk any of our lives with the truth."

Eyja sighed and sat up straighter to stretch her back. "I suppose he is right on that, sister. We'll come up with a suitable story as we don't know what would happen if word got out, but it would be no surprise to the people of our village." She gave her husband another hard look. "Everyone knows how Falcon loved her."

Thrand sighed and stood up. "I have things to do before dark."

The women watched him go. Eyja smiled and reached over to squeeze Svana's hand. "I will let him between my legs tonight and that way he won't be such a brute to you tomorrow."

Svana smiled and her tears glistened as she held Eyja's hand to her lips and kissed it. "If only I had the chance to be with my love once more…"

* * *

The weather was clear and warm and the horses made good time in their return to the Kirkelte Valley. Thrand eased his mount closer to Svana's as a dozen men of his house rode behind and flanking them.

"We are almost there," he said. "Are you sure you want to do this?"

Svana nodded. "I have to. Don't ask me why, because I don't understand it myself. I only know that Falcon was a man like no other and that's how we loved each other." She cast a glance at Thrand and gave him a little smile.

"What?" he asked, when she didn't speak the cause for the knowing look in her eyes.

"It's nothing. Just thank you for bringing me here."

Thrand grunted as he shifted in the saddle. "Don't thank me yet. Thousands of little bones, and perhaps even pieces of flesh and strands of hair caught in the grass is a sight you'll not soon forget."

Svana nodded and swallowed hard. She had tried to put those

images out of her mind that had insisted to her that Falcon would be no different. Yet a deep knowing in her heart told her that Falcon would be nothing of the sort, because what man had a spirit and life force like his.

They reached the edge of the valley and Thrand reined to a stop. He turned to his men and said, "All of you remain here. There is no need for you to relive that saddest victory any men have had to endure." Several looked at him as if asking for permission. He sighed. "Fine, if you feel you must take the field, then only a few at a time."

"Yes, my lord," their voices murmured and several turned their backs and wouldn't look out at the valley still dotted with spots of color as the earth's retaking of its own was slow.

Thrand reached up to help Svana from her mount. He held her a moment as she steadied her feet beneath her. She looked up at him and reached up to touch his face, clean shaven for the coming of summer.

"You don't need to come with me either, dearest brother. The battle you could care less about, but you know how I have always known you, and your love for him was always in your eyes."

Thrand turned away, his throat tightened. "I will come. You might need help coming back up the rise."

Svana took his arm and he escorted her to the edge of the broad valley. She paused and looked out over the land. The spring rains and warm days had made the grasses grow and partially obscured the rotting dead. Only a faint hint of the stench remained, but not enough to deter her from seeing this mystical sword and the remains of her love.

"You know, don't you," Svana said quietly as they descended the shallowest slope, "that Falcon cherished you above all of his men, and even before he cast his eyes upon me."

"He had many men under his command and throughout his kingdom. I would not presume such a thing."

"It is no presumption, but the truth as he told me many times. He always told me he saw great things for you."

Thrand smiled sadly and adjusted their course through the field. "But now he's gone, and I'm only one of many jarls who owes fealty to the new king."

Svana nodded with a smile but said nothing more. Her eyes had caught sight of the one and only sword that stood on its point in spite of wind and weather and knew that was where Falcon lay. She paused a moment and took a deep breath. She fought the tears that crept to her eyes and the trepidation that pounded in her heart.

The last time they had seen each other, he had spent the entire night making love to her and while he was sometimes rough in his passion, the way his eyes softened and his lips kissed her gently rounding belly spoke of his happiness, his desire to hold and nurture the child she carried.

She felt Thrand's emotion as much as she felt her own and gave his arm a squeeze and moved toward the place of which neither of them would speak.

"Even from here I can see that the sword didn't come from one of our smiths," Svana said.

"Without warning," Thrand said softly, "it flew at him directly from out of the sky, higher and more accurately than any man could throw, and it shattered his shield as if it belonged to a boy."

Svana let go of Thrand and walked through the fragrant grass to where Falcon lay. Tears ran and she paused, her mouth open in shock as she stared down. Just as she believed with all her heart, Falcon lay pale, fully formed, as if he slept, except for the horrific sword that stood as a silent sentinel through his heart.

She glanced toward Thrand and wondered if he would see the same, but the sight of her beloved, whole and handsome, drew her back and she knelt next to him. Gently, she put a trembling hand upon his face. She didn't know if the warmth she felt was from the shining sun, or if somehow, as they had said, the mystic sword held his life to him but at the same time wouldn't let him live or die.

She couldn't help herself and as she bent to kiss him, her tears fell on his face. "Oh gods, Falcon, my love, I miss you so. The days pass and still my grief for you refuses to part from me." She paused and stroked his face, his hand. She put her hand on his chest, but his heart was still and she dared not touch the accursed sword. If Falcon's child didn't move and flutter in her belly, she would have been tempted to try to pull the sword from him, but she feared that the great magic had felled him might also take their child from her.

Her hand squeezed his and it was almost as if she could feel him watching her. She kissed him again and smelled the sweet flowers that grew around his face and shoulders. She plucked a handful of wildflowers and laid them over the top of his sword that still rested upon his chest.

"War brought you to this accursed place, but new life grows around you, beautiful and fragrant." Her hand traced over his face, lingering on the bridge of his nose, the softness of his lips. "Your child moves within, beloved, and I beg the gods to give me a son as beautiful and handsome as you. Strong and brave... Thrand, whom you loved well, brought me here, and perhaps, someday, he will bring me again."

She laid herself carefully across his chest, careful not to touch the mystical sword, held him, and let her grief come, which didn't last as long as she thought it would. "Oh, my love, why did the gods wait so long to bring you to my door and then take you so soon? But soon, a part of you will live again..."

"Svana," Thrand's voice called quietly to her. "The smell of sulfur rises and we must go. I don't know what it means, but it's never good."

She turned to look at him and he looked at her as if something revolted him other than the growing smell.

"Why do you make such a face?" she asked.

"I shouldn't have brought you here."

"Why not?" She turned back to Falcon, kissed him again and whispered, "Forever you are with me, my love."

Thrand came closer and held out his hands to her. He closed his eyes again at the sight of his liege. Nature had done its work and Falcon, once a vibrant and valiant warrior was now nothing more than bones, his clothing hiding the worst of his decay. The ground around him, around the hundreds of others, was brown and dead, making little islands of death drifting across the vast, green sea.

"Your grief has made you mad, sister," Thrand said, pulling her up. He saw nothing but dried weeds lying atop the rusting sword. "You apparently see things as you want them, not as they are."

"The others are dead and rotting, brother, but my lord has been enchanted. He is as beautiful in death as he was in life," Svana said, and finally turned to head up the hill.

"No, Svana, he is just as corrupted as the others."

"He isn't. His skin was cool, but his lips were as soft as when he kissed me."

Thrand looked up at the sky as he gently pushed her up the incline. "Love, grief and pregnancy... who can say what a woman sees," he sighed and decided not to argue with her. If he did, Eyja would make him pay for it and right now, though he was loath to admit it, he needed her more than she needed him.

* * *

Falcon heard the soft sounds of subdued voices and felt the vibration of footfalls tremble gently through the earth. He ignored them at first. Nothing but more scavengers coming to strip the dead of weapons and anything else they deemed valuable. But then he heard the soft cadence of voices coming toward him, a man and a woman, and he realized he knew them well.

A moment later he felt Svana's gentle touch and felt the warmth of her tears falling on his face. Her words made his heart ache, and in his altered state, he felt her love flowing over him as did the torrents of the spring rain. He opened his eyes to look at her and if he still had breath, he would have had it no more as her beauty struck him even more now than it had at the beginning, when he had spotted her watching him from a nearly hidden space in the upper galleries of her brother's house.

Her eyes, her heart had loved him from the beginning without cause, without reason, just that she did, and he was grateful that his enchantment kept the horrors of his decay from her eyes.

It was now three months that he lay in the field, suffering Hede's torments, but for Svana, time continued on and he saw that her body swelled with his child. A shiver of fear quivered through him. He wondered if Hede would sense his child. He wanted to shout to Svana to leave this accursed ground and never come back. To take his son, which he knew it would be, and raise him far from this place. And then he glanced to Thrand, who he realized saw him as his earthly body showed. He saw his concern for his sister, who continued to kiss what Thrand saw as a skeletal corpse.

Falcon's heart grew heavy. How, in the end, they were so fragile, something to be protected, and yet... perhaps he should have surrendered to the witch. No, impossible. Giving in to her demands once would only make her future demands more terrifying. Perhaps his earthly son wouldn't live so long, but better than siring a creature of darkness, as would happen with Hede, and one who could live for a time without reckoning.

He knew Thrand smelled the odor of sulfur just as quickly as he did. Yes, my brother, take her from here before the witch comes or there will be hell to pay.

* * *

Eyja looked from Thrand to Svana and wasn't sure which of them frustrated her more. "I think, my lord husband, you are most certainly out of sorts and need to take some of your men and go hunting for a few days in the lower mountains. It wouldn't hurt to have more meat in the smokehouse, and as we lost men to the recent battles, we have orphans and widows to think about, especially with winter coming."

"Besides," Svana said and sat awkwardly as the baby within stretched and rolled, "what sort of trouble can two women, eight months pregnant get into anyway."

"I don't know, but if it can be done, the two of you will do it," Thrand said crossly and folded his arms across his chest. The thought of leaving them was at once enticing and terrifying. "I will consider it, but I'm not promising."

"Then while you are considering it," Eyja said and got to her feet, "I need you to bring those few work baskets up to our room. And then you can go stomp around with your distemper in the barn or take the practice field."

"If you two would just stop with your nonsense, I wouldn't be in such a mood. Gods, how often must we argue this? The past is done and there is no changing it," Thrand said as he stacked the baskets and picked them up. "Lord Falcon was only a man and if I need to, I will take you again and maybe this time you will see bones as I saw." Svana glared at him, but dutifully he followed Eyja up the spiral staircase and was still amazed that she could climb the stairs as easily as she did.

"Put them by my chair, please," she said as she stepped aside to allow him into the room.

"At least I got a please," Thrand grumbled and did as she asked. When he turned back around, Eyja grabbed him by his short beard and pulled his lips to hers. He felt her hand sink into his groin. "What is this now?" he asked, but didn't really care and took her into his arms and kissed her back.

Eyja pulled away and stroked the side of his face. "I feel like I'm going as crazy as you and Svana are with your arguing about Falcon's fate." She smiled as she untied his breeches. "But, the old women do say that a wife often does crave her husband toward the end."

Thrand smiled and sat her on the edge of their bed and knelt in front of her. His hands pushed under her skirt. "But... I see sadness in your eyes..."

"Because now, with the babes soon to arrive, I feel so much more Svana's loss. And... and..." Tears splashed down her face, but she quickly wiped them away. "And what if something happens to me when it's my time... how long will your heart be broken? You and your sister are much alike."

Thrand withdrew his hands and gently stroked the hair from Eyja's face. "The women in your family are strong, as you are, my love. There's not a one I know of who has not borne many children."

"I know," Eyja said and tried to smile. "I just want Svana to be happy again. Sometimes I feel guilty, because I have you."

"And she will have another when she's ready. Already men have approached me about her."

"Really? Who?"

Thrand smiled and wagged a finger at her. "I'm not telling either of you. When I have determined their motives, then I will decide who may speak to her."

"Motives? What does that mean?"

Thrand pushed her lips to his and he kissed her soundly. "One who will raise Falcon's son up to be a good man and warrior, not use him to usurp the throne."

"But who—"

Thrand was kissing her again as he gently laid her back and grabbed a pillow for her head and shoulders. He grinned at her. "Oh, nay, woman. You motives have me completely undone."

* * *

Svana looked back furtively as she and Eyja walked through the village toward the edge of town.

"What bothers you, sister?" Eyja asked.

"I just keep thinking Thrand is somehow going to see us."

Eyja laughed and slipped her arm through Svana's. "Even if he does, what can he say? Women about to give birth always visit the old woman at least once. He certainly wouldn't know which charms are useful for a birthing bed."

Svana smiled. "No, he wouldn't. I suppose none of them do, do they?" Her voice was wistful as she thought of Falcon.

"No, indeed. And we don't need to tell anyone but the old woman about your other questions."

Women smiled and nodded at them as they passed by. Several stopped them to ask how they were feeling and when the babes were due. It was always a happy event when the current jari was expecting, and more was the interest with the jarl's unmarried sister. Though there was still speculation, they all knew that when the dark-haired child was born, there would be no doubt that their fallen king was his sire. And for that, they overlooked the fact that the child would be a bastard.

The dirt road was lined with late summer clover, fragrant, the flowers a brilliant yellow. Stepping from the road that passed through the town, they traversed the damp, mossy footpath to the old woman's hut.

Before they could ring her little bell, they noticed her door stood open and more sweet and calming fragrances wafted out to greet them; both were surprised that the sudden smells didn't make either of them queasy. The old woman stood just inside and greeted them.

"Welcome, my ladies," she said with a nod as her old back prevented her from bowing to them. "Do come in. I had expected you somewhat sooner than now."

Eyja gave a little laugh as she stepped into the neat and tidy hut. "It was our plan, Bera, but you are no stranger to Lord Thrand's whims on the subject. He doesn't believe much in the power of charms. In fact, he has lost belief in much since that battle."

"Hmmm," Bera hummed as she went to stir a simmer pot.

"And does he deny the sword that pierced his lord? The one that still stands firmly embedded in the ground five months after that battle and not a spot of rust has appeared."

"So he does," Svana said and sat on one of the two chairs prepared for them. "Two months ago, we went to see it together and still he will not believe that Lord Falcon is enchanted in the way I do. He accepts the sword as the will of the gods, but nothing more."

"Tis rumored that his beliefs, not only in the gods, but in many things, were shaken that day on the field. Makes a few men wonder if he'll bring calamity on us all for denying the gods." Bera drew her hands down the sides of Svana's face and gently kissed the top of her head. "And did you see Falcon as bones or as a man?"

"As a man. Just as he always was to me," Svana answered. "But Thrand saw him as bones, because he won't believe."

Eyja sighed and sat down next to Svana. "And she and Thrand have been arguing about that ever since."

"I see... well... perhaps that is just as well," Bera said and rummaged through several boxes. "Ahh, here we go." She handed each of them a leather thong with several charms suspended from them. "Now, put these on and let them touch your skin. These are the birthing charms and before you go, I will give you little pouches of chamomile and other herbs to help you when it is time."

"Thank you, Bera," Eyja said. "How much do we owe you? And my lord husband will be sending you meats and stores at the end of autumn harvest."

Bera took the simmer pot from the fire and put on a larger pot and started it simmering. "This will not smell very good in a little bit. If it bothers you, we will continue outside in the garden. Now, about who owes who..." She went to a dark corner of her hut and pulled something from an old trunk. Bringing it back to the light shining through the small doorway, she sat on a stool. "I really don't know how to read, but the pictures and stories I learned as child, and someday, my daughter will take all of this over from me."

From a woolen wrap, Bera took out an old, wood-bound book and gently leafed through the delicate parchment pages that were sewn into its spine. Finding the picture she was looking for, she turned the page so the ladies could see.

"This tells the story of Falcon, as it has been told since any storyteller can ever remember," Bera said as the women looked at the picture of a warrior and then of a great bird soaring through the sky.

"But… but there is no god that I have ever heard about with such a name," Eyja said.

"True," Bera agreed and turned the page, "because he is a world spirit, but still has some god powers. Falcon was a very brave man who performed many great deeds and helped to slay the monsters alongside the gods. For his valor, and on the point of death, great Odinn gave him the choice to go to Valholl, or to become a powerful world spirit. Falcon was still a young man, burning with life, and he chose the gift of the gods. There are more than a few immortal beings who are not really gods and goddesses in these tales." She leafed through several more pages and paused to point at a bare-breasted woman with long hair flying in the wind. "Her name is Hede and she, you know."

"The witch of the valley," Svana whispered.

Bera nodded. "The very one. One day she caught a glimpse of Falcon, and she has desired him ever since, taunting him with her firm breasts, a beautiful face, but the rest of her is corrupted flesh. That's why you sometimes smell the sulfur in the valley. Through all of time she has desired him, pursued him, but he, ever a man of honor, will never submit to her evil. Seeresses greater than I have said she wants his child and then she will leave him in peace. But now…"

"Oh gods," Svana said with sudden clarity and tears ran down her face. "Lord Falcon told me of the strangeness of the battles they lost prior, pushing them ever back to that valley. They had no choice but to fight there, and that sword… she conjured that sword to capture him, because she knew he wouldn't leave Thrand and the others. He was their king, world spirit aside."

Eyja's face paled. "Then Svana's story, her suppositions, are correct…?" she asked hesitantly.

"Yes, my lady. And as I have done, twice now, I go to the edge of the valley on the full-moon night when Hede takes form in the field, and I hear Falcon's anguish and sorrow from midnight until the sun rises," Bera said, closed the book and kept it on her lap.

Svana's tears ran faster and she wept softly. "Tell me how I can free him from this terrible fate. I know him. He will never capitulate to something like her. It isn't right."

Eyja looked at Svana. "Don't even think the thoughts I think you are."

"I have to. If I give her my child, then Falcon will be set free."

"But... but if he rises again, he will never forgive you."

Svana shook her head. "He might hate me forever, but at least he will be free. I can't bear the thought that every full moon she tortures him, and what god will release him when it is the Sword of Fate that holds him... maybe forever."

"But what do we know of the Fates and their plans for man or god?" Eyja asked. "What, perhaps, he has done that no man knows and this is his just fate."

"And maybe this is my fate..." Svana said softly and both women heard the resolve in her words.

* * *

"Oh gods," Thrand said as he paced and tugged at his beard. Eyja's labor had started slow and easy at mid-day, but now it was well past midnight. "How long does this take?"

His mother smiled and patted the bench next to where she sat. "As long as it takes. Come and sit a while. She's doing just fine."

Thrand sat down a for short time and then he was on his feet again. "And then in what, a few days, a week, we have to do this again with Svana..."

"It was nice of you to take her to be with Kori and Olava. But you know, I'm surprised Olava agreed to marry him so soon after Ranvald's death."

Thrand gave a little laugh. "Not really when you know what really went on between the three of them. They pursued her relentlessly, but she couldn't choose, and her father demanded an end to the chaos they created for him. So, she devised a game of three tasks. Ranvald won two out three, and that only by the slimmest margin." He sat down as the sounds from their bedchamber subsided somewhat. "Ranvald's daughter was born a scant month before that last battle. Kori will take good care of them."

Eyja's sudden cry put him back on his feet and he tugged at his hair. "How do you just sit there? Go check on her. Do something."

His mother laughed quietly. "The first is always the hardest, my son. Be patient."

Thrand just looked at her and drank down a mug of ale. She laughed again.

"Yes, you were long coming into the world, but your brothers and sisters, and especially Svana, were nothing more than a pause on a spring day."

Thrand frowned and spent the next hour sitting, pacing and thinking he was near to losing his mind.

* * *

Svana cried out as she doubled over and sat in the night forest just at the edge of the witch's valley. Her contractions were strengthening and she knew that before long she was going to have to walk or crawl into the accursed valley to where she could see the Sword of Fate gleaming in the bright, full moonlight.

She had told Kori and Olava that she was tired and wanted to go to bed early, but already she had felt the subtle stirrings in her body. As the house settled for the night, she had silenced the moans of the first harder contractions into the denseness of her down pillow. But once the house was quiet, she was out the door and to the stable where she had managed to mount one of the smaller horses and rode bareback, using the horse's mane to guide it to the valley.

But now, with a last wailing cry to the goddess, and clutching at her amulets, she felt her body go suddenly quiet and knew this was the point that Olava had told her about; the transition from contractions to feeling the need to push the child into the light of life. Now was the time for her to enter the valley. Grabbing up her staff, and holding the weight of her belly in her other hand, she walked slowly down the gentle slope.

The smell of sulfur was overpowering and as the moon was high, she knew Hede was present and her torture of Falcon had begun. As before, Falcon lay upon the grass as though he were only asleep, while the whiteness of other men's skulls and bones partially hidden between the summer grass and flowers made her shiver.

"Ohhh," she moaned and stopped as she felt heaviness, a pressure wanting to push down between her legs. "A few more steps…"

She dropped to her knees, put a wine flask to her lips and drank the wine mixed with the chamomile and herbs. There wasn't much left, but it would be enough. She groaned again and as Olava said, the need to push became overpowering. Tears poured down her face and she felt so alone, so afraid, but Falcon's dreaming face gave her the courage to continue.

"Hede, you witch," Svana cried. "I know what you want. You want Falcon's child and I will give you his child for his freedom." She cried out as the pain overtook her and gasped when the contraction released. "You know I speak...the truth. You have walked in my dreams. Aaaahhhhh!" She choked on her tears and clutched the staff. "But until you have withdrawn the sword, I will not give you the child. Do you hear me?"

Svana felt the overwhelming need to push again and her scream tore into the night. The pain, sharp and tight, made her breath catch in her throat. She leaned into the staff, her body bearing down again and again, trying to relieve the pressure, the cutting and burning sensation. Her hands clutched the staff, her body insisting that the child should come forth and she screamed again and suddenly the pain was gone. Slippery and wet, the babe slid from her flesh, fell to the earth and bumped against her knee.

The smell of sulfur increased to a nearly intolerable level. Svana let go of the staff and let her hands drop to the earth. Beside her appeared the hem of Hede's long, black skirts. The reek of her nearly made Svana pass out and she wept bitter tears that her precious child should be given to such a creature. She reached beneath her own chemise and quickly cleared the child's mouth.

"Give me the child!" Hede demanded. Her voice was raspy and vicious.

"Not until that sword has vanished from Falcon's chest. From this entire valley," Svana said, rubbing the child and heard its first cry that grew louder with each breath.

In a bright flash, the sword was gone and Hede's hands were reaching for her. "Give it to me!"

Svana's hands trembled and her tears blinded her as she lifted the child, black feathers sticking to its body, and in but a second, her son, Falcon's son, was wrapped in the witch's shawl and both disappeared from sight.

Svana watched Falcon's chest heave with breath and knew by the sudden look in his eye that he knew exactly what she had done. Without hesitating, she flung herself on top on him to keep him from rising. Her tears fell on his face. "I'm so sorry, my love, but I want you to live, and live free. Forgive me… forgive me."

Falcon opened his mouth to inhale and speak, to shout his anger at what she had done, when hers suddenly closed over his.

Oh gods. No! Svana, no! What have you done?

Falcon's mind reeled when she released him and pushed his mouth closed. The gold coin her tongue had pushed into his mouth was sweet and precious and the falcon within was called forth.

No, Svana, my love!

And compelled by the force of his nature, he rolled from Svana's weak grip and his wings unfurled. The great bird took shape and moments later he was aloft, flying above the valley, desperately wanting to land next to Svana, to lift her from that horrific place, but the need to take the gold and secure it safely in the place of the bird's treasure store made him wheel to the north and Svana heard the falcon's call fade into the distance.

Falcon flew as fast as ever he could fly to reach the tree that grew next to the walls of Thrand's keep. His mind was a whirl of lingering pain from Hede's turn of the sword as well as from watching Svana give his son to the vile creature. How and why could she have done it? And then he knew why, when he realized the answer from her point of view rather than his own. For her, it was simply that she would bring forth another life to replace the one she had given for him.

But it was not so simple and Falcon's heart broke at his loss, at Svana's knowing that the gold would take him from the field, and that perhaps it would be long enough for the sun to rise and the power of the witch to fade. He needed to go back to her. He could hardly be angry now when he realized the totality of what she had just done.

The bird soared over the forest and in a time, that seemed an eternity, Thrand's keep came into sight. The moon was setting and dawn was not far away when he came to roost on the sturdy branch that held the falcon's nest.

Falcon looked into the twigs and moss and dropped the coin where it joined several others and pieces of broke chain and other shiny things that caught the bird's attention.

A sudden cry similar to Svana's came from the window not far below. A moment later it was followed by women screaming in fear. Falcon leaped from the branch and flew to the sill of the chamber window.

The women screamed again and he heard a voice shouting as it came up the stairs. He stared at the bed and realized the woman was Eyja, Thrand's wife, and between her legs lay another child, a boy, covered on his head by tiny feathers as was his torso, but his arms and legs were bloody and pink.

"Clean his mouth!" Eyja shouted to the women and struggled to sit up. Sweat soaked her hair and chemise and both clung to her wet body. Her face showed her exhaustion, but there was no fear in her for what lay on the bloody sheets.

It was then Falcon felt his world spin again into another level of fear and heartbreak. The child Svana had handed to Hede was not like this one. This was his true son, but whose was the other?

Thrand burst through the door, his hair as wild and unkempt as was the look in his eye. He stared around the room wondering why the women huddled in a corner and Eyja was abandoned on the bed, struggling to wipe the babe and clear its mouth and nose.

"What the hell..." Thrand muttered, staring at the strange creature in his wife's hands.

"Kill it!" one of the women screamed and the others screamed again. "Kill it! It's unnatural. A creature from Hel!"

Thrand drew his dagger and Eyja hugged the strange, crying babe to her, tears running down her face.

"Stay where you are, husband," Eyja warned Thrand, her voice hard and forceful. "If you think to kill this child, then you will have to kill me first."

Thrand stared at her unsure what to do.

"Did you hear me?" she demanded.

Falcon felt the last of the gold spell leave him and he flapped for a moment into the room. The women screamed again at his sudden whoosh and screech. Half of them fainted when suddenly a king who was dead was now alive and stood between Thrand and Eyja.

Thrand fell to his knees and leaned heavily on the edge of the bed for support. His heartbeat pounded, showing in the tenseness of his neck. His breathed great gasps of air. The dagger dropped to the floor.

"Do not you dare to touch my son," Falcon said, staring down at Thrand and truly he felt everything that was on his beloved warrior's face.

And suddenly Thrand was angry, furious, but he had no strength to stand. "Wasn't it enough I gave you my sister? You had to take my wife as well?"

"Thrand! How dare you!" Eyja said just as furious, but Falcon turned and motioned for her to be quiet and gave her a sad smile. He knew then what had happened.

Falcon knelt in front of Thrand, who shook and trembled in anger and wouldn't look at his lord. With a thought that suddenly stilled his body, wanting to make him crumple to the floor in shame, Thrand realized that Svana was right. Falcon was more than just a man.

"The women have put their mark upon us this night and we are at their mercy," Falcon said quietly. "Svana came to me in the field."

"What?" Thrand looked at him, stricken. "No, she couldn't have. I sent her to Koris for safe keeping."

Falcon shook his head. "She may have been there the day, but she pushed out a child, yours, I believe, on the field next to me and gave it to the witch in exchange for my life and freedom."

"What?" Thrand said again and slowly his head turned side to side. "What?" he repeated, trying to understand. "No… she couldn't have… no, but Eyja… my son…" He looked up at his wife who was gently rocking the strange babe, but silent tears slid down her red cheeks. "Eyja… but where is my son… what is he saying… I…"

She looked at him and slowly nodded her head, but words failed her.

"Listen to me," Falcon said and shook Thrand by the shoulder. "I need to go back for Svana. She's all alone on that wretched field. Do nothing until I return. Do you understand?"

"Svana… I should have listened…" Thrand mumbled, his mind reeling, unable to comprehend what he plainly saw in front of him.

"Thrand!" Falcon shook him again. "Do nothing until I return. Care for your wife if nothing else."

"Yes… my lord…"

Falcon picked up Thrand's dagger and tossed it to Eyja. She smiled and tucked it beneath the sheets. Falcon pulled Thrand to his feet and made him sit on the bed. "Stay there until I return." He rounded on the women still huddled in the corner. "All of you, out! Your use and skills have come to an end."

When they were gone, Falcon closed the door and dropped the wooden beam into the brackets. He paused by the bed and looked down at the child, still messy, but sleeping peacefully. As he turned to the window, he hoped beyond hope that he didn't find what his nightmarish precognition was telling him. In the wink of an eye, he was gone and a lone feather fell from his wing and fluttered to the floor.

Halfway back to the field, the sun rose golden and warm, but Falcon felt cold to the very center of himself. The witch would be gone and for that there was no end to his relief, but the closer he came, the heavier the wind was against his wings.

And isn't it written that even you, All-Father Odinn, can be merciful to one of us if it pleases you? His feet touched the ground and saw that Svana had tried to flee, but only made it partway up the slope. He walked to where she lay, pierced through her body with the rusted sword that had lain on his chest, the body of the child not far from her, his skin bluish and neck broken. Great tears rolled down his face and if he wasn't a world spirit, surely, he would have died a thousand times by now. What have I not done in serving your children, Great Father, for you to have let the Fates give me this day, this sorrow, this wound from which I will never recover?

He knelt next to Svana and lifted the edge of her bloody chemise. If miracles were possible, he would have smiled at her cleverness in tricking Hede as he saw dozens of black feathers loosely sewn around the inside of her garment. And what great magic had been wrought between the two women to switch the babes, he could only guess at, and cursed the enormous price his sweet love had paid.

A great cry was ripped from his throat as he pulled the rusted sword from her body and hurled it far afield. He gathered her into his arms and wept. He didn't understand why this piece of mortal flesh meant more to him than all the others. He looked down at her face, now peaceful and beautiful in its stillness. As she had done for him, he kissed her cooling lips, wanting her to know that his love for her transcended the veil between life and death.

Her likeness to Thrand reminded him of his duty to her brother. And perhaps he understood why he loved them so. Their courage, their pure hearts, the kindnesses they showed to lord and pauper were as one, as was the love they had for each other, a rarity in this place of harsh and unforgiving life.

Gently, he laid Svana back down and went to retrieve Thrand's rightful son. When he laid the child on Svana's chest, his heart felt pressed by a hundred stones making him wonder if even his great wings could lift them all from the wretched, mortal earth.

He flew and his sorrow nearly grounded him several times before he touched down on the roof of Thrand's home. Carefully, he laid Svana on its warmth. For Thrand to see his son like this was enough. He didn't need to see what had become of Svana on this day that should have brought him joy. He wrapped the child in Svana's wrap to hide the worst of his injuries and flew down the tower and into the room.

Instantly, Thrand was on his knees, his color returned, but his face was ravaged by the tears he had wept.

"Forgive me, my Lord Falcon," Thrand said, his voice quivering. He knew it was his son, his dead son that Falcon held in his arms. "Eyja told… told me what… has happened. I… I…"

Falcon walked to him and pressed Thrand's head and shoulders to him. Thrand's arms went around Falcon and his body shook with grief that warred with his joy that his king lived. With his shame that he hadn't heeded Svana's words.

Gently, Falcon rubbed his hand over Thrand's forehead, easing his sorrow as much as his god-fire would allow. He looked to Eyja and knew by the anger that set her face and the sadness in her eyes that likely they had fought the entire time he was gone.

"Thrand, my beloved warrior, I want you to hear my words," Falcon said, but realized he wouldn't as long as he held his dead child. "Come, sit on the bed with Eyja whom you love as deeply as ever I loved Svana."

Thrand nodded and pulled himself to sit on the bed with the movements of a defeated man.

Falcon gave him a bit of a smile and motioned him to move closer to Eyja. "We cannot hate them for what they've done, brother." Then he turned to the washbasin that had been prepared to wash the newborn.

Falcon let his tears fall again and they dropped unseen by Thrand and Eyja onto the child and into the water. He unwrapped the babe and placed him in the basin. With gentle strokes he washed the blood, the dirt, the evil of Hede into the water blessed by his tears. With each stroke of the cloth, the babe turned pinker, his wounds healed, he breathed and opened his blue eyes. Falcon reached over to the cup of wine sitting nearby and wet his fingers. He let the red wine drip onto the tiny lips that opened, wanting to suckle, and wet his fingers again and washed the inside of the tiny mouth, cleansing him of the last of Hede's evil.

The splash of water sounded loudly in the silent room and a great wail came forth from strong lungs and a solidly beating heart.

Eyja felt her heart sink and looked down at the strange creature she held and who breathed no more. "Oh gods," she murmured and realized what Falcon had done and looked up at him when he turned to them cradling the fussing child. "Why my Lord Falcon? The son of a world spirit is more important than anything our poor flesh could ever create. We are here to serve you."

Falcon shook his head slowly. "Nay, my lady, you have it reversed. I'm charged with serving and helping all of mortal flesh," he said and stepped forward to hand the child to his father.

"In spite of my anger, my despair," Thrand said, not quite knowing how to cradle the babe as easily as Falcon or Eyja, "she is right. Take back the life of your son as well as you take back your own." He looked up. "And Svana…?"

Falcon smiled sadly and shook his head as he lifted his still son from Eyja's arms. "Hede killed her, but I have brought her from that sad place and will take them both with me."

Eyja burst into tears and Thrand felt his heart soften for her. In spite of it all, and as Falcon had said, he loved her deeply. He got up and sat closer to her, then looked up at Falcon. "Please, my lord, take back your son."

"Nay, warrior," Falcon said. He pulled Thrand to him once more and leaned down to kiss the top of his head. "Once, in a time growing harder to remember, I was no more than a flesh and blood man just as you... and a man's time is short upon this world... its many tragedies overly burden his heart. And I realize, in spite of myself, my essence rejoices in the freedom that Svana's courage has given me, and as the two of you do, I loved her without measure. The measure of my love for you is that you take care and raise well our son. Let him grow strong in the love of his parents that he may know the honor of his father, and," he paused to smile at Eyja as his hand softly stroked her face, "the cleverness and strength of his mother. And like you, warrior, let him become a just lord to your people."

"I don't know what to say..." Thrand said and looked up at Falcon, his face distraught.

Falcon turned and walked to the window. "This day is sorrowful indeed, but when people see without understanding and wonder why our son is without peer, you will tell the tragic tale of Falcon and Svana."

In a flash of light, and the dropping of many feathers, Lord Falcon was gone from their sight.

Thrand and Eyja sat and stared out the window, lost in their own sorrows, until the child cried and Thrand gave him over to his mother. He watched as she settled the babe to her breast and knew his and Falcon's line would grow strong in the child and carry them well into the next generations. He watched tears trickle down Eyja's face as she gently ran her fingers over the child's head and knew Falcon was right. He couldn't fault either of the women and felt his love for his wife deepen, but knew he only understood a small portion of Falcon's grief.

Thrand looked back to the floor and slid off the bed to his hands and knees. Slowly, reverently, he picked up the scattered feathers. Tears of sorrow blinded him and his chest ached for Svana, alone in her steadfast faith in Falcon, alone on that wretched field in the throes of childbirth, and then what must have been a moment of incomparable joy at seeing Falcon free before dying, alone, a death no less tragic and valorous than any of his men.

"By all the gods, Svana, why didn't I believe you? I knew it, but I didn't believe it could be. If I had, would all of this have come to pass?" he whispered and held the feathers to his chest. "How do I tell Mother and expect her to believe me...? How do I live with the guilt of not protecting the one of her children that she favors the most...?"

"Thrand..." Eyja called softly to him, but he ignored her. "Husband, come. Sit on the bed with me."

Slowly, Thrand turned to her, but he remained where he was, head bowed. "And how much do you blame me?"

"I don't."

"You should. Even if I didn't believe this, I shouldn't have been so angry with her, with you, but just let it be."

"And what man can truly understand the ways of the gods, both good and evil?"

"Apparently, that is the realm of the womenfolk," he said, bitterness tightening his voice.

"The important thing is that even if your faith wavers, if you have doubts, I know you will raise your son to honor both men and gods.

He looked up at her, disheveled, the bloody sheets beneath her, hair still damp and clinging to the sides of her face and neck, and yet she was beautiful. The child had fallen asleep again and was lying beside her, covered with a corner of the bedding. She had pulled her chemise up a bit, but still her breasts were mostly bare.

In the moment, he would surely swear that he saw the face of Frigg, radiant and peaceful, looking back at him. The eternal mother, the strength of the earth, of life, and the women apparently understood these things much better than he did. And perhaps the goddess did give strength and understanding to his beloved Eyja.

He rose up and went to sit with her, and put the feathers near their son. Gently, he touched her face and smoothed back her hair. "I will bring the women to you."

"In a while," she whispered and pulled his face to hers, encouraging him to kiss her back.

"I can't, Eyja..." Thrand whispered and pulled away from her, stroking her face. "You are so beautiful to me... but my heart is so broken..."

"As is mine, but your son is your victory on this sad day, and we will face the family later after our hearts have settled a bit."

"Promise me you will never say again that he is my son, but our son. I can't bear to live with this day alone."

Eyja nodded and gave him a hesitant smile. They fell into each other's arms and held each other long. Thrand knew it would take both of them to raise Falcon's son, and though Falcon lived in their hearts, they never saw him again.

* * *

A fist hammered on the door to Falcon's chamber and the latch lifted. A page entered and brought in food and drink and set it on the sideboard.

"My lord, the All-Father wishes to see you."

Falcon's gaze, hard and angry, focused on the servant. "My answer is the same as it was yesterday. Can a man not have a few days to mourn his love, his son? Leave."

The page bowed quickly and was gone. Falcon sat a moment more staring out the window of his high, mountain retreat. He drew in a deep breath, stood and walked to the window where Svana and his son, wrapped in a soft blanket and nestled in her arm, lay in a granite crypt with a clear, crystal cover. He stared down at them. The soft light made Svana's beauty glow as if she lived again, and wondered when he could say the same for himself.

The door opened quietly and Falcon was angry. "I told you to leave me, boy. What do you want now?"

"Hmmmm," came a rumbling sound as the door closed. "I don't recall being a boy anymore."

Falcon turned quickly to see Odinn All-Father standing in the center of his room. "Great lord, forgive me."

Odinn shook his hand and waved away the words. "I think it's time you rejoined the world, Falcon. The people cry out to you, but you do not hear. A world spirit, just as a god, really must listen now and then."

"I will, someday, when my heart has healed of its grief, but now is too soon. A few days is not enough to forget my love for her or what happened in that valley," Falcon said and turned back to Svana. His fingers rubbed against the crystal cover wanting desperately to feel her lips on his once more.

Odinn stepped closer and turned Falcon to face him. "Have you forgotten, my son, that— why such a look as that?"

Falcon was sullen. "Why do you call me your son, when I'm not? I was a bastard in life."

Odinn smiled and pulled him into a tight embrace. "And did you not love Ranvald, Thrand and Eyja, and all the others, almost as your children, with you as their guardian."

"Love is not something I wish to experience right now."

Odinn shook his head. "Love is the only thing that makes eternity worth enduring. All other emotions and thoughts are worthless compared to that one, and it's time you answer those who cry out to you," Odinn said.

"And as I said before, can I not have a few days for my heart to mend?"

Falcon glanced behind to the open window, when he heard the flapping of wings and the caws of two black ravens, Hunr and Munr, as they settled on the ledge.

"You have shut yourself off from the world. In the nights you have allowed yourself to touch the god sleep, but below in the mortal realm, two centuries have passed," Odinn said and watched shock come to Falcon's face. The All-Father nodded. "Yes, Falcon, in those slumbers to ease your heart, time has slipped from your grasp, from your knowing, and all those you loved are no more. The living fire of your son, that you so graciously gave to Thrand and Eyja, long ago entered Valholl as a warrior of renown and many were his victories. But, their names have been lost to memory and their bones long since turned to dust."

Odinn turned him back to Svana's bier, the crystal cover now flowing with the image of muddy and broken ground, gray skies and rain. The surface roiled with mist to reveal the solitary image of a golden-haired youth kneeling before a small altar and all around him the great keep of his family was in ruins. Collapsed beams burned with spotty fires and the rain poured down beyond the tiny enclosure that housed the altar where a small fire burned.

His hands bloody and dirty, the young man peeled off but a few black strands from a feathery nub and carefully placed them into the fire. A golden spark flared as the fire consumed the tiny pieces.

Falcon barely heard the words he spoke, faint and flowing away in the torrents of rain.

"Great Falcon, god of my father and many fathers before him beginning with Thrand, hear my plea. We have fought the battle these many years, but now defeat is ours. We go to new lands that we do not know, and ask your favor to protect us from our enemies and give us safe passage. Help us establish again the line of our family and make it strong."

Another voice shouted to the young man, but Falcon couldn't hear the words, only the urgency of the plea. The young man quickly put the necklace fashioned of a gold coin and the stubs of several feathers bound together around his neck. He grabbed his sword and put the blade into the tiny fire.

"Please, I beg you, give us Thrand's strength, Svana's courage, and Enar's victories…" And with that, he dashed out into the rain. A gust of wind blew into the shelter and extinguished the flame, just as Falcon realized he had quit burning for them.

Falcon looked stricken and fell to his knees. How did he not realize this? He had wanted to watch the boy grow. He hadn't meant to abandon them and wondered how many times Thrand, Kori and all the others might have called to him. On what occasions did their descendants light ritual fires over the many years for his help, and who was the desperate young man in the All-Father's vision…? At the least he would have given them his subtle support as he gave their hearts the strength to bear their burdens, if not more.

"I… I have no words. I did not mean…their faith continued and grew stronger, and I abandoned them, and selfishly so…" and his grief deepened when he thought of it all. He looked up at Odinn. "I have failed them… and you. Let my time end here and now. You've given me more than I ever deserved."

Odinn All-Father motioned to Hunr and Munr. They flew forward and landed on Falcon's shoulders. Falcon felt them attempting to impart their wisdom to him, but he was too overcome to hear.

"Your time is not finished," Odinn said with a sigh. "Sometimes the gods of the realm are too concerned with themselves and their petty feuds and they forget the land of men."

"As I have forsaken them...when their courage, their steadfast faith in me, and perhaps even my renewed leadership might have softened, even prevented, this blow..."

"Perhaps. But the Fates will weave their cloth as they please and no god has say over them... Nevertheless, you are of them and you are of us. Thrand, your shared son, their descendants have never forgotten you, but their mortal faith can only be strong and true for so long without feeling you with them from time to time."

"But there are others of my immortal brothers and sisters to care for them..."

Odinn All-Father smiled and nodded. He reached down to help Falcon to his feet. "Yes, but there is a huge divide between them and you. You lived with them, loved them and Svana gave you the purest heart of all, and even so, it is time for her memory to become one with all." He paused when tears rolled down Falcon's face and he turned to look at her. Odinn put his hands on Falcon's head.

Falcon let his head drop back and felt the oneness with all that is, was and will be in the vastness of time until their proscribed destruction, when the Midgard Serpent would awaken and destroy the world. He felt a reconnecting with the godhead of Valholl, with the struggling souls of Midgard, tempered with a hint of the All-Father's compassion coursing through him.

"How can I let any of them go? How can I let any of that little village fade into nothing but a memory forgotten in time?"

"That is why they need you now, Falcon. Memories of long-ago victories are dying in them as they are driven from their land and into strange places. But you are the living source of their steadfast faith. You know that you will once again find men worthy of your love, your service to them, and your world-spirit circle, broken these many years, will complete again."

Odinn gave a sharp whistle and Falcon felt himself pulled across the floor and lifted to the windowsill by the two ravens. Before he realized their intent, they pulled him out of the window.

"What is this? For what purpose do they seize me?" He looked down and saw the valleys and fjords of the hard land far below. "Where are they taking me?" Falcon shouted as the ravens flew higher still and suddenly dropped him. He tumbled end over end as he fell toward the great sea below.

Falcon heard Odinn's voice ring through his being.

"The age of the warrior has come upon the land. It's time for you to live, fight, and love again."

Odinn watched Falcon's form shrink smaller and smaller as he fell and the ravens called out in fear for him. The All-Father said nothing, watching unconcerned and smiled when Falcon's great wings unfurled and the cry of the solitary bird echoed up from the canyon far below.

AFTERWORD

By CA Morgan

We hope you've enjoyed this first anthology by the Tucson Science Fiction and Fantasy Writers Meetup group. With the publication of this book, what was said on a whim one night during a gathering, has become a reality--at least in our version of the multiverse.

Having been a member of many organizations over the years, and having dealt with unfortunate circumstances, I want to thank all of our participating members for their stories, but more importantly, for their refreshing enthusiasm and willingness to be a part of the process—and a learning process for some.

Projects like these can be potential pitfalls for disaster as a result of personality, opinion, creative subjectiveness, and other things that drive people apart rather than together. Instead, this experience has made the group stronger, and more cohesive and helpful to all of our members. Helping each other succeed in this sometimes difficult and frustrating creative process makes us all stronger as writers and eventually, published authors.

If, by chance, you found a new favorite author, there will be more! We are working hard on new stories and are looking forward to welcoming several new authors to our next "adventures in the multiverse."

Join the Meetup

If you live in Tucson or the surrounding area and would like to become a member of our group, simply visit Meetup.com or download the Meetup app and join us at: *Tucson SF and Fantasy Writers.*

Not sure you want to join just yet? Then stop by and say "hi" during one of our meetings and meet the group.

Current times and locations as of October, 2018 are:
Every other Saturday from 1 to 4pm at Old Chicago located at 2960 N. Campbell Ave. This meeting is a "quiet" meeting more along the lines of "write-in" in the company of like writers. Asking for help is fine, but shhhhh...!

Every other Wednesday from 6 to WheneverPM at the IHOP located at 5101 E. Grant Road. People say that writers are quiet and extremely introverted souls...well, not at this meeting! We love to chat about our new works, new movies, new books, anything and everything, and we will be more than happy to learn about you and your projects. Small group critique sessions can be had for the asking,

For more information, check out our website at:

https://tucsonscififantasywriters.weebly.com

What's Next?

Beyond Tucson:
Peak Experiences

Tucson is surrounded by approximately five mountain ranges visible from the city center. As with many places in this rugged Southwestern state, the areas are sparsely populated. Just what *really* goes on in and around those desolate areas. Find out in our next installment of the *Beyond Tucson* anthology series due out in 2019. Check the website for updates.

Who's on Amazon?

Karen Funk Blocher (January 2019)

Erik Hertwig

CA Morgan

Joni Parker

Jessica Priester

G. E. Zhao